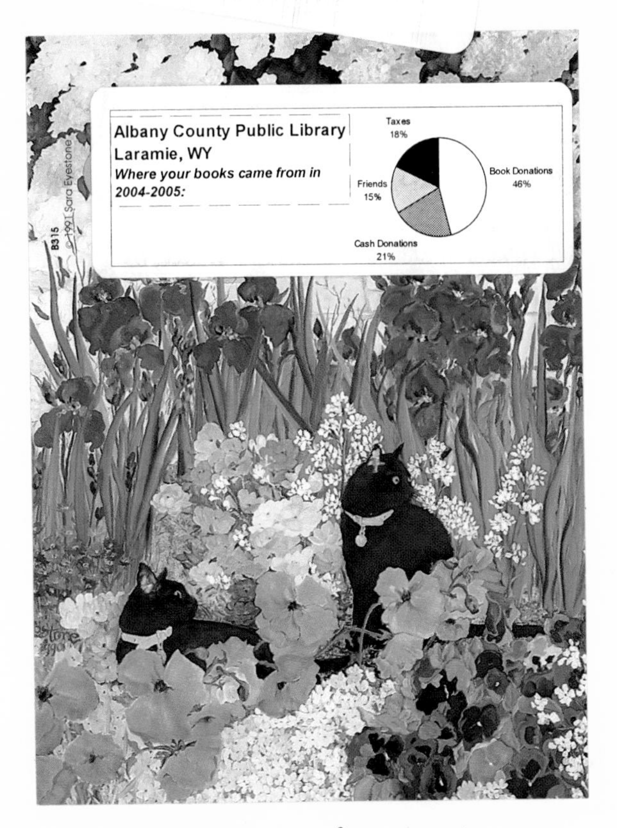

Dubois - Brooks Lake

A BREACH OF PROMISE

By Anne Perry
Published by Fawcett Books

Featuring William Monk

The Face of a Stranger
A Dangerous Mourning
Defend and Betray
A Sudden, Fearful Death
The Sins of the Wolf
Cain His Brother
Weighed in the Balance
The Silent Cry
A Breach of Promise

Featuring Charlotte and Thomas Pitt

The Cater Street Hangman
Callander Square
Paragon Walk
Resurrection Row
Bluegate Fields
Rutland Place
Death in the Devil's Acre
Cardington Crescent
Silence in Hanover Close
Bethlehem Road
Highgate Rise
Belgrave Square
Farriers' Lane
The Hyde Park Headsman
Traitors Gate
Pentecost Alley
Ashworth Hall
Brunswick Gardens

A BREACH OF PROMISE

Anne Perry

FAWCETT COLUMBINE
The Ballantine Publishing Group • New York

A Fawcett Columbine Book
Published by The Ballantine Publishing Group

http://www.randomhouse.com

ISBN 0-449-90849-6

Designed by Holly Johnson

Manufactured in the United States of America

To Ken Weir for his friendship

CHAPTER ONE

Oliver Rathbone leaned back in his chair and let out a sigh of satisfaction. He had just successfully completed a long and tedious case. He had won most substantial damages for his client over a wrongful accusation. The man's name was completely cleared and he was grateful. He had told Rathbone that he was brilliant, and Rathbone had accepted the compliment with grace and appropriate humility, brushing it aside as more a courtesy than truth. But he had worked very hard and had exercised excellent judgment. He had once again used the skills which had made him one of the finest barristers in London, if not in England.

He found himself smiling in anticipation of a most pleasant evening at Lady Hardesty's ball. Miss Annabelle Hardesty had been presented to the Queen, and had even earned an agreeable comment from Prince Albert. She was launched upon society. It was an evening in which all manner of victories might be celebrated. It would be a charming affair.

There was a knock on the door, interrupting his reverie.

"Yes?" He sat up straight. He was not expecting anyone. He had rather thought he would go home early, perhaps take a short walk in the park and enjoy the late-spring air, see the chestnuts coming into bloom.

The door opened and Simms, his chief clerk, looked in.

"What is it?" Rathbone asked with a frown.

"A young gentleman to see you, Sir Oliver," Simms replied very seriously. "He has no appointment, but seems extremely worried."

His brow puckered with concern and he looked at Rathbone intently. "He's quite a young gentleman, sir, and although he's doing his best to hide it, I think he is more than a little afraid."

"Then I suppose you had better ask him to come in," Rathbone conceded, more from his regard for Simms than conviction that the young man's difficulty was one he could solve.

"Thank you, sir." Simms bowed very slightly and withdrew.

The moment after, the door swung wide again and the young man stood in the entrance. He was, as Simms had said, deeply troubled. He was not tall—perhaps an inch less than Rathbone himself—although his slender build and the squareness of his shoulders gave him an extra appearance of height. He had very fair skin and fine, regular features. Strength was given to his face by the width of his jaw and the level, unflinching gaze with which he met Rathbone's eyes. It was difficult to place his age, as it can be with those of a very fair complexion, but he could not have been far on either side of thirty.

Rathbone rose to his feet.

"Good afternoon, sir. Come in, and tell me in what way I may be of service to you."

"Good afternoon, Sir Oliver." The young man closed the door behind him and advanced towards the chair in front of Rathbone's desk. He was breathing very steadily, as if it were a deliberate effort, and when he was closer it was possible to see that his shoulders were tense, his body almost rigid.

"My name is Killian Melville," he began slowly, watching Rathbone's face. "I am an architect." He said it with great meaning; his light voice almost caressed the word. He hesitated, still staring at Rathbone. "I am afraid that I am about to be sued for breach of promise."

"Promise to do what?" Rathbone asked, although he was all but certain he knew. That particular phrase held one meaning above all others.

Melville swallowed. "To marry Miss Zillah Lambert, the daughter of my patron, Mr. Barton Lambert." He obviously found difficulty even in saying the words. There was a kind of despair in his face.

"Please sit down, Mr. Melville." Rathbone indicated the chair opposite him. "By all means tell me the details, but I think it is quite possible I may be unable to help you." Already his instinctive liking for the young man was waning. He had little sympathy for people who flirted and made promises they did not intend to keep, or who sought to improve their social and financial situations by using the affections of a woman whose position might be an advantage to them. They deserved the blame and the misfortune which followed.

Melville sat down, but the bleakness of his expression made it apparent he had heard the disapproval in Rathbone's voice and understood it only too well.

"I had no intention of hurting Miss Lambert," he began awkwardly. "Of causing injury either to her feelings or to her reputation. . . ."

"Is her reputation in question?" Rathbone asked rather coolly.

Melville flushed, a wave of color rising up his fair cheeks.

"No it is not, not in the way you mean!" he said hotly. "But if a . . . if a man breaks off an engagement to marry—or seems to—then people will raise questions as to the lady's morals. They will wonder if he has learned something of her which is . . . which has changed his mind."

"And have you?" Rathbone asked. That at least could prove some excuse, both ethically and in law, if it could be proved.

"No!" Melville's reply was unhesitating. "As far as I know she is blameless."

"Is the matter financial?" Rathbone pursued the next most likely problem. Perhaps Melville required a wife of larger fortune. Although if her father was able to be a patron to architects, then he must be of very considerable wealth. A social disadvantage seemed more likely. Or possibly Melville could not afford to keep her in the manner which she would expect.

Melville stiffened. "Certainly not!"

"You would not be the first young man not in a financial position to marry," Rathbone said a little more gently, leaning back in his chair and regarding the young man opposite him. "It is a common enough state. Did you perhaps mislead Mr. Lambert about your prospects, albeit unintentionally?"

Melville let out his breath in a sigh. "No. No, I was very candid with him." The shadow of a smile crossed his face, an unexpected light of humor in it, rueful and self-mocking. "Not that there would have been any point in doing any less. Mr. Lambert is largely responsible for my success. He would be in a better position to estimate my financial future than my banker or my broker would."

"Have you some other encumbrance, Mr. Melville? A previously incurred relationship, some reason why you are not free to marry?"

Melville's voice was very quiet. "No. I . . ." He looked away from Rathbone, for the first time avoiding his eyes. "I simply cannot bear to! I like Zillah . . . Miss Lambert. I regard her as a good and charming friend, but I do not wish to marry her!" He looked up again quickly, this time meeting Rathbone's eyes, and his voice was urgent. "It all happened around me . . . without my even being sensible to what was occurring. That may sound absurd to you, but believe me, it is true. I took it to be a most pleasant acquaintance." His eyes softened. "A mutual interest in art and music and other pleasures of the mind, discussion, appreciation of the beauties of nature and of thought . . . I—I found her a most delightful friend . . . gentle, modest, intelligent . . ." Suddenly the desperation was back in his face. "I discovered to my horror that Zillah's mother had completely misunderstood. She had read it as a declaration of love, and before I knew where I was, she had begun to make arrangements for a wedding!"

He was sitting upright in the chair opposite Rathbone, his back straight, his hands strong and square, the nails very short, as if now and then he bit them. He clasped the chair arms as if he could not let them go.

"I tried to explain that that was not what I had meant," he

went on, biting his lips as he spoke. "But how do you do that without appearing grossly hurtful, offensive? How do I say that I do not feel that kind of emotion for her without insulting her and wounding her feelings unforgivably?" His voice rose. "And yet I never said anything, so far as I can recall, that sounded like . . . that was intended to mean . . . I have racked my brain, Sir Oliver, until I now no longer have any clear recollection of what I did say. I only know that announcements have been made in the *Times*, and the date is set, and I had no say in the matter at all." His face was pale, except for two spots of color in his cheeks. "It has all happened as if I were a prop in the center of some stage around whom the whole dance revolves, and yet I can do nothing at all to affect it. And suddenly the music is going to stop, and they are all going to wait for me to play my part and make everyone happy. I can't do it!" He was filled with quiet despair, like a trapped creature who can no longer fight and has nowhere to run.

Rathbone found his sympathy touched in spite of his better judgment.

"Has Miss Lambert any idea of your feelings?" he asked.

Melville's shoulders lifted slightly.

"I don't know; I don't think so. She is . . . she is caught up in the wedding plans. I sometimes look at her face and it seems to me as if it is quite unreal to her. It is the wedding itself which has occasioned such enormous preparation, the gown, the wedding breakfast, who will be invited and who will not, what society will think."

Rathbone found himself smiling with the same half-ironic appreciation of frailty and fear that he had seen in Melville's eyes. He had some slight experience of society matrons who had successfully married a daughter, to the envy and the chagrin of their friends. Appearance far outweighed substance at that point. They had long ago ceased to consider whether the bride was happy, confident, or even what she actually wished. They assumed it must be what they wished for her, and acted accordingly.

Then he was afraid Melville might think he was laughing at him, which was far from the case. He leaned forward.

"I sympathize, Mr. Melville. It is most unpleasant to feel manipulated and as if no one is listening to you or considering your wishes. But then, from those of my friends who are married, I believe it is a not uncommon experience at the time of the ceremony itself. The bridegroom can seem little more than a necessary part of the stage property and not a principal in the act. That will pass, immediately after the day itself is over."

"I am not suffering from nervousness of the day, Sir Oliver," Melville said levelly, although such self-control obviously cost him a great effort of will. "Nor do I feel any pique at being placed at the side of events rather than in the center. I simply cannot"—he seemed to have difficulty forming the words with his lips—"bear . . . to find myself married to Zillah . . . Miss Lambert. I have no desire to be married to anyone at all. If at some time I shall have, it will be of my own choosing, and of theirs, not something that has been assumed by others and organized around me. I . . ." Now at last there was a thread of real panic in him, and his knuckles were white where he gripped the ends of the chair arms. "I feel trapped!"

Rathbone could see that he spoke the truth.

"I assume you have done what you can to escape the contract—"

"There was no contract!" Melville cut across him. "Simply an assumption, which I did not realize soon enough to deny with any dignity or sensitivity. Now it is too late. My refusal, all my arguments, will be seen as a breach of promise." His green-blue eyes were growing wilder, his words more rapid. "They forget what was actually said and remember the facts quite differently from the reality. I cannot stand there and argue 'You said this' and 'I said that.' " He jerked one hand up sharply. "It would be absurd and degrading, and achieve nothing but mutual blame and hurt. I assure you, Sir Oliver, Mrs. Lambert is never going to admit she presumed something which was not so and that I gave her daughter no proposal of marriage, literal or implicit. How could she, now that she has announced it to the world?"

Rathbone could see that that was indeed so unlikely as to be considered impossible.

"And Mr. Lambert?" He made a last attempt, more out of habit than a belief he would learn anything which would provide a defense.

Melville's expression was difficult to read, a mixture of admiration and despair. He sank back in the chair. "Mr. Lambert is an honest man, straightforward in word and deed. He drives a hard bargain, which is how he made his fortune, but strictly fair." The lines around his mouth softened. "But of course he loves his daughter, and he's fiercely loyal. He's sensitive about his northern roots and he sometimes fancies high society thinks the less of him because he earned his money in trade . . . and for that matter, so they do." He winced a little. "I suppose it was unnecessary to say that. I apologize."

Rathbone waved it aside. "So he would be quick to defend her from anything he saw as an insult," he concluded.

"Yes. And there is hardly a greater insult than to break a contract of marriage." The fear was sharp in Melville's voice again. "He cannot afford to believe me that there was none. Mrs. Lambert is a formidable woman—" He stopped abruptly.

"I see." Rathbone did see, extremely clearly, the nature of the predicament. He also felt increasingly certain that Melville was withholding something which he knew to be of importance. "Have you told me all the facts, Mr. Melville?"

"All that are relevant, yes." Melville spoke so unhesitatingly that Rathbone was sure he was lying. He had been expecting the question and was prepared for it.

"You have not found your affections engaged elsewhere?" He looked at Melville closely and thought he saw a faint flush in his cheeks, although his eyes did not waver.

"I have no desire or intention of marrying anyone else," Melville said with conviction. "You may search all you care to, you will find nothing to suggest I have paid the slightest court to any other lady. I work extremely hard, Sir Oliver. It is one of the most difficult things in the world to establish oneself as an architect." There was a ring of bitterness in his voice, and something which was almost certainly pride. His clear eyes were filled with light. "It requires time and skill in negotiation, patience, the art of diplomacy, as well as a vision of precisely what makes a building both beautiful and functional, strong enough to endure through generations of time and yet not so exorbitantly expensive that no one can afford to construct it. It requires magnitude of ideas and yet note of the minutest detail. Perhaps the law is the same." He raised his brows and stared questioningly, almost challengingly. For the first time Rathbone was conscious of the man's remarkable mind, the breadth and the power of his intellect. He must indeed have an extraordinary strength of will. His present problem was not indicative of his character. He was certainly not a man of indecision.

"Yes," Rathbone agreed ruefully, many of his own past romances, or near romances, fleeting through his mind. He had been too busy, too ambitious, to allow the time necessary to enlarge them into courtship. This he could understand with no effort at all. But he had not been unmindful enough of others, or of the way of the world, to allow himself to be so misunderstood that anyone, even a socially avaricious would-be mother-in-law, had missed his intentions.

"Yes, the law is a hard taskmistress, Mr. Melville," he agreed. "And one requiring both imagination and exactitude if one is to succeed. And it also requires an ability to judge character. I confess that I do not think you are telling me the whole truth of this matter."

He saw Melville's face tighten and the skin around his lips turn pale.

"Many men are not particularly in love with the women they marry," he continued, "but find the alliance quite tolerable. Even more young women accept marriages which are based upon financial or dynastic necessity. If the person is honorable, kind, and not physically repellent, they very frequently learn to love one another.

At times such a union is happier than one entered into in the heat of a passion which is based upon dreams and fades when the first hunger is assuaged, and there is no friendship left to feed it or to tide them over the later times." As he said it he knew it was true, and yet he would not have entered such an arrangement himself.

Melville looked away. "I am aware of all that, Sir Oliver, and I do not deny it. I am not prepared to marry Zillah Lambert in order to satisfy her mother's ambitions for her, or to try to be what she desires in a husband." He rose to his feet rather awkwardly, as if he were too rigid to coordinate his limbs as he normally might. "And profoundly grateful as I am to Barton Lambert for his patronage of my art, my obligation does not extend to the ruin of my personal happiness or peace . . . of life."

Rathbone drew in breath to ask him yet again what it was he was concealing, then saw in Melville's face that he would not answer. Perhaps if the Lamberts did indeed sue him he would change his mind. Until then the matter was speculative anyway, and he felt increasingly that it was something in which he did not wish to become involved. Melville could not win. And frankly, Rathbone thought he was being melodramatic about something which was no more than the lot of a vast proportion of mankind, and not so very bad.

"Then perhaps you had better see what transpires, Mr. Melville," he said aloud, "before presuming the worst. Perhaps if you were to explain the situation to Miss Lambert herself and give her the opportunity to break the engagement, for whatever reason you can agree upon that does her no dishonor, then such an ugly and expensive matter as a legal suit could be avoided. And your relationship with Mr. Lambert would suffer far less. I assume you have taken that into your considerations? If you break your promise to Miss Lambert, you can hardly expect his future patronage."

"Of course I have taken it into consideration!" Melville said bitterly, standing now at the door. "I cannot win! It is only a question of how much I lose. But I am not prepared to marry in order to further my professional career." He looked at Rathbone with contempt, as if he believed Rathbone would do such a thing himself, and yet beneath the anger and the disgust there was still the deep fear—and a flickering light of hope. "I am a very good architect, Sir Oliver," he added softly. "Some have even said brilliant. I should not need to prostitute myself in order to obtain work."

Rathbone was stung by the words. He realized with a flush of shame that he had half intended to insult Melville, without having the slightest idea of his professional ability or anything other of his personal situation than the one problem of which he had spoken. There were numerous personal reasons why a man might not wish to marry, many often too delicate to explain to others, whatever the pressure.

"I will help you if I can, Mr. Melville," he said more gently. "But I fear that from what you have told me, there would be very little I could do. Let us agree to leave the matter until you have done your best to persuade Miss Lambert to break the engagement herself." He sounded more encouraging than he meant to. He did not intend taking the case. He had already given his best advice in the matter.

"Thank you," Melville said with his hand on the door, his voice flat. "Thank you for your time, Sir Oliver."

Rathbone put the subject from his mind and carried out his original intention of leaving his chambers in Vere Street early. It was still a lovely afternoon and he stopped the hansom cab and walked the last half mile with pleasure. He passed a couple of fashionable ladies of his acquaintance out taking the air, their crinolined skirts obliging him to step almost to the curb in order not to be in their way. He bowed to them, raising his hat, and they smiled charmingly and continued their excited conversation.

The slight breeze carried the sound of an organ grinder, and children shouting to one another, and the rapid clip of a horse's hooves as it pulled a light carriage or gig.

He reached his home in plenty of time to eat supper, then sat and read the day's newspapers before changing into his evening clothes and leaving for Lady Hardesty's ball.

He arrived amid a crowd of other carriages and alighted, paid his driver, and went up the steps and into the blaze of lights and the swirl and glitter of enormous skirts, white shoulders, jewels of every sort, the sound of music and laughter and endless talk. Footmen moved about with trays of champagne, or lemonade for the more abstemious and the young ladies who should not overindulge, and perhaps behave in a less than seemly manner, or forget for an instant why they were there. A girl who did not make a fortunate impression in her first season was in perilous shape, and if she had not found a husband by her second, could be written off as a disaster.

Rathbone had been told these facts of life often enough, but he took them with a smile. It was an intellectual rather than emotional knowledge. Whether a man married or not was immaterial, except to himself. Society thought neither more nor less of him. All around him he heard snatches of conversation.

"What happened to Louisa?" an elderly lady in burgundy silk asked rhetorically, her eyebrows raised. "Why, my dear, she left the country. Went to live in Italy, I think. What else could she do?"

"What else?" her companion asked, her thin face expressing bewilderment, then a sudden rush of understanding. "Oh, my goodness! You don't mean she divorced him, do you? Whatever for?"

"He beat her," the lady in burgundy replied tersely, leaning her head a trifle closer. "I thought you knew that."

"I did . . . but really . . . I mean . . . Italy, did you say?" Her eyes widened. "I suppose it was worth it . . . but a terribly bad example. I don't know what the world is coming to!"

"Quite," the first matron agreed. "I shan't let my daughters know of it. It is very unsettling, and it doesn't do to allow girls to be unsettled." She lowered her voice confidentially. "One is far happier if one knows precisely what to expect of life. Rose Blaine just had her ninth, you know. Another boy. They are going to call him Albert, after the Prince."

"Speaking of whom," her friend continued, leaning even closer and moving her skirts absently, "Mariah Harvey told me he is looking quite poorly these days, very pasty, you know, quite lost his good complexion, and his figure. Dyspeptic, they say."

"Well, he is a foreigner, you know," the thinner of the two said, nodding as if that explained everything. "He may be our dear Queen's husband, but—oh, you know I do wish she would stay with pink, and not ever that fierce shade of fuchsia. She looks hot enough to burst into flames any moment! They say she never ever chooses a thing without taking his advice. Some men are color-blind, I hear. It's that German blood."

"Nonsense!" came the instant retort. "English men can be just as color-blind, if they choose."

Rathbone concealed a smile and moved away. He was well acquainted with the insularity of mind which still regarded the Prince Consort, given that official title three years before, in 1857, as being a foreigner, in spite of the fact that he was so deferred to by the Queen that he was king in all but name. He had a wide reputation for being painfully serious and more than a trifle pompous, not merely given to good works but completely overtaken by them to the point where pleasure of any sort was deeply suspect. Rathbone had met him once and found the experience daunting, and one he did not seek to repeat.

He passed a group of pretty girls, seventeen or eighteen years old, their fair skin gleaming in the light from the myriad candles in the chandeliers, their eyes bright, their voices high with nervousness, full of giggles and little squeaks. Their mothers or aunts were only yards away. One must never be without a chaperone. Reputations could be ruined.

A couple of young men were eyeing them from a distance of a few yards, standing self-consciously, pretending not to notice. One of them was so stiff his back was almost arched. They reminded Rathbone of bantam cocks.

He felt a hand on his arm and turned to see a man in his middle forties with a lean and humorous face.

"Rathbone, how are you?" he said cheerfully. "Didn't expect to see you at this sort of thing!"

"Hello, FitzRobert!" Rathbone replied with pleasure. "I was invited, and I rather fancied a little idle amusement, a spot of champagne and music."

FitzRobert's smile broadened. "Just won a notable victory?"

"Yes, as a matter of fact," Rathbone admitted, reliving his satisfaction. "I have. How are you?" He regarded his friend more closely. "You look well." It was not entirely true, but he felt tact was the better part of perception.

"Oh, I am," FitzRobert said a shade too quickly. "Busy, you know. Politics is a demanding mistress." He smiled briefly.

Rathbone struggled to remember the man's wife's name, and it came to him with a sudden picture of her face, very beautiful in a smooth, oddly discontented way. "And how is Mary?" he added.

"Very well, thank you." FitzRobert put his hands in his pockets and looked away. His eye caught a group of people several yards in the distance. The man was stocky, balding, with a plain but genial face. His features were strong, and no skill of expensive tailoring could hide the awkwardness of his stance or the weight and power of his shoulders. The woman next to him, presumably his wife, was a head shorter than he, and extremely pretty, almost beautiful, with regular features, a long, straight nose, and wide eyes. The girl with them was demurely dressed in the customary white for a first season, only barely enhanced with trimmings of pink. The gown was doubtless extremely costly, but she did not need it to make her stand out among her peers. She was a little over average height, slender, and with quite the most beautiful hair Rathbone had ever seen. It was thick, of a muted golden bronze in color, and with a heavy curl which no art could have imitated.

"Are you acquainted with them?" Rathbone asked.

"Only slightly," FitzRobert answered without changing expression. "He is in trade of some sort. Made himself a fortune. But of course that hardly endears him to society, although they will put up with him for his money's sake. And he has had the grace to patronize the arts to the extent of tens of thousands of pounds." He shrugged slightly. "Which, of course, does not make him a gentleman but at least lends him some respectability." FitzRobert turned back to Rathbone, smiling because they both knew precisely what he meant: the subtle grades of acceptance which came so easily to those born to it and were nigh on impossible to those who were not.

Even Prince Albert was regarded with coolness by some, just as he disdained the frivolity, the wit, the self-indulgence and the sheer arrogant grace of some of the oldest aristocracy in the country, whose fortunes certainly equaled his own and whose wives had a better sense of fashion than the Queen—and jewels to match. Until very recently they had considered him a political upstart, and his endless notes and letters to be interfering.

Rathbone smiled back. He allowed FitzRobert to see in his eyes that he was going to pretend he had not noticed the shadow of unhappiness there, nor understood its deeply personal nature.

"Who is he?" he asked. "He does not look familiar to me."

"Barton Lambert," FitzRobert replied. "His daughter, Zillah, is engaged to marry Killian Melville, the architect. I don't see him here tonight." He looked around. "Devoted to his work. Not a very social man."

Rathbone was suddenly uncertain whether he wanted to know more or not. When there were crimes and desperate injustices to fight, why on earth should he spend his time and his skills in defending a foolish young man from the consequences of his ambition and his lack of forthrightness towards a young woman who had taken him at his behavior, if not his word—as it turned out, mistakenly. It was not a matter which should waste the time of the law. It could be settled with a few well-chosen words and a little sensitivity, and strategic realignment.

"Brilliant fellow," FitzRobert went on. "Probably one of the most original and daring thinkers of his generation. And has the technical skill and personal drive and persistence to see his ideas from the dreams into the reality."

"With suitable help from Barton Lambert," Rathbone added dryly.

FitzRobert was surprised. "Thought you didn't know him!"

"Not a great deal." Rathbone retreated with more speed than grace. "Only what I have heard. A word or two—you know how one does."

FitzRobert smiled. "Well, I suppose he has been on people's tongues lately. The engagement was in the *Times*."

Rathbone spoke almost before thinking. "Perhaps you could introduce me?"

"Of course," FitzRobert agreed. "Delighted to. For all his northern brashness, and a certain quickness to see insult where it is not intended, he is a very decent fellow. Honest as you like, and loyal. Once a friend, always a friend."

"I don't want to intrude." Rathbone took a step backwards, already regretting his words. "Perhaps . . ."

"Not at all," FitzRobert said with an expansive gesture. He took Rathbone by the arm. "Come on, by all means."

Rathbone had little choice but to follow, and a few moments later he was being introduced to Barton Lambert and his wife and daughter.

"How do you do, sir," Lambert said with a strong northern accent. His manner was open and friendly, but he seemed not to be too impressed by Rathbone's title.

Delphine Lambert, on the other hand, had a very different air. Closer to her, it was apparent that her marvelous jewelry was real—and almost certainly worth more than Rathbone made in half a year, although he did extremely well. And she was a remarkably pretty woman. Her skin was blemishless and the arch of her brows and delicate curve of her hairline were quite unique, as was the slope of her cheekbones. Her intelligence was apparent in her wide, clear eyes.

"How do you do, Sir Oliver," she said with charm, but marked reserve. Rathbone had an instant feeling that were her daughter not engaged to be married, her interest in him would have been quite different. He felt a surge of relief, which was ridiculous. He was perfectly capable of declining politely! He had done it for years.

Zillah was lovely. There was a naturalness and a spontaneity about her which Rathbone liked immediately. Also, she was unashamedly happy. The knowledge of how soon it would be shattered bothered Rathbone more than he had expected.

They spoke of the usual kind of trivia, and he could see her parents' pride in her, the quick glances of obvious affection from her father. Her pain would be his pain; her embarrassment would cut him more deeply than his own. Rathbone doubted Barton Lambert would forgive a man who hurt his daughter, privately or publicly. It was not difficult to understand. He was not a foolish man, nor one without worldly wisdom, or he could not have made the wealth he had in a harsh and highly competitive trade. Manchester—that was the area where his accent proclaimed him to have lived—was not a soft city nor one easily to refine the rough edges from a man's manner. But neither did it have the weary sophistication of London, the cosmopolitan mixture of cultures and the press and vigor of the world's traffic. There was a kind of innocence to Barton Lambert, and looking at his face, Rathbone was sure his anger would be of the same spontaneous and unstoppable character.

The conversation was about politics. FitzRobert had just said something about Mr. Gladstone.

"Fine man," Lambert agreed. "Knew his family." He nodded.

Of course. William Ewart Gladstone, "God's vicar in the Treasury," as he had been mockingly called, was a Manchester man. There was a ring of pride in Lambert's voice.

"Couldn't be less like the Prime Minister," FitzRobert went on, referring, no doubt, to Lord Palmerston's reputation for wit and good fellowship and the distinct enjoyment of life, its pleasures as well as its duties.

A thought crossed Rathbone's mind about Mr. Gladstone's

fairly well-known vigor regarding the opposite sex, and the occasionally understandable interpretation of his hospitality for the less fortunate of them, whose souls he believed he might save. However, in deference to the ladies present, especially Zillah, he forbore from making any remark. He caught FitzRobert's eye and kept his face perfectly composed, but with difficulty.

They were joined a moment later by another handsome woman, accompanied by two unmarried daughters. They were all dutifully introduced, and Rathbone saw the lady's eyes sparkle with interest as she automatically assessed his eligibility, his social status and his probable income. Apparently she found them all satisfactory. She smiled at him generously.

"I am delighted to make your acquaintance, Sir Oliver. May I present my elder daughter, Margaret."

"How do you do, Sir Oliver," Margaret replied obediently. She was a comely enough girl with candid blue eyes and rather ordinary features. Her brown hair had been elaborately curled for the occasion. It probably became her better in its natural state, but an opportunity such as this was not to be wasted by informality. No artifice for glamour was left untried.

"How do you do, Miss Ballinger," Rathbone said civilly. He hated these forced conversations and wished more than ever that he had refused to come across with FitzRobert. Nothing he could possibly learn about Barton Lambert or his daughter would compensate for the awkwardness of it. In fact, it would be of no use whatever, because he did not intend to take Killian Melville's case, should it arise. It was Melville's own fault he was in this predicament, and he should use his common sense to get himself out of it, or else abide the consequences, which were more than likely to be only the same as those experienced by the majority of men in the world. Zillah Lambert was most attractive and would come with a handsome dowry. Left to his own choice he might well do very much worse.

"And my younger daughter, Julia," Mrs. Ballinger was saying to him.

"How do you do, Miss Julia." Rathbone inclined his head towards her. She was no prettier than her sister and had the same frank, almost amused stare.

"Did you attend the concert at Lady Thorpe's house yesterday evening?" Mrs. Ballinger was asking Mrs. Lambert. "We went for Margaret's sake. She is so fond of music, and of course is a most accomplished violinist, if I do say so myself." She turned to Rathbone with a bright smile. "Are you fond of music, Sir Oliver?"

Rathbone wanted to lie and say he was tone-deaf. He saw the eagerness in Mrs. Ballinger's face and the embarrassment in Margaret's. She must feel as if she were bloodstock being paraded in front of a prospective buyer. It was not far from the truth.

Mrs. Lambert smiled with inner satisfaction. She had already won and no longer needed to compete. The triumph of it was luminous in her eyes. Zillah herself looked serenely happy.

Rathbone felt like part of a group picnicking in the sun, and he was the only one aware of the clouds thickening over the horizon, and growing chill in the air.

Mrs. Ballinger was waiting for a reply.

Rathbone looked at Margaret, and his compassion overcame his sense and he answered with the truth.

"Yes, I am very fond of music, particularly the violin."

Mrs. Ballinger's answer was immediate.

"Then perhaps you would care to visit with us some occasion and hear Margaret play. We are holding a soirée next Thursday."

Margaret bit her lip and the color mounted up her face. She turned away from Rathbone, and he was quite certain she would have looked daggers at her mother had she dared. He wondered how many times before she had endured this scene, or ones like it.

He had walked straight into the trap. He was almost as angry as Margaret at the blatancy of it. And yet neither of them could do anything without making it worse.

Delphine Lambert was watching with an air of gentle amusement, her delicate mouth not quite smiling.

It was Julia Ballinger who broke the minute's silence.

"I daresay Sir Oliver does not have his diary to hand, Mama. I am sure he will send us a card to say whether he is able to accept, if we allow him our address."

Margaret shot her a look of gratitude.

Rathbone smiled. "You are perfectly correct, Miss Julia. I am afraid I am not certain of my engagements a week ahead. My memory is not as exact as I should like, and I should be mortified to find I had offended someone by failing to attend an invitation I had already accepted. Or indeed that a case kept me overlong where I had foreseen it might . . ."

"Of course," Margaret said hastily.

But Mrs. Ballinger did not give up so easily. She produced a card from her reticule and passed it to him. It noted her name and address. "You are always welcome, Sir Oliver, even if you are not able to confirm beforehand. We are not so very formal as to admit only those we expect when an evening of social pleasure is to be enjoyed."

"Thank you, Mrs. Ballinger." He took the card and slipped it into his pocket. He was sufficiently annoyed with her insensitivity that he might even go, for Margaret's sake. Looking at her now, standing stiffly with her shoulders squared, horribly uncomfortable, and knowing this ritual would be observed until she was either successfully married or past marriageable age, she reminded him faintly of Hester Latterly, whom he had come to know in some ways so well in the last few years. There was a similar courage and vulnerability in her, an awareness of precisely what was going on, a contempt for it, and yet a knowledge that she was inevitably caught up in it and trapped.

Of course, Hester was not any longer similarly caught. She had broken free and gone to the Crimea to nurse with Florence Nightingale, and returned changed forever. It was her personal loss that both her parents had died in the tragedy which indirectly had brought about her meeting with William Monk, and thus with Rathbone. It had also spared her the otherwise inevitable round of parties, balls, soirées, and attendances at any conceivable kind of social occasion until her mother had found her an acceptable husband. Acceptable to her family, of course, not necessarily to her.

But Hester must be about thirty now, and too old for most men to find her appealing—of which fact she could not be unaware. Standing in this glittering room with the music in the background and the press and hum of scores of people, the clink of glasses, the faint smells of warmth, champagne, stiff material and sometimes of flowers and perfume, he could not help wondering if it hurt her. And yet only a few months ago he had been so close to asking her to marry him. He had even led into an appropriate conversation. He could remember it now with a sudden wave of disappointment. He was certain she had known what he was going to say, and she had gently, very indirectly, allowed him to understand that she was not ready to give him an answer.

Had that been because she loved Monk?

He did not wish to believe that; in fact, he refused to. It would be like ripping the plaster off a wound to see if it was really as deep as one feared. He knew it would be.

And he would go and listen to Margaret Ballinger play her violin. Damn Mrs. Ballinger for insulting her so!

The conversation was going on around him, something to do with a house they had all seen recently, or a public building of some nature.

"I am afraid I do not care for it," Delphine Lambert said with feeling. "Most unimaginative. I am disappointed they chose such old-fashioned ideas. There was nothing new in it at all."

"Restricted budget, I daresay," her husband offered.

She gave him an odd look. "Mr. Melville could have designed something far better, I am sure. Don't you think so, my dear?" She looked at Zillah.

"He is quite brilliant," Zillah agreed, unable to hide her enthusiasm. "He is so sensitive. He is able to create beauty where one would never have imagined it possible and to draw designs so it can be built. You cannot imagine how exciting it is to see drawings on a page and then to see them come to life. Oh!" She blushed. "I mean—to reality, of course. But such grace and inventiveness almost seem as if they have a life, an existence of their own." She looked from one to another of them. "Do you know what I mean?"

"Of course we do, my dear," Lambert assured her. "Only natural for you to be proud of him."

Delphine smiled at Rathbone. "Perhaps you did not know, Sir Oliver, but Zillah is engaged to marry Mr. Melville. It is quite charming to see two young people so devoted to one another; they cannot but be happy. He really is a most talented man, and yet not in the least immodest or overbearing. His success has never gone to his head, nor has he lost his sense of gratitude to Mr. Lambert for his patronage. You believed in him from the very beginning, didn't you, my dear?" It was a rhetorical question. She did not wait for an answer but turned again to Mrs. Ballinger. "Mr. Lambert was always good at seeing a man's character. Makes a judgment from the first meeting, and never wrong that I know of."

"How fortunate," Mrs. Ballinger said dryly, "we have not the opportunity of having to exercise such a gift. So much in society is already known of a person." She did not add the implicated aside that the Lamberts were not part of society, but it hung in the air unsaid.

Mrs. Lambert merely smiled. She could afford to. Society or not, she had successfully accomplished her principal role in life. She was not only married to a wealthy man herself, she had engaged her only daughter to a man of good looks, good manners, brilliant talent, and excellent financial prospects. What more was there to do?

The orchestra had begun to play a waltz. Rathbone turned to Margaret Ballinger.

"Miss Ballinger, will you do me the honor of dancing with me?"

She accepted with a smile and he excused himself and offered her his arm to lead her to the floor. She took it lightly—he could barely feel her hand—and followed him without meeting his eyes.

They had been dancing for several minutes before she spoke, and then it was hesitant.

"I am sorry Mama is so . . . forward. I hope she did not embarrass you, Sir Oliver."

"Not at all," he said honestly. It was she who had been embarrassed. He had been merely angry. "She is only behaving as all mothers do." He wanted to think of something else to add which would make her feel easier, but he could imagine nothing. This would go on, and they both knew it. It was a ritual. Some young women found a certain excitement in it or had a self-confidence which bore them along. Some were not sufficiently sensitive or imaginative to suffer the humiliation or to perceive the young man's awkwardness or knowledge of being manipulated, almost hunted, and the burden of expectation upon him.

He must find a conversation to hold with Margaret. She was dancing with her head turned away, self-conscious, almost as if she feared he had invited her only to save her embarrassment. It was half true. He wished to make it wholly a lie. She seemed so very vulnerable.

"Do you know this architect, Killian Melville?" he asked.

"I have met him three or four times," she answered, a slight lift of surprise in her voice, and she looked up towards him. "Are you interested in architecture, Sir Oliver?"

"Not especially," he said with a smile. "I suppose I tend to be most aware of it when it offends me. I am rather used to agreeable surroundings. Perhaps I take them for granted. What is his work like? A less biased opinion than Miss Lambert's, if you have one. . . ."

She laughed. "Oh, yes indeed. I did like him. He was so easy to talk to. Not in the least . . . brash or—oh, dear, I don't know how to pursue it without sounding . . ." She stopped again.

"Now you have me fascinated," he admitted. "Please tell me. Speak frankly, and I promise not to take offense—or to repeat it."

She regarded him uncertainly, then relaxed, and her eyes lost the anxiety they had held until that moment. He realized that without the artificial necessity to be charming, biddable, pretty and accommodating, she was almost certainly an intelligent and most likable person.

"Yes?" he prompted.

She laughed. "I found Mr. Melville one of the most comfortable people I ever encountered," she said, swirling gracefully in his arms as they negotiated a complicated corner, her huge, pale skirts flying. "He never seemed to misunderstand or to need to prove himself and—and parade . . . as so many young men do . . . I—" She bit her lip. "I hope that does not sound too unkind?"

"Not at all," he assured her. "Merely very candid. I know precisely what you mean. I have observed it, and I daresay if I were to glance around now I should see a score of examples. I was doubtless guilty of it myself . . . a few years ago."

She wanted to laugh. He could see it in her eyes, but good manners, and the slightness of their acquaintance, forbade it.

"Perhaps I still do. . . ." He said it before she could complete the thought.

"Oh no," she denied. "I'm sure not now. You don't need to, and you must know that."

"The advantage of age." He laughed at himself.

Suddenly the vulnerability was back in her eyes, and he knew she was afraid he had referred to the difference in their ages to distance himself from her, to let her know gently that this was merely a courtesy acquaintance and could be nothing more. That was true, but because of his feelings for Hester, not anything to do with Margaret Ballinger. Were it not for Hester, he might well have sought to know Margaret a good deal better.

He was chilled by the realization of how easy it was to hurt, without the slightest intention, simply because one was thinking of something else, watching some other imperative.

"Well, perhaps it is more the assurance one gains from some professional success," he amended, then wished he had not. He was only making it worse. "Tell me more about Mr. Melville's architectural designs. Is he really innovative?"

"Yes, quite definitely," she replied without hesitation. "His designs seem to have far more light than most people's. They are full of windows and curves where I have never seen them before. There is a house in Hampshire he built, or should I say Mr. Lambert had built, which is wonderful inside. Every room seems to be full of sunlight, and the windows are quite irregular. It is extraordinarily comfortable to be in. One always seems to be looking outside either at trees or at the sky. I felt so at peace in it. And yet when I asked the housekeeper if it was difficult to care for, she assured me it was actually highly practical. I was most surprised."

So was Rathbone. He had not judged Melville to have such courage.

"I think perhaps he is a genius," Margaret said very quietly. He only heard her because the music had stopped. They swung to a standstill. He offered his arm again, and she took it.

"Would you care for a glass of champagne?" he asked. "Or lemonade?"

"Lemonade, if you please," she accepted.

He fetched it for her and they spent a little further time in conversation, now not in the least difficult. Then he returned her to where Mrs. Ballinger was standing alone looking remarkably pleased with herself.

"I can see how much you have enjoyed your dance," she said with a smile. "You are excellently matched." She turned to her daughter. "Mr. Edwin Trelawny has been asking for you, my dear. He remembered you from your meeting in Bath. I think we should return Lady Trelawny's call . . . perhaps this week."

It was a ploy to make sure Rathbone did not think Margaret too available. No one wished to pursue a young lady if he was alone in the chase. If he were, then she could not be worth a great deal.

"Yes, Mama," Margaret said dutifully, cringing at the obviousness of it.

Mrs. Ballinger was undeterred. In order to marry off daughters one had to develop an exceedingly thick protective armor against disapproval or other people's embarrassment. She ignored Margaret's pleading look.

"Does your family live in London, Sir Oliver? I don't believe I am acquainted with your mother."

Margaret closed her eyes, refusing to look at Rathbone.

Rathbone smiled with quite genuine amusement. He was now being judged as to whether he was socially fully acceptable.

"My mother died some years ago, Mrs. Ballinger," he answered. "My father lives in Primrose Hill, but he mixes very little in society. In fact, I suppose it would be more honest to say he does not mix at all." He looked at her directly. "Of course, he is quite well acquainted with most of the scientific and mathematical community because of his work . . . before he retired. And he always had a high regard for Lord Palmerston."

He knew instantly he should not have mentioned the Prime Minister. She was immensely impressed.

"How very agreeable," she answered, momentarily at a loss for words. She recovered rapidly. "I hope I shall have the good fortune to meet him someday. He sounds quite delightful."

Margaret looked as if she wanted to groan.

"I am afraid my opinion is hopelessly biased," Rathbone said, excusing himself with a smile. He was actually extremely fond of his father. He liked him quite as much as anyone he knew. "Now I must not monopolize your time, Mrs. Ballinger. Miss Ballinger, I have greatly enjoyed your company, and I hope we shall meet again. Good evening."

They replied appropriately and he turned and walked away, perhaps a little more rapidly than usual. In spite of his intellectual knowledge of what was happening, and why, and his wry amusement at it all, he still felt pursued, and only his certainty of escape kept the panic from welling up inside him.

He must not seem to be fleeing. It would hurt Margaret and be inexcusably rude. He should dance with at least three or four other young ladies, and perhaps one or two older ones, before he could decently leave.

An hour later he was preparing to excuse himself to Lady Hardesty and thank her for a delightful evening, when he found himself standing next to Zillah Lambert, who had just been left by a companion who had gone to seek refreshment for her. She looked flushed and happy, her skin glowing, her eyes bright.

"Good evening again, Miss Lambert," he said politely. She really was a very charming girl.

"Good evening, Sir Oliver. Isn't it a lovely ball?" She looked around at the sea of lace and tulle and silk, the blaze of lights, the laughter and the music and the sway and swirl of movement. "I wish everyone could be as happy as I am."

He felt acutely awkward. He knew that almost all of her joy rested in her engagement to Melville, and she obviously had not even the slightest idea that his feeling was utterly different. What to her was a prospect of excitement and unshadowed delight was to him a prison closing in, so unbearable he would risk social ruin—and very probably financial and professional ruin also—rather than endure it.

Why? There had to be far more to it than he had told Rathbone. Was Zillah really completely different from the way she seemed?

He looked at her again. She was certainly comely enough to please any man, and yet not so beautiful as to be vain or spoiled because of it. If she was extravagant, she would probably bring a dowry with her which would more than offset that. And her nature seemed most agreeable.

"You must meet Mr. Melville, Sir Oliver," she was saying enthusiastically. "I am sure you would like him. Everybody does, or nearly everybody. I would not wish to give the impression he is so obliging as to be without character or opinion. He certainly is not."

"You are very fond of him, aren't you?" he said gently.

"Oh yes!" She seemed to radiate her happiness. "I think I am the most fortunate woman in England, if not the world. He is everything I could wish. I have never felt so extremely at ease in anyone's company, and yet at the same time so invigorated in thought and so filled with the awareness of being on the brink of the greatest adventure life has to offer." There was not a shadow of doubt in her. "We shall be the envy of everyone in London for the blessings of our lives together. I know he will make me a perfect husband, and I shall do everything I can think of to please him and make him proud of me. I wish that never in all the years we shall live together should he even for an hour regret that he chose me." She looked at him with wide, soft eyes filled with hope and trust.

Suddenly, like a hand clenching inside him, he understood Melville's fear. It was unbearable to think of being responsible for so much in the life of another human being, one who sees you not as the fallible, sometimes self-conscious, sometimes weary and frightened creature that you are, just as frail as they, but as some kind of cross between a genius and a saint, whose every thought bears examination and whose every act will be both wise and kind. One could never relax, never admit to weakness or doubt, never simply lose one's temper or confess terror, failure or despair. What intolerable loneliness! And yet a loneliness without privacy.

Was she aware of the intimate facts of life? Looking at her bright innocence, and knowing a little of the tragic lives of some of his clients, he thought very possibly not. And even if she was, could any man live up to her expectations?

His own skin broke out in a prickle of sweat as he placed himself in Melville's situation for a moment. Now he understood only too sharply why the young architect could not bear it. With Delphine Lambert engineering everything, her clever, prying eyes seeing every fleeting expression of her daughter's face, nothing he said or did would go unknown. He could not ever fail in decent privacy.

And it had been arrogant of Rathbone to imagine he could not have found himself in the same position. He was at least twelve or fifteen years older than Melville, if not more. And yet he had been neatly enough maneuvered by Mrs. Ballinger.

"I imagine you will be very happy, Miss Lambert," he said awkwardly. "I certainly hope you will. But . . ."

She looked at him without the slightest comprehension. "But what, Sir Oliver? Can you doubt my good fortune? You would not, if you knew Killian, I promise you."

What could he possibly say to be even barely honest? What should he say to her? Melville had asked Rathbone to defend him in court, should the need arise, not to conduct any negotiations to break the engagement. He might change his mind. It might simply be the sort of nervousness many people experience before marriage.

"But nothing, Miss Lambert," he said, shaking his head. "Perhaps I merely envy you. I wish you every joy. Good evening." And before he could find himself any further embroiled, he took his leave and made his way towards Lady Hardesty.

The following day Rathbone sent Melville a message saying that on further consideration he had changed his mind, and if Melville should, after all, find himself sued for breach of promise, Rathbone would be willing to represent him. Although he feared it would be a most difficult case, and his change was not based upon any alteration in his belief that the chances of success were very small. Still, he would do his best.

CHAPTER TWO

While the thought of her had crossed Rathbone's mind during Lady Hardesty's ball, Hester Latterly herself was sitting quietly in the room she had been given for her accommodation during her stay in the elegant house at the northwest corner of Tavistock Square. It was the house of Lieutenant Gabriel Sheldon and his new young wife, Perdita. Lieutenant Sheldon had served honorably in the army in India. He had survived the hideous Mutiny, the siege of Cawnpore, and been one of the few survivors of that atrocity. He had remained in India afterwards, only to fall victim to appalling injuries just over two years later, in the winter of 1859–60. He had lost an arm, been severely disfigured, and at first was not expected to live.

By January his partial recovery was deemed sufficient for him to be shipped home to England and invalided out of the service. However, he was far from well enough to manage without skilled nursing, and the damage done to the skin and flesh of his face was such that it required a particular sensitivity, as well as medical knowledge of and experience with such wounds, to care for him. The stump of his arm was also far from satisfactory. The wound still was raw in places and not entirely free from infection. Even the danger of gangrene could not yet be disregarded.

Perdita Sheldon had been young and pretty and full of high spirits when her handsome husband of a few months had been obliged to return to his regiment and departed for India in the late autumn of 1856. She had wanted to go with him, but she had been newly with child and not at all well. She had miscarried in the spring. And then in 1857 the unimaginable had happened. The native sepoys had mutinied, and the revolt had spread like wildfire. Men, women and children were massacred. The tales that reached England were almost too monstrous to be believed. Daily, almost hourly, people rushed to read the latest news of the besieged cities of Cawnpore and Lucknow, the battles that raged across the country. The names of Nena Sahib, Koer Singh, Tanteea Topee, and the Ranee of Jhansi became familiar to everyone's lips. For two years the continent of India seethed with inconceivable violence. The question of whether Perdita Sheldon, or any other woman, should leave England to go there did not arise.

When it was over and calm had been restored once more, nothing could ever be the same again. The trust was shattered forever. Gabriel Sheldon was still on active service with his regiment, mostly in the rugged country of the northwest, near the borders of the Khyber Pass, leading through the Himalayas into Afghanistan. Perdita remained in England, dreaming of the day he would come back and she could once again have the life he had promised her, and which she had equally promised him.

The man who did return was unrecognizable to her either in body or in spirit. He was wounded too deeply, broken too far to pretend, and she had not the faintest idea even how to understand, let alone to help. She felt as abandoned as he did, confused and asked to bear a burden heavier than anything her life had designed her to face.

Hence Gabriel's brother, Athol Sheldon, had engaged the best nurse he could find, through the agency of his excellent man of affairs, and Hester Latterly was installed in Tavistock Square to nurse Gabriel for as long as should prove necessary.

Now it was late in the evening for the household of an invalid, and they had already dined: Perdita downstairs with her brother-in-law, Athol; Gabriel in his room with Hester's assistance. Hester herself had eaten only briefly, in the servants' hall, and then left as soon as his tray was ready to bring upstairs.

This was a time of day when she had no specific duties, simply to be available should she be required. Gabriel would ring the bell beside his bed when he was ready to retire or if he felt in need of assistance. There was no mending to do and her other duties had long since been attended to. She had borrowed a book from the library but was finding it tedious.

It was just after ten when at last the bell rang, and she was delighted to close the book, without bothering to mark her place, and walk the short distance along the landing to Gabriel's room. She knocked on the door.

"Come in!" he answered immediately.

It was the largest room on this floor, turned into a place where he could not only sleep at night but read or sleep during the day, and in time write letters, or receive visitors, and feel as much at ease as was possible in his circumstances.

She closed the door behind her. His bed was at the far end, a magnificent piece with elaborately carved mahogany headboard and footboard, and presently piled with pillows so he could sit up with some comfort. A special rest had been designed and made both to support his book or paper and to hold it open so he could read, or keep it from moving if he was writing. Fortunately he was right-handed, and it was his left arm he had lost.

But on first seeing him it was not the empty sleeve one noticed but the terrible disfigurement to his face, the left side of which was so deeply scarred from cheekbone to jaw that the flesh had not knitted and the features were distorted by the pull of the muscles and the healing skin. There was a raw red line which would never change, and white crisscross fine ridges where it had been stitched together hastily on the battlefield. After the initial shock it was possible to imagine quite easily how handsome he had been before the injury. It was a face almost beautiful in its simplicity of line, its balance between nose and cheek and jaw. The clear brow and hazel-gray eyes were unblemished even now. The dark brown, wavy hair was thick. His mouth was pinched with pain.

"I've had enough of this book," he said ruefully. "It's not very interesting."

"Neither was mine." She smiled at him. "I didn't even bother to mark my place. Would you like me to find you something else for tomorrow?"

"Yes, please, although I don't know what."

She took the book away and carefully removed the stand and folded it up. It was well designed and quite light to manage. His bed was rumpled where he had moved about restlessly. He was not only in physical distress from his amputation, the flesh not healing properly, the phantom pain of a limb which was not there; even more acute was the emotional distress of feeling both ugly and incomplete, powerless. He was without a role in a life which stretched interminably ahead of him containing nothing more than being dependent upon the help of others, an object of revulsion to the uninitiated in the horror of war, and one of pity to those familiar. Perhaps the greatest burden of all was the fact that he was unable to share his feelings with his wife. His existence shackled her to a man she was embarrassed even to look at, let alone touch. He had offered to release her from the marriage, as honor required. And as honor required, she had refused.

"Any subject in particular?" Hester asked, stretching out her hand to assist him in throwing back the covers and climbing from the bed so she could remake it. He was still quite often caught off balance by the alteration in his weight since the arm had gone.

He forced himself to smile, and she knew it was an effort, made for her sake, and perhaps from a lifetime of good manners.

"I can't think of anything," he admitted. "I've already read everything I knew I wanted to."

"I'll have to see if I can find you something quite different," she said conversationally, leaving him to sit on the bedside chair and beginning to strip off the bedclothes to replace them smoothly. She did not want to talk of trivialities to him, and yet it was so difficult to know what to say that would be honest and not hurtful, not intrusive into areas he was perhaps not yet ready to explore or to expose to anyone else. After all, she had been there only a few days and was in a position neither of family member and friend nor yet of servant. She already knew a great many of his intimate physical feelings and needs far better than anyone else, but could only guess at his history, his character or his emotions.

"What were you reading?" he asked, leaning back in the chair.

"A novel about people I could not bring myself to like," she replied with a laugh. "I am afraid I did not care in the slightest whether they ever found a solution to their problems or not. I think I shall try something factual next, perhaps a description of travels or places I shall almost certainly not visit."

He was silent for several moments.

She worked at the bed without haste.

"There's quite a lot about India," he said at last.

She caught an inflection in his voice of more than a mere remark. He must be appallingly lonely. He saw few people but Perdita, and in her visits neither of them knew what to say and struggled with platitudes, silences and then sudden rushes of words. He was almost relieved when she went, and yet was sharply aware of his isolation and overwhelming sense of despair and helplessness.

His brother, Athol, was what was known as a "muscular Christian"—a man given to unnatural ebullience, overbearingly vigorous views about health and morality, and an optimism which at times was beyond enduring. He refused to acknowledge Gabriel's pain or attempt the slightest understanding of it. Perhaps it frightened him, because his philosophy had no answer for it. It was something beyond anyone's control, and Athol's sense of safety came from his conviction that man was, or could and should become, master of his life.

"You must know India better than most writers," she said, forgetting the linen for a moment and looking at Gabriel, trying to read the expression in his eyes.

"Parts of it," he agreed, watching her equally intently, also seeking to judge her reaction, what he could tell her with some hope she would not be overwhelmed or distressed by events beyond her comprehension. "Are you interested in India?"

She was not particularly, but she was interested in him. She moderated the truth. "I am in current affairs, especially military ones."

His eyes clouded with doubt. "Military ones, Miss Latterly?" There was a hint of doubt in his voice now, as if he mistrusted her motives, fearing she was accommodating him. He must be very sensitive to condescension. "Have you a brother in the army?"

She smiled that he automatically assumed it would not be a lover. He must see her as too old for such a thing, or not comely enough. It was unthinking. He would not mean to hurt.

"No, Lieutenant, my elder brother is in business, and my younger brother was killed in the Crimea. My interest in military history is my own."

He knew he had been clumsy, even though he was not sure how. It was there in his cheeks and his eyes.

She realized how little she had told him of herself, and perhaps Athol had been equally unforthcoming. Possibly he considered her only a superior servant, and as long as her references were adequate, everything else was superfluous. One did not make friends of servants, especially temporary ones.

She smiled at him. "I have strong opinions about army medical matters, most of which have got me into trouble since I returned to England."

"Returned?" he said quickly. "From where?"

"The Crimea. Did Mr. Sheldon not tell you?"

"No." His interest was sharp now. "You were in the Crimea? That's excellent! No . . . he simply said you were the best person to nurse extreme injuries. He did not say why." He was leaning forward a little in his chair, his face eager. "Then you must have seen some terrible things, starvation and dysentery, cholera, smallpox . . . gangrene . . ."

"Yes," she agreed, pulling the last cover over the bed and

straightening it. "And anger and despair, and incompetence almost beyond belief. And rats . . . thousands of rats." The memory of them was something which would never leave her, the sound of their fat bodies dropping off the walls to run among the men as they lay on floors awash with waste no one had had time or equipment to clean. It was that heavy plop and scamper which chilled her flesh even now, four years after and myriad experiences since.

He was silent while she helped him back into bed and smoothed the covers over him.

"No . . ." he said quickly as she made to remove the pillows. "Please leave them. I'm not ready to go to sleep yet."

She drew back.

"Miss Latterly!"

"Yes?"

"Tell me a little about the Crimea . . . if you don't mind, that is?"

She sat down in the chair and turned to face him.

"I expect much of it you are familiar with," she began, sending herself in memory back six years to early in the war. "Crowds of men, some new and eager, with no idea of what to expect, jostling together, full of courage and ready to charge the moment the order should be given. Your heart aches for them because you know how different it will all be in only a few weeks. No one else would believe such a short time could change anyone so much. . . ."

"I would!" he said instantly, leaning forward to twist around towards her, losing his balance for a moment as instinctively he tried to put out the hand that was not there.

She ignored it and allowed him to right himself.

"Did you know that the whole siege of Cawnpore lasted only from June fifth to July seventeenth?" he asked. He was studying her to see what it meant to her. Had she read anything of the accounts of that unspeakable event? Did she have any idea what it meant? Most people had not. He had tried to speak of it to his brother, but Athol had nothing with which to compare it. Gabriel might as well have been speaking of creatures and events on another world. Such emotions were not describable; one had to live them. The thought of telling Perdita never entered his mind. She would be confused and distressed by the little she might grasp. His passion and grief would frighten her, perhaps revolt her. And yet bearing the knowledge alone was almost more than he could endure.

"I could not have timed it," she confessed. "But I know that events which destroy the flower of a generation and leave wounds which never heal can happen in a day or two."

He was uncertain. Hope flickered in his eyes that he might not be alone in his memories and his understanding.

"I saw the Charge of the Light Brigade at Balaclava," she said very quietly. She found she still could not control her voice when she spoke of it. Even the words choked in her throat and brought a prickle of tears to her eyes and an ache to her chest. The sweet, cloying smell of blood always brought it back to her, the drowning pain would never leave her, the bodies of so many mutilated and dying men, many of them barely into their twenties. Behind her closed eyelids she could see them bent in fantastic attitudes, trying to staunch their own wounds with scarlet hands.

Gabriel shook his head silently, and in that moment she knew he had seen things just as terrible. They brimmed behind his eyes, a haunting of the dreams, needing to be shared, not openly, but enough to break the terrible aloneness of being among those who were unaware, who could speak of it as history, as from the pages of a newspaper or a book, to whom the pain was only words.

She asked him the inevitable question. The Mutiny had ravaged all India from Calcutta and Delhi to the mountain passes into Afghanistan where the altitude thinned the air and peaks towered into the sky, the snow unmelted in millennia.

"Were you at Cawnpore?"

He nodded.

"In the relief column?"

"No . . . I . . ." He looked at her very steadily. "There were over nine hundred of us, counting women and children and civilians. I was one of the four people who survived." He looked at her, his eyes filled with tears.

What could one possibly say to that?

"I have never faced such savagery." She spoke very quietly, a simple, bare truth. "All the death I have seen has been either on the battlefield, incredibly stupid, senseless and pointless, men outmatched by numbers and by guns, ordered to charge impossible targets, but still soldiers even though their lives were squandered. Or people dying of starvation, cold and disease. Far more died of disease than of gunfire, you know." She shook her head a little. "Yes, of course you know. But I have never seen hatred like that, barbarism that would massacre every living soul. The siege of Sebastopol was at least . . . military."

He clung to her understanding, his eyes fixed on hers unwaveringly.

"It began on the fifth of June," he said. "The Mutiny had already been sweeping across the country since the end of February. There had been disturbances because of the cartridges in Meerut and Lucknow. You know all about the cartridges?" He was watching her face. "They were greased with animal fat. If it was pork it was unclean to the Muslim soldiers, and if it was beef it was blasphemous to the Hindus, to whom the cow is a sacred animal. On May seventh open mutiny broke out in Lucknow; on May sixteenth the sappers and miners mutinied in Meerut. By the twentieth it had spread to Murdan and Allygurh. The day after that we began our intrenchment at Cawnpore."

She nodded.

"On the twenty-fourth Gwalior Horse mutinied at Hattrass," he went on. "By the twenty-eighth it had spread to Nuseerbad. On the thirty-first it was Shahjehanpoor. June third, Alzimghur, Seetapoor, Mooradabad and Neemuch. The day after, Benares and Jhansi. On the fifth it was us." He took a deep breath, but his voice did not alter. "I learned after that on the sixth it was Allahabad, Hansi and Bhurtpore. The following week, Jullunur, Fyzabad,

Badulla Derai, Sultanpore, Futtehpore, Pershadeepore . . . and on and on. I could name every garrison in India. There was no one to help us."

She could not imagine it. The isolation, the consuming terror must have been like a tidal wave, drowning everything.

He needed to know she could bear to hear it.

"How did it begin?" she asked. "Guns?"

"No. No, the whole of the native troops set fire to their lines and marched on the treasury, where they were joined by the troops of Nena Sahib . . . which is a name I can still hardly say." His face was tight with misery and the spectacle of horror was dark in his eyes.

She waited, sitting quite still.

"He had thousands of native soldiers," he went on after a moment. "We were only a couple of hundred, with three hundred women and as many children, and of course the civilian population, ordinary people: merchants and shopkeepers, servants, pensioners. General Sir Hugh Wheeler was in command. He ordered us to retreat to the barracks and military hospital. We couldn't possibly hold the whole town." He frowned, as if even now uncertain and puzzled. "Why he didn't choose the treasury instead I don't know. That was on high ground and had far more solid walls. In there we might have held out. I think . . . I think he couldn't really believe we would have to face them alone. He couldn't imagine that the sepoys wouldn't be loyal to us when it came to it." He stopped again. His hand curled and uncurled on the edge of the sheet. "Of course he was wrong."

"I know," she said softly. "Did you have food and ammunition?"

He looked at her steadily.

"Food was modest; ammunition was good. But there was no shelter. After only a few days the walls were so riddled with shot we dug trenches and pulled carts and trunks and furniture over us to protect ourselves as much as we could. The heat was unbearable for many."

She tried to imagine India in July. It was hotter than anything she had ever known.

"I don't know how many died of it," he said, still watching her closely. He needed to speak of the loss of his friends, the human beings he had seen in the utmost extremity of suffering, and yet a part of him was still aware of what such knowledge might do to her. And he needed to know they were not empty descriptions she could not follow. He needed her companionship in his grief.

"I imagine it was worse than the cold," she said thoughtfully. "I've seen men freeze, and animals too."

"The smell," he answered. "It was the smell . . . and the flies I hated most. I still can't bear the sound of flies. It makes me sick and I can't get my breath. I feel as if I am suffocating and my heart is going to burst."

"You weren't relieved?" She remembered reading it in the *Illustrated London News*. The account had been terrible, even after censorship for the general public.

"No." The word fell like a stone. "Every day we kept expecting help would come. We didn't know the whole country was under the sword. We fell one by one, taking as many of the enemy with us as we could. I've never seen greater courage. Every able-bodied person did what they could, men and women alike. Every man stood his watch. The women nursed the sick, carried food and water, tried to protect the children."

His hand rubbed the edge of the sheet, gripping it so hard the fabric must have hurt his skin. The movement was some kind of release of tension, even though his muscles were locked tight. She had seen it before in men recalling events of nightmare proportions. The room was silent in the spring evening.

"We were good shots," he resumed. "We kept them at bay. They didn't charge us and overrun. But there were so many of them, and their guns could reach us easily. They fired at everything that moved. Every day we thought help would come. It was so hot. No escape from it. You could smell the heat, feel it everywhere. The sweat dried the instant it broke. Skin hurt to touch. It cracked and blistered." He shrugged very slightly. "I don't know why I mentioned that. It hardly mattered. We died of heat stroke and dysentery . . . those who didn't die of their wounds. What did it matter if groins or armpits were on fire?"

"The one thing too much to bear," she answered. "For me it was the rats . . . rats everywhere, dropping off the walls."

He smiled, a sudden wide grin, beautiful in spite of his disfigured face. It was not any kind of amusement, simply the dazzling, wonderful relief of being not alone.

"But you survived," she said. She guessed that was part of the private torture inside him. She had known it before in men who had seen companions fall all around them, for no reason other than chance as to where they were standing. A yard this way or that and it would have been someone else. One moment they were alive, full of intelligence and feeling, the next just mangled blood and bone, torn flesh and pain . . . or nothing at all, the fire and the soul gone. One could not get rid of the guilt of being the one who survived. Part of you wanted to be with them.

His smile vanished, but he did not avoid her eyes.

"On June twenty-fourth Mrs. Greenway came to the intrenchment with a note from Nena Sahib. I can still see her face. She was old, very old indeed. She seemed like an embodiment of Time to me . . . or of Death. She had been a prisoner of the rebels and they sent her with terms of surrender." His voice was harsh, filled with emotion so great it almost choked him. "Nena Sahib promised that if we gave up all the money, stores and arms in the intrenchment he would not only allow all the survivors of the garrison to retreat unmolested but he would provide means of conveyance for the women and children as well."

She looked steadily at his eyes. The horror was still so deep inside him it seemed to fill his being. It was like a storm about to break.

"The treaty was agreed." His voice became strained almost to a whisper. "On June twenty-seventh we surrendered according to the terms and filed out of the garrison. The women and children were led aboard boats on the river . . . there were small thatched coverings on them . . . protection from the sun. The man in charge was called Tanteea Topee. He was sitting on a platform watching it all. A bugle sounded at his command, and they ran out the guns which had been concealed up to that point. They fired on the boats. The thatch caught alight. Women and children were burned alive. Some jumped into the stream, but the sepoys rode their horses into the water and clubbed and sabered them to pieces. Some managed to struggle to the farther shore."

Hester closed her eyes and put her hands up to cover her face. She had not meant to, but she did it without thinking.

"Then Nena Sahib ordered all the remaining men shot," Gabriel went on as if he could not now stop himself. "The women and children who had made it as far as the shore he had taken to his residence. They were hacked to pieces too, and their bodies thrown down the well."

She looked up at him again. She must not run away from this. It was all past. They could hurt no more. But Gabriel needed not to be alone in his horror. He was the only one still alive she could help.

He went on talking.

"When General Havelock's men found it eventually, the floor of the room was two inches deep in human blood. They found the hacked-up limbs and bodies in the well. They pulled up the body of one of General Wheeler's daughters. They sent a lock of her hair home as a memento, to her family in England." His voice was low in the quiet room smelling of clean linen and candle wax. "The rest of the scalp they divided up among themselves and then each man counted the individual hairs in his portion and swore an oath by heaven, and by the God who created him, that he would kill one mutineer for every hair he had. I know, because one of those men was a friend of mine. He wept even as he told me of it. He used to scream in his sleep when he remembered that house and what they found in it."

"How did you escape?" she asked him.

"I was hit on the head and nearly drowned," he replied. "But I was washed up by the river further downstream. I lay senseless for so long I suppose they thought I was dead and not worth bothering with. When I came to myself they had taken the plunder and the prisoners who were still alive and gone. Then followed the worst two weeks of my life. . . . I don't know how I lived, but I made my way towards Futtehpore and met up with General Havelock's men. I was nearly dead and no use for the fight, but they took care of me. I recovered." He smiled as if it still surprised him. "I wasn't even badly hurt, just burned and half starved and on the point of exhaustion." He glanced at his empty sleeve. "I didn't lose that until a few months ago. It was a stupid street brawl I tried to stop. But you don't need to hear about that."

What he meant was that he did not want to relive it.

"No, of course not," she agreed, standing up slowly, finding her legs shaking and her balance not very good. She put out a hand to steady herself.

"Thank you for listening to me," he said gravely. "I . . . I hope I haven't disturbed you too much . . . but there is no one else. They don't wish to know. They think it would be much better for me if I were to forget . . . but how can I? It would be such a betrayal . . . even if it were possible!" He wanted reassurance he was right. "What kind of man would I be if I could just go on as if they had never lived . . . and died like that?"

"One never forgets," she agreed, thinking of some of her own memories, men, and women too, who had been fragile and brave and who had died terribly. "But you can't expect other people to share what they don't understand." She straightened the bedclothes unnecessarily. "It is a part of your life, and it always will be . . . but it isn't all of it."

He looked at her ruefully, acknowledgment in his eyes, but he did not answer.

She glanced at his bedside table to make sure he had water and a clean glass.

"Is there anything else you would like?"

"No," he said flatly. "No, thank you. Are—are you going to sit with Perdita?"

She knew what he really meant. She was aware of his deep sense of inadequacy to be the husband, companion and protector that he had promised his wife he would be. Instead he was in need of her strength and help, not only physically but emotionally.

"Yes," she said with a smile of assurance. "As soon as I can see you are settled I shall go and find her."

He relaxed. At least for tonight he need not worry. "Thank you. Good night, Hester." Without being aware of it he had used her Christian name.

"Good night, Gabriel," she answered from the doorway, then went out and closed the door quietly.

It was after eleven o'clock, but since she had promised, she made her way downstairs to see if Perdita was still up. Most probably she was not, but she must look.

However, as soon as she opened the withdrawing room door Perdita sat up from the sofa where she had been curled half asleep. Her hair was tousled and she blinked even in the dim light of the one wall lamp still lit.

"How is he?" she asked anxiously. "Is he all right?"

Hester closed the door and walked over to the chair near Perdita and sat down. She looked at the younger woman's frightened eyes and her soft cheek, marked now where she had lain against the crease in the cushions. She was about twenty-two, but in some ways no more than a child. She had been married at eighteen after a year's betrothal to a man who was in every way her ideal. She had seen him through the eyes of a girl who expected everything of marriage. It was not only what was required of her, it was her own dream, and Gabriel Sheldon was the perfect husband: handsome, brave, charming, well-bred and with a promising career. And for all that it had been a socially suitable marriage, they had also been in love.

Now her whole world was in ruins, for no reason she could comprehend, and she was overwhelmed by it.

"He is settled for the night," Hester answered. "I think he will sleep well." She had no idea whether he would or not, but there was no purpose in saying that to Perdita.

Perdita frowned. "Are you sure? You were in there a long time. . . ."

"Oh . . . I suppose I was. We were just talking. There was nothing wrong, I promise you."

Perdita looked unhappy, twisting her hands together in her lap. "I never know what to say to him," she murmured. "I can't keep asking how he is feeling. He only says he's all right. And I know he isn't, but there's nothing I can do." She glanced up suddenly. She had very blue eyes, but in this somber light they seemed almost black. "What do you find to say, Miss Latterly?"

Hester hesitated. She should not answer with the truth. He had not said so, but what Gabriel had told her was implicitly a confidence. It was something neither of them could share with anyone else. As close as she had been to William Monk at times—all the causes they had fought for together, the tragedies they had seen—she would not share her experiences of the battlefield or the siege or the hospital at Scutari with him. But Gabriel understood.

She must find an answer which did not make Perdita feel even more helpless and excluded.

"It is easier for me," she began, watching Perdita's face. "We are not emotionally concerned with each other. There cannot be the same . . . the same sort of hurt. We were discussing places we had been to, what it was like, the things that are different, and those that are the same."

"Oh . . ."

Had Perdita disbelieved her? It was impossible to tell from her downcast expression and the hesitation in her voice. Her loneliness was so sharp it was almost like a cry.

"I told him a few of my experiences in the Crimea," Hester went on, impelled to add to what she had said.

"The Crimea?" Perdita did not immediately understand. Then realization flooded her face. "You were in the Crimea?"

Hester perceived instantly that she had made a mistake. Perdita had heard and read enough to know that that conflict, with its horror and its losses, had had so much in common with the Mutiny in India that Hester and Gabriel must share feelings and memories she could never know. It was clear in her eyes that she was uncertain how she felt about it. Part of her was relieved, grateful that there was someone he could turn to; another part, easily as great, felt frightened and excluded because it was not her.

"Yes." It would be absurd to deny it. "That is where I learned my nursing abilities. I imagine that is why your brother-in-law chose me to come here."

"So you could talk to Gabriel?"

"Rather more so I would have some knowledge of what his needs would be," Hester answered.

Perdita stared at the embers of the fire. "He doesn't think I can learn to do that. He doesn't think I will be any use or comfort at all."

What was there to say that was even remotely honest and yet not so hurtful it was destructive?

"Sometimes there isn't anything you can do," Hester began, thinking what more to say, feeling for words. "At times he may wish to speak of the Mutiny and of what happened at Cawnpore, other times he will want to forget it. No one can know when each will be."

"You mean it is easier for you?" Perdita said.

"In some ways, yes, of course it is. Not just because I have seen a battlefield . . ."

"Can you tell me what it is like?" Perdita asked, eagerness and dread mixed in her voice. "So I can understand Gabriel? He won't tell me anything about it. I was at home when he was in India, and my father wouldn't even allow me to read about it in the newspapers. He said it was not suitable . . . for me or for my mother." She bit her lip. "He said we didn't have to know things like that, and anyway it was only a journalist's idea of the truth and might be inaccurate and overdramatic. Now it's too late because the newspapers are all thrown away ages ago."

"You can always go to the library and find the back copies, if you want to," Hester pointed out. "But I am not sure if that would be a good thing. Do you wish to know about it . . . as much as can be understood by reading?"

The fire crackled and threw up a shower of sparks.

Perdita sat very still. "I don't know. Sometimes I think so, then there are times when I wish it never had to be thought of again and I'm glad I know nothing." She took a long breath and shook her head a little. "I just wish it would go away and everything could be as it used to . . . before the Mutiny. None of that mattered then." She sniffed. "I could have gone out to Delhi, or Bombay, or wherever was the nearest place to where Gabriel was. I could have been with him, and none of these things would have happened!"

"He wouldn't have seen things like the massacre at Cawnpore," Hester agreed. "But he would still have lost his friends, and he might still have received his own injuries. That can happen anywhere."

"Not in England!" Perdita said, looking up quickly.

"Yes, it could. People can be dragged by horses, or burned by fires, or any number of other things. There isn't anywhere where life is completely safe. And even if there were, it doesn't matter now. The only way is forward through reality, through what we have."

"You make it sound so easy!" There was resentment in Perdita's voice, and fear, and self-pity.

"No, it isn't," Hester contradicted her. "It's very difficult indeed. It's just that there isn't any alternative worth having. And perhaps Gabriel doesn't want you to know about the Mutiny."

"You mean he thinks I'm not strong enough to bear it!" Perdita challenged. "But you are! He can talk to you about it for hours."

Hester took a deep breath. "I am here temporarily. In a while I shall leave again. It doesn't matter to him what I know or what I think. I shall be gone after a while. And he doesn't care so much about my feelings . . . beyond what courtesy dictates. I am a stranger, not part of his life."

Perdita's face softened a little, a flare of hope in her eyes.

"But if he doesn't want me to know, if I can't share it with him, how can I ever be of any use?" The sharp edge in her voice was fading but still discernible.

Hester thought very carefully. "Wait a little while," she suggested. "Feelings don't always remain the same. He has only been home a few days. You cannot make tomorrow's decision until tomorrow comes. I know that is hard. One wants to see the way ahead . . . but it is not possible."

Perdita sat silently for several minutes and Hester waited without interrupting.

Eventually, Perdita stood up and straightened her dress. She seemed unaware that her hair was coming out of its pins, long, fair brown hair with a wave in it.

"I suppose I had better go to bed. I'm terribly tired, but I can't seem to sleep these nights."

"Would you like me to make you a draft?" Hester offered, rising to her feet as well. "Or a lavender pillow? Do you have one? They can help."

"I expect so. I think there's one in my handkerchief drawer or in the linen." She went to the door without looking at Hester. "I can ask Martha. Good night, Miss Latterly."

"Good night, Mrs. Sheldon."

Perdita went out and Hester heard her walk across the hall and then silence. She went out herself a few moments afterwards, and upstairs to her room. She washed quickly in cold water and went to bed. She was too tired to lie awake.

In the morning she accomplished her usual duties for Gabriel, changing the linen and seeing that his bandages were fresh and the wound clean. The doctor had called the day before and there was no need to trouble him today.

She was in the stillroom sorting through the various herbs and oils kept in stock in the house when Perdita's lady's maid came in.

Martha Jackson was a thin, dark woman who had probably been handsome enough in her youth, but now, in her middle forties, she was a little gaunt. The lines of hardship were etched deeply into her face but there was no bitterness in them, and no self-pity. Hester had liked her from the moment they met. She had gathered from the odd remark let slip that Martha had originally been Perdita's governess but that circumstances had dictated that she remain in a secure position, and become her maid, rather than leave and seek another post as governess somewhere else, which could only be temporary again, as children's schoolroom years always pass. Once she had been a senior, almost independent employee. Now she was a servant, albeit a necessary and trusted one.

"Good morning, Miss Latterly," she said with forced cheerfulness. "How are you today? I hope you are settling in well. If there is anything I can do, please let me know."

Hester smiled at her. "Good morning, Miss Jackson. Yes, I am very comfortable, thank you."

Martha busied herself with making a paste for reviving the luster of tortoiseshell which had lost its shine and depth. She was carefully putting drops of olive oil into a teaspoon of jeweler's rouge.

"Are you needing anything in particular, Miss Latterly?" she asked after a moment or two. "Perhaps there is something missing that you could use?" She started to apply the paste to the comb, rubbing the soft cloth around in small circular movements.

"More lavender," Hester answered. "I think Mrs. Sheldon is not finding it easy to sleep at the moment."

Martha was rubbing with the cloth automatically. She turned to face Hester.

"She's so frightened," she said quietly. "Is there anything you can say to comfort her? I've racked my brains, but I know so little about his condition; if I tell her something that isn't true, she'll never trust me again. She has no one else to turn to. Mr. Sheldon is no use—" She stopped abruptly. She had betrayed a family confidence, even if it was one Hester could have worked out for herself, and probably had. It was not what others knew that mattered, it was the breach of trust.

Hester saw the compassion in Martha's face. It was more than duty or the pity anyone might have felt; it was the kind of love which cannot escape once obligation has been fulfilled, or walk away when conscience is satisfied. Martha had known and cared for Perdita since Perdita was a child. Perhaps she was the only one who had, closely, daily, seeing the weaknesses as well as the strengths, the temptations and disappointments, the failures; the only one who knew what effort or what price lay behind the outward joys.

"I don't know," Hester confessed. "But I am trying to think."

"She loved him so much," Martha went on. "You should have seen him before he went away. He was so full of life, so happy. He believed in everything . . . at least he seemed as if he did." She pushed a strand of hair off her brow. "You can't ever get back that innocence, can you." It was a statement not a question, and it appeared as if she was thinking of other things as well, tragedies that had nothing to do with this.

Hester knew exactly what she meant. She had seen the raw soldiers arrive from the troopships, and then seen their faces again after one of the battles where men were slaughtered by the hundreds, cut down uselessly, human beings sheared off like corn before the harvest. You could not ever get that hope, that unknowing, back.

"No," she agreed. "She asked me last night if she should read about the Mutiny, about Cawnpore and Lucknow. I didn't know what to say."

Martha stared at her, her eyes dark, her cheeks hollow, as if she had borne all Perdita's suffering; but there was still a kind of softness in her in spite of the angles and the sharp cheekbones.

"She mustn't!" she said urgently. "She couldn't bear it. You don't understand, Miss Latterly, she's never experienced anything . . . violent . . . in her life." She lifted her hands helplessly, waving the cloth. "She's never seen anyone . . . dead. In families like the Lofftens they don't ever mention death. People don't die, they 'pass over,' or sometimes they 'take the great journey.' But it is always peaceful, as if they have fallen asleep. She will have to learn this . . . very slowly."

Hester reached for the jar of dried lavender flowers. "I don't think there is time to be very slow," she replied, realizing how little she knew of Perdita Sheldon or of the tenor of her marriage, the strength of her love for her husband. Hester could hardly ask Martha if Perdita was really only in love with the idea of love, of a handsome husband and a dream of happiness which simply moved, untrammeled by pain or reality, into an endless future. Asking Martha would be almost like making such an inquiry of her own mother.

And yet if she did not she might be losing the only chance anyone had to help Perdita—and Gabriel. He was maimed; he was disfigured. He had seen horror he would never forget and had lost too many of the flower of his friends not to be reminded—with every hot day, every military tune, every buzzing of flies—of what he had seen.

"Perhaps she should start with a history of India?" Hester suggested. "Begin forty or fifty years ago. Then the Mutiny would make more sense. By the time she reached it, she would understand at least a little of why it happened." She smiled, remembering schoolbook Latin. "*Peccavi,*" she said wryly. "That is what Clive said when he had conquered the province of Sind. He sent it in the dispatch home."

Martha blinked.

"*Peccavi,*" Hester repeated. "It is Latin. . . . It means 'I have sinned.' "

"Oh. I see." Martha smiled back, some of the tension easing out of her face. "Of course. It is so long since I taught . . . and then it was mostly French, and a little Italian for music. I'm sorry." She blushed, and began to buff the tortoiseshell gently. "Things have changed . . . but that has nothing to do with Miss Perdita now. Do you think Indian history would help? I suppose . . . she does have to know? You don't think he—Lieutenant Sheldon—would be better if he could forget it, bit by bit? Would it be easier if she didn't know?"

"If you were she, what would you want?" Hester asked, searching Martha's face.

Suddenly Martha's eyes filled with tears and she turned away, wiping her hand quickly across her cheek. "I should want to know!" she said fiercely. "No matter what the truth was . . . I should want to know!" Her voice was tight and brittle with the power of her emotions, and for a moment some pain within her was naked.

Hester could not pretend not to have noticed, but she could at least refrain from making any remark.

"Then we had better find her some appropriate books," she said, pulling down the next jar, which held comfrey leaves. It was less than half full. "And I think we should replenish our stock of herbs and oils before it gets too low."

Martha regained control of herself and continued polishing. "Yes, certainly, Miss Latterly," she agreed. "I think that would be excellent. Thank you for your counsel." She shot her a swift look of gratitude, and for a moment there was great understanding between them.

In the afternoon Hester was upstairs with Gabriel, reading to him from a book of poetry, a world utterly removed from the physical immediacies or the emotional pains of reality. It was Shelley's epic "Endymion," and its lovely cadences soothed without turmoil.

There was a brisk knock on the door, and almost before Gabriel had spoken, it opened and Athol Sheldon came in. He was Gabriel's height, but broader in shoulder and chest, and he walked on the balls of his feet, as if he were about to break into a run. He had a long, straight nose and an extremely direct stare.

"Good afternoon, good afternoon," he said cheerfully, looking first at Gabriel, then at Hester. "Getting on well? Good." He always enquired after people's well-being, but never waited for an answer, assuming it would be positive. He had extremely robust health himself, and regarded it as an attainable ideal for everyone, if not immediately, then certainly in time, with the right attitude. As a matter of principle, he never complained about anything.

"Hello, Athol," Gabriel replied guardedly. In his present state he found such vigor exhausting. "How are you?" He asked from habit.

"Very well, very well," Athol replied, sitting on the edge of the bed. "Saw Perdita before I came up." His face shadowed. "Not in good spirits, poor girl. Bit worried, if you ask me. Have to see what we can do about it."

Gabriel sighed soundlessly. "She seemed all right when she came in just before luncheon. She said she would take a walk this afternoon . . . later."

"Good," Athol agreed. "She ought to get out more. Brisk walk is the best thing in the world. Sure you agree, Miss Latterly. Not enough fresh air. Read somewhere that your Miss Nightingale said that." He looked pleased with himself.

"Yes," Hester agreed reluctantly. Athol's insensitivity annoyed her. He reminded her of many soldiers she had known, always convinced they were right, wearing an air of impenetrable confidence like armor against any kind of doubt, seldom listening to anyone else. Only heaven could count the number of lives they had cost.

She knew she was probably being unfair to Athol Sheldon. He was not a soldier. Being the eldest brother, he had inherited the family estate in Buckinghamshire and most of the time managed it, sufficiently well at least to allow him to offer financial assistance to his injured brother.

"There you are." Athol rubbed his hands together. "Duties of a wife are first, of course; but she should find an occupation of some sort to fill her hours. Plenty of good works to be done. Vicar's wife would know all about it. Need younger women on some of their charities. Fresh ideas . . . energy." He looked a little uncomfortable.

"I expect she will," Gabriel agreed, easing himself up a little higher on his pillows.

"Have another one," Athol offered immediately, leaning forward.

"It's all right!" Gabriel refused, using his one hand. "I can manage."

" 'Course you can. Apologies." Athol retreated. "You'll get used to doing all manner of things. A few weeks will make all the difference. A year from now you'll have put it all behind you."

He did not seem to notice Gabriel's face tighten.

"Time will heal the memories," Athol went on cheerfully. "Perdita will help you to forget. Lovely girl. Look towards the future. Now, is there anything I can do for you? Anything you need?"

Gabriel smiled. "No, thank you. You have done extremely well for me."

"Pleasure, my dear fellow." Athol smiled back, looking a little less uncomfortable. "Don't worry, everything will sort itself out. Only got to do our part and we'll be able to put all this behind us."

Hester cringed. Athol had not the faintest idea what he was talking about. For him the Indian Mutiny and its horror were only mistakes on the pages of history, momentary darknesses in the grand procession of empire.

Athol stood up. "Won't interrupt you." He put his hands under the lapels of his jacket and rearranged it on his shoulders. "Must see if I can call on the vicar and have a word with him about Perdita. I am sure something can be arranged. Do her the world of good. Always does. Busy, that's the thing."

Gabriel looked quickly at Hester, his eyes searching.

Hester stood up. "I'll see you to the door, Mr. Sheldon."

"No need, my dear Miss Latterly," he said graciously. "Don't want to interrupt you. What are you reading? Shelley? Bit miserable, isn't it? I'll bring you something with a bit more fire to it, something more uplifting."

Hester controlled herself with an effort. After all, they did not have to read it. "Thank you. That is very kind." But she still walked to the door with him and accompanied him onto the landing and slowly down the stairs.

"Mr. Sheldon . . ."

He stopped, hesitant for an instant, as if he too had considered speaking to her. "Yes, Miss Latterly?"

"Please reconsider asking Mrs. Sheldon to participate too fully in other activities just at the moment," she said gravely. "I—I don't think it will help."

"Always good to be busy, Miss Latterly," he said quickly, almost as if he had decided how to answer before she spoke. "Needs to get out. Mustn't brood, you know." His voice lifted, not as if his last comment were a question but rather as if he sought to encourage her somehow. "Can think about things too much. Get inward. Not healthy."

"But—"

He frowned. "Know you mean the best for them," he went on, interrupting. "Gabriel's your patient, and all that. Er . . . speaking of which . . . most natural thing in the world, only thing for a woman, really . . . faith, modesty . . . good works . . ." He colored faintly and ceased meeting her eyes. "I . . . ah . . . well . . . do you think she will have children, Miss Latterly? Perdita . . . of course . . . ."

"I know of no reason why not, Mr. Sheldon," she replied. "Gabriel's injuries are not of that nature, and I fully expect his general health to return in time. However . . ."

"Good . . . good. Hope you don't mind my asking? Indelicate, I know . . ."

"I don't mind at all," she assured him.

He started to move down the stairs again, relieved.

She kept pace with him, then went a step ahead and stopped.

He stopped also, more or less obliged to, if he were not to push past her.

"Mr. Sheldon, I think it is important that Mrs. Sheldon learn something of what actually happened in the Mutiny, in time about the massacre at Cawnpore."

"Good God!" He blushed deeply. "I mean . . . good heavens!" he corrected himself. "I simply cannot agree. You are quite mistaken, my dear Miss Latterly. I know something of it myself. Read the newspapers at the time, having a brother out there, and all that. Quite terrible. Not a suitable thing for a woman to know at all. You can't have any idea, or you would not have said such a thing. Absolutely out of the question." He waved his hand to dismiss it.

"I know it was terrible." She refused to retreat, obliging him to remain where he was, even though he loomed over her. "I also read the newspapers at the time, but rather more important than that, and possibly truer, Gabriel himself has told me some of his experiences—"

He shook his head sharply. "You should not have encouraged him, Miss Latterly. Never good to dwell on tragedies, unpleasant things in general. Too easy to become morbid . . . downcast, you know. And all that is quite unsuitable for Perdita. Distress her needlessly."

"I don't think it is needless, Mr. Sheldon," she answered. "It is the most emotionally profound thing that has happened in his life—"

"Oh, really . . ."

"And he cannot forget it," she went on, disregarding his interruption. "One does not forget friends simply because they are dead, and all of it is too big and too recent not to intrude into his thoughts every day. If she is to be any sort of wife and companion, as she has said she wishes, she must share at least some part of his experience."

"You are asking far too much, Miss Latterly," he corrected, shaking his head again. "And if I may say so, quite inappropriately. A young woman, a lady, of Perdita's background, a gentlewoman, should not know of such barbarities as occurred in India. Part of her charm, her great value in a man's life, is precisely that she keeps an island safe for him, unsoiled by the tragedies of the world. That is a very beautiful thing, Miss Latterly. Do not try to damage that or rob them both of it." He smiled as he finished speaking, a calm, assured expression returning to his face, except for the faintest shadow in his eyes. She knew he was speaking to convince himself as well as her. He needed that island to exist, to visit it in mind if nothing more. It was his own dreams he was protecting as much as Gabriel's.

And perhaps it was his way of protecting himself from Gabriel's pain. There was a fear in him of the darkness he only guessed at in acts like those in the Mutiny. Like many people, he preferred to think they could not really have happened, not as had been reported.

Was there any purpose in trying to force him to see the reality? "Mr. Sheldon, when we share our terror and pain with someone else, we create a bond with that person which is seldom broken. Should we not give Mrs. Sheldon the chance to be the one to share Gabriel's experiences?"

He frowned at her.

"I mean," she went on hastily, "allow her to decide whether she will or not, rather than deciding it for her?"

"Not very logical, my dear Miss Latterly," he said with a quick smile. "Since she can have no idea what she would be offering to share, she cannot make such a decision. No, I am quite certain we should not burden her." His voice gathered conviction. "It is our duty to protect—my duty, in which you will be of great assistance."

"Mr. Sheldon . . ." she persisted.

But he raised his hand, smiling widely. "We must have fortitude and strength, Miss Latterly. We shall overcome. I trust you are a woman of Christian faith? Yes, of course you are. You could not do the great good works which I already know of you, were you not. Onward!" He thrust his hand out, holding it high. "We must go forward, and we shall overcome." And he brushed past her and went on down the stairs with a spring in his step.

Hester swore under her breath, words she would have been ashamed to use aloud, and returned the way she had come.

In the evening Hester sat restlessly fiddling with mending which did not really need to be done. Martha attended to such things and left little from one week to the next. But she could not keep her mind on mending, and sitting idle was even worse.

There was a knock on the door.

"Come in," she said with relief.

Martha entered and closed the door behind her. She looked tired and dispirited.

"Have you time to sit down?" Hester invited. She set her sewing aside. "Would you like a cup of tea?"

Martha smiled. "I'll get it. I'm sure you would like one too, wouldn't you?"

"Thank you," Hester accepted. "Yes, I really would."

Martha held out a letter. "This came for you in the last post."

"Oh!" Hester took it with pleasure. It was written in Lady Callandra Daviot's hand and postmarked from Fort William, in the north of Scotland. "Oh, good!"

"A friend?" Martha said with a smile. "I'll fetch the tea. Would you like some shortbread as well?"

"Yes, please," Hester accepted, and the moment after Martha had gone, she tore open the letter and read:

> My dear Hester,
>
> What a marvelous country! I had never imagined I would enjoy myself so much. I have the undeniable urge to try painting again. It should all be done on wet paper, I think, to catch the softness of the colors and the way the light strikes the water. Yesterday I came back from the Isle of Skye. The Cuillin Mountains are so beautiful they make me ache inside because the moment I look away I know I shall need to see them again. And I cannot spend the rest of my life standing on the spot staring at shifting sunlight and mist and the shadows across the sea.
>
> Today I am resting and doing very little, except writing to friends, of whom you and William are the only ones who might begin to understand how I feel, and therefore the only ones in which I shall have pleasure, rather than the

mere knowledge of duty performed. What slaves we are to conscience! I wonder how much the postman carries that is no more than obligation satisfied?

How are you? Have you any cases which you care about intensely? Or are you nursing bored old ladies with the vapors, and nothing to do with their time and money but make somebody else run around after them, and irascible colonels with gout whose only cure would be to abstain from the Port and Stilton, and who will never do that?

Have you seen William lately? I missed his last case of real interest. Of course, he told me about it afterwards, but that is hardly the same thing. He is doing so well recently that he does not need my occasional financial intervention—which of course pleases me immensely. I wish him to succeed. Of course I do. My support was only intended to be temporary, or I know he would not have accepted it. Men are very odd when it comes to money—unless, of course, they marry it. In which case they consider it theirs by right, as indeed it is by law.

However, I do miss the excitement of being with you, the urgency of learning the truth about some violence in secret, even though it may in the end prove to be tragic. I am not used to drifting on the surface of life, and I find the calm of it sometimes drives me into a terrible state of loneliness, as if the reality were passing me by. Am I sitting behind a window observing the world, separated by impenetrable glass?

Hester read more description of the majestic and lyrical beauty of the Highlands, but her mind was more fully tuned to the emotions which underlay it, and her own memories of the warmth of Callandra's friendship—and the honesty. In a sense, Callandra had replaced the family she was no longer close to, and she looked forward to her return.

Martha came back with a tray of tea and a rather large plate of fresh shortbread from the kitchen. She set it down and poured for both of them.

Hester put the letter aside.

Martha held her cup, waiting till it should cool sufficiently to sip. She was frowning and obviously troubled.

Hester guessed. "Did Mr. Sheldon say anything to Mrs. Sheldon about reading Indian history?" she asked. "I tried to argue him out of it, but I am almost sure I failed."

"I am afraid you did," Martha agreed, looking at her over the top of her cup. "He believes that the least that is said the soonest it will be mended—which is absolute nonsense!" Her voice was urgent with an anger she knew she should not express. "She is so lonely because she has no idea even what he is closing her out from. It isn't just the physical pain . . . or the memories." She stared ahead of her, her eyes on something far beyond this quiet, domestic room and the household around them, settled for the night, no sound but the hissing of the gas and the occasional creak of a floorboard.

Hester did not interrupt her.

"It is not being whole," Martha went on. "It is being used to beauty and then suddenly having to accept ugliness, deformity . . ." She obviously found even the word painful to say.

"Disfigurement," Hester contradicted her. "It isn't really the same."

Martha looked at her quickly. "No—no, of course not. I'm sorry. I was half thinking of something else. I . . ." She regarded Hester with a curious almost shyness, and yet her eyes were searching.

"You have experienced it before?" Hester asked very quietly, then took the first hot sip of her tea, not to press too hard.

Martha turned away again, pushing the plate of shortbread across closer to Hester. "My brother Samuel married a very pretty woman . . . twenty-five years ago now, it must be—or nearly. Dolly, her name was. She had the most perfect skin. Not a blemish anywhere. And lovely eyes . . . and fine features." She stopped, anger, pity and confusion in her face. The memory hurt her and there was something in it still fiercely unresolved.

Hester waited.

"They were happy, I think," Martha went on. "Sam adored her. They had a baby, a little girl. Phemie, they called her. That was Dolly's idea. Sam wanted to call her by a biblical name, something old-fashioned." She sipped her tea. "I can remember the day he came to tell me." She stopped and took a moment or two to master her emotions. She breathed deeply, her thin chest rising and falling with the effort. "She wasn't right." Her voice was choked. "Little Phemie was deformed. Her face. Her mouth. Her lips were all twisted. Dolly couldn't suckle her herself. She was too upset. She got a wet nurse in, but even she had terrible difficulty getting the baby to feed. She was a poor little thing for long enough, but in the end she did survive."

"I'm sorry," Hester said quietly. She had almost no knowledge of caring for babies. All her experience had been with the results of violence and disease, and always with adults. There was something particularly wrenching to the heart about a tiny creature, new in the world, struggling to live.

Martha drank some of her tea. "It wasn't until Leda was born about two years later that they realized Phemie was deaf too."

Hester said nothing. She knew from Martha's face that she was trying to collect her self-control sufficiently to say something else which still tore at her, over twenty years afterwards, intruding into Perdita Sheldon's grief and confusion and, for a moment at least, pushing it aside.

"Leda was deformed as well," Martha said in a whisper. "It was her mouth and an eye. She could see, but she couldn't hear either, except a tiny bit." She looked at Hester, waiting for her to say something.

"I'm so sorry." Hester could only try to imagine what the mother must have felt, the overwhelming tide of pity, anger, confusion, guilt, and also consuming fear for the future of the children she had borne into a world which would treat them with terrible cruelty, sometimes without even realizing it. What would become of them when she was not there to protect and defend and love them?

"What happened?" she asked.

"Sam loved them," Martha answered, biting her lip and staring straight ahead. "He looked after them, even when Dolly was too distraught to manage." She stopped again, unable for a moment to continue.

Hester sat motionless, ignoring the tea and the shortbread; in fact, she had forgotten them.

"Then Sam died," Martha said abruptly. "It was something with his stomach. It was very quick. Dolly couldn't manage without him. She was completely distracted with grief. Phemie and Leda were put into an institution and Dolly went away. She didn't tell us where. I expect she meant to, but something inside her just . . . collapsed." She looked at Hester, her eyes filled with tears. "I would have taken the girls, if I could have. But I was in service. There was no place for two little children. Phemie was barely three, and Leda only a year . . . and—and they weren't pretty children. They were . . . deformed. And they couldn't hear, so they would never be any use to anyone. . . ."

Hester reached out and took Martha in her arms, holding her thin body closely and feeling the dry sobs that racked through her.

"Of course, there was nothing you could do," Hester said gently. "You had to work to eat. So do all of us. Sometimes it is all you can do to support yourself, and if you go under, what use is that to anyone?"

"I wish I knew where they were!" Martha said desperately. "I look at Lieutenant Sheldon with his face all twisted and burned like that until half of him hardly looks human, and I see the look in Perdita's eyes, and she was so in love with him . . . and now she can hardly bring herself to look at him straight, let alone touch him . . . and I wonder what happened to those poor little souls. I should have found some way to help! Who's going to love them, if not me?"

"I don't know," Hester said honestly. False words of comfort now would only leave Martha thinking she did not understand or believe the enormity of her anguish. Hester held her even closer. "We can't change what has already happened, but we can try to do something about Gabriel and Perdita. She's got to learn to understand, to forget his disfigured face and see the man inside . . . that beauty matters so much more. That is what will love her in return. To the devil with Athol Sheldon and his ideas."

Martha gave a jerky little laugh, half choking. "He means well," she said, straightening herself up and pushing back some of her hair which had fallen askew from its pins. "He just doesn't realize . . ."

Hester poured fresh tea, which was still hot and steaming fragrantly. She passed one of the cups over to Martha.

Martha smiled and fished in her pocket for a handkerchief to blow her nose.

Hester sipped her own tea and took a piece of shortbread.

"Thank you for bringing my letter up," she said conversationally. "It was written from Scotland. Have you ever been there?"

Martha dabbed her eyes and settled to listen with interest to Callandra Daviot's account of her journeys.

CHAPTER THREE

The Lamberts were not open to negotiation of any sort. Killian Melville was sued for breach of promise and the case came to trial very rapidly. It was naturally attended by a great deal of gossip and speculation. Such an event had not happened in society in some while, and it was on everyone's lips.

Oliver Rathbone had given his word to defend Melville, so although he still had no further information which he could use, he was in court with a calm face and a steady smile to face Wystan Sacheverall, acting for Miss Zillah Lambert but, of course, paid by and instructed by her parents.

The jury had already been selected: a group of men more embarrassed by their position than usual and—quite obviously to even the casual eye—wishing they were not involved in what was a private and domestic matter. Looking at them, Rathbone wondered how many of them had daughters of their own. Above half of them were of an age to be considering their own children's marriages.

How many of them had made rash promises in their youth and lived to regret them, or at least attempted to retract them? Were their own marriages happy? Were their experiences of domestic family life ones they would wish upon another? So much might hang upon things Rathbone would never know. They would remain two rows of well-to-do men of varying ages, different appearances and characteristics, with only two things in common: the reputation and the personal means to become a juror; and a degree of discomfort at finding themselves obliged to make a decision they would much rather not.

The judge was a smallish man with mild features and remarkably steady, candid blue eyes. He spoke very quietly. One was obliged to listen in order to hear what he said.

The first witness called was Barton Lambert. He looked angry and unhappy as he strode across the open space in the front of the room and climbed the steps to the witness-box. His cheeks were flushed and his arms and body stiff.

Beside Rathbone, Killian Melville bit his lip and looked down at the table. He had seemed thoroughly wretched throughout their preparation, but no matter what Rathbone had said, any argument or estimate he had offered about the probable outcome, Melville had refused to be swayed from his decision to fight.

Sacheverall moved forward. He was a plain man with rather large ears, but he had a confidence which lent him a certain grace, and he had a good height and broad shoulders. His fair hair was in need of cutting, and curled up at his collar. His voice was excellent, and he knew it.

Barton Lambert took the oath to tell the truth, the whole of it, and nothing else.

Sacheverall smiled at him. "We all appreciate that this is a most distressing experience for you, Mr. Lambert, and that you bring this action at all only to defend your daughter's good name. We realize that there is no animosity in your action, and no desire to inflict embarrassment or pain upon anyone—"

The judge leaned forward. "Mr. Sacheverall, there is no need to state your case. We require you simply to prove it, if you will be so good," he said gently. "If you will give us the facts, we shall draw our own conclusion. We assume all parties to be honorable, until shown otherwise. Please provide your evidence."

Sacheverall looked taken aback. Apparently he did not know Mr. Justice McKeever.

Rathbone knew him only by repute. He hid his smile.

"My lord," Sacheverall acknowledged. "Mr. Lambert, will you

please tell the court how you first made the acquaintance of Killian Melville, and in what circumstances he was introduced to your daughter, Miss Zillah Lambert, upon whose behalf you are bringing this suit."

"Of course," Lambert said gruffly, and cleared his throat and then coughed, raising a large hand to his mouth. "I had a little capital I wanted to spend. Create something beautiful out of what I had earned." He looked at Sacheverall for approval and continued when he saw him nod. "I thought of a building . . . something real handsome . . . different . . . new. I had several architects recommended to me." He moved uncomfortably. "Saw all their plans. Young Melville was one of 'em. Liked his the best, by a long way. The others were adequate . . . but pedestrian compared wi' his." He took a deep breath, filling his lungs. "I sent for him. Liked him straight off. Modest enough, but sure of 'imself. Looked me straight in the eye." He coughed again. "He wanted the job, I could see that, but he wasn't going to curry favor for it. His designs were good, and he knew it."

"You commissioned him to draw the plans for your new building?" Sacheverall concluded.

"Yes sir, I did. And it was the admiration of all my acquaintances, and many strangers, when it was built. In Abercorn Place, it is, in Maida Vale." There was a ring of pride in Lambert's voice when he said it. Whatever his feelings for Melville currently, he still regarded his work with delight. "You may have seen it . . ." he added hopefully.

"Indeed I have," Sacheverall agreed. "It is very beautiful. Was it at this time that you came to know Mr. Melville socially and invited him to your home?"

"It was. Not at first, you understand," he explained, "but as the building was nearing completion. Naturally he had to come and consult with me from time to time. Very diligent, he was. Left nothing to chance."

"Not a careless man?" Sacheverall noted.

Rathbone knew what he was doing, but he could not stop him.

He looked at the jurors' faces. They were all men of property, by definition, or they would not be jurors. They would understand Lambert's feelings and identify with them, even if their own estates were on a vastly smaller scale.

"Not at all," Lambert said vehemently. "Wouldn't employ a careless man. I couldn't have got where I am, sir, if I couldn't judge a man's ability in his profession." He took another deep breath, as if steadying himself. "Thought I could judge a man's personal character as well. Would have sworn Melville was as honorable as any man I've known. Looks as if I'm not as clever as I thought, doesn't it?"

"I am afraid it does, sir," Sacheverall agreed. "Did you introduce Melville to your family, most specifically to your daughter, Miss Zillah Lambert?"

"I did."

"Forgive me for asking you this, sir, when it must sound highly indelicate, but did you introduce Mr. Melville as a socially acceptable person, a fit companion for your daughter, a friend; or as an employee, a person of inferior rank?"

"Certainly not!" Barton Lambert was affronted. Of all things, he was not socially arrogant. No one impressed him by birth or rank, except Her Majesty the Queen. She was an entirely different matter. He was intensely patriotic, and she was the head of his country and the seat of his ultimate loyalty. "Killian Melville was good enough to speak to anyone, and I introduced him as such," he said sharply. "My daughter was brought up to respect a man who earned his way and left the world a better place than he found it." It was said with a note of challenge, and he swiveled around to look at the jurors as he spoke. If he had to parade his family's shame before the gentlemen of society, he would do it with his head high and his standards unmistaken by any.

Against his will, Rathbone liked the man already.

"Quite." Sacheverall nodded, inclining his head a trifle towards the jurors. "You introduced him to your home and family as an equal. You offered him complete hospitality." That was a statement, not a question. He proceeded to the point. "And he became friendly with your wife and daughter?"

"He did."

"He visited regularly and was at ease in your company . . ." Sacheverall glanced at Rathbone. "Or should I say he appeared at ease?" he corrected.

"Yes sir."

"You became fond of him?"

"I always liked him," Lambert acknowledged. In all the time he had been on the stand he had not looked at Melville. Rathbone was acutely aware of it, and he was certain Melville was also.

"Did you take him with you to social events outside your home?"

"From time to time. He wasn't one for a lot of dining out and polite conversation, and I don't think he danced."

Rathbone stood up. "My lord, no one disputes that Mr. Lambert and his family were gracious and friendly towards Mr. Melville and showed him the greatest hospitality, and that Mr. Melville in turn was grateful to them and held them in the highest personal regard. The only matter of issue is whether he feels himself suited to marry Miss Lambert, desired to do so, and actually contracted such an agreement. Mr. Melville contends that Miss Lambert mistook the nature of his regard for her and Mrs. Lambert assumed something that was not in fact so. It is even imaginable that Miss Lambert herself knew this but did not feel able to extricate herself from what had become an embarrassing situation."

Mr. Justice McKeever smiled. "All manner of things are imaginable, Sir Oliver. We will restrict ourselves to what is demonstrable. However, Mr. Sacheverall, I take Sir Oliver's point that no one disputes the fact that a warm friendship developed between Mr. Melville and Mr. Lambert's family, especially his daughter. Such friendships do not always end in marriage. Please proceed with your case."

Sacheverall bowed, but he turned back to Lambert with perhaps a fraction less confidence in his stance and the set of his shoulders.

"During the course of their friendship, did Mr. Melville on occasion escort your daughter to certain functions, keep her company, walk and talk with her, tell her of his exploits, adventures, plans for the future? Did he share ideas with her, tastes in art, literature and music? Did he read poetry together with her, show her the drawings of his work, share jokes and humorous episodes? In general, did he pay court to her, Mr. Lambert?"

Rathbone glanced sideways at Melville, but he was staring straight ahead.

"He did all of those things, sir, as you well know," Lambert answered grimly. Sacheverall's words must have brought back memories to him, because now his reluctance was gone and he was plainly both hurt and angry. He no longer avoided Melville but looked straight at him, challengingly, all his bewilderment clear in his face.

Rathbone felt a sinking inside him. There was no defense against his kind of honesty. Had he been a juror he could have found only one way. Killian Melville was guilty, and it was almost impossible to believe well of him. No man could court a girl in the manner Lambert described and not expect that she would read it as a declaration of love. Anyone would. Not even a fool could mistake it.

He looked sideways again at Melville now. His fair head was bent forward and there was a flush in his cheeks. His eyes were filled with despair, as if he were trapped with no escape.

Rathbone was not sure whether he felt sorry for him or simply so overwhelmed with anger he wanted to slap him for his irresponsible cruelty.

"So it came as no surprise to you in the least when a betrothal followed, in the natural course of events?" Sacheverall concluded.

"Of course not!" Lambert responded. "No one was surprised! It was as night follows day."

"Quite so." Sacheverall smiled sadly. He pursed his lips, frowning as he looked up at Lambert. "Arrangements were made for the wedding?"

"Yes. Announcement in the *Times*. All society knew." Lambert pronounced the words sharply, showing his pain and perhaps a certain feeling of alienation, as if he were only too aware of the whispers and the amusement which would be enjoyed at his family's expense.

"Naturally," Sacheverall murmured. "And then what happened, Mr. Lambert?"

Lambert squared his shoulders. "Melville broke it off," he said quietly. "No reason. No warning. Just broke it off."

"It was Killian Melville, not your daughter?" Sacheverall stressed, anger plain in his voice.

Rathbone looked at Melville, and he was sitting forward, one hand to his lips, biting his nails.

"It was." Lambert's face showed the strain. He was being publicly humiliated. He refused to look at anyone in the gallery. Rathbone was sharply aware of how much better it would have been for everyone if Zillah Lambert had consented to be the one to break the betrothal, regardless of whether she wished to or not. Apparently she had simply not believed Melville meant what he said.

Although, of course, Rathbone had only Melville's word for it that he had actually tried to approach her. Perhaps he had failed in courage when it came to the moment.

"Have you any idea whatever what caused Mr. Melville's extraordinary behavior, sir?" Sacheverall asked, his fair eyebrows raised, his whole stance conveying bewilderment.

"No idea at all," Lambert said, shaking his head. "Can't begin to understand it. Makes no sense."

"Not to me," Sacheverall agreed. "Unless there are things we do not know about Mr. Killian Melville. . . ."

Rathbone rose to his feet.

Sacheverall waved at him airily. "Your witness, Sir Oliver." He smiled, knowing he was almost invulnerable, and returned to his seat.

Rathbone felt somehow wrong-footed. He had never opposed Sacheverall across a court before. He knew his reputation, but somehow he had underrated him. His plain, rather foolish-looking face was deceiving. The quality of his voice should have warned him.

He walked to the middle of the open space surrounded by the lawyers' positions, the witness-box, the judge and the high double row of jurors. He looked up at Barton Lambert. Apart from his own respect for the man, he knew better than to antagonize him. The jurors were already by nature and inclination in sympathy with him.

"How do you do, Mr. Lambert," he began. "I am sorry for the circumstance which brings us together again. I need to ask you a few questions about this affair, in order to clarify it and to do my duty by my client."

"I understand, sir," Lambert said graciously. "That's why we're here. Ask away."

Rathbone acknowledged with a nod of courtesy.

"During this time that Mr. Melville called frequently at your home, sir, was he employed by you to design and oversee the construction of buildings you had commissioned?"

"He was."

"And he was friendly with all your family?"

"Not the way you're putting it, sir," Lambert argued. "You're trying to say he was equally friendly with all of us, and that's not so. He was civil and pleasant to Mrs. Lambert. He was always pleasant with me, but he would be, wouldn't he?" He raised his eyebrows. "I was his patron in his profession—his employer, in a sense. He'd have been a fool to be less than polite to me." But his eyes avoided Melville as he spoke. "Not that I didn't think he liked me, mind; and I liked him. Well-spoken, intelligent, decent-thinking young man, I thought him. But it is my daughter he spent time with, laughed and talked with, shared his ideas and his dreams with, and no doubt all of hers too."

His face was full of the sharpness of the regret and the sense of betrayal he felt. "I can see them clear in my mind's eye even as I stand here, heads bent together, talking and laughing, looking in each other's eyes. You can't tell me he wasn't courting her, because I was there!" His look defied Rathbone, or anyone, to contradict him.

Rathbone had nothing to fight with, and he knew it. It angered him more than he had expected that all this distress could have been avoided. The rows of avid faces in the gallery need never have witnessed these people's humiliation. Their private quarrels and griefs should have remained exactly that, known only to their own circle. It was no one else's concern. He hated what he was doing, what they were all doing here. The whole forced performance of grooming every young woman for marriage and parading her before what amounted to the market, judging her human worth by her marriageability, was offensive.

"Mr. Lambert," he said, rather more brusquely than he had meant to, "when did Mr. Melville ask you for your daughter's hand in marriage?"

Lambert looked startled.

Rathbone waited.

"Well . . . he didn't," Lambert admitted. "Not in so many words. He should have, I grant you. It was an omission of good manners I was willing to overlook."

"Possibly it was an omission of good manners," Rathbone agreed. "Or possibly it was an omission of intent? Is it possible he was very fond of Miss Lambert, but in a brotherly way, rather than as a suitor, and his affection was misinterpreted . . . with the best of intentions, and in all innocence?"

"By a man of our age, perhaps, Sir Oliver," Lambert said dryly. "Although I doubt it. A man of Melville's years does not normally feel like a brother towards a handsome and good-natured young woman."

There was a faint titter around the room, almost like the rustle of leaves.

Rathbone kept his composure with difficulty. He did not like being taken for Lambert's age—and was startled by how much it offended him. Lambert must be at least fifty.

"There are many young ladies I admire and find pleasant company," he said rather stiffly, "but I do not wish to marry them."

Lambert said nothing.

Rathbone was obliged to continue. He was not serving Melville's cause.

"So Mr. Melville did not ask you for your daughter's hand, and yet it was assumed by you all that he wished to marry her, and arrangements were made, announcements were given and so forth. By whom, sir?"

"My wife and myself, of course. We are the bride's parents." Lambert looked at him with raised eyebrows. He had a very broad, blunt face. "That is customary!"

"I know it is," Rathbone conceded. "I am only trying to establish that Mr. Melville took no part in it. It could have been conducted without his awareness of just how seriously his relationship with Miss Lambert was being viewed."

"Only if he was a complete fool!" Lambert snorted.

"Perhaps he was." Rathbone smiled. "He would not be the first young man to behave like a fool where a young lady is concerned."

There was a burst of laughter in the gallery, and even the judge had a smile on his face.

"Is my learned friend saying that his client is a fool, my lord?" Sacheverall enquired.

"I rather think I am," Rathbone acknowledged. "But not a knave, my lord."

The judge's bright blue eyes were very wide, very innocent. The light shone on the bald crown of his head, making a halo of his white hair.

"An unusual defense, Sir Oliver, but not unique. I hope your client will thank you for it, should you succeed."

Rathbone smiled ruefully. He was thinking the same thing. He turned to Lambert again.

"You say, sir, that the breaking of the betrothal came without any warning at all. Was that to you, Mr. Lambert, or to everyone?"

"I beg your pardon?" Lambert looked confused.

"Is it not possible that Mr. Melville, when he realized how far arrangements had progressed, spoke to Miss Lambert and tried to tell her that matters had proceeded further than he was happy with, but that she did not tell you that? Perhaps she did not believe he was serious, or thought he was only suffering a nervousness which would pass with time?"

"Well . . ."

"It is possible, is it not?"

"Possible," Lambert conceded. "But I don't believe it."

"Naturally." Rathbone nodded. "Thank you. I don't think I have anything more to ask you."

Sacheverall declined to pursue the subject. He was in a strong position, and he was thoroughly aware of it.

Rathbone wondered why he had not asked Lambert about the damage done to his daughter's reputation, and why indeed he was pursuing this case instead of allowing the matter to remain at least somewhat more private. The omission was not one he would have made himself.

The answer came immediately.

Sacheverall, looking extremely pleased with himself, called Delphine Lambert to the stand.

She came in looking harassed and distressed, but with a supreme dignity. She was a small woman, but carried herself so superbly she gave the impression of regality. She was dressed in deep blue, which flattered her complexion, and the huge skirts with their crinoline hoops emphasized her still-tiny waist. She mounted the witness-box with difficulty, because of the narrowness of the steps, and turned to face the clerk who swore her in.

Sacheverall apologized for the distress he would cause her in having to speak to her on so delicate a matter, with the implication that this too was Melville's fault, then proceeded with his first question.

"Mrs. Lambert, were you present during most of the growing relationship between Mr. Melville and your daughter?"

"Naturally!" Her eyes widened. "It is usual for a mother to chaperon her daughter at such times. I have only the one daughter, so it was easy for me."

"So you observed everything that took place?" Sacheverall asked.

"Yes." She nodded. "And I assure you there was never anything in the least out of order. I thought myself a good judge of character, but I was completely duped." She looked lost, and innocent, as if she still did not fully understand what had happened.

Rathbone wondered if Sacheverall had schooled her brilliantly or if he had simply been given the perfect witness.

Sacheverall was too astute to belabor the point. The jurors had seen her. He even forbore from glancing at Rathbone.

"Mrs. Lambert," he continued, "would you be good enough to describe for us a typical encounter between Miss Lambert and Mr. Melville, one as like many others as you may be able to recall."

"Certainly, if you wish." She straightened her shoulders even more, but without the slightest exaggeration. She was not doing it for effect. This truly was an ordeal for her. Her bearing and her voice were full of fear, and she understood the darkness this cast over her daughter's future.

Again Rathbone felt himself cold with anger that Melville had allowed this to happen. He was not merely a fool, he was irresponsible. Rathbone had been instinctively sorry for him in the beginning, but now he was annoyed that Melville had not somehow managed to make his feelings plain enough that the Lamberts would have withdrawn from the betrothal themselves and avoided this fiasco. He looked at his client, in the chair next to him, avoiding Rathbone's eyes, staring at nothing. He seemed closed in a world of his own.

The court was waiting.

Delphine Lambert selected her occasion and began. "Mr. Melville had been to speak to my husband about some architectural matter—something to do with oriel windows, I believe. My husband went out, and Mr. Melville came down into the withdrawing room to take tea with Zillah and myself. This was last autumn. It was one of those late, golden days when everything looks so beautiful and you know it cannot last. . . ."

She blinked and made an effort to control emotions which were obviously raw.

Sacheverall waited sympathetically.

"We talked of all sorts of slight things, of no consequence," Delphine continued. "I remember Killian—Mr. Melville—sat in the chair next to the sofa. Zillah sat on the sofa, her skirts all swirled around her. She was wearing pink and she looked wonderful." Her eyes were soft with memory. "He remarked on it. Anyone would have. When you see her you will understand. We talked and laughed. He was interested in everything." She said it with the pleasure of surprise still in her voice. "Every detail seemed to please him. Zillah was telling him about a party she had been to and recounting several anecdotes which really were very funny indeed. I am afraid we were a trifle critical, and our amusement was sometimes not altogether kind . . . but we laughed so hard we had tears running down our cheeks." She smiled and blinked as if the tears came again, but this time of sorrow. "Zillah has a delicious turn of phrase, and Killian so enjoyed her observations. She was a perfect mimic! Perhaps it is not very ladylike," she apologized. "But we had such fun."

Sacheverall nodded in satisfaction. Even the jurors were smiling.

Rathbone glanced at Melville.

Melville bit his lip and moved his head an inch in acknowledgment. He looked wretched. Perhaps it was the look of innocence, but it had all the air of guilt. The jury could not have missed it.

"Please continue," Sacheverall prompted.

"We had tea," Delphine resumed. "Hot crumpets with melted butter. They are not easy to eat delicately. We laughed at ourselves over that as well. And toasted tea cakes. They were delicious." She made a little gesture of deprecation. "We ate them all. We were so happy we did not even notice. Then Killian and Zillah got up and went for a walk in the garden. The leaves were turning color and the very first few had fallen. The chrysanthemums were in bloom." She glanced at the judge, then back to Sacheverall. "Such a wonderful perfume they have, earthy and warm. They always make me think of everything that is lovely . . . rich but never vulgar. If only we could always have such perfect taste." She sighed. "Anyway, Killian and Zillah remained outside for some time, but I was in every proper sense still a chaperone. Zillah told me afterwards they were discussing their ideas for a future home, all the things they would most like to have, and how it would be . . . colors, styles, furniture . . . everything two people in love would plan for their future."

Rathbone looked at Melville again. Could any man really be such a complete fool as to have spoken to a woman of such things and not know perfectly well she would take it as a prelude to a proposal of marriage?

"Is that true?" he demanded under his breath.

Melville turned to him. His face was deep pink with the rush of blood to his cheeks, his eyes were hot, but he did not avoid looking straight back.

"Yes . . . and no . . ."

"That won't do!" Rathbone said between his teeth. "If you are not honest with me I cannot help you, and believe me, you are going to need every ounce of help I can think of—and more!"

"That may be how she saw it," Melville answered, looking down now, not at Rathbone. His voice was low and tense. "We did talk about houses and furnishings. But it wasn't for us! I'm an architect . . . houses are not only my profession, they are my love. I'll talk about design to anyone! I was making suggestions to her about the things she wanted in a home and how they could be achieved. I told her of new ways of creating more warmth, more light and color, of bringing to life the dreams she had. But it was for her—not for both of us!" He turned to face Rathbone again. "I would have spoken the same way to anyone. Yes, of course we laughed together—we were friends. . . ." His eyes were full of distress. Rathbone could have sworn he held that friendship dear and the loss of it hurt him.

Delphine Lambert was still talking, describing other occasions when Melville and Zillah Lambert had been together, their easy companionship, their quick understanding of each other's thoughts, their shared laughter at a score of little things.

Rathbone looked across at the jurors' faces. Their sympathy was unmistakable. To change their minds it would take a revelation about Zillah Lambert so powerful and so shocking it would shatter any emotion they felt now so that they would be left angry and betrayed. And Melville had sworn there was no such secret. Was it conceivable he knew something of her which made it impossible to marry her, yet he still cared for her too deeply to expose it—even to save himself?

It would have to be something her parents did not know, or they would never have risked his revealing it. They could not rely on Melville's self-sacrifice.

And Zillah herself would not dare to tell them, even to save Melville, and thus this whole tragic farce.

Rathbone would have to press Melville harder, until he at last spoke of whatever it was he was still hiding. And Rathbone had felt certain from the first that there was something.

He turned his attention back to the court.

Delphine was describing some grand social event, a ball or a dinner party. Her face was alight with remembered excitement.

"All the girls were simply lovely," she said, her voice soft, her slender hands on the rail in front of her, lightly touching it, not gripping. She might have held a dancing partner so. "The gowns were exquisite." She smiled as she spoke. "Like so many flowers blown in the wind as they swirled around the floor. The chandeliers blazed and were reflected on jewels and hair. The young men were all so dashing. Perhaps it was happiness which made everything seem so glamorous, but I don't think so. I believe it was real. And Killian danced the whole evening with Zillah. He barely spoke with anyone else at all. He sat a few dances out, but I swear I did not see him pay the slightest heed to any other lady, no matter how beautiful or how charming." She gave a little shrug of her shoulders. "And there were many titled ladies there, and heiresses to considerable fortunes. On that particular occasion Lady—"

Sacheverall held up his hand. "I am sure a great many people of note were there, Mrs. Lambert. What is important is that Mr. Melville paid very obvious court to your daughter, for everyone to see, and his intent could hardly be mistaken or misinterpreted. Now, madam, I must bring you to a far more painful area, for which I apologize. I most truly wish I could avoid it, but there is no way in which it is possible."

"I understand." Delphine nodded, the light going from her face, her body seeming almost to shrink as she dismissed past happiness and faced the present icy disillusion. "Do what is necessary, Mr. Sacheverall."

"You have just told me how publicly and how obviously Mr. Melville courted your daughter. It must have been common knowledge among all your acquaintances, indeed in all society, that they were to be married?"

"Of course." She raised her beautiful eyebrows. "She did not hide her joy. What young girl does?"

"Exactly." Sacheverall took several paces to one side, then to the other. He moved elegantly, and he was aware of it. He stopped and faced her again. "When Mr. Melville suddenly, and for no reason that we may observe, broke off the engagement and refused to go through with the ceremony, what effect did this have upon Miss Lambert's reputation, the way in which she is regarded by society, and her hopes for any future marriage?"

"Of course it will ruin her!" The panic rose in Delphine's voice. "How could it possibly do anything else? People will ask why, and when there is no answer, they will assume the worst. Everyone does, don't they?"

"Yes, Mrs. Lambert, I am afraid it is one of the less attractive characteristics of human nature," Sacheverall said with ardent sympathy. "Even when it is unjustified." He smiled ruefully. "And beauty has its disadvantages in that it increases envy among those less fortunate."

Delphine looked on the verge of tears. "And she is innocent of everything!" she said desperately. "It is so unfair!" Her eyes swept across the jury and then back to Sacheverall. "How could he do this to her—to anyone? It is wicked beyond belief! I can hear them already, beginning to ask each other what can be wrong with her. What does he know about her that he is not saying?" She looked at him defiantly. "And there is nothing! Nothing at all! She is modest; clever enough, but not too clever; lovely but not too proud or self-obsessed; and as honorable as it is possible to be." She gulped, and her voice dropped huskily. "And she was so in love with him. It is so wicked I just cannot imagine why he is doing it! You have to find out! You have to prove it is Killian Melville, not Zillah, who is evil and perverse."

"We shall do, Mrs. Lambert," Sacheverall said gently. "We will prove to the court, and to society, that Miss Lambert has been wronged without cause. Her reputation shall be restored. It would be monstrous that she should have her entire future ruined because of one young man's irresponsibility at best, dishonesty or immorality at worst. Will you be so good as to remain there in case Sir Oliver wishes to ask you anything? Thank you, Mrs. Lambert." He turned to Rathbone invitingly.

The expression of confidence in his face was sufficient warning. Rathbone knew he would get nothing from Delphine Lambert. Almost alone she had built the case. And she had done it without exaggeration. Such breaking of a betrothal after what seemed to everyone a natural love affair would suggest to even the well disposed that there was something profoundly wrong with Zillah Lambert but that Melville was too much of a gentleman to expose her.

Rathbone rose to his feet. He dare not fail to speak to her. That would be an open admission of defeat.

There was a rustle of anticipation in the room. The jurors were watching him.

"We sympathize with you in your concern, Mrs. Lambert," he said courteously, his mind racing for anything whatsoever to mitigate her testimony. "Perhaps you will tell me something more about these wedding arrangements that you mentioned . . ."

"All made!" Her voice rose again. "Of course, the official invitations had not gone out, but everyone knew who was invited, so it comes to virtually the same thing! I have never been so mortified in my life. You cannot imagine the humiliation of having to tell people!" She flung her arms out, hands graceful even in her extreme emotion. "How do I explain? What is there anyone can possibly say? Poor Zillah." She turned to the judge. "Can you begin to imagine how she feels? Every time anyone laughs, if we didn't hear the reason, we think it is at our misfortune."

Rathbone forced himself to remain friendly. "I am sure that is natural. We have all experienced such fears when we are aware of some . . ." What word could he use without seeming critical? He had given himself an impossible sentence to finish. She was looking at him again. "Self-consciousness is to be expected," he said instead. "But to these arrangements, Mrs. Lambert . . ."

"The dressmaker, the wedding attendants, the church, of course, the flowers in season," she listed them off. "I spent hours seeing that everything should be perfect. It is the most important, the most exquisitely beautiful day of a woman's life. I would have given anything I had to ensure that nothing whatever went wrong for her. No time, trouble or expense was to be spared. Not that it was the money. Never think for an instant that it was that." She dismissed it with a wave of her hand.

Curiously, he believed her. It was honor which concerned her. What should have been entirely happiness and beauty instead had become a source of embarrassment and cruel jests, the golden future tarnished beyond repair. She had not mentioned it, maybe she had not even thought of it yet, but it was not impossible that the sense of rejection which Zillah felt would make it hard for her to believe the next man who claimed to love her. No one could say what seeds of future misery had been sown.

"I am sure that is so, Mrs. Lambert," he agreed soothingly. "I do not doubt it. But my question is, how much did Mr. Melville participate in all these plans and decisions?"

She looked blank. "Mr. Melville? It is the bride's parents who make these arrangements, Sir Oliver. It was nothing to do with him."

"My point precisely." He was careful not to show any feeling of victory, however slight. It would offend the jury. He stood in the center of the open space, aware of everyone's eyes on him. "He did not agree to the style of the wedding gown, the amount or kind of flowers, or even the church. . . ."

She looked completely bemused.

"My lord." Sacheverall rose to his feet with a gesture of disbelief. "Is my learned friend suggesting that Mr. Melville broke the engagement to marry in a fit of pique because he was not consulted on these matters? And further, that such absurd behavior is somehow justified? If that were so, my lord, no man would ever marry!" He laughed as he said it, turning towards the jury.

Rathbone kept his temper only through great practice.

"No, my lord, I am not suggesting anything of the kind, as my learned friend would have known had he waited a moment or two. What I am suggesting is that these arrangements, excellent as they no doubt were, were made without Mr. Melville's knowledge. He did not ask for Miss Lambert's hand in marriage, nor did he intend to. The matter was anticipated and, in all good faith, acted upon without his participation. He did not break his agreement, because he did not make one. It was assumed—perhaps with good cause, but nonetheless it was an assumption."

"Sir Oliver is making a clumsy argument!" Sacheverall protested. He stared at Rathbone. "Are you finished? Have you no better case than that to offer?"

Rathbone had not, but this was certainly not the time to say so.

"Not at all," he denied blandly. "I am explaining what I intended by the question, since you misinterpreted it."

"You are saying Mrs. Lambert organized a wedding without any assurance that there was a bridegroom?" Sacheverall challenged, the laughter of derision all but bubbling through his words.

"I am suggesting it was a misunderstanding, not villainy," Rathbone answered, aware how lame the argument was, in spite of its probable truth. Except that he was convinced Melville was holding something back so important it amounted to a lie. There was something elusive about the man, and he had no idea what it was. He had taken his case on impulse, and he regretted it.

Sacheverall dismissed the idea and returned to his seat, with his back half towards Rathbone.

"Sir Oliver?" the judge enquired.

There was nothing more to say. He would only make it even worse.

"No, thank you, my lord. Thank you, Mrs. Lambert."

Sacheverall had nothing more to add. He was wise enough not to press the issue. He was winning without having to try.

It was already late for luncheon. The court adjourned.

Rathbone walked out with Melville. The crowd stared at them. There were several ugly words said quite clearly enough to hear. Melville kept his eyes straight ahead, his face down, his cheeks flushed. He must have been as aware of them as Rathbone was.

"I didn't know about the wedding until it was all planned!" he said desperately. "I heard, of course, bits and pieces. I didn't even realize it was supposed to be me!" They were passing through the entrance hall of the courthouse. Rathbone held open the doors.

"I know that sounds ridiculous," Melville went on. "But I didn't listen. My mind was on my own ideas: arches and lintels, colonnades, rows of windows, depths of foundations, front elevations, angles of roofs. Women are often talking about fashion and who is going to marry whom. Half the time it is only gossip and speculation."

"How can you have been so stupid?" Rathbone snapped, losing his temper at the idiocy of it, all the unnecessary embarrassment.

"Because I suppose I wanted to," Melville answered with astounding honesty. "I didn't want it to be true, so I ignored it. If you care about one thing enough, you can exclude other things." Now they were outside in the sharp wind and sunlight. His eyes were the blue-green of seawater. "I care about buildings, about arches, and pillars and stone, and the way light falls, about color and strength and simplicity. I care about being able to design things that will long outlast me, or anyone I know, things that generations after us will look at and feel joy."

He pushed his hands into his pockets hard and stared at Rathbone as they walked along the street towards the busy restaurant where they could purchase luncheon. They brushed past people barely noticing them.

"Have you ever been to Athens, Sir Oliver?" he asked. "Have you seen the Parthenon in the sunlight?" His eyes were alight with enthusiasm. "It is pure genius. All the measurements are slightly off the true, to give an optical illusion of perfect grace to the observer . . . and it succeeds brilliantly." He flung his arms out, almost hitting a middle-aged man with a gray mustache. He apologized absently and continued to Rathbone. "Can you imagine the minds of the men who built that? And here we are two thousand years later struck silent with awe at its beauty."

Unconsciously he was walking more rapidly than before, and Rathbone had to increase his pace to keep up with him.

"And Tuscany!" he went on, his face glowing. "All Italy, really—Venice, Pisa, Sienna; but the Tuscan Renaissance architecture has a sublime simplicity to it. Classical without being grandiose. A superb sense of color and proportion. One could look at it forever. The arcades . . . the domes! Have you seen the round windows? It all seems part of nature, sprung from it, not vying against . . . there is a mellowness. Nothing jars. That is the secret. A unity with the land, never alien, never offending the vision or the mind. And they know how to use terraces, and trees, especially cypress. They lead the eye perfectly from one point to the next—"

"The restaurant," Rathbone interrupted.

"What?"

"The restaurant," the barrister repeated. "We must have luncheon before we return."

"Oh. Yes . . . I suppose so." Obviously it had slipped Melville's mind. It was an irrelevance.

The first witness of the afternoon was Zillah Lambert herself. She took the oath with a grave, trembling voice and looked up to face Sacheverall. She was very pale, but so far composed. She wore cream trimmed with palest green and it complemented her perfectly. Her glorious hair was piled richly on her head rather than tied severely back, and she looked vulnerable and very young. Yet there was a brightness about her like the glancing sunlight of April, as if she brought a breath of the spring countryside with her.

Without realizing, the jurors smiled at her. She was utterly unaware of them, looking only at Sacheverall. Not once did her eyes stray to Melville, as if she could not bear to look at him. No one could have failed to be aware of it.

"I regret the necessity for this, Miss Lambert," Sacheverall began, as Rathbone had known he would. "But it is absolutely unavoidable, otherwise I should not subject you to this embarrassment, and an ordeal which must be terribly distressing to you."

"I understand," she whispered. "Please do what you must."

Sacheverall smiled warmly at her. "Miss Lambert, has Mr. Killian Melville been a constant visitor at your home over the last two years?"

"Yes sir."

"To see only your father, or also your mother and yourself?"

"He spent a great deal of time with us too," she replied. "He often dined with us and would stay afterwards late into the evening. He and I would talk of all manner of things, our hopes and beliefs, our experiences, whatever we found beautiful or interesting, funny or sad." She blinked hard, trying to keep away the tears. She glanced momentarily at Melville, and then away again. "He was the best and gentlest companion I ever had. He was wise and honest and yet he could make me laugh more than anyone else I knew. He told me wonderful tales of some of the places he had visited, what he had seen and how he felt about them . . . and the things he planned to build. He knows a great deal about history, most particularly the history of art in Italy. I—I find it wonderful to listen to him, because he cares so much."

A certain tightness pulled Sacheverall's mouth and his eyes were sharp.

"Quite so," he said tensely. "In short, Miss Lambert, one might say he courted you." That was a conclusion, not a question. He went straight on. "He spoke of his feelings, he shared his hopes for the future, he showed an extraordinary trust in you that we may assume he did with no one else. Did he make it unmistakable that he cared for you deeply, whatever ways, or words, he chose to use?"

"Yes . . . I believed so." She was obliged to reach into her reticule for a handkerchief with which to dab her eyes. "Excuse me."

"Of course." Sacheverall was instantly tender. "I imagine every man in this room will understand how you feel—except for Melville, and possibly his counsel."

Rathbone considered objecting, but it was not worth the trouble. The remark had already been made, and its impact would be less than that of Zillah herself. One could feel the sympathy for her filling the room. Even the gallery was totally silent. If anyone had been disposed to laugh or feel any sense of satisfaction in her misfortune, either they had changed their minds or they had sensed the atmosphere and wisely concealed it.

"Miss Lambert," Sacheverall continued, "was Mr. Melville fully aware of all the wedding plans and arrangements?"

She sounded surprised. "Of course."

"He was present when you discussed such matters as the choice of church? He was consulted in that, wasn't he?"

"Yes, of course he was." She gazed back at him. "Do you imagine we would arrange such a thing without making certain of his feelings?"

"No, I do not, Miss Lambert, but Sir Oliver seems to have considered it the case." His very slight sneer derided it. "Did Mr. Melville at any time give you the slightest idea he was going to break your agreement?" He jerked his head in Melville's direction.

"No," she said simply.

"And has he since offered you any reason for his behavior?" Sacheverall persisted.

"No." She was having difficulty restraining her emotions and it was plain for everyone to see. Some of the jurors were staring at her intently, others were embarrassed for her and did not wish to seem to intrude into her distress. If Sacheverall was not careful he would risk losing their sympathy towards himself. Perhaps that did not matter to him, as long as he retained it for her. What Rathbone knew of his reputation suggested he was a man who wished to win, even if it should be at considerable cost.

Sacheverall bit his lip and made some show of reluctance.

"Miss Lambert, has he given you any reason for his actions, any reason at all?"

"No," she said so quietly it was barely audible.

The judge leaned forward but he did not ask her to repeat it.

"Only one more question, Miss Lambert," Sacheverall promised. "Have you any idea whatever why he has done this? Have you done anything at all to give him cause? Is there anything he could have discovered about your situation, your family or your personal conduct which could explain it or justify it?"

"That is at least three questions, Mr. Sacheverall," the judge pointed out.

"It will require only one answer, my lord," Sacheverall said with a wave of his hands. "After that the witness is Sir Oliver's."

"Miss Lambert?" the judge prompted.

"No, my lord, I know of nothing," she assured him.

Sacheverall shrugged and looked back towards the jury, then Rathbone. "Sir Oliver, your witness."

Rathbone rose to his feet. "Thank you, Mr. Sacheverall. I feel you have made my point for me." He smiled, largely to unnerve

Sacheverall and irritate him. Then he turned to Zillah, still smiling, but now gently. He walked towards her and looked up, his expression mild. "Miss Lambert, you have just told my learned friend that you know of no reason whatever why Mr. Melville should have broken your engagement to marry. There is no shadow of any kind upon your family, your financial position, or your personal reputation."

There was a murmur of resentment from the gallery and the jurors' faces darkened.

Rathbone continued to smile. "I have no cause to doubt that what you say is the truth, absolutely. Have you a quick temper, Miss Lambert, or a sulky disposition?"

She looked surprised. "I don't think so, sir. No one has ever suggested such a thing to me."

"Are you disposed to gossip, perhaps?"

"No sir. I consider it a vicious habit."

Again there was a rustle of dislike from the gallery and several of the jurors were glaring at him.

Judge McKeever frowned, but he did not interrupt.

Melville was drumming his fingers tensely.

Sacheverall looked more and more satisfied.

"And is your health good?" Rathbone continued. "You do not have any chronic problems, no more than the usual afflictions that upset us all from time to time?"

"No sir, my health is excellent." She still looked totally bemused.

"Your patience with my intrusiveness is witness to your equable temper and your good nature, Miss Lambert," Rathbone said gently. "And it is apparent to any of us here that you are of a remarkably pleasing appearance." He disregarded her blush. "And becoming modesty. Oh . . . I forgot to ask, are you extravagant?"

She looked down at her hands. "No sir, I am not."

"And your father's abundant success ensures your financial position. In all you seem to me a bride any man might consider himself most fortunate to win."

"Thank you, sir."

"I cannot imagine why Killian Melville cast aside his opportunity, but the shortcoming is with him, most certainly not in you."

Melville jerked up his head.

Sacheverall stared at Rathbone, then at the judge.

McKeever leaned over his bench. "Your point, Sir Oliver? You seem to be maligning your own client."

"My point, my lord, is that Miss Lambert is not a young lady who will receive only one offer or opportunity of marriage," he replied expansively, looking at her as he said it. "She is most desirable in every way. She does not seem to have a failing or a weakness, above the merest frailties we may all expect in any human person. She will undoubtedly receive many more offers of marriage, at least as fortunate as that of Mr. Melville, possibly more so. She may easily win the heart of a man with title and fortune to offer her. I cannot agree with my learned friend Mr. Sacheverall"—he waved his arm at him—"that she has suffered a great injury, or indeed with her mother, Mrs. Lambert. I do not refer to her feelings, of course, which are undeniably injured. She has been insulted and her trust betrayed. But her worldly future has not been injured. Unfortunately, our personal feelings cannot be protected from the wounds of love. To accept the gift of life is to accept also the risks."

"Really!" Sacheverall protested, starting to his feet and walking forward.

McKeever raised his scant eyebrows and his wide blue eyes were innocent. "Yes, Mr. Sacheverall?"

"I . . ." Sacheverall gave up in disgust and returned to his seat.

"Have you anything further to put to Miss Lambert?" McKeever asked them both.

They each declined, and he adjourned the court until the following day.

Rathbone left feeling thoroughly miserable. He had scored a slight victory over Sacheverall on the point of Zillah Lambert's very evident charm and apparent innocence, but it would not win him the case, and they both knew it. It made Melville's behavior all the more incomprehensible, and the thought that filled Rathbone's mind as he walked smartly along the footpath, avoiding the eyes of the few professional acquaintances he passed and heading for the nearest hansom cab, was just what did Melville know about Zillah, or her family, that he refused to say? And that thought must also sooner or later cross the mind of almost every one of her friends and enemies in society as well. Certainly it would cross the lips of the mothers of her rivals. And they would make doubly sure that it entered the ears of the mothers of suitable young gentlemen, heirs to titles and fortunes.

If anyone was marrying Zillah Lambert for love, it would seem he could not do better, but that was not the majority of those whom her mother would seek. Even if no one was vulgar enough to say so, the jurors were men of the world, and no doubt married themselves, perhaps with sons who would soon seek brides. Would they accept willingly a girl about whom there were questions?

It was beginning to rain and he had to run to catch a hansom before a couple of gentlemen in short temper could beat him to it. He heard their cries of frustration as he slammed the door and gave the driver his address.

Two hours later, after he had dined without enjoying it and then paced the floor for thirty-five minutes, he went out again to look for another cab to Melville's rooms.

He had only been there once before, Melville had come to him during their preparation for trial. The building was a handsome Georgian town house, but in no way different from its neighbors on either side. However, once he was past the vestibule, across the hall and up the stairs to the second floor, where Melville had his rooms, it was utterly individual. The inside had been gutted and the new walls were curved and washed with colors giving a unique appearance of space and light. They had been used to create optical illusions of both distance and warmth. One room seemed to blend into the next. Ivories and golds and the shades of brown sugar blended with the richness of polished wood. One brilliant fuchsia-red cushion caught the eye. Another in hot Turkish pink echoed it.

Killian Melville sat in the middle of the floor on an embroidered camel saddle. He looked wretched. He barely glanced up as Rathbone came in and the maid disappeared.

"I suppose you want to resign the case," he said gloomily. "I can't blame you. I appear to be a complete cad."

"Appear to be?" Rathbone said with sarcasm.

Melville looked up. There were shadows around his eyes and fine lines from nose to mouth and around his lips. He was handsome in a refined, ascetic manner, but the most outstanding impression in his countenance was still one of overriding honesty. There was a directness in him, a sense of courage, even daring.

"Are you asking to resign?" he repeated.

"No, I am not!" Rathbone said sharply, stung more by pride than by sense, and certainly not by any belief that he could win. "I shall fight the case to the end, but the least I can realistically hope to do for you is mitigate the scale of the disaster. On what you have given me, I cannot beat Sacheverall; he has all the weapons."

"I know," Melville agreed. "I do not expect miracles."

"Yes, you do." Rathbone sat down on the sofa without waiting to be invited. "Or you would not have entered this case at all. It is not too late to make some excuse of nervousness, indisposition, and still ask her to marry you. She may well refuse now—heaven knows, you have given her cause—and then at least her honor will be satisfied and you will have extricated yourself."

Melville smiled with self-mockery. "But what if she accepts?"

"Then marry her," Rathbone responded. "She is charming, modest, intelligent, good-tempered and healthy. Her father is rich and she is his only heir. For heaven's sake, man, what more do you want? You have admitted you like her, and she obviously cares for you."

Melville looked away. "No," he said quietly, but there was infinite resolution in his voice. "I cannot marry her."

Rathbone was exasperated. He felt helpless, sent into battle robbed of both armor and weapons.

Melville sat in the camel saddle staring at the floor, shoulders hunched, miserable and obstinate.

"Then for God's sake, give me a reason!" Rathbone heard his own voice getting louder, filled with anger. "If you forbid me, then I won't use it, but at least let me know! What is wrong with Zillah Lambert? Does she drink? Has she some disease? Is there madness in her family? What is it?"

"Nothing," Melville said stubbornly, still staring downwards. Rathbone could see only his profile. "So far as I know, she is as charming and as innocent as she looks." He continued, "I know of nothing else."

"Then it must be you," Rathbone accused. He could not remember ever having been so angry with a client before. Melville was brilliant, handsome, highly individual, and had a very real charm . . . and he was destroying himself over something which, compared with the tragedies and violence Rathbone usually dealt with, was utterly trivial. That a young woman's reputation was being questioned and her feelings were being hurt were not light matters, but they were so very much less than the imprisonment, ruin and often death which he dealt with in cases of murder. And Melville's problem seemed so much of his own making. Why did he lie? What could there possibly be that was worth concealing at this cost?

Melville sat hunched and silent.

"What is it?" Rathbone demanded. "Is it Zillah Lambert you won't marry, or anyone at all?"

Melville turned to look at him, his face puzzled, something dark in his eyes which Rathbone thought might have been fear.

"Well?" Rathbone said urgently. "Are you free to marry? Whatever you tell me I am bound by oath to keep in confidence. I cannot lie for you in court, but I can and will keep silent. But I cannot help you if I don't know what I am fighting."

Melville turned away again, his face set. "I am free to marry . . . but not Zillah Lambert. That is an end to it. There is nothing wrong with her. I'll take the punishment. Just do the best you can."

Rathbone remained another half hour, but he could get nothing more from Melville. At quarter to ten he left and went home through rising wind and squalls of rain, still surprisingly cold.

He poured himself a draft of single-malt whiskey and drank it neat, then went to bed. He slept very badly, troubled by dreams.

CHAPTER FOUR

The trial resumed the next morning with Sacheverall providing witnesses to Zillah's blameless character, as Rathbone had known he would. It was hardly necessary—her own appearance had been sufficient—but then he could not be certain that Rathbone had no witness of his own in store, someone who could cast doubt on the innocence and charm they had seen.

The first was a Lady Lucinda Stoke-Harbury, a girl of Zillah's own age who was newly betrothed to the second son of an earl, and impeccably respectable. She stood with her head high, her eyes straight ahead, and spoke clearly. Sacheverall could not have found anyone better, and the very slight swagger with which he walked to and fro on the open space of the floor showed his confidence. He smiled like an actor playing to the gallery, and seemed just as sure that the rest of the cast would respond as if according to a script.

"Lady Lucinda, please tell us how long you have been acquainted with Miss Lambert, if you would be so kind."

"Oh, at least five years," she replied cheerfully. "We have been great friends."

Sacheverall was delighted; it was exactly the reply he wanted. He hesitated long enough to make sure the jury had fully digested the statement, then continued.

"Have you many friends in common?"

"Naturally. We attend all the same parties, dinners, balls and so on. And we have often been to art galleries and lectures together."

"So you know her well?"

"Yes, I do."

It was all very predictable, and there was nothing Rathbone could do to affect it. To cast doubt on Lady Lucinda's judgment, or her honesty in expressing it, would only play directly into Sacheverall's hands. It could both turn the jury against him, and indirectly Melville, and show them his own desperation. If he had any evidence of his own he should produce it, not insult Lady Lucinda.

Sacheverall grew more and more enthusiastic, seeking praise and affirmation for Zillah with many new avenues of questioning.

Rathbone looked around the gallery. He saw the range of expressions on the faces as they craned forward, listening to every word. For a woman in black bombazine with a ribboned hat it was an avid interest showing in her eyes, her lips parted. For a man with gray side-whiskers it was more relaxed, even a trifle cynical, a half smile. A well-dressed young woman with straight brown hair under her bonnet looked at Melville with undisguised contempt. Her neighbor seemed more curious as to why a young man with such golden opportunities before him should risk losing it all for such an absurd reason. Rathbone could almost read the speculation in their eyes as to what was unsaid behind the polite words from the witness stand. What was the real reason behind this charade?

More than once he caught someone looking at him, speculation easily read as to what he could do, what he knew and would spring on them, when he was ready.

He wished there were something!

He saw several studying the jury, and perhaps trying to guess their thoughts, although at this point there seemed only one possible verdict.

Melville sat through it all sunk in unhappiness but without moving, except occasionally to put his fingers up to his mouth, and then away again, but he did not speak. He did not offer any contradictions or suggestions of help.

Rathbone declined the offer to question Lady Lucinda. There was nothing whatever to ask.

The next witness was another young woman of impeccable reputation, and she reaffirmed everything that had already been said.

The judge looked enquiringly at Rathbone.

"No, thank you, my lord," he said, rising briefly to his feet and then sitting down again.

Sacheverall was delighted. His contempt, not only for Melville but for Rathbone also, was vivid in his face and the entire attitude of his body.

He called the Honorable Timothy Tremaine and asked him for his opinion of the most admirable Miss Zillah Lambert. As Tremaine spoke, his own admiration for her grew more and more apparent. He smiled, he met her eyes, and his eager expression softened. He spoke of her with a warmth which was more than mere sympathy. An idea began to form in Rathbone's mind, not clearly, and only a thread, but he had nothing else.

"Your witness, Sir Oliver," Sacheverall said finally, with an ironic half bow towards Rathbone.

Rathbone rose to his feet. "Thank you, Mr. Sacheverall." He was acutely aware of all eyes upon him. There was a hush as if awaiting a startling event. He would disappoint them, and it rankled with him more sharply than he had expected. He felt the defeat already.

"Mr. Tremaine," he began quietly, "you spoke of Miss Lambert as if you are quite well acquainted with her. May I assume that is so?"

"Yes sir, you may," Tremaine answered politely. He too must have been waiting for some retaliation at last.

Rathbone smiled. "And you expressed some regard for her yourself—indeed, some admiration?" It was not really a question.

"Yes sir." Tremaine was more guarded now.

Rathbone's smile widened. He knew what the gallery was waiting for, what Tremaine himself quite suddenly feared. It was there in his face. He drew in his breath as if to add something, then changed his mind.

"Yes?" Rathbone enquired helpfully.

"Nothing . . ."

"There is no need to apologize for your feelings," Rathbone assured him. "It is only natural. She is most attractive. Indeed, Mr. Sacheverall himself has been unable to conceal a very considerable"—he hesitated delicately—"personal regard towards her. . . ."

He heard Sacheverall's indrawn breath behind him and ignored it.

"I . . ." Tremaine realized the trap and sidestepped it rather obviously. "Yes sir. I think we all feel a certain . . . friendship towards her which—" He stopped, uncertain how to complete the thought.

"Is your regard as . . . warm as Mr. Sacheverall's?" Rathbone asked blandly.

"Well . . ." Tremaine looked at him squarely. "I could say I regard her more as a friend . . ."

Sacheverall stood up, his face only very slightly pink. "My lord, the depth of my regard for Miss Lambert is irrelevant. It is Mr. Melville's behavior towards her which is at issue here. If Sir Oliver is trying to suggest that I have in any way overstepped the bounds of the strictest propriety, or that Miss Lambert has regarded me as other than her legal counsel, then I would warn him that he is not above the laws of slander either, and I will protect Miss Lambert's good name with every skill at my disposal . . . and every weapon also!"

Rathbone laughed very lightly and swiveled to look at Sacheverall.

"My dear Sacheverall, you have spent the morning persuading me of Miss Lambert's virtue, charm and total desirability. Is it really now slanderous for me to suggest that you are not immune to charm yourself? Surely it would be more so to suggest that you are? Then you might think I accused you of being less than a natural man. Or at the very least of speaking insincerely, saying something which you yourself did not believe."

"You are—" Sacheverall began.

But Rathbone overrode him. "Your sincerity seemed to ring

through your words, your choice of adjectives to describe her, the very ardor of your tone and the grace of your gestures. You made your argument superbly."

"What is your point?" Sacheverall snapped, his cheeks flushed. "There is nothing improper for you to find!" He gestured towards Melville, who was sitting staring at him. "That is where the fault lies. You have paved the way for that yourself! Indeed, it would be an unusual man—perhaps, to borrow your own phrase, something less than a natural man—who would not admire Miss Lambert!" His face twisted into an expression suddenly far uglier than perhaps he knew. "Have you considered, Sir Oliver, that you do not know your own client as well as you imagine? You are the last man I would have supposed naive, but I could be mistaken." His meaning was masked, but it was clear enough. There was a gasp around the room. One or two of the jurors looked taken aback. The remark was indelicate at best, at worst slanderous.

The judge looked expectantly at Rathbone.

Rathbone had turned immediately to Melville. Sacheverall was right in that he had not known his client as well as he wished to.

But the look on Melville's face was one of bitter but quite honest laughter. No one could doubt he found the remark genuinely funny. There was no embarrassment in him, not a shred of shame or even discomfort.

The judge blinked.

One or two jurors looked at each other.

Sacheverall colored very slightly, as if aware he had stepped a little too far. For the first time he had lost the sympathy of the jury. But he would not retreat.

"There may be many reasons for a man to shrink from marriage," he said rather loudly. "Reasons he would not be willing to acknowledge to anyone. I make no accusations, please be clear; I speak only in general. He may be aware of disease in himself, or in his family." He waved his arms in a gesture Rathbone had come to recognize was characteristic. "There may be a strain of madness. He may have a burden of debt he cannot meet, and therefore could not keep a wife. He may even be in danger of prosecution for some offense or other. He may already be married!"

There was a buzz of excited conversation as people in the gallery turned to whisper to one another.

"Silence!" Mr. Justice McKeever ordered, his voice surprisingly penetrating for one so soft. "Silence, or I shall clear the court!"

Obedience was instant. A man in the gallery cleared his throat, and it sounded like a minor explosion.

"Or he may be unable to consummate the union," Sacheverall finished.

One of the jurors, an elderly man with thick white hair, clicked his teeth and shook his head disapprovingly. The remark obviously offended him as being in exceedingly poor taste. Gentlemen did not discuss such things.

Again Rathbone glanced at Melville, and saw only laughter in his light, sea-blue eyes.

"Of course," Rathbone agreed, equally penetratingly. "And there may be many reasons why a man may decline to marry a particular lady, many of them disagreeable, coarse and offensive even to suggest, so I shall not." He saw out of the corner of his eye one of the jurors nod. "I am loathe to have this already sad situation descend to such a level," he finished.

McKeever smiled bleakly. He had seen too many civil cases to hold out any such hope.

"I am sure you are," Sacheverall agreed sarcastically. "And I daresay your client even more so. But he should have thought of that before he humiliated and insulted Miss Lambert and used her affections so lightly. It is too late for such regrets now, even more for the fear of how it may reflect upon his own reputation."

The fragile advantage had slipped away already. Thank heaven it was Friday and Rathbone had two days in which to try to prevail on Melville to tell him the truth. If he did not, then he could see no strategy at all which would avoid defeat. Perhaps Melville had not realized quite how damaging that would be to him, not only financially but also professionally. Barton Lambert would certainly cease to support him or employ him. Lambert was a man of influence. Melville might very well find his entire career jeopardized, regardless of his brilliance.

Rathbone forced himself to smile and face Sacheverall.

"This is not over yet," he said with infinitely more confidence than he felt. "Let us await the conclusion before we assess the damage, and to whom. I have no wish to cause injury, but I shall represent my client's interests with all the vigor at my disposal."

"Naturally." Sacheverall was not disturbed. He had regained his composure and he knew he had little to fear. Victory was only an inch from his grasp, and in his mind he could already feel it. "One would expect no less of you," he added, but his smile lacked any anxiety that Rathbone might win.

He called one more witness, and then the court was adjourned for the weekend. The crowd dispersed from the gallery with unusual quietness and good order. It was an ominous sign. They were not expecting any surprises, no turn in events to spark their interest or change what to many was already a foregone conclusion.

Melville rose to leave also and Rathbone put his hand out and grasped his arm, gripping it unintentionally hard. He saw Melville wince.

"You're not going," he said grimly, "until you tell me the truth. I don't think you realize just what you're facing. This could ruin you."

Melville sat down again, turning to stare at him. Around them the crowd had moved away. There was hardly anyone left except the ushers and court officials.

"You need a lot more than talent to succeed in the arts," Rathbone went on quietly but clearly. "You need patronage, in architecture more than almost anything else. Your plans are stillborn if they never get off the paper." He saw the pain tighten Melville's face but he had to go on. If he did not succeed in persuading him now it could be too late. "You have to have a wealthy patron who believes in you and is willing to spend tens of thousands of pounds to build your halls and houses and theaters. You are not big enough yet to defy society, and you will very soon find that out if you lose this case without any excuse to offer."

Melville blushed. "You want me to try to blacken her name?" he asked angrily. "Suggest that I suddenly found out something about her so appalling I couldn't live with it? That she was a thief? A loose woman? A drunkard? A spendthrift? A gambler? I can't. And if I could"—his lip curled in disgust—"would that endear me to society, do you suppose? How many wealthy men would then wish to have me in their close acquaintance, to observe their wives and daughters and then tell the world their weaknesses!"

"I don't want you to tell the world!" Rathbone answered back with equal sharpness, and still holding Melville's wrist, ignoring the last few people leaving the room, looking at the lawyer and his client curiously. "I meant you to tell me so I can understand the battle I am supposed to be fighting. I don't need you to tell me that blackening Zillah Lambert's name, with or without justification, will not help you. But with the truth, I may be able to reach a settlement out of court. It wouldn't be victory, but it would be a great deal better than any other alternative facing you now."

"I know nothing to her detriment," Melville insisted. "Do you think I am being noble and letting her family sue me without a word in my defense? Is that what you imagine?" There seemed to be a brittle ring of amusement in him, as if the idea were funny.

"I don't know what to think." Rathbone half turned as the last woman went out of the doors and the usher looked at him enquiringly. "But if there is nothing about Zillah, then I must conclude that Sacheverall is right and it is something to do with you."

He had longed to read an answer, a vulnerability or a fear in Melville's eyes which would give him the clue he needed, but there was nothing. Melville remained staring at him with a blank, defiant despair.

"Is there someone else you love?" Rathbone guessed. "It doesn't excuse you, but it would at least explain—to me, if no one else."

"There is no one else I wish to marry," Melville replied. "I have already told you that." He gave a little shiver. "There is no purpose in your asking me, Sir Oliver. I have nothing to tell you which can help. The only truth of the matter is that I never asked Zillah to marry me. I have no intention of ever marrying anyone." There was a curious bleakness in his eyes as he said it, and a momentary pull at his lips. "It was arranged without consulting me and I was foolish enough not to realize that all the chatter was taken to be sufficient notification. I was blind, I fully acknowledge that; naive, if you like." His chin came up. "I admit to carelessness of her feelings because I did not think of her as more than a friend I cared for dearly. It did not cross my mind that she felt otherwise. That was clumsy, looking back with the clarity of hindsight. I will not make that error again."

"That's not enough," Rathbone said bitterly.

"That is all there is." A self-mockery filled Melville's eyes. "I could say I had suddenly discovered madness in my family, if you like, but since it is not true, it would be impossible to prove. They'd be fools to believe me. Any young man could say that to escape an engagement if no proof were required."

"Except that it would disqualify him from all future engagements as well," Rathbone pointed out. "And possibly other things. It is not a tragedy one would wish upon anyone."

The irony vanished from Melville's face, leaving only pain behind. "No, of course it isn't. I did not mean to make light of the affliction of madness. It is just that this whole situation invites the thought of farce. I am sorry."

"It won't feel like farce when the jury finds against you and awards costs and damages," Rathbone replied, watching Melville's expression.

"I know," Melville answered in little above a whisper, looking away. "But there is nothing I can do except employ the best lawyer there is and trust in his skill."

Rathbone grunted. He had done his utmost, and it was insufficient. He let go of Melville's arm and stood up. The ushers were waiting. "You know where to find me if you should change your mind or think of anything at all which may be useful."

Melville rose also. "Yes, of course. Thank you for your patience, Sir Oliver."

Rathbone sighed.

At first Rathbone decided to go home and have a long, quiet evening turning the case over in his mind to see if he could discover something which had so far eluded him. But the prospect was unpromising, and he had been in his study only half an hour, unable to relax, when he abandoned the whole idea and told his manservant that he was going out and did not know when he would be back.

He took a hansom all the way to Primrose Hill, where his father lived, and arrived just as the shadows were lengthening and the sun was going down in a limpid sky.

Henry Rathbone was at the far end of the long lawn staring at the apple trees whose gnarled branches were thick with blossom buds. He was a taller man than his son, and leaner, a little stooped with constant study. Before his retirement he had been a mathematician and sometime inventor. Now he dabbled in all sorts of things for pleasure and to keep his mind occupied. He found life far too interesting to waste a day of it, and all manner of people engaged his attention. His own parents had been of humble stock; in fact, his maternal grandfather had been a blacksmith and wheelwright. He made no pretensions to superiority, except that when he judged a man to have sufficient intelligence to know better, he suffered fools with great impatience.

"Good evening, Father," Rathbone called as he stepped through the French doors across the paved terrace and onto the grass.

Henry turned with surprise.

"Hello, Oliver! Come down and look at this. Do you know the honeysuckle in this hedge flowered right on until Christmas, and it's coming well into leaf again already. And the orchard is full of primroses. How are you?" He regarded his son more closely. The evening light was very clear and perhaps more revealing than the harsher sun would have been. "What is wrong?"

Oliver reached him and stopped. He put his hands in his pockets and surveyed the hedge with the aforementioned honeysuckle twined through it, and the bare branches of the orchard beyond. His father frequently read him rather too easily.

"Difficult case," he answered. "Shouldn't really have taken it on in the first instance. Too late now."

Henry started to walk back towards the house. The sun was barely above the trees and any moment it would disappear. There was a golden haze in the air and it was appreciably colder than even a few minutes before. A cloud of starlings wheeled above a distant stand of poplars, still bare, although in the next garden a willow trailed weeping branches like streamers of pale chiffon. The breeze was so slight it did not even stir them.

Henry took a pipe out of his pocket but did not bother even to pretend to light it. He seemed to like just to hold it by the bowl, waving it to emphasize a point as he spoke.

"Well, are you going to tell me about it?" he asked. He gestured towards a clump of wood anemones. "Self-seeded," he observed. "Can't think how they got there. Really want them in the orchard. What sort of case?"

"Breach of promise," Oliver replied.

Henry looked at him sharply, his face full of surprise, but he made no comment.

Oliver explained anyway. "At first I refused. Then the same evening I went to a ball, and I was so aware of the matrons parading their daughters, vying with one another for any available unmarried man, I felt like a quarry before the pack myself. I could imagine how one might be cornered, unable to extricate oneself with any grace or dignity, or the poor girl either."

Henry merely nodded, putting the pipe stem in his mouth for a moment and closing his teeth on it.

"Too much is expected of marriage," Oliver went on as they came to the end of the grass and stepped across the terrace to the door. He held it open while Henry went inside, then followed him in and closed it.

"Draw the curtains, will you?" Henry requested, going over to the fire and taking away the guard, then placing several more coals on it and watching it flame up satisfactorily.

Oliver walked over towards the warmth and sat down, making himself comfortable. There was always something relaxing about this room, a familiarity, books and odd pieces of furniture he remembered all his life.

"I'm not decrying it, of course," he went on. "But one shouldn't expect someone else to fill all the expectations in our lives, answer all the loneliness or the dreams, provide us with a social status, a roof over our heads, daily bread, clothes for our backs, and a purpose for living as well, not to mention laughter and hope and love, someone to justify our aspirations and decide our moral judgments."

"Good gracious!" Henry was smiling but there was a shadow of anxiety in his eyes. "Where did you gather this impression?"

Oliver retracted immediately. "Well, all right, I am exaggerating. But the way these girls spoke, they hoped everything from marriage. I can understand why Melville panicked. No one could fill such a measure."

"And did he also believe that was expected of him?" Henry enquired.

"Yes." Oliver recalled it vividly, seeing Zillah in his mind. "I met his betrothed. Her face was shining, her eyes full of dreams. One would have thought she was about to enter heaven itself."

"Perhaps," Henry conceded. "But being in love can be quite consuming at times, and quite absurd in the cold light of others' eyes. I think you are stating a fear of commitment which is not uncommon, but nevertheless neither is it admirable. Society cannot exist if we do not keep the promises we have made, that one above most others." He regarded him gently, but not without a very clear perception. "Are you certain it is not your rather fastidious nature, and unwillingness to forgo your own independence, which you are projecting onto this young man?"

"I'm not unwilling to commit myself!" Oliver defended, thinking with sharp regret of the evening not long before when he had very nearly asked Hester Latterly to marry him. He would have, had he not been aware that she would refuse him and it would leave them hesitant with each other. A friendship they both valued would be changed and perhaps not recapturable with the trust and the ease it had had before. At times he was relieved she had forestalled him. He did value his privacy, his complete personal freedom, the fact that he could do as he pleased without reference to anyone, without hurt or offense. At other times he felt a loneliness without her. He thought of her more often than he intended to, and found her not there, not where he could assume she could listen to him, believe in him. There were times when he deeply missed her presence to share an idea, a thing of beauty, something that made him laugh.

Henry merely nodded. Did he know? Or guess? Hester was extraordinarily fond of him. Oliver had even wondered sometimes if part of his own attraction for her was the regard she had for Henry, the wider sense of belonging she would have as part of his family. That was something William Monk could not give her! He had lost his memory in a carriage accident just after the end of the Crimean War, and everything in his life before that was fragments pieced together from observation and deduction, albeit far more complete now than even a year ago. Still, there was no one in Monk's background like Henry Rathbone.

Could that be it? Was it not Zillah who was unacceptable but someone else in her family? Barton Lambert? Delphine? No, that was unlikely in the extreme. Barton Lambert had been Melville's friend far more than most men could expect of a father-in-law. And Delphine was proud of her daughter, ambitious, possibly overprotective, but then was that not usual, and what one expected, even admired, in a mother? If she disliked Melville now, she certainly had ample cause.

"There seems to be no defense," he said aloud.

"What does he say?" Henry asked, taking the pipe out of his

mouth and knocking the bowl sharply against the fireplace. He looked enquiringly at Oliver as he cleaned out the pipe and refilled it with tobacco. He seldom actually smoked it, but fiddling with it seemed to give him satisfaction.

"That's it," Oliver replied with exasperation. "Nothing! Simply that he did not ask her in the first place and he cannot bear the thought of marrying anyone at all. He states emphatically that he knows nothing to her discredit, and has no impediment to marriage himself, and trusts in me to defend him as well as may be done."

"Then surely there is something he is not telling you," Henry observed, putting the pipe between his teeth again but still not bothering to light it.

"I know that," Oliver agreed. "But I have no idea what it is. Every moment in court I dread Sacheverall facing him with it. I imagine he is going to produce it, like a conjurer, and any hope I have will evaporate."

"Is that Wystan Sacheverall?" Henry asked, raising his eyebrows.

"Yes. Why?"

Henry shrugged. "Knew his father. Always thought him very ambitious socially, something of an opportunist. Big man with fair hair and large ears."

Oliver smiled. "Definitely his son," he agreed. "But he is a very competent man. I shall not make the error of underrating him simply because he has a clownish face. I think he is extremely serious beneath it."

"Then you had better find out for yourself what your client will not tell you," Henry stated. "Have you told Hester about this situation? A feminine point of view might help."

"I hadn't thought of it," Oliver admitted. She had been in his mind on many occasions, but not as a possible source of help. "Actually, I have not been in touch with her for a few weeks. She will almost certainly be with a new patient."

"Then you can ask Lady Callandra Daviot," Henry pointed out. "She will know where Hester is."

"Callandra is in Scotland," Oliver replied stubbornly. "Traveling around from place to place. I had a letter from her posted from Ballachulish. I believe that is somewhere on the west coast, a little short of Fort William in Inverness-shire."

"I know where Fort William is," Henry said patiently. "Then you will have to enquire from Monk. It should not be beyond his ability to find her. He is an excellent detective . . . assuming he does not already know."

Oliver loathed the idea of going to Monk to ask him where Hester was. He would feel so vulnerable. It would entirely expose his disadvantage that he did not know himself, and yet he assumed Monk would. His only satisfaction would be if Monk did not know either. But then he would be no further forward. Now that Henry had suggested it, he realized how much he wanted to consult Hester. In fact, this case could provide the perfect reason to go to her again without their personal emotions intruding so much that the whole meeting would be impossibly awkward. On reflection, it had been a mistake not to see her more often in the intervening time. It would then have been so much easier.

Now he was reduced to going to Monk, of all people, for help.

Henry was watching him reflectively.

"I suppose it would be quite a good idea," Oliver conceded. "I may even end up employing him myself!" He meant it as a joke. He could not use a detective against his own client, but he was tempted to do it simply to have the weapon of knowledge in his hand.

"What will happen to him if you lose?" Henry asked after another few moments of thoughtful silence by the fire.

"Financial penalty and social ruin," Rathbone answered. "And considering his profession, probably professional catastrophe as well."

"Does he realize that?" Henry frowned.

"I've told him."

"Then you must find out the truth, Oliver." Henry leaned forward, his face very grave, worry creasing his brow. "What you have told me so far does not make any sense. No man would throw away a brilliant career, about which he obviously cares passionately, for such a reason."

"I know," Oliver agreed. He sat a little lower in his chair. It was soft and extremely comfortable. The whole room had a familiar feeling that was far more than mere warmth; it was a deep sense of safety, of belonging, of values which did not change. "I'll ask Monk. Tomorrow."

Monk was startled to see Rathbone on his step at half past eight the following morning. He opened the door dressed in shirtsleeves, his dark hair smoothed back off his brow and still damp. He surveyed Rathbone's immaculate striped trousers and plain coat, his high hat and furled umbrella.

"I can't guess," he said with a shrug. "I cannot think of anything whatever which would bring you, dressed like that, to my door at this hour on a Saturday morning."

"I don't expect you to guess," Rathbone replied waspishly. "If you allow me in, I shall tell you."

Monk smiled. He had a high-cheekboned face with steady gray eyes, a broad-bridged aquiline nose and a wide, thin mouth. It was the countenance of a man who was clever, as ruthless with himself as with others, possessed of courage and humor, who hid his weaknesses behind a mask of wit—and sometimes of affected coldness.

Rathbone knew all this, and part of him admired Monk, part of him even liked him. He trusted him unquestioningly.

Monk stood back and invited him in. The room where he received his prospective clients was already warm with the fire bright in the hearth, the curtains drawn wide and a clock ticking agreeably on the mantel. That was new since the last time Rathbone had been there. He wondered if it had been Hester's idea, then dismissed the thought forcibly. The rest of the room was filled with her suggestions. Why not this, and what did it matter if it were?

Monk waved to him to sit down. "Is this professional?" he asked, standing by the fire and looking down at Rathbone.

Rathbone leaned back and crossed his legs, to show how at ease he was.

"Of course it is. I don't make social calls at this hour."

"You must have an appalling case." Monk was still amused, but now he was also interested.

Rathbone wanted to make sure Monk understood it was professional, and not that he wanted to find Hester for personal motives. For him to believe that would be intolerable. In his own way he would never allow Rathbone to forget it.

"I have," he said candidly. "I am out of my depth, because of the nature of it, and I know I am being lied to. I need a sound judgment on it, one from a very different point of view." He saw Monk's interest increase.

"If I can be of help," Monk offered. "What is the case? Tell me about it. What is your client accused of? Murder?"

"Breach of promise."

"What?" Monk could hardly believe it. "Breach of promise? To marry?" He laughed in spite of himself. "And you don't understand it?" It was not quite contempt in his voice, but almost.

"That's right," Rathbone agreed. He was a past master at keeping his temper. Better men, more skilled at these tactics than Monk, had tried to provoke him and failed. "My client stands to forfeit not only money but his professional reputation if he loses. And he has a brilliant career. Some might even say he has genius."

The humor vanished from Monk's face. He stared at Rathbone with gravity, and the curiosity returned.

"So why did he court someone and then break the engagement?" he asked. "What did he discover about her?"

"He says there was nothing," Rathbone replied. Now that it had come to it, he might as well hear Monk's opinion as well. Whatever his emotions towards Monk, and they were wildly varied, he respected Monk's intelligence and his judgment. They had fought too many issues side by side, embraced too many causes together passionately, at any cost, not to know each other in a way few people are privileged to share.

"Then either he is lying," Monk responded, watching Rathbone closely, "or there is something about himself he is not telling you."

"Precisely," Rathbone agreed. "But I have no idea which it is or what the something may be."

"Are you employing me to find out . . . against your own client?" Monk asked. "He'll hardly pay you for that! Or thank you, either."

"No, I'm not," Rathbone said sharply. "I would like a woman's judgment on the situation. Callandra is in Scotland. I want to ask Hester." He searched Monk's face and saw his eyes widen very slightly but no more. Whatever Monk thought, he kept it concealed. "I don't know her present case. I thought you might."

"No, I don't," Monk answered without a flicker. "But I know how to find out. If you wish I shall do so." He glanced at the clock. "I assume it is urgent?"

"Are you expecting someone?" Rathbone misunderstood deliberately.

Monk shrugged very slightly and stepped forward from the mantel. The half smile touched his lips again. "Not for breakfast," he answered, crossing the room. He managed to move with the grace of suppressed energy. Always, even when weary or seeming beaten, he gave the air of one who might be dangerous to antagonize. Rathbone had never tested his physical strength, but he knew that not even the despair or the defeats of the past, the close and terrible personal danger which had plumbed the bottom of his emotional power, had broken him. The last dreadful moments of the affair in Mecklenburg Square must have come close. Hester had seen the worst extreme, but she had not betrayed it, and he knew she never would—just as she would never have told Monk anything about the moments between herself and Rathbone.

"I suppose you have eaten?" Monk asked with assumption of the answer in his voice. "I haven't. If you want to join me for at least a cup of tea, you're welcome. Tell me a little bit more about this life-and-death case of yours . . . for breach of promise, hurt feelings and questioned reputation. Business must be hard for you to be reduced to this!"

It was nearly noon before Monk arrived at Rathbone's rooms and simply handed him a slip of paper on which was written an address and the name "Gabriel Sheldon." He passed it to Rathbone with a slight smile.

Rathbone glanced at it. "Thank you," he said simply. He did not know what else to add. It was a strangely artificial situation. They knew each other in some ways so well. Rathbone knew far more of Monk than anyone else except Hester—and possibly Callandra Daviot and John Evan, the sergeant who had worked with Monk before Monk left the police force following a violent quarrel with his superior. But Evan had seen him only intermittently since then; Rathbone had worked with him every few months. They had stood together in victory and despair, in mental and physical exhaustion, in the elation of triumph and the strange, acute pain of pity. Even if they had never voiced it, they each understood what the other felt.

Rathbone knew that Monk had lost his past, everything, until four years ago. He had discovered himself as a man in his forties, not a man he always liked, sometimes a man he despised, even feared. Rathbone had watched Monk struggle to regain memory, and had seen the courage it required of Monk to look at what he had been: the occasional cruelty, the hasty judgments, made too often in ignorance and from fear. Monk had hesitated at times, flinching from what he would find, but in the end he had never refused to look.

Rathbone admired him for it. Indeed, he would have protected him and defended him were it possible. A part of him liked Monk quite naturally, despite their widely differing backgrounds. Rathbone was born to comfort and had received an excellent education with all the grace and social status which such an eduction afforded. Monk was the son of a fisherman from the far northeast, on the Scottish borders. His education had been struggled for, given as charity by the local vicar, who appreciated a boy of intellectual promise and driving will, and was prepared to tutor him for nothing. He had come south to London to make his fortune, assisted quickly by a man of wealth who had trained him in merchant banking until his own unjust prosecution and ruin.

Then, burning with indignation, Monk had joined the police, driven by anger and filled with passion to right the intolerable wrongs he saw.

That was so unlike Rathbone, who had studied law at Cambridge and risen easily from one position to another assisted by a mixture of patronage and his own brilliance.

Only his sense of purpose was similar, his ambition to achieve the highest, and perhaps his love of the beautiful things of life, of elegance and good taste. In Rathbone it was natural to dress perfectly. He looked and sounded the gentleman he was. It took no effort whatever.

For Monk it was an extravagance which had to be paid for by going without other things, but he never hesitated. Rathbone could not accuse him of vanity, but someone else might have, possibly even Hester herself, certainly Callandra Daviot. Rathbone had never known a woman who gave less considered thought to her appearance. But for all Monk's natural elegance and carefully attentive grooming, he would never have the assurance Rathbone did, because it came with breeding and could not be acquired.

"Thank you," he repeated. "I'm obliged. If you will excuse me, I will go and see her immediately. I have no time to lose."

Monk nodded, a very slight smile on his lips. "But everything else," he said dryly. "Let me know if I can help with your case, but it sounds hopeless to me. What is she like, this jilted lady?"

"Young, pretty, even-tempered, sufficiently intelligent to be interesting and not enough to be daunting, and an heiress," Rathbone replied, putting on his coat and opening the door for Monk, satisfied at the surprise in Monk's face. "She also has a spotless reputation," he added. "And she does not drink nor is she extravagant, sharp-tongued nor given to gossip. Have you a hansom waiting, or would you care to share one?"

"I have one waiting," Monk replied. "I assume you would like to share it with me?"

"I would," Rathbone agreed, and strode out briskly.

The door of the Sheldon house was opened by a very young footman and Rathbone gave his name but did not offer him a card. He did not wish to make it appear a professional call.

"I am a friend of Miss Latterly, who I believe is staying here temporarily," he said. "I realize it is probably not a convenient time to call, but the matter is of some urgency, and I am prepared to wait, should that be necessary. Would you tell her this and ask Mr. Sheldon if it is permissible for one to interrupt Miss Latterly?" Then he offered the card.

The footman took it, glanced at its expensive lettering and noted the title.

"Yes, Sir Oliver, I'll take it straightaway. Would you care to wait in the library, sir?"

"Thank you, that would be excellent," Rathbone accepted, and followed the man across a modest hallway to a most agreeable room lined on two sides with books and overlooking a small, rather exuberant garden, now full of lots of narcissi and early leaves of lupines. The stone wall he could see was festooned with the bare branches of honeysuckle and climbing roses, all greatly in need of pruning.

The fire was not lit and the air was chilly. The house had the small signs of a family home acknowledging certain financial restrictions—not stringent, but there in the background. Resources were not unlimited. There was also a certain recent inattention to detail, as if the mind of the mistress had been upon other things. He was forcibly reminded of Hester's occupation, and with it came an unwelcome understanding of how important it was to her. He had never before known a woman who had any profound interest outside the home and family. He admired it—wholeheartedly and with an instinctive emotion he could not deny. It brought them closer together. It made her in many ways more like a man, less alien, less mysterious. It meant she could understand his devotion to his work, his dedication of time and energy to it. She would know why at times he had to cancel social engagements, why he would stay up all night pursuing a thought, a solution, why every other normal routine of life had to be bent, or even broken, when a case was urgent. It made her so much easier to talk to. She grasped logic almost without seeming effort.

It also made her quite unlike the women whose lives were familiar to him, his own female relatives, the women he had courted in the past, or been drawn to, the wives of his friends and acquaintances. It made her somehow in another way unknown, even unknowable. It was not entirely a comfortable emotion.

The door opened and a large, ebullient man came in. He was dressed in a Norfolk tweed jacket of an indeterminate brown, and brownish gray trousers. His stance, his expression, everything about him was full of energy.

"Athol Sheldon!" he announced, holding out his hand. "I understand you've come to see Miss Latterly? Excellent woman. Sure she'll care extremely well for my brother. Hideous experience, losing an arm. Don't really know what to say to help." For a moment he looked confused. Then by force of will and belief he assumed an air of confidence again. "Best a day at a time, what? Courage! Don't meet tomorrow's problems before they're here. Too easy to get morbid. Good thing to have a nurse, I think. Family's too close, at times." He stood in the middle of the room, seeming to fill it with his presence. "Do you know Miss Latterly well?"

"Yes," Rathbone said without hesitation. "We have been friends for some years." Actually it was not as long as it seemed, if one counted the actual span of time rather than the hectic events which had crowded it. There were many other people he had known far longer but with whom he had shared little of depth or meaning. Time was a peculiarly elastic measurement. It was an empty space, given meaning only by what it contained, and afterwards distorted in memory.

"Ah . . . good." Athol obviously wanted to say something else, but could find no satisfactory words. "Remarkable thing for a woman, what? Going out to the Crimea."

"Yes," Rathbone agreed, waiting for Athol to add whatever it was he really wanted to say.

"Don't suppose it's easy to settle down when you come back," Athol continued, glancing at Rathbone curiously. He had very round, very direct eyes. "Not sure it's entirely a good thing."

Rathbone knew exactly what he meant, and thought so too. It had forced Hester to see and hear horror that no person should have to know, to experience violence and deprivation, and to find within herself not only strength but intelligence, skill and courage she might not have conceived, let alone exercised, at home in England. She had proved herself the equal of many men whose authority she would never have questioned in normal circumstances. Sometimes she had even shown herself superior, when the crisis had been great enough. It upset the natural, accepted order of things. One could not unlearn knowledge so gained. And she could not and would not pretend.

Rathbone agreed, but he found himself resenting the fact that Athol Sheldon should remark it. Instantly he was defensive.

"Not entirely painless, certainly; but if you consider the work of someone like Miss Nightingale, you cannot but be enormously grateful for the difference she will make to medical care. We may never count the millions of lives her methods will save, not to mention the sheer suffering relieved."

"Yes . . ." Athol nodded, but there was no easing of the expression in his face. He pushed his hands into his pockets and then took them out again. "Of course. Admirable. But it changes one."

"I beg your pardon?"

"Changes one," Athol repeated, moving restlessly around the room before turning to face Rathbone. "A woman is designed by God and by nature to create a gentle and safe place, a place of inner peace and a certain innocence, if you like, for those who are obliged to face horror or evil." He frowned, looking intensely at Rathbone. "It changes a person, you know, the sight of real evil. We should protect women from it . . . so they in turn can protect us from ourselves." He spread his large hands wide. "So they can renew us, revive our spirits, and keep a haven worth striving for, worth . . . fighting or dying in order to—to protect!"

"Has Miss Latterly done something that disturbs you, Mr. Sheldon?" Rathbone asked anxiously.

"Well . . ." Athol bit his lip. "You see, Sir Oliver, my brother Gabriel has seen some appalling sights in India, quite shocking." He frowned and lowered his voice confidentially. "Unfortunately he cannot put them from his mind. He has spoken of them to Miss Latterly, and she is of the opinion that my sister-in-law, Mrs. Sheldon, should learn a little of Indian history, and then of this wretched Mutiny, in order to be able to understand what Gabriel has experienced. So he can share his feelings with her, you understand?" He watched Rathbone's expression closely. "You see? Quite inappropriate. Perdita should never have to know about such things. And poor Gabriel will recover far more rapidly, and more completely, if he can spend his time with people who won't keep reminding him. It is amazing, Sir Oliver, what an effort of will a man can make to live up to a woman's expectations of him, and what he can do in his determination to guard her from ugly and degrading knowledge." He shook his head, pursing his lips. "Miss Latterly does not seem persuaded of it. And of course I do not have the authority to command her."

Rathbone laughed. "Neither do I, believe me, Mr. Sheldon. But I shall certainly put the point to her, if you wish me to."

Athol's face cleared. "Would you? I should be most obliged. Perhaps you had better come up and meet my brother. Miss Latterly will be with him. She is very good reading to him, and the like. An excellent woman, please never think that I mean otherwise!"

"Of course not." Rathbone smiled to himself and followed Athol out of the library, up the stairs and into a large bedroom where Hester was sitting in a rocking chair with a book open on her lap, and in the freshly made bed a young man was propped up on pillows, turned towards her. Rathbone did not immediately notice his empty sleeve; his nightgown almost camouflaged it. But the disfigurement to the left side of his face was horrifying and it took all the effort of will of which he was capable to keep it from showing in his expression, or even in his voice.

He realized as the young man swung around at the entrance of a stranger how insensitive it was of Athol not to have asked first if he was welcome and to have warned them both, Gabriel of the intrusion, and Rathbone of what he would see.

Anger flickered across Hester's face and was disguised only with difficulty, and perhaps because it was superseded by surprise at recognizing Rathbone. Apparently it was Athol to whom the footman had delivered his message, and possibly Perdita.

After the first shock, Hester seized the initiative. She rose to her feet, smiled briefly at Rathbone, then turned to the man in the bed.

"Gabriel, this is my friend Sir Oliver Rathbone." She looked at Rathbone, ignoring Athol. "Oliver, I should like to introduce you to Lieutenant Gabriel Sheldon. He was one of the four survivors of the siege of Cawnpore and was subsequently wounded while still serving in the Indian army. He has only been home a very short time."

"How do you do, Lieutenant Sheldon," Rathbone said gravely. "It is very good of you to allow me to call upon Miss Latterly in your home and without the slightest warning. I would not have taken such a liberty were it not a matter of urgency to me, and to my present client, who may face ruin if I cannot defend him successfully."

Gabriel was still overcoming his self-consciousness and sense of vulnerability. This was the first time since his return that he had been faced with a stranger.

"You are welcome," he said a little hoarsely, then coughed and cleared his throat. "It sounds a most serious matter." It was not a question. He would not have been so inquisitive.

"I am a barrister," Rathbone replied, determined to keep a normal conversation going. "And in this have a present case of which I should like a woman's view. I admit I am utterly confused."

Gabriel was interested. His eyes were intelligent and direct and Rathbone found himself meeting them very easily, without having to make a deliberate effort to avoid staring at the appalling scar and the lips pulled awry by it.

"Is it a capital case?" Gabriel asked, then instantly apologized. "I'm sorry; I have no business to intrude. Forgive me."

"Not at all," Rathbone replied quite spontaneously. "It is serious only in the damages if my client loses, but the offense is relatively slight. It is suit for breach of promise."

"Oh!" Gabriel looked surprised and Rathbone felt as if he had disappointed him by dealing with anything so trivial. In comparison with what Gabriel had experienced, which Rathbone had read about only in newspapers, no doubt robbed of much of its horror and detail, a broken romance seemed an insult even to mention. It was certainly painful, but a common affliction of mankind. Surely everyone suffered such disappointment, in some degree or another, if they were capable of love at all?

He looked at Hester to see what she might feel. Would she consider it absurd too?

"Breach of promise?" she said slowly, staring back at him.

Suddenly he was aware of how much of her he did not know. Why had she gone to the Crimea in the beginning? Had someone let her down, just as Melville had Zillah Lambert? Had she felt that humiliation, the laughter of friends, the sense of utter rejection, the whole of her certain and happy world shattered at a blow?

Now, instead of with Melville, his whole sympathy was with

Zillah. He saw Hester in her place, and burned with anger for her and with shame for his own clumsiness.

"Yes . . ." He fumbled for the words to try to mend things. "I think it arises out of misunderstanding rather than intentional callousness. He swears that he did not even ask her to marry him. It was merely assumed. That is the reason I was prepared to accept the case. Now I find I cannot comprehend his motive at all, and I cannot help believing that he is concealing something of the utmost importance, but I have no idea what."

Athol shook his head. "A man of no honor," he said, speaking for the first time since they had entered the room. "Once you have given your word you must abide by it, regardless of what you may then wish. A man's word should bind him for life . . . even to death, if need be." He glanced at his brother. "Of course, if circumstances change, then you say so, and offer to set a woman free. That is a different thing." He frowned at Rathbone. "Was she changed, this woman? Has she had to lie about something? You said she was virtuous, didn't you? Or did I assume it?"

"So far as I know she is perfectly virtuous," Rathbone replied. "She seems in every way all that one could wish. And my client swears she has no faults that he is aware of."

"Then he is a bounder, sir, a complete outsider," Athol pronounced. "You cannot defend him; he is indefensible. Your clearest duty is to persuade him to honor his promise, with the utmost apology."

"She would be unlikely to want him now," Hester pointed out. "I certainly shouldn't. It might make me feel better to have him offer, but I would most certainly decline."

"I suggested that," Rathbone explained. "He was afraid she might not decline and then he would be back in his present situation, and he refuses absolutely to go through with it, but he will not tell me why."

Hester burst into laughter, then controlled herself again instantly.

"How marvelously arrogant!" she exclaimed. "She would be quite mad to accept him in those circumstances. All it would do would be to give her the opportunity to be the one to turn him down. There has to be more to it than you have been told."

"Perhaps he is already married?" Gabriel suggested. "Perhaps it is unhappy, an arrangement over which he had little control, a family obligation, and he has run away from it, fallen in love with her, but now realizes he cannot commit bigamy. Only he does not tell anyone, because he does not wish his wife to find out." He looked pleased with himself, forgetting to be conscious of his disfigurement.

"That is quite plausible," Rathbone thought aloud. "Providing his family are some considerable distance away, perhaps Scotland or Ireland. He is bent on making a name for himself in London."

"Has his eye on someone higher," Athol said dismissively. "More money, better connected family."

"Well, he is ruining his chances completely by losing a suit for breach of promise," Gabriel pointed out. He looked at Rathbone. "Didn't you say this young lady is an heiress?"

"Yes, very considerable," Rathbone agreed. He turned back to Hester. "And I have the strong impression that his emotion is fear, even panic, rather than greed. He is quite aware that this girl's father is ideally placed to assist him in his career, and has done so already. No, he is definitely a man caught in a situation which is intolerable to him, but I don't know why!"

Athol snorted. "If he won't tell you, then it is something he is ashamed of! An honorable man would explain himself."

It was a very bald statement, without sensitivity or allowance, and yet before Rathbone could frame a contradiction, he realized it was true. Were there not something profoundly wrong, real or imaginary, Melville would have explained his situation to Rathbone, if not to Zillah Lambert.

"Perhaps he is in love with somebody else?" Hester suggested.

"Then why doesn't he simply tell me?" Rathbone continued.

"It is a plain enough thing to understand. I might not agree, but I would know what arguments I was facing."

Hester thought for a moment.

"Cannot always have what you want just because you want it," Athol observed sourly. "There is such a thing as duty."

"Maybe it is someone he cannot approach?" Hester looked up at Rathbone, who was still standing, as Athol was, because there was no suitable place to sit.

"Cannot approach?" Rathbone repeated. "Why not? You mean someone already married? Perhaps a close friend of—" He stopped just before he mentioned the Lamberts' name.

"Why not?" she agreed. "Or . . ."

"It happens," he said, shaking his head. "That is not anything to be ashamed of. It is simply awkward, possibly embarrassing, but not worth this public disgrace."

"What about her mother?"

"What?" Rathbone was incredulous. The idea was inconceivable.

Athol misunderstood completely. "Don't suppose the poor woman knows," he put in. "Wouldn't have brought the action if she did." He shook his head, his face still bland and certain.

"Hester means what if the man is in love with the girl's mother," Gabriel enlightened him. "And even if she did know, it wouldn't stop her bringing the suit, because she will hardly be likely to tell the father, will she?"

"Good God!" Athol was astounded.

Rathbone collected his wits. "I suppose it's possible," he said slowly, remembering Delphine's lovely face, her delicacy, the grace with which she moved. Melville would not be the first young man to fall in love with an older woman. It had never entered Rathbone's thoughts, and even now he found it exceedingly difficult. Delphine had seemed so genuinely betrayed. But then maybe she had no idea.

Hester's mind was racing ahead. "Or perhaps the girl is in love with someone else and your client knows it," she suggested. "It could be a matter of honor with him, the greatest gift to her he could give . . . and she dare not tell her parents, if this other person is unsuitable. Or on the other hand, it might be pride—he could not marry a woman he knew did not love him but did love someone else. I wouldn't! No matter how willing he was to go through with it."

Rathbone smiled. "I'm sure you wouldn't. But there is an optimism, or an arrogance, in many of us which makes us believe we can teach someone to love us if only we have the chance." Then he wondered immediately if he should have said that. Was it not too close to the unspoken, vulnerable core of what lay inside himself? Did he not dream that with the chance, the time, the intimacy, Hester would learn to love him with the passion of her nature, not merely the abiding friendship? It had never occurred to him before that he might have anything in common with Melville beyond a terror of being trapped into a marriage he did not want. But perhaps he had?

He found himself unable to meet her eyes. He looked away, at the curtains, through the window at the trees, then at Gabriel.

He saw a flash of something in Gabriel's face which could have been understanding. Gabriel was intelligent, sensitive, and before his injury he must have been remarkably handsome. His was a world of loss which made Melville's situation, and even Zillah Lambert's hurt feelings, seem so trivial, so easy to settle with a word or two of goodwill and an ability to forgive. If they were to smile and remain friends, society would talk about it for a brief while, but only until the next scandal broke.

"I shall put it to him." He turned to Hester at last. "Thank you for helping me to clarify my mind. I feel as if I have the case in better perspective." He smiled at her, then looked again at Gabriel. "Thank you for your indulgence, Lieutenant Sheldon. You have been most gracious. I wish you a speedy return of health."

Gabriel bade him good-bye, as did Athol, and Hester rose and went with him to the door. Out on the landing, she looked at him gravely, studying his face. Was she imagining something personal rather than professional in his coming? He would very much rather she did not. He was not ready to commit himself again.

"Thank you," he repeated. "I—I find myself at a loss to understand the case, and I am afraid I shall be of little help to my client until I do. It all seems like needless pain at the moment. I have no defense to offer for him."

"There must be something vital that you don't know," she said seriously. There was no disappointment in her face that he could see, and certainly no withdrawing, or sense of criticism, or hope deferred. The knot of anxiety eased inside him. He found himself smiling at nothing.

"I think you need to know what it is," she went on. "It may be . . . physical."

"I have thought of that," he said truthfully. "But how do you ask a man such a thing? Most men would suffer anything, even imprisonment, rather than admit it."

"I know," she answered so softly it was little more than a whisper. "But there are euphemisms which could be used, white lies. A doctor could be found to swear he had some illness which would make marriage impossible. Her father would understand that, even if she did not."

"Of course . . . thank you for clarifying the thought so well. I . . ." He bit his lip ruefully. "I admit I had not known how to phrase it to ask him. Although I am not at all sure that is the answer."

"Well, if it is not, you need to learn what is." She was perfectly direct. "You cannot afford to lose the case because you were unaware of the personal facts."

"I know. Of course you are right. I suppose I shall have to learn them for myself"—he smiled suddenly, widely—"and charge my client accordingly. In which case I had better win!"

She smiled back and put out her hand to touch his with quick warmth, then started down the stairs to introduce him to Perdita Sheldon, who was standing at the bottom looking puzzled.

CHAPTER FIVE

Monk stood near the fireplace in his rooms and stared at the flames as the coals settled in a shower of sparks. Oliver Rathbone had just left. He had been there for nearly two hours explaining all he knew about his present case and the details which troubled him. And indeed he had looked less assured than usual. The difference was subtle, an inflection of the voice, something in the way he stood, but to Monk, who knew him well, it was unmistakable.

From what he had said, one could only conclude that Killian Melville had not told him the entire truth of the reason for his sudden refusal to marry Zillah Lambert. What was less easy to understand was why he still refused to tell Rathbone, who was bound to keep his confidence.

As Monk stood warming himself by the dying embers he could not rid his mind of the fear that the problem was criminal. For all his urbane appearance, his smooth good manners, his supreme confidence, Oliver Rathbone was a man who took some extraordinary risks with his career. Perhaps he did not intend to be a crusader, but lately he had unwittingly become one. The Rostova case had nearly ruined him. This one, taken on impulse, looked unlikely to improve his reputation. Realistically, there seemed little he could accomplish for his client or gain for himself.

Their interview had been awkward. Rathbone hated coming to Monk for help when it was personal rather than because a client had requested it. He had begun a trifle stiffly.

Monk had been careful to hide his sardonic amusement—well,

moderately careful. Such moments were too rare, and too pleasing, not to savor a little.

Now he must decide what to do, where to begin. It was also his professional reputation being tested now. Why does a young man court a woman, apparently in every way a desirable match, and then on the brink of marriage risk his financial, professional and social well-being by breaking off the betrothal?

Only for the most powerful of reasons.

It must be the Lambert family, Zillah herself, or something to do with Melville's own situation. Presumably, since he seemed to have courted her up until the last moment, it was something he had only just discovered. Or else it was some matter to do with his own life which he had believed he could keep hidden, and circumstances had proved him mistaken.

Was he being blackmailed? It was a dark possibility, but one which would make sense of the presently inexplicable. Monk would begin, this afternoon, with Melville himself. The trial resumed on Monday morning, which gave him less than a day and a half in which to find something to help Rathbone.

He put on his coat. It was already half past three, and he expected to be out until late evening—in fact, as long as he had any hope of finding someone awake who could be of assistance.

Outside the weather was bright and mild, but there were clouds banking to the east beyond the rooftops and he was only too aware from experience that conditions could change in the space of ten or fifteen minutes from pleasant weather to a chill close to freezing and a soaking rain.

He had made his decision to begin with a past client of his own, a man for whom he had solved a sensitive domestic problem and avoided a situation which could have become very ugly. Mr. Sandeman was correspondingly grateful, and had promised to give any assistance he was able should Monk ever need it. Monk was not sure if he had spoken impulsively, without any belief that he would ever be taken up on it, but this seemed like an excellent time to put it to the test.

Accordingly, he arrived at Upper Bedford Place just after three o'clock, and asked if he might see Mr. Sandeman on a matter of urgency.

"If it were not, I should not trouble him on a Saturday, and without writing first," Monk explained to the butler, taking off his gloves and passing the man his hat and stick as if there were no question as to whether he would be received.

"Certainly, sir," the butler said, masking his surprise with long practice. "I shall see if Mr. Sandeman is at home." That was the conventional way of saying he would see if the visitor could be welcomed or not. Naturally, he was perfectly aware who was in the house and who was not. It was his job to be. "If you care to wait in the green room, sir, I am sure you will be comfortable."

The green room was very attractive, full of afternoon sunlight from white-painted windows which overlooked a garden where silver birch leaves shimmered in the breeze, making the air seem to dance. Inside the walls were papered with an unusually plain dark green, and two were hung with many paintings of landscapes. Monk remembered the room from his previous visit, when Sandeman had been so concerned about an apparent theft from his wife's bedroom. But that had been satisfactorily dealt with, and it would be tactless to raise the issue now.

Monk had not long to wait. The door opened and Robert Sandeman came in, a look of apprehension on his broad, good-natured face. He was a very wealthy man who continued to look as if he were wearing secondhand clothes, even when they were the best Savile Row could offer. They seemed to have been made for someone of an entirely different shape. He was the despair of his tailors.

"Hello, Monk!" he said with evident surprise. "Nothing new arisen, has it?" He could not keep the anxiety out of his eyes.

"Nothing at all," Monk assured him. "I am looking into another matter entirely, for a friend, and hoped you might be able to give me a little assistance. I have to learn enough to provide some sort of answer by Monday morning, or else I would not have disturbed you like this."

Sandeman's relief was almost palpable. He closed the door behind him and waved at one of the large chairs, sitting in one of the others.

"My dear fellow, by all means. Whatever I can do."

"Thank you," Monk accepted immediately. On the journey there he had tried to decide exactly how to approach the subject without appearing intrusive in areas no gentleman would discuss. There was no easy solution. "It is another matter of delicacy," he began. "Perhaps a domestic issue, or possibly financial. It is all so undefined at the moment. And I do not wish to break anyone's confidence or jeopardize their privacy."

"Quite so," Sandeman said quickly. "Quite so." He looked relieved. He leaned back in his chair and crossed his legs, wrinkling his trousers hopelessly. "So what can I tell you that may be of service?"

Monk began very carefully. "Are you familiar with the work of an architect named Killian Melville?"

Sandeman was quite openly surprised. "Yes! Yes, I am. Brilliant fellow. Unique. His work is quite new, you know? Nothing like anybody else's. Not in the least vulgar," he added quickly, in case Monk should misunderstand him. "He manages to make spaces look larger than they are. Don't know how he does it. Something to do with shades of color and the way lines are directed. Uses curves and arches in an unusual way." He drew breath to go on, then closed his mouth again. "Mustn't ask why you want to know."

Monk knew he was very conscious of his own need for privacy, and if Monk were to betray Melville or Lambert, then Sandeman would assume he would do the same to him. The situation required the most subtle handling. And yet if he were to be of any use to Rathbone he must discover Melville's secret, and do it before Monday morning. He was rash to have accepted the case, but he could never resist a challenge from Oliver Rathbone, however it was placed before him, however disguised. He thought wryly that probably Rathbone knew that when he had come.

He smiled at Sandeman. "I daresay it will be in the evening newspapers, if it was not in the morning ones," he acknowledged. "Unfortunately, those things cannot be kept private, as I believe they should be."

Sandeman raised his eyebrows. "Oh? I am sorry to hear that. Poor fellow. Surprised, mind you. Never heard the slightest whisper against him, myself." His eyes narrowed and he regarded Monk deceptively closely. His mild manner hid a more astute mind than many had supposed, to their cost. Still he refused to ask the nature of the charge.

"Not the slightest?" Monk pressed, knowing he must tread extremely carefully.

"Nothing but praise," Sandeman affirmed. "Not everyone likes his work, of course. But then if they did it would mean he was mediocre, safe, and pedestrian. And he is certainly not that. Everyone's friend is no one's, you know?" He regarded Monk quizzically, although he knew he agreed. "Can't bear a man who trims his sails to meet the prevailing wind all the time and never stands for anything himself. Melville is not one of those." He frowned, wrinkling his brows together. "But that is hardly a thing one would sue a man for, or have him charged in law. You did not say whether it was a civil suit or a criminal one."

"Civil."

"Not a building less than standard." Sandeman made it a statement. "I don't believe that. He knows his job superbly. I would be prepared to say he is the best architect of his generation, perhaps of the century." He stared at Monk as if prepared to defy a challenge.

"Where did he study?" Monk enquired.

Sandeman thought for a moment. "You know, I have no idea," he said with evident surprise. "I haven't heard anyone mention it. Is it of importance?"

"Probably not," Monk answered. "It is unlikely the difficulty stems so far back. I assume that you have never heard suggestion that he is financially untrustworthy or—"

Sandeman did not allow him to finish. "He is an architect, Monk. A man of vision, even genius. He is not a banker or a trader. He sells ideas. I think rather than beating around the circumference of this, you had better tell me, in confidence, the nature of this difficulty. If it is the subject of a court case, then it will soon enough become public."

Monk was more than ready. "He is being sued for breach of promise."

Sandeman sat perfectly still. He did not speak, but disbelief was in every line of him.

"I am in the employ of the barrister seeking to defend him," Monk answered to the question in Sandeman's face.

Sandeman let out his breath slowly. "I see." But there was doubt in his voice. He looked at Monk now with a certain carefulness. Something was unexplained. The debt between them was not sufficient to override his other loyalties, and there was a perceptible coolness in the room. "I doubt I can help you," he continued. "As far as I know Melville, he is a man of complete probity, both publicly and privately. I have never heard anything whatever to his discredit." He met Monk's gaze steadily. "And I can tell you that without any discomfort of mind, knowing that I owe you a great deal for your assistance to me when I depended upon you."

Monk smiled with a harsh twist of his lips. "The case may become ugly. I expect the family of the girl to suggest serious flaws in his character in order to explain his behavior in terms other than some fault in their daughter. If Melville is vulnerable in any way he has not told us, or even is not aware of, we need to know it in advance in order to defend him."

Sandeman's face eased, and his large body relaxed in his chair, crumpling his suit still further. "Oh, I see." He did not apologize for his suspicion, it was too subtle to have been voiced, but it was there in his eyes, the suddenly warmer smile.

"Who is the lady?"

Monk did not hesitate; there was nothing to be lost. "Miss Zillah Lambert."

"Indeed?" Sandeman was silent for a moment. "I still cannot help you. I know a little of Barton Lambert. Not a sophisticated man, but on the other hand he is nobody's dupe either. He made his own fortune by hard work and good judgment—and a certain amount of courage. In my limited experience he has not been one to be socially ambitious, nor to take a slight easily."

"And his wife?" Monk said with the shadow of a smile.

Sandeman drew in his breath and there was a flicker in his eyes which expressed possibly more than he was willing to say.

"A very pretty woman. Met her several times. Even dined at their home once." He put his head a trifle to one side, a look of mild surprise on his face. "I confess I had not expected to find it so extraordinarily beautiful. And it was, believe me, Monk. I have dined with some of the wealthiest families in England, and some of the oldest, but for its scale, nothing outdid Lambert's home. It was full of invention . . . architectural invention, I mean, not scientific. It was brilliantly innovative. That was Killian Melville." He began to smile as he spoke, and his eyes took on a faraway shine as he retreated into memory. "As we went into the hall the floor was red oak, lovely warm color to it, and the walls were in different shades like . . . like sweet and dry sherry . . . no, more like brown sugar. But because of the windows it was full of light. It was one of those rare places where instantly one feels both a warmth and a curious sense of peace. There was a width, a space about it. All the lines pleased the eye. Nothing intruded or was cramped."

Monk did not interrupt, although he found the impression he was gaining more of Killian Melville than of Lambert. He did not want to like Melville, because he believed the case was hopeless. It would be so much more comfortable to believe him a knave, a fool, or both. It would be emotionally expensive to feel a desperate need to save him, to struggle, and fail, and have to watch him ruined. He pushed away the thought.

Sandeman was still recalling the house. He obviously enjoyed it.

"The dining room was marvelous," he said enthusiastically and leaning forward a little. "I had seen a lot of magnificent rooms before and was a bit blasé. I thought I had seen every possible combination and variation of line and color, but this was different." He was watching Monk's reaction, wanting to be sure Monk appreciated what he was saying. "Not so much in obvious construction but in smaller ways, so the overall impression was again one of lightness, simplicity, and it was only on reflection one began to realize what was different. It was largely a matter of perfect proportion, of relation between curve and perpendicular, circle and horizontal, and always of light."

"You are saying Melville is a true genius," Monk observed.

"Yes . . . yes, I suppose I am," Sandeman agreed. "But I am also saying that Lambert understood that and appreciated it. I am also saying that Mrs. Lambert was fully sensitive to it too, and that she complemented it perfectly. Everything in her dining room was superb. There was not a lily in the vases with a blemish on it, not a smear or a chip on the crystal, a scratch on the silver, a mark or a loose thread in the linen." He nodded his head slightly. "It was all in equally exquisite taste. And she was the perfect hostess. The food, of course, was delicious, and abundant without ever being ostentatious. The slightest vulgarity would have been abhorrent to her."

"Interesting," Monk acknowledged. "But not helpful."

"I don't know anything helpful." Sandeman shrugged his heavy shoulders. "Barton Lambert's reputation is impeccable, both professional and personal. I have never heard anyone make the slightest suggestion that he was less than exactly what he seems, a shrewd but blunt north country businessman who has made a fortune and came to London to enjoy his success, patronize the arts—by the way, that is also painting and music, though principally architecture—and give his wife and daughter the pleasure of London society. You can try, by all means, and see if you can find evidence he patronizes the brothels in the West End or has a mistress tucked away somewhere, or that he gambles at his club, or occasionally drinks a little too much. I doubt you'll find it, but if you do, it won't help. So do most men in his position. None of it would be grounds for not marrying his daughter."

Monk knew it. "What about Mrs. Lambert?" he asked.

"Just as spotless, so far as I know," Sandeman replied. "Her reputation is excellent. A trifle ambitious for her daughter, but I am not sure that is regarded as a fault. If it is, you can charge nine tenths of the mothers in London with the same offense."

"Where does she come from?"

"No idea." Sandeman's eyes widened. "Do you imagine Melville cares?"

"No. I suppose I am trying any possibility. Could their daughter be illegitimate?"

"No," Sandeman said with a slight laugh. "I happen to know that she is eighteen years old, and the Lamberts recently celebrated the twentieth anniversary of their wedding. It was mentioned the evening I was there. It was several months ago now, seven or eight. And would it change Melville's view of her?" He shrugged again, wrinkling his clothes still further. "Yes, I suppose it could. Might not know who the father was. Could be anybody."

Monk forbore from observing that that could be said of many people. It was a point Sandeman might find offensive. He could think of nothing else to explore, no more to ask that might elicit a useful answer. He rose to his feet and offered his thanks.

"I hope you can help," Sandeman said with a frown. "It seems like an ugly situation which should never have happened. Lovers' quarrel, do you suppose? Two young people with more feeling than sense, high temperament of an artist crossed with the emotions of a young girl, overexcited, perhaps suffering a little from nervousness?"

"Could be," Monk conceded. "But it's gone too far now. It is already in the courts."

"What a shame," Sandeman said sincerely. "If I hear anything, I shall advise you."

And Monk had to be content with that.

He spent a chilly and exhausting afternoon viewing the latest building close to completion to the plans of Killian Melville. First he had to seek the permission of a dubious caretaker, then pick his way over planks and racks of plaster and past busy craftsmen.

It was an uncomfortable experience. He did not want to feel any involvement with Melville, and already a sense of the young architect's vision was forcing itself upon him. There was light everywhere around him as he stood in the main floor, where Carrara marble was being laid. It was not cold light, not pale, bleaching of color or fading, but giving an air of expansion and freedom. It was almost as if the interior could be as unrestricting as the outside with its clean, soaring lines and uncluttered facades. It was extremely modern, avant-garde, and yet also timeless.

Walking in the still uncompleted galleries, Monk found himself relaxing. He went through an archway into a farther hall, sun reflecting through a huge rose window along a pale floor, this time of wood. The other windows were very high and round, above the picture line, filling the arched ceiling with more light. He found himself smiling. He enjoyed being there, almost as if he were in the company of someone he liked. There was a kind of communication of joy in beauty, even in life.

What would make a man who could create such things ask a woman to marry him and then break his word? Was it as he had told Rathbone, simply that he had been so naive to the ways of the world that he had allowed himself to form a friendship which was misunderstood? The whole wedding had been arranged around him, and he had at no time the grasp to understand it—or the courage to disclaim and retreat?

These buildings were created by a mind of burning clarity and aspiration, a strength of will to dare anything. Such a man could never be a coward. Nor could he be a deceiver. There was a simplicity of line and conception which was in itself a kind of honesty.

Without realizing it, Monk had clenched his fists; his whole body was stiff with determination and an inner anger in his will to preserve this, to defend whoever was the person whose spirit was embodied there. He had always judged a man not by what he said but by what he did, the choices he made, when it was difficult, dangerous, when he had much to lose. This building soared to the sky with Killian Melville's choices.

He had entered not wanting to like Melville, not wanting to care one way or the other. He walked out rapidly, his feet loud and brisk on the wood and marble floors, and through the entrance door down steps to the square. He did not even bother to excuse himself to the caretaker. The wind was sharp and growing colder. The sun was already lowering and filling the west over the rooftops with an apricot glow. How could he help Melville? What was he hiding, and above all, why did he not trust Rathbone with it?

Was he protecting himself or someone else? Zillah Lambert herself?

There was no time before Monday morning and the trial's resumption to discuss anything but the most superficial facts. The most urgent thing to learn was if there had been some incident in Melville's life he was afraid might come to light and ruin him. It must be something Sacheverall could find out, or Rathbone would have no need to fear it.

It was late Saturday afternoon. No professional organizations would be open for him to ask questions. He would have to call on more acquaintances, people who might help him for the sake of old friendship, or more likely old debt. He had no relationships more than four years long. Everything before that was part of the past he knew so imperfectly, although now that he at least understood why Runcorn hated him, and why their quarrel and his dismissal from the police force had been inevitable, that no longer troubled him.

He seldom looked backward anymore. The old ghosts had lost their power.

He stood still on the pavement for several minutes. People passed by him, two ladies chattering, their crinoline skirts swaying, curls blown in the increasing wind, hands held up to keep their bonnets from flying away. A carriage and four went by at a fast clip, horses' manes streaming, harness jingling loudly. Someone shouted, and a young man darted out into the street.

An elderly man with magnificent whiskers passed an angry remark about the state of society.

Monk remembered the name of someone he could ask about architects and money. He turned and walked briskly across the square and through an archway into a main thoroughfare where he found a hansom and gave the driver an address in Gower Street.

George Burnham was an elderly man with a prodigious memory, and was happy to exercise it to help anyone, even to show off a little. The days were very long now that he was alone, and he delighted in company. He piled more coals on the fire and ordered supper for himself and Monk, and settled comfortably for an evening of companionship and recollections, after shooing away a large and very beautiful black-and-white cat so Monk might have the best chair.

"Known every new architect, painter and sculptor to come to London in the last forty years," he said confidently. "Do you like pork pie, my dear fellow?" He waved casually at the cat. "Off you go, Florence."

"Yes, I do," Monk accepted, sitting down carefully so as not to crush the skirts of his jacket, trying to disregard the cat hairs.

"Excellent!" Mr. Burnham rubbed his hands together. "Excellent. We shall dine on pork pie, hot vegetables and cold pickle. Mrs. Shipton makes the best pickle in this entire city. And what about a little good sherry first? A nice mellow amontillado? Good, good!" He reached out and pulled the bell cord. "Now, my dear fellow, what is it you wish to know?" He smiled encouragingly.

Monk had met him during a sensitive case concerning missing money. It had been solved very much to Mr. Burnham's satisfaction. A collection of such clients was invaluable. At first Monk had despised the smaller cases, thinking them beneath his talents and no more than a demeaning necessity in his newly reduced circumstances. Now he began to appreciate the value of the clients far beyond the nature of the problems they had presented to him. Sandeman had been one such; Mr. Burnham was another.

"What do you think of the work of Killian Melville?" he asked candidly.

Mr. Burnham cocked his head to one side, his blue eyes bright with interest.

"Sublime," he answered. "In a word—sublime! Finest architect this century." He did not ask why Monk wished to know, but he did not take his gaze from Monk's face.

"Where did he study?" Monk frowned.

"No idea," Mr. Burnham said instantly. "No one does. At least, no one I have met. Appeared in London about five years ago from God knows where. Can't place his accent. Tried to. Don't think it matters. Man is a genius. He can be a law unto himself. Although don't mistake me," he added earnestly. "He's a very pleasant fellow, no airs or graces, no filthy temper, doesn't keep a mistress or practice any excesses, so far as I know." Still he did not ask why Monk was enquiring.

"Could he have studied abroad?" Monk asked.

Florence leaped up into Mr. Burnham's lap, turned around several times and then settled.

"Of course he could!" Mr. Burnham answered. "Probably did, in fact. He is far too original to have gathered all his inspirations here. But if you doubt his technical ability, you have no need. I know Barton Lambert quite well enough to stake all I possess on his having assured himself, beyond even the slightest question, that all Melville's drawings are structurally perfect before he would put forward a halfpenny to have them built." He stroked Florence absentmindedly. "You may rely absolutely upon that as you would upon the Bank of England! Stand as long as the Tower of London, I assure you." There was absolute conviction in his face, and he smiled as he spoke.

The door opened and a stout and very agreeable woman came in. Mr. Burnham introduced her as Mrs. Shipton, his housekeeper, and requested that supper be served for two. She seemed pleased to have a guest and disappeared briskly about her business.

"A man whose word you would trust?" Monk asked. "And his judgment?"

"Absolutely!" Mr. Burnham answered instantly. "Ask anyone."

Monk smiled. "I am not sure 'anyone' will tell me the truth, or even that they know it."

"Ah!" Mr. Burnham smiled and settled a little farther down in his chair. Florence was purring loudly. "You're a skeptic. Of course you are. It's your job. Silly of me to have forgotten it."

Monk found himself recalling how much he had liked Mr. Burnham in their previous acquaintance. He had been almost sorry when the case was concluded. It was not a feeling he indulged in often. All too frequently he saw pettiness, spite, a mind too willing to leap to prejudiced assumptions, instances where unnecessary cruelty or greed had opened the way for acts of impulse which were beyond the borders of selfishness and into the area of actual crime. Sometimes there was a justice to be served, too often simply a law. The case here had been one of the happy exceptions.

Mr. Burnham put more coals in the fire. It was now roaring rather dangerously up the chimney, and he regarded it with a flicker of alarm before deciding it would not set the actual fabric of it alight, and relaxed again, folding his hands across his stomach and resettling the cat to its satisfaction.

"Let me tell you a little story about Barton Lambert," he began with candid pleasure. He loved telling stories and could find too few people to listen to him. He was a man who should have had grandchildren. "And you will see what I mean."

Monk smiled, amused at both of them. "Please do." It was just possible the tale would even be enlightening, and he was extremely comfortable and looking forward to a very fine supper. He had tasted Mrs. Shipton's cooking twice before.

Mr. Burnham settled himself still deeper into his chair and began.

"You must understand one thing about Barton Lambert. He loves beauty in all its forms. For all his rather unrefined exterior, frankly, and his"—he smiled, not unkindly, as he said it—"rather plebeian background—he was in trade—he has the soul of an artist. He has not the talent, but instead of envying those who do, he supports them. That is his way of being part of what they create."

A coal fell out of the fire and he ignored it, in spite of the smoke it sent up.

Monk recovered it with the tongs and replaced it in the blazing heap.

"He is a man without envy," Mr. Burnham carried on without apparently having noticed. "And that of itself is a very beautiful thing, my dear fellow. And I think he is entirely unconscious of it. Virtue that does not regard itself is of peculiar value."

Monk wanted to urge him to begin the story, but he knew from past experience it would only interrupt his thought and hurt his feelings.

Mrs. Shipton came in and set the small gate-legged table with a lace-edged cloth, silver, salt and pepper pots and very fine crystal glasses, and a few moments later carried in the supper and served it. Mr. Burnham continued with his story, barely hesitating as he removed Florence from his lap and conducted Monk to his chair, and thanked Mrs. Shipton. They began to eat.

"Lord . . ." He hesitated. "I think I shall decline, in the interests of discretion, to give him a name. In any case, someone approached Mr. Lambert about building a civic hall for the performance of musical concerts for the public." He passed Monk the dish of steaming vegetables and watched with satisfaction as he took a liberal helping. "Excellent, my dear fellow," he applauded. "The hall would have been most expensive, and milord was prepared to put forward at least half of the cost himself if Lambert would put forward the other half. He had connections with the royal family." He put a small piece of pie on a saucer and put it on the floor for Florence. "The prestige would have been enormous, and something not open to Lambert from any other source. You may imagine what it would have meant to such a man, who is genuinely most patriotic. The mere mention of the Queen's name will produce in him a solemnity and a respect which is quite marked. Only a most insensitive person would fail to be affected by it, because it is sincere. No honorable man mocks what is honest in another."

Monk was enjoying his meal very much. The rich home baking was a luxury he was offered far too seldom, and the thought that all this was so far of no professional value was overridden by physical pleasure, and possibly also by the knowledge that Mr. Burnham was enjoying himself.

"This hall," Mr. Burnham went on, helping himself to more dark, spicy pickle and pushing the dish across the table towards Monk, "was to be dedicated to Her Majesty. It was some time ago now, and Killian Melville was not the architect, but some other fellow put forward by milord. The plans were given to Lambert and he was cock-a-hoop with excitement. He seemed on the brink of stepping into a circle he had previously barely dreamed of. He was man of the world enough to know his rough origins would never allow him to be accepted in such society ordinarily. Mrs. Lambert, on the other hand, has all the bearing of a lady; whether that is bred in her or learned, no one knows. Women seem to acquire these things more easily. It is in their nature to adapt. I daresay it has to be!"

Monk did not comment. His mouth was full.

"She is a remarkably pretty woman, and has the art to please without ever seeming to seek to or to be overeager," Mr. Burnham continued. "And yet in her own way she is a perfectionist too, an artist in domestic detail, a woman who can create an air of grace and luxury so natural it appears always to have been there." He watched Monk to assure himself he understood, and was apparently satisfied.

The first course was finished and treacle tart was offered with cream. Monk accepted with undisguised pleasure, and Mr. Burnham beamed at him in delight. He gave Florence a teaspoonful of cream.

"You may imagine," he said, resuming his tale, "Mrs. Lambert's happiness when milord's only son took a marked fancy to her only daughter, a charming, high-spirited girl, not yet of marriageable age but fast approaching it. In a couple of years the two families could have made a most acceptable arrangement, and in due course young Miss Lambert would have become a lady in every sense of the word, the chatelaine of one of the finest country seats in England."

"But something spoiled it?" Monk was now truly interested.

"Indeed," Mr. Burnham agreed, without losing a shred of his satisfaction. He was quite obviously not on the brink of recounting a tragedy. "Indeed it did." He leaned forward across the table, his face gleaming in the candlelight and the reflected glow of the spring evening beyond the tall window. "This hall was to be magnificent," he repeated urgently. "Lambert was enthralled with the idea. He took the plans and drawings home with him and pored over them like a man studying holy writ. He was alight with the idea. After all, it is a kind of immortality, is it not? A work of art which can last a thousand years or longer. Do we not still revere the man who designed the Parthenon? Do we not travel halfway around the world like pilgrims to gaze on its beauty and dream of the minds who thought it up, the genius which brought it into reality, even the men and women who daily passed beneath it in their ordinary lives?" He gazed at Monk steadily.

Monk nodded. Words were not necessary.

"He sat up night after night reading those plans," Mr. Burnham said in little above a whisper. "And he found a flaw in them . . . a fatal flaw! At first he could hardly believe it—he could not bear to! It was the shattering of his dreams. And not only his, but his wife's as well, and such possible future happiness for his daughter; although that, of course, was more problematical. She was a very charming girl and would no doubt find other suitors. I don't think it was a matter of the heart—at least not deeply." He smiled with some indulgence. "Shall we say a touch of glamour, to which we are most of us susceptible?"

"But Lambert chose to decline the building?" Monk concluded, eating the last piece of his treacle tart. It was an illuminating story, although not helpful to his cause. It said much of Barton Lambert but shed no light upon Melville's reason for abandoning Zillah.

"Yes . . . much to milord's anger," Mr. Burnham agreed. "Lambert's withdrawal provoked questions, and the flaws in the plan were exposed. Reputations were damaged."

"Lambert made powerful enemies?" It was hardly a motive for Melville's act, but he had to press every point.

"Oh no, my dear fellow," Mr. Burnham said with a broad smile. "On the contrary, he came out of it rather well. We may be a society with our share of sycophants and hypocrites, but there are still many who admire an honest man. It was milord who suffered."

"I see."

"You look disappointed," Mr. Burnham observed, regarding Monk keenly. "What had you hoped?"

"An explanation as to why a young man might be reluctant to marry Miss Lambert," Monk confessed. "I suppose her reputation is as impeccable as it seems?" Florence wound herself around his ankles, doubtless leaving long, silky hairs on his trouser legs.

Mr. Burnham's sparse eyebrows shot up. "So far as I know, she has the normal share of high spirits, and a young and pretty girl's desire to flirt and trifle more than is modest, to play the game dangerously from time to time. That is no more than healthy. Let us say she is not tedious and leave it at that?"

Monk laughed in spite of himself. The evening had been most enjoyable, and as far as he could see of no use whatever to Rathbone. He thanked Mr. Burnham sincerely and remained another half hour listening to irrelevant stories, then went home without removing the cat hairs, in case it should offend Mr. Burnham, and considered his tactics for the morrow.

He spent Sunday morning equally fruitlessly. He called upon two or three acquaintances, who merely confirmed what he had already heard. One of them owned a gambling house in the less-reputable part of the West End and occasionally loaned money to gentlemen temporarily embarrassed in a financial way. He usually knew who owed money, and to whom. He was expert in assessing precisely what any given man was worth. He was better at it than many a legitimate banker. He had never heard of Killian Melville, and he knew of Barton Lambert only by repute. Neither of them owed a halfpenny to anyone, so far as he was aware. Certainly neither of them gambled heavily.

Another acquaintance, who owned a couple of brothels in the Haymarket area and was familiar with the tastes and weaknesses of many of the leading gentlemen in society, also knew neither man.

By early afternoon Monk was irritable, chilly in the intermittent showers of rain, and profoundly discouraged. It appeared Killian Melville was simply a young man who had made a rash offer of marriage, perhaps in a moment of physical passion, and now regretted it and was foolish enough to believe he could walk away unscathed. Perhaps he had prevailed upon her virtue and now despised her, wondering if he were the first or would be the last. It was a shabby act, and Monk had little patience with it. If one wished to satisfy an appetite, there were plenty of women available without using a respectable girl who believed you loved her. She would be ruined in reputation, whatever her emotional distress or lack of it. Melville must know that as well as anyone.

And yet as Monk fastened his coat more tightly at the neck and put his head down as the rain grew harder, he could not think that the man who had designed the building he had walked through yesterday, so full of soaring lines and radiant light, would be such a hypocrite or a coward as to run away from responsibility for his own acts. Could a man be of such a double nature?

Monk had no idea. He had never known a creative genius. Some people made excuses for artists, poets and composers of great music. They believed such men did not have to live by the standards of ordinary people. That thought provoked in him a deep disgust. It was fundamentally dishonest.

Was it possible Melville was merely naive, as he had told Rathbone, and had been maneuvered into a betrothal he had never intended? Was the marriage really unbearable to him?

Monk stepped off the pavement over the swirling gutter and ran across the cobbled street as a hansom driver came around the corner at a canter and swore at him for getting in the way. The wheels threw an arc of water over his legs, soaking his trousers, and he swore back at the man fluently.

He reached the far side and brushed the excess water and mud off himself. He was filthy.

How would he feel in Melville's place? Suddenly his imagination was vivid! He would no longer have any privacy. He could not do so simple a thing as decorate his room as he wished, have the windows open or closed according to his own whim, eat what and when he liked. And these things were trivial. What about the enormous financial responsibility? And the even greater emotional commitment to spend the rest of his life with one other human being, to put up with her weaknesses, her foibles, her temper or occasional stupidity, to be tender to her needs, her physical illness or emotional wounds and hungers! How could any sane person undertake such a thing?

But then the other person would also promise the same to him. It would be better than passion, stronger than the heat of any moment, more enduring. It would be the deepest of friendships; it would be the kindness which can be trusted, which need not be earned every day, the generosity which shares a triumph and a disaster with equal loyalty, which will listen to a tale of injury or woe as honestly as a good joke. Above all it could be closeness to one who would judge him as he meant to be, not always as he was, and who would tell him the truth, but gently.

He was walking more and more rapidly. He was now in Woburn Place, and the bare trees of Tavistock Square were ahead of him. The sky was clearing again. A brougham swept by, horses stepping out briskly. Two young women walking together laughed loudly and one clasped the other by the arm. A small boy threw a stick for a black-and-white puppy that went racing after it, barking excitedly. "Casper!" the boy shouted, his voice high with delight. "Casper! Fetch!"

Monk turned into Tavistock Square and stopped at number fourteen. Before he could give himself time to reconsider, he pulled the bell.

"Good evening," he said to the parlormaid who answered. "My name is Monk. I should like to call upon Miss Latterly, if she is in and will receive me. That is, if Lieutenant Sheldon will permit?"

The maid looked less surprised than he had expected, then he remembered that Rathbone would have been there only the day before. Somehow that irritated him. He should not have come without a better reason, but it was too late to retreat now without looking ridiculous.

"I shall understand, of course, if she is occupied," he added.

But she was not, and less than ten minutes later she came into the small library where he was waiting. She looked neat and efficient, and a little pale. Her hair was pulled back rather too tightly. It was no doubt practical, and she might have done it in a hurry, but it was less than flattering to her strong, intelligent face and level eyes.

She regarded him with surprise. Obviously she had not expected to see him. He was now acutely aware of being wet and his trousers splashed with filth.

"How are you?" he asked stiffly. "You look tired."

Her face tightened. It was apparently not what she wished to be told.

"I am quite well, thank you. How are you? You look cold."

"I am cold!" he snapped. "It is raining outside. I'm soaked."

She regarded his trousers, biting her lip.

"Yes, I can see that. You would have been better advised to take a hansom. You must have walked some distance."

"I was thinking."

"So I see," she observed. "Perhaps you should have been watching where you were going." A tiny flicker of amusement touched the corner of her mouth.

"You have been nursing too long," he criticized. "It has become a habit with you to tell people what to do for their welfare. It is extremely unattractive. You remind me of one of the more miserable type of governess. Nobody likes to be ordered around, even if the person doing it is correct."

Two spots of color burned on her cheeks. He had hurt her, and he saw it. There were times when her composure bordered on arrogance, and this was one of them. He was aware of having stepped in front of the hansom without looking. He was actually fortunate not to have been run over.

She lifted her eyebrows in sarcasm. "Is that what you waded through the gutter to tell me?"

"No, of course it isn't!" He had not meant to quarrel with her. Why did he allow her to make him feel so defensive? He would not have spoken to any other woman that way. The very familiarity of her face, the curious mixture of vulnerability, bravado and true strength, made him aware of how much she had woven herself into the threads of his life, and it frightened him. She could not leave without tearing it apart, and that knowledge left him open to more hurt than he had armor to deal with. And yet he was driving her out himself.

He breathed in and out slowly, making an effort to control his temper. Even if she could not do that, he could.

"I came because I thought you might be of some assistance in the case I am investigating for Rathbone," he explained. "The trial continues tomorrow, and he is in considerable difficulty."

Her concern was immediate, but who was it for, himself or Rathbone?

"You mean the architect who broke his word? What are you trying to learn?"

"The reason for it, of course," he replied.

She sat down, very straight-backed. He could imagine some governess in her childhood had come and poked the middle of her spine with a sharp ruler. She sat now as if there were a spike behind the padding of the chair.

"I meant what is wrong with him, or wrong with her," she explained patiently, as though he were slow-witted.

"Either," he answered. "He takes precedence, so if there is anything, at least Rathbone can be forewarned—if there is any defense." He sat down on the other chair.

She stared at him solemnly. "What did you learn?"

He was ashamed of his failure. The expectancy in her eyes stung him. She had no idea how difficult it was to acquire the sort of information Rathbone needed. It could take weeks, if it was possible at all. He was seeking the most intimate details of people's lives, things they told no one. It had been a hopeless request in the first place.

"Nothing that is not in the public domain," he replied with an edge to his voice. "I might know if Rathbone had asked me a month ago. I don't know what possessed him to take the case. He has no chance of winning. The girl's reputation is impeccable, her father's even better. He is a man of more than ordinary honor."

"And isn't Melville, apart from this?" she challenged.

"So far as I know, but this is a very large exception," he returned. He looked at her very directly. "I would have expected you to have more sympathy with a young woman publicly jilted by a man she had every reason to suppose loved her."

The color drained from her face, leaving her white to the lips.

He was overtaken with a tide of guilt for his clumsiness. The implication was not at all what he had intended; he had meant only that she was also a young woman. But it was too late to say that now. It would sound false, an artificial apology. He was furious with himself. He must think of something intelligent to say to contradict it, and quickly. But it must not be a retreat.

"I thought you might be able to imagine what she might have done to cause him to react this way," he said. He wanted to tell her not to be so idiotic! Of course he did not think she had been in this position herself. Any man who would jilt her this way was a fool not worthy of second thought, still less of grief, and certainly not worthy of her! If she applied an atom of sense to the matter, she would know what he had meant. And even if he thought it, he would not have said so. It was completely unjust of her even to entertain such an idea of him.

"Did you?" she said coldly. "I'm surprised. You never gave the impression you thought I had led a colorful life . . . in that respect. In fact, very much the opposite."

He lost his temper. "For heaven's sake, Hester, don't be so childish! I never thought of your early life, painted scarlet or utterly drab! I thought that as a woman you might understand her feelings better than I, that's all. But I can see that I was clearly—" He stopped as the door opened and a burly, muscular man came in, his face agitated. He closed the door behind him, ignoring Monk and turning to Hester.

She stood up, Monk forgotten. The anger fled out of her eyes, her mouth, and was instantly replaced by concern.

"Is something wrong?"

The large man's eyes flickered at Monk.

"This is Mr. Monk," Hester said, introducing him perfunctorily as he too rose to his feet. "Mr. Athol Sheldon." She gave them no time to speak to each other but hurried on. "What is wrong? Is it Gabriel?"

Athol Sheldon relaxed a fraction, his powerful shoulders stopped straining his jacket and he let out his breath in a sigh. Apparently, having found her he already felt better, as if somehow the problem were in control.

"Yes—I'm afraid he fell asleep and seems to have had a

nightmare. He is—quite unwell. I . . . I don't know what to do for the best for him, and poor Perdita is dreadfully upset." He half swiveled on his foot to acknowledge Monk. "I am sorry to intrude," he said briefly; it was lip service to courtesy. He looked back instantly to Hester. It was not necessary to request she come; she was already moving towards the door.

Monk followed her because he could not simply ignore what was obviously an emergency of some sort. It was an unbecoming curiosity to go with them, and callous indifference to stay. The former was instinctive to him.

Athol led the way across the hall and up the stairs. If he found Monk's presence odd he was too involved in his own concern to remark it. There was a maid standing at the top of the stairs, a woman of perhaps forty or so, her thin face creased with worry, her eyes going swiftly not to Athol but to Hester. A younger woman with a lovely, frightened face stood a yard away from her, her cheeks pale, her lips trembling. She twisted her hands together, the light catching the gold of her wedding ring. She too looked at Hester desperately. She seemed on the verge of tears.

The door ahead of them was ajar, and Hester went past them after only the briefest hesitation, not as if she was undecided, certainly not afraid, but simply allowing herself time to be reassured. Then she went into the room, and Monk could see over her shoulder a wide bed with a young man lying crumpled over in it, his fair hair tousled, his face buried in the pillow. It was a moment before Monk realized his left sleeve was empty.

Hester did not speak at first. She sat on the bed and put her arms around her patient, her cheek against his hair, holding him tightly. It was a gesture which startled Monk; there was a spontaneity in it and a tenderness he had never seen in her before. She did not wait to be asked. It was a response to his need, not to any touch or plea he had made. It moved the whole scene to a new level of gravity.

Beside Monk, Athol Sheldon was also taken aback, but he

seemed embarrassed. He cleared his throat as if about to speak, then changed his mind and said nothing. He shifted his weight from one foot to the other and back again.

"Gabriel," Hester said quietly, as if she were unaware of the group outside the open door. "Was it James Lovat again?"

Gabriel nodded.

Perdita looked questioningly at Athol.

"I've no idea," Athol said. He moved forward at last. "Really, my dear chap," he said to his brother, addressing the back of his head where he half lay in Hester's arms. "You must put all this behind you. It is a tragedy which cannot be helped now. You did your part, splendidly. Put it from your mind."

Hester looked up at him, her eyes wide and bright.

"One cannot forget at will, Mr. Sheldon. Some memories have to be faced and lived with."

"I think not," Athol contradicted, his voice firm. He stood very square on the balls of his feet.

"Then if it should happen to you, Mr. Sheldon," Hester said without flinching, "we shall know what best to do for you. But for Gabriel we shall do as he wishes."

"Gabriel is ill!" Athol said angrily. He was frightened by emotion he could neither understand nor share; it was sharp in his voice. He had no idea what demons were in his brother's head. He was afraid of them for himself, and he did not want anyone to have to look at them. "It is our duty, as well as our—our love for him to make decisions in his interest. I would have thought as a nurse you would have perceived that!" That was an accusation.

Monk drew breath to defend Hester, then saw her face and realized it was her battle and she needed no assistance. She understood Athol better than he understood himself.

"If we want to help, we will listen to him," she answered, equally levelly. "Grief for the death of a friend should not be smothered. You wouldn't say that if James Lovat had died in an accident here in England instead of from gangrene in Cawnpore."

"I should not encourage dwelling on it!" Athol argued, his face pink. "But that is beside the point. He didn't die here, poor fellow. The whole matter of the Indian Mutiny is better not dwelt upon, and the siege of Cawnpore and its atrocities especially so." His voice was final, as if what he said were an order, but he did not move away. Suddenly Monk realized Athol depended upon Hester. He might condescend to her, his conscious mind might think of her as a woman and necessarily of inferior intellect and ability in almost everything, but he knew there was a strength in her to meet and deal with the horror and tragedies of life greater than anything within himself.

A ripple of ridiculous pride surged through Monk.

"Mr. Sheldon"—Hester let go of Gabriel gently and rose to her feet, straightening her rumpled skirts with one hand—"if it had been Gabriel who had died in Cawnpore, or a wife or child of yours—and there were hundreds of women and children among the dead—what would you think of their friends who chose to forget them?"

"Well, I—I think I would understand if it was to save their own minds from nightmare—" Athol began to answer.

"Oh, it's not to save Gabriel," she interrupted. "It is because you don't wish to hear about it . . . and because you think we don't."

"Nonsense!" he said too quickly. "I want Gabriel to get well, to be able to take up his life again here at home—at least . . . at least, as much as he can. And I want to protect Perdita from horrors no woman should have to know about. Really, Miss Latterly." His voice was growing stronger, his confidence gathering. He squared his shoulders. "We have discussed this before. I thought we had reached an understanding. This house is to be a refuge from the ugliness and violence of the world, a place where Gabriel, above all, will be at peace, may heal his mind and body from the tragedies of war and its barbarities, where he may feel utterly safe. . . ." He was becoming enthusiastic now; his face was composed again, his body easily balanced. He even had the shadow of a smile on his lips. "It is Perdita's calling most properly to establish and master that, and ours to be of whatever assistance to her we may." He swung around and looked at Perdita, his lips parted, his eyes brighter. "And you may rest assured, my dear, we shall be equal to it!"

"Thank you, Athol," she said helplessly. It was impossible to judge from her expression whether she was relieved or terrified.

The maid beyond her was still looking at Hester.

Monk swiveled back to her.

The man in the bed was sitting up, turned towards them. His skin was flushed, his face appallingly disfigured. Monk felt a rush of pity for him that was almost physical.

"I know you will, Mr. Sheldon." Hester's voice was soft but very clear, very insistent. "And it will be a very safe place. . . ."

"Good—good. . . ." he began.

"But it will not help if you try to force Gabriel into it before he is ready," she continued. "A prison is simply a place you don't want to be and from which you cannot escape."

"Really! Miss Latterly—" Athol protested.

"Stop speaking about me as if I am not here, Athol."

Gabriel had spoken for the first time. His face was damaged beyond healing, but his voice was still beautiful, clear and of unusual character and timbre.

"I've lost an arm, not my wits. I don't want wrapping away from reality as if I were a case of nervous collapse or hysteria. Pretending Cawnpore never happened isn't going to take the nightmares out of my sleep, and I don't want to forget my friends as if they never lived or died. It would be a betrayal. They don't deserve that. God knows, they don't!" Suddenly the anger and the overwhelming pain drenched his voice and was raw in the room, silencing even Athol.

Only Hester had seen war as he had. Monk knew even he was excluded, for all the poverty and death and daily intolerable misery he had seen in the city slums not more than a mile from where they stood. But he felt grateful for it, not angry, not put aside.

He looked at Hester, not smiling at her with his lips, but willing her to understand that he knew what she was doing, and that she was right, and that he admired her intensely for it. Gabriel Sheldon must need desperately to speak openly to someone. One can wrap the truth in palatable euphemisms for only so long, then it chokes in the throat and the lies suffocate. One ends in hating those who force the deceit upon you by their expectancy, their fear, their cowardice, their sheer lack of understanding of the reality of pain and loss.

"Perhaps we should go downstairs?" Monk said aloud. "I am sure the matters about which I consulted Miss Latterly can wait a while longer."

"Oh . . ." Athol had apparently forgotten who he was. "Good . . . good. Yes, perhaps we should. Talk about something else, what? Would you like a glass of whiskey, Mr. . . . ?"

"Monk. Thank you." He turned and followed Athol across the landing and towards the stairs. He wanted to stay and talk to Hester, but he knew it was impossible now.

However, she surprised him. He had barely closed the withdrawing room door, and Perdita asked the butler to bring the decanter, when Hester came in as well.

"Is he all right?" Perdita said immediately, her voice rapid, the decanter forgotten.

"Yes," Hester assured her with a softness around her mouth which was almost a smile. "Don't worry for him. These memories are bound to intrude at times. They would with all of us."

Athol frowned and took half a step forward, but Perdita seemed unaware of him; her attention was entirely upon Hester.

"It isn't in me," she whispered. "I've never seen anything really terrible. I feel a thousand miles away from him, as if there were an ocean between us and I don't know how to cross it. I don't even understand. I don't have nightmares."

"Don't you?" Hester looked doubtful. "Didn't you feel shattered, terrified, broken inside—"

"Miss Latterly!" Athol said sharply.

"No!" Monk put his hand on Athol's arm, his fingers gripping hard enough to silence him.

". . . when you saw Gabriel for the first time after he came home?" Hester finished.

"Well . . ." The memory was so clear in Perdita's face, her mouth pulled as if the pain were physical inside her. She struggled for words and did not know which to choose. "Well . . . I . . ." Her eyes filled with tears. "Yes . . . I felt . . . just like that."

"Haven't you forgotten sometimes, and woken up as if it were all just the same as before, then remembered?" Hester asked. "And had to live it all over again?"

"Yes!" Suddenly Perdita knew; she grasped the reality of it as if it could save her from drowning. "Yes, I have."

"Then you know what nightmares are like," Hester assured her. "It is that same shock of seeing and feeling all over again, just as sharp as the first time, only it happens again and again."

"Poor Gabriel. Do you think if I read"—she looked at Hester with desperate earnestness, stumbling towards knowledge—"if I read the history of India, as you said, that I shall be able to listen to him and be of some use?"

"I really don't think—" Athol began.

Perdita swung around on him. "Oh, be quiet!" she said sharply. "I don't want to hear about all their tortures and deaths. I'd much rather imagine the world is all as safe as we are here and nothing really unspeakable ever happens. But it isn't true, and in my heart I know that. If I try to stay a child forever, I shall lose Gabriel."

"Nonsense, my dear—"

"Don't tell me it's nonsense!" She stood still with her hands straight by her sides, her fists clenched. "He has to be able to speak properly to survive. If it isn't to me, it will be to Hester. It certainly won't be to you! You don't know anything more about India than I do! Not about the reality of it, the heat and dust and disease, the flies and the cruelty, the death. You don't know what happened to him. Neither do I . . . but I'm going to find out!"

"You are overtired," Athol said, nodding with assurance. "It is hardly surprising. You have had a most distressing time. Any woman would—"

"Stop it!" she said loudly, her voice cracking she was so close to tears. "Stop talking at me as if I were feeble! I am! I know I am! Hester has been out to the Crimea and nursed dying men, faced bullets and swords, seen atrocities we haven't even read about in our nice ironed newspapers the butler brings us on a tray. And what have I done? Sat at home painting silly pictures and stitching samplers and mending the linen. Well, I refuse to stay useless! I'm—I'm terrified!"

Athol was appalled. He had no idea what to say or do. He stared at her, then at Hester with a mixture of anger and appeal. He loathed her for precipitating this crisis, and yet he needed her to cope with it, which he resented profoundly.

Monk was waiting for Hester to show her impatience with Perdita. She was quite right; she was useless and had been hiding from reality like a child.

"Being terrified doesn't matter," Hester said confidently, walking forward to stand beside Perdita. "So are most of us. It isn't what you feel, it's what you do that counts. Gabriel won't mind you being frightened, then he'll know you understand at least something of it. Nobody understands it all."

"You do."

Hester laughed. "Nonsense! I simply know what it feels like to see pain you can't help, to be terrified yourself, overwhelmed and hideously uncomfortable in body, and so tired you haven't even the strength to weep. If you haven't felt that yet, one day you will." She took her by the arm. "Now have a stiff sherry or something and go up to him."

"But it's you he wants to talk to," Perdita protested. "You understand. He doesn't want to have to explain to someone who knows nothing." There was reluctance in every line of her.

"Frightened?" Hester said with a smile.

"Yes!" Perdita pulled back physically.

"So now is the time to have courage," Hester pointed out. "Imagine how much worse soldiers must feel at the order to charge. What is the worst that can happen to you? Your husband will think less of you? You will still have all your arms and legs. You will not bleed or—"

"That's enough!" Athol said sharply. "You exceed yourself, Miss Latterly!"

Perdita gulped and then swung around very deliberately and glared at him.

"She is quite right! I am going up to see Gabriel. Please don't wait for me. I don't know when I shall be down." And without stopping to see his response, or Hester's, she marched out of the room and they heard her feet cross the hall floor, sharp and determined.

"Have some whiskey," Monk suggested to Athol, although it sounded like an offer. He felt enormously proud of Hester, as if he had had some part in her actions, which was absurd. But they were friends, closer in ways than many a man and wife. They had shared extraordinary triumphs and disasters; they knew each other, both the best and the worst. He trusted her above anyone else. There was a way in which friendship was the deepest and the best of bonds.

Athol took the whiskey and drank it, then poured himself another. He did not think to offer Monk one. It was not rudeness, he was simply too lost in his own perplexity.

Hester turned to Monk. She had not the slightest idea what had been going through his mind or his heart.

"Do you still care to discuss the case which concerns you?" she asked as if they had only just left the subject a few moments ago.

He did not. There was really nothing to say. But on the other hand, he did not want to leave yet.

"If you can spare the time, I should," he answered.

"Certainly." She turned to Athol. "I shall be upstairs if I am needed, Mr. Sheldon, but I think I will not be, at least until bedtime."

"What? Oh. Yes, I think you have done quite enough for one day." He was displeased, and he intended her to know it.

Monk watched her closely and saw no sign of embarrassment or doubt in her face.

She led the way out of the room and up the stairs to the small sitting room she shared with the gaunt lady's maid, Martha Jackson. They sat in the deep, chintz-covered armchairs and he told her about his fruitless search for information which might help Rathbone, mentioning that apparently Melville had studied abroad, because no one in England knew of him until about five years ago. He also told her the story of Barton Lambert and the unnamed lord who had been involved with the flawed building plans.

None of it mattered insofar as he expected her to offer any helpful remark; it was simply good to clear his own thoughts by putting them into words, and he was comfortable sitting with her.

It was almost an hour later when Martha Jackson came in. At first Monk was annoyed. It was an intrusion. But she was an agreeable woman. There was an honesty to her which pleased him, and he sensed the quiet courage to bear sorrow without complaint that seemed marked in the lines of her face. There was no bitterness in her mouth, no self-pity.

It was Hester who raised the subject of Martha's brother's children and their deformities—and the fact that no one now knew their whereabouts.

"How long ago?" Monk asked, turning to Martha.

"Twenty-one years," she replied, the hope she had allowed for a moment dying out of her eyes. She had been living in the past, telling him about it, talking as if it were only recently, when it was still possible to do something. Now it was foolish even to think of it.

He was startled. Samuel would have been an elder brother. It was a hard thing. He felt for her as he watched her tired face with the grief washing back into it and the realization of pain lost in the past, irretrievable now, children who could not be found, helped or given the love which had been missed too long ago.

He looked quickly at Hester. She was watching him steadily, her eyes so direct he had the feeling she was seeing his mind and his heart as clearly as anyone else might have seen his outward features. Surprisingly, it was not an intrusion and he did not resent it in the slightest.

What he resented was the fact that he would let her down. He could not do what she wanted, and he knew it as exactly as if he had heard the words.

Martha looked down at her hands, knotted in her lap. Then she made herself smile at Monk. "It wouldn't matter even if I could find them," she said quietly. "What could I do to help? I couldn't take them then, and I couldn't now. I just wish I knew. I . . . I wish they knew that they had somebody . . . that there was someone who belonged to them, who cared."

"I'll look into it," Monk said quietly, knowing he was a fool. "It may not be impossible."

Hope gleamed in Martha's eyes. "Will you?" Then it faded again. "But I have very little money saved. . . ."

"I don't think I can succeed," he said honestly. "And I wouldn't charge for failure," he lied. He avoided Hester's eyes although he could feel her gazing at him, feel the warmth as if it were sunlight, hot on his cheek. "Please don't hope. It is very unlikely. I'll simply try."

"Thank you, Mr. Monk," Martha said as levelly as she could. "It is very good of you . . . indeed."

He stood up. It was not good at all, it was idiotic. Next time he saw Hester, he would tell her just how ridiculous it was in the plainest terms.

"Save your thanks till I bring you something useful," he said rather less generously. He felt guilty now. He had done it for Hester, and he would never be able to help this woman. "Good day, Miss Jackson. It is past time I was leaving. I must report to Sir Oliver. Good night, Hester."

She stood up and moved closer to him, smiling. "I shall accompany you to the door. Thank you, William."

He shot her a glance which should have frozen her and seemed to have no effect whatever.

CHAPTER SIX

Rathbone went into court on Monday morning with not a scrap more evidence than he had possessed on the previous Friday afternoon. He had spoken with Monk and listened to all he could tell him, but it offered nothing he could use. Thinking of it now, he had given Monk an impossible task. It was foolish of him to have allowed himself to hope, but sitting at his table in the half-empty courtroom, he realized that he had.

The gallery was filling only slowly. People were not interested. They had no feeling that the case was anything but the rather shabby emotional tragedy Sacheverall had made it seem and, to be frank, Rathbone had been unable to disprove. If Melville were hiding any excuse, no whisper of it showed.

Rathbone looked sideways at him now. He was sitting hunched forward like a man expecting a blow and without defense against it. There seemed no willingness to fight in him, no anger, even no spirit. Rathbone had seldom had a client who frustrated him so profoundly. Even Zorah Rostova, equally determined to pursue a seemingly suicidal case, had had a passionate conviction that she was right and all the courage in the world to battle her cause.

"Melville!" Rathbone said sharply, leaning forward to be closer to him.

Melville turned. His face was very pale, his eyes almost aquamarine colored. He had a poet's features, handsome yet delicate; the fire of genius in him was visible even in these miserable circumstances, a quality of intelligence, a light inside him.

"For God's sake," Rathbone urged, "tell me if you know something about Zillah Lambert! I won't use it in open court, but I can make Sacheverall speak to his client, and they might withdraw. Is it something you know and her father doesn't? Are you protecting her?"

Melville smiled, and there was a spark of laughter far behind the brilliance of his eyes. "No."

"If she's worth ruining yourself over, then she won't let you do this," Rathbone went on, leaning a little closer to him. "As things are, you can't win!" He put his hand on Melville's arm and felt him flinch. "You can't avoid reality much longer. Today, or tomorrow at the latest, Sacheverall will conclude his case, and I have nothing to fight him with. Just give me the truth! Trust me!"

Melville smiled, his shoulders sagging, his voice low. "There is nothing to tell you. I appear to have given you an impossible case. I'm sorry."

He got no further because Sacheverall came across the floor, looking at them with a faint curl to his lips, his head high, a swagger in his walk. He was even more satisfied with himself than he had been when they adjourned. He sat down in his chair, and the moment after the clerk called the court to order. It was still half empty.

McKeever took his place.

"Mr. Sacheverall?" he enquired. His face was almost devoid of expression, his mild blue eyes curious and innocent. If he had come to any conclusions himself he did not betray them in his manner.

Sacheverall rose to his feet. He was smiling. There was satisfaction in every inch of him. Even his floppy hair and protruding ears seemed cavalier, a mark of individuality rather than blemishes.

"I call Isaac Wolff," he said distinctly. He half turned towards Melville, then resisted the temptation. It was a sign of how sure he was of himself. Rathbone recognized it.

"Who is Wolff?" he said under his breath to Melville.

"A friend," Melville replied without turning his head.

"Of whose? Yours or Lambert's?"

"Mine. Lambert has never met him, so far as I know." His voice was so soft Rathbone had to strain to hear it.

"Then why is Sacheverall calling him?" Rathbone demanded. Sacheverall was not bluffing. He showed that in every inch of his stance, his broad shoulders, the angle of his head, the ease in him.

"I don't know," Melville answered, lifting his eyes a little to watch as a tall man with saturnine features walked across the open space of the floor and climbed the steps of the witness-box. He faced the court, staring at Sacheverall. His eyes seemed black under his level brows, and his thick hair, falling sideways over one temple, was as dense as coal. It was a passionate, compelling face, and he stared at Sacheverall with guarded dislike. No one could mistake that he was there against his will.

"Mr. Wolff," Sacheverall began, relishing the moment, "are you acquainted with Mr. Killian Melville, the defendant in this case?"

"Yes."

Rathbone looked across at the jury to see their reaction. There was a stirring of interest, no more. They were inexperienced in courtroom tactics. They did not understand Sacheverall's confidence and were only half convinced of it.

"Well acquainted, sir?" Sacheverall's voice was gentle and he smiled as he spoke.

A flicker of annoyance crossed Wolff's eyes and mouth but he did not allow it into his words.

"I have known him for some time. I do not know how you wish me to measure acquaintance."

Sacheverall held up his hand in a broad gesture. "Oh! But you will, Mr. Wolff, you will. It is precisely the point I am coming to. Give me leave to do it in my own way. How did you meet Mr. Melville?"

The judge glanced towards Rathbone, half inviting him to object that the question was irrelevant. Rathbone knew there was no point in doing so. To challenge would only show Rathbone's desperation. He shook his head momentarily and McKeever looked away again.

"Mr. Wolff?" Sacheverall prompted. "Surely you recall?"

Wolff smiled, showing his teeth. "It was some years ago, about twelve. I'm not sure that I do."

It was not the answer Sacheverall had wished. Rathbone could tell that from the sharp way he moved his arm back. But he had opened the way for it himself.

"Was it a social occasion, Mr. Wolff, or a professional one?"

"Social."

"You have recalled it, then?"

"No. We have no professional concerns in common."

Rathbone rose to his feet, more as a matter of form than because he thought it would actually affect Sacheverall's case. The tension was becoming palpable. Beside him at the table, Melville was rigid.

"My lord . . ."

"Yes, yes," McKeever agreed. "Mr. Sacheverall, if you have a point to this, please come to it. Mr. Wolff has conceded that he is acquainted with Mr. Melville. If there is something in that which bears upon his promise to marry Miss Lambert, then proceed to it."

"Oh, a great deal, my lord," Sacheverall said impassively. "I regret to say." He swung around to face the witness-box. "Are you married, Mr. Wolff?"

"No."

"Have you ever been?"

"No."

McKeever frowned. "Mr. Sacheverall, I find it hard to believe that this is indeed your point."

"Oh, it is, my lord," Sacheverall answered him. "I am about to make it." And disregarding McKeever, he swung back to Wolff, on the stand. "You live alone, Mr. Wolff, but you are not a recluse. In fact, you have a close and enduring friendship, have you not . . . with Mr. Killian Melville?"

Wolff stared back at him unflinchingly, but his face was set, his eyes hard.

"I regard Mr. Melville as a good friend. I have done so for some time."

Rathbone knew what Sacheverall was going to say next, but there was no way in which he could prevent it. Any protest now would make it worse, as if he had known it himself and therefore it must be true. He felt hollow inside, a strange mixture of hot and cold.

"Is that all, Mr. Wolff?" Sacheverall raised his eyebrows very high. "Would you not say an intimate friend, with all the subtle and varied meanings that word can carry? I use it advisedly."

There was a hiss of indrawn breath in the gallery. One of the jurors put his hand to his mouth, another shook his head, his lips compressed into a thin line. A third was pale with anger.

McKeever cleared his throat but said nothing.

Rathbone looked at Melville. His eyes were hot with misery and his fair skin was flushed. He was staring straight ahead. He refused absolutely to look back at Rathbone.

"You may use what word you like, sir," Wolff replied steadily, his voice thick. "If your implication is that my relationship with Killian Melville is of an unnatural kind, then you are mistaken." There was a rush of sound in the gallery, exclamations, sudden movement, a cry of disgust. A journalist broke a pencil and swore. "The acts lie in your imagination, and nowhere else," Wolff continued more loudly to be heard. "I am under oath, and I swear to that. I have never had an intimate relationship with another man in my life, nor can I imagine such a thing." This time the noise was louder, sharper voices. Someone shouted an accusation, another an obscenity.

McKeever banged his gavel angrily, commanding silence.

"I do not expect you to admit it, Mr. Wolff." Sacheverall did not appear disconcerted. He gave a very slight shrug as he walked a few paces away and then swiveled on his heel and suddenly raised his voice accusingly. "But I shall call witnesses, Mr. Wolff! Is that what you want, sir? Never doubt I will, if you force me to! Admit your relationship with Killian Melville, and advise him, as your friend, your lover, to yield in this case." He said the word *lover* with infinite disgust, his lips curled. "Stop defending the indefensible! Do not put it to the test, sir, because I warn you, I shall win!"

Melville sat as if frozen. His face was ashen white and the freckles stood out like dark splashes. He did not take his eyes from Wolff, and the pain in him was so powerful Rathbone could all but feel it himself. He was unaware for seconds that his own hands were clenched till his nails gouged circles in his palms.

The courtroom prickled with silence.

Isaac Wolff stood perfectly motionless. His look towards Sacheverall was scorching with contempt. A man less arrogant would have withered under it, would have faltered in self-doubt, instead of smiling.

"If it is your intention to attempt to blacken my name, or anyone else's, through calling people up to this stand to say whatever it is they wish, then you will have to do so," Wolff said very carefully, speaking slowly, as if he had difficulty forming the words and keeping his voice steady. "That is a matter for your own concern, not mine. I am not going to admit to something which is not true. I have already sworn that I have never had an intimate relationship with another man, only with women." There was a buzz of titillation and embarrassment at the use of such frank words.

"I cannot and will not alter that statement, whatever threats you may make," Wolff went on. "And if you persuade someone to forswear or perjure themselves, that is your responsibility, and you are a great deal less than honest, sir, if you try to make anyone believe the answer, for that lies with me."

Sacheverall pushed his large hands into his pockets, dragging the shoulders of his coat.

"You force me, sir! I do not wish to do this to you. For heaven's sake, spare yourself the shame. Think of Melville, if not of yourself."

"By admitting to a crime of which neither of us is guilty?" Wolff said bitterly.

Rathbone rose to his feet. "My lord, may I ask for an adjournment so I may speak with my client and with Mr. Sacheverall? Perhaps we can come to some understanding which would be preferable to this present discussion, which is proving nothing."

"I think that would be advisable," McKeever agreed, reaching his hand towards the gavel again as there was a murmur of disappointment in the gallery and several of the jurors muttered, whether it was in agreement or disagreement, it was not possible to say. "Mr. Sacheverall?" He did not wait for the answer but assumed it. "Good. This court is adjourned until two o'clock this afternoon."

Rathbone leaned towards Melville, still sitting motionless. He grasped his arm and felt the muscles locked.

"What can he prove?" he whispered fiercely. "What is Wolff to you?"

Melville relaxed very slowly, as if he were waking from a trance. A smile with a hint of hysteria in it touched his lips and then vanished.

"Not my homosexual lover!" he said with a gasp of disbelief, as if the idea had a kind of desperate humor to it. "I swear that in the name of God! He is as normal, as masculine, a man as ever drew breath."

"Then what? Is he some relative by blood or marriage?" Even as he asked, Rathbone could not believe it was blood. The two men were physically as unalike as possible. Wolff must have been four or five inches the taller and two stones heavier. He was as dark as Melville was fair, as brooding, mystic and Celtic as Melville was open, direct and Saxon. "What?" he repeated firmly.

But Melville refused to answer.

The bailiff was beside the table.

"Mr. Sacheverall is waiting for you, Sir Oliver. I'll take you to him, if you come with me."

"Do you want to withdraw?" Rathbone demanded, still facing Melville. "I can't make that decision for you. I don't know what Sacheverall will find or what these witnesses may say."

"Neither do I!" Melville said jerkily. "But I am not going to marry Zillah Lambert." He closed his eyes. "Just do what you can. . . ." His voice cracked and he turned away.

Rathbone had no choice but to go with the bailiff and meet with Sacheverall, not knowing what he could salvage of the chaos he had been thrown into. Except that if he were honest, he had not been thrown, he had leaped, more or less open-eyed. His own lack of thought had earned him this.

Sacheverall was half sitting on the bare table in the small room set aside for just this sort of meeting. He did not stand when Rathbone came in and closed the door. His fair eyebrows rose quizzically. "Ready to retreat?"

Rathbone sat in one of the chairs and leaned back, crossing his legs. He realized he disliked Sacheverall, not because he was losing—he had lost cases before, to adversaries he both liked and admired—but for the way in which Sacheverall savored the misfortune this would bring to Melville, and his own part in making it happen. The prosecutor was not serving justice but some emotion of his own. Rathbone resented giving him anything.

"If you mean ready to capitulate, no, I'm not. If you mean discuss the situation, then of course. I thought I had already made that plain in asking for an adjournment."

"For God's sake, man!" Sacheverall said with a half laugh. "You're beaten! Give in gracefully and I won't call my witnesses who can place Wolff and Melville together in the most intimate and compromising circumstances. Of course the man doesn't want to marry!" His voice was rich with scorn. "He's a homosexual. . . . I'll use the politest word I can for what he does." His expression made all too evident what manner of word was running through his mind.

"You can use whatever word is natural to you," Rathbone answered with a sneer he did not bother to hide. "You have no reputation to guard in here."

Sacheverall flushed. Perhaps he was more aware than he showed that he was awkward beside Rathbone, clumsy, inelegant, that his ears were too large.

"If you think I won't drag it up, you are mistaken!" Sacheverall said angrily. "I will! Every sordid detail necessary to prove my client's case and claim the damages she's due. Melville will end in prison . . . which is where he belongs."

"If that is what Barton Lambert wants," Rathbone said very quietly, his voice as calm as if he were addressing an elderly lady disposing her will. His mind was racing. "Then he must hate Melville . . . or fear him . . . far more than would be explained by anything we know so far. Although I do have an excellent detective working on the case, and if there is anything whatsoever in the history of any one of the Lambert family, from the day they were born, then he will find it."

He saw Sacheverall's face darken with anger, and ignored it. "And, of course, once you have opened the door for this kind of slander then anything will be permissible. The gallery will love it. The press will tear them apart like a pack of dogs." Rathbone adjusted his legs a little more gracefully. "You and I are aware of that, naturally. We have seen it before. But are you sure the Lamberts are? Are you perfectly sure Mrs. Lambert is prepared to have her every act—every flirtation, every gift, every incident, letter, confidence—examined this way and interpreted by strangers? Can anyone at all be so certain of every moment of their lives?"

Two furious spots of color marked Sacheverall's cheeks and he sat forward, his back straight, shoulders hunched.

"How dare you?" he grated. "You have sunk lower than I thought possible. Your client is guilty of acts that all civilized society regards as depraved. He has pursued and deceived an utterly innocent young woman for the furthering of his own ambition—and you threaten her with slander in order to aid him in escaping the consequences of his actions." He jabbed his finger in the air and his lips were drawn into an almost invisible line. "You show that behind that facade of a gentleman you are without honor or principle. The best I can think of you is that you are ambitious and greedy. The worst is that you have a sympathy with your client which extends a great deal further than you would wish it supposed."

Rathbone felt an absurd moment of chill as he realized what Sacheverall meant, then laughter. Then his dislike turned into something much greater.

"You have a prurient mind, Sacheverall, which seems to be fixed in one area. The reason for my refusing to admit to this act on my client's behalf is extraordinarily simple. He has instructed me not to. I am bound by his wishes, as you are—or should be—bound by those of Miss Lambert and her family." He put his fingertips together. "I do not know why Mr. Melville is so unwilling to marry her after having grown to know her as well as is undisputed between us. But if you have a jot of intelligence between your ears"—he saw Sacheverall flush; he had referred to them deliberately—"then you will consider the possibility that the reason has nothing to do with Isaac Wolff and everything to do with Miss Lambert herself."

"She has nothing whatever to hide!" Sacheverall said between his teeth. "Do you imagine she would be foolish enough to go into this if she had? Her father is not an imbecile."

Rathbone smiled patiently. "If he imagines he knows everything about his daughter's life, then he is more than an imbecile," he replied. "He is a babe abroad in the land, and not only deserving your protection, for the fee he pays you, but needing it, in common humanity."

Sacheverall was shaken. It was in his eyes and his mouth. He was also very very angry indeed. His hand on the table was trembling.

Rathbone uncrossed his legs and stood up. "Give the matter a little more thought before you call these witnesses of yours and open up the area of private conduct in an effort to ruin Melville. I think you will find it is not what Lambert wishes. Perhaps you should speak to Miss Lambert alone? You may find she has been maneuvered into this suit by circumstances and now is unable to withdraw without explaining far more than she wishes to. Fathers, on occasions, can be very . . . blind . . . where their daughters are concerned. It is not too late to settle this matter privately."

"With damages?" Sacheverall demanded. "And a statement that Miss Lambert is innocent of any fault whatever?"

"Mr. Melville has never implied that she was less than totally charming and desirable, an excellent bride for any man," Rathbone said truthfully. "He simply does not wish to marry her himself. His reason is no one else's concern. Perhaps Miss Lambert's feelings are engaged elsewhere but she cannot afford to admit it—if the gentleman is unsuitable. Perhaps married already."

"That's untrue!" Sacheverall responded instantly and with considerable heat.

"Probably," Rathbone agreed, standing by the door now. "I am merely pointing out that the possibilities are many, and none of them need to concern the law or the general public. Consult with your clients and let me know." And before Sacheverall could make any further response, Rathbone went out and closed the door, surprised to find his own throat tight and his hands clammy.

As it happened, the court did not resume for another two days, and Rathbone spent the time desperately trying to capitalize on the brief respite he had gained. First he went to see Isaac Wolff, having obtained his address from Melville. He had not known what to expect. Perhaps at the back of his mind was the fear that Sacheverall was right and that visiting Wolff would confirm it beyond anything he could argue to himself—and therefore ultimately to the court.

As he walked along Wakefield Street, just off Regent Square, looking for the correct number, he realized how little defined was the impression he had of Killian Melville. He did not know the man at all. He was usually aware of intense emotion in him; his revulsion, almost terror, at the idea of marrying Zillah Lambert was so real it was almost palpable in the air. His love of his art was real. One had only to look at the work itself to lose all possible doubt of that. The light and beauty that flooded it spoke more of the inner man, of his dreams and his values, than anything he might say.

But there remained in him something concealed, elusive. The core of the man was shielded and, to Rathbone at least, inaccessible. He had made no judgment within himself.

He reached the house in which Wolff had rooms and pulled the bell at the door. A manservant showed him in and up the stairs to a very gracious hall opening into apartments which took up the whole of the front of the house.

Isaac Wolff admitted him and led him to a sitting room which overlooked the street, but the windows were sufficiently well curtained that the sense of privacy was in no way marred. It was old-fashioned. There was nothing of the grace and imagination of Killian Melville's architecture, but it was also restful and extremely pleasing. The furniture was dark and heavy, the walls lined with books, although there was no time to look and see what subjects they covered.

Wolff stared at him levelly and with a cold intensity. It was not unfriendly, but it was guarded. He was anticipating attack. Rathbone wondered if it had happened before—suspicion, accusation, innuendo. It must be a wretched way to live.

"Good afternoon, Mr. Wolff." Rathbone found himself apologetic. This was an intrusion any man would loathe. "I'm sorry, but I have to speak to you about today's evidence. I have already consulted with Mr. Sacheverall, and it is possible he may persuade Mr. Lambert to settle without returning to court, but it is a very slender hope, and we certainly cannot count on it."

Wolff took a deep breath and let it out silently. A very slight smile touched his lips.

"You must be extremely effective, Sir Oliver. What on earth did you say to him that he would even consider settling? He seems to have won outright. What he says is untrue, but there is no way I could prove it."

"No one can ever prove such things," Rathbone agreed, coming a step or two farther into the room and taking the seat Wolff indicated to him. "That is the nature of slander. It works by innuendo, belief and imagination. It plays upon the ugliest sides of human nature, but so subtly there is no armor against it. It is the coward's tool, and like most men, I despise it." He looked at Wolff's dark face with its brilliant eyes and curious, sensitive mouth. "But as I pointed out to Sacheverall, it is a weapon that fits almost any hand, mine as well as his, if need be."

"Yours?" Wolff looked surprised. He remained standing, his back now to the window, silhouetted against it. "Who could you slander, and how would it help? Would it not simply reduce Melville to the appearance of a viciousness born of desperation?"

"Yes, probably. And it is not inconceivable he would refuse to do it anyway," Rathbone conceded. "But Sacheverall does not know that, nor dare he rely upon it. He cannot be certain that if Melville is staring ruin in the face, he may not alter his hitherto honorable character and strike anywhere he can."

"He wouldn't," Wolff said simply. There was no doubt in his eyes, only a kind of bitter, powerful laughter.

"I believe you," Rathbone acknowledged, and he spoke honestly. He surprised himself, but he felt no uncertainty at all that Melville would accept complete destruction before he would sink to saying something of Zillah Lambert he knew to be untrue. He was a man whose behavior in the whole affair was a succession of acts which did not have any apparent logical or emotional line of connection. Rathbone was assailed again with an overwhelming conviction that there was something, one powerful, all-consuming fact, which he did not know but which would explain it all.

Something eased in Wolff's demeanor, something indefinable it was so slight. He was waiting for Rathbone to explain.

"Sacheverall is risking his client's well-being as well as his own, so he has to be certain." Rathbone crossed his legs and smiled up at Wolff, not in humor or even comfort, but in a certain sense of communication that they were in alliance against an attitude, a set of beliefs which they both found repellent but that was too delicate to be given words. "And he may guess or judge that Melville will not react with attack, but he will not judge it of me. He knows better. I too will behave in the interests of my client, not necessarily having sought his permission first."

"Would you?" Wolff said quietly.

"I don't know." Rathbone smiled at himself. It was true; he did not know what he would reveal were Monk to discover anything. What he did know, without doubt, was that he would drive Monk to learn every jot there was to know: about Zillah Lambert, her father, her mother, and anyone else who could conceivably have any bearing on the case. "I don't know if there is anything, but then neither does Sacheverall."

Wolff let out his breath slowly.

"But I must know what they can learn about Melville," Rathbone went on reluctantly. "Not what is true or untrue . . . but what witnesses can he call and what will they say?"

Wolff stiffened again and his voice was unnaturally steady. "That Melville and I are friends," he replied without looking away. "That he has visited me here, sometimes during the day, sometimes in the evening."

"Overnight?"

"No."

Rathbone was not sure if there had been a hesitation or if he had imagined it. He was not even sure how much it mattered. Once an idea was sown in someone's mind, without realizing it, memory became slanted towards what was believed. No deception need be intended, nevertheless it was carried out, and when a thing had been put into words it assumed a kind of reality. No one wanted to go back upon testimony. It was embarrassing. The longer one clung to it and the more often it was repeated, the harder it was to alter.

"Anything else?" Rathbone asked. "No more than that? Please tell me the truth, Mr. Wolff. I cannot defend Melville, or you, from what I do not know."

But Wolff was as stubborn as Melville. He gave the same blank stare and denied it again.

"How long have you known Melville?" Rathbone pursued.

Wolff thought for a moment. "About twelve years, I think, maybe a little less."

"Do you know why he changed his mind about marrying Miss Lambert?"

Wolff was still standing with his back to the window, but the light was shining on the side of his face, and Rathbone could see his expression clearly. There was no change in it, no shadow.

"He didn't," he replied. "He never intended to. He liked her. It was a friendship which he believed she shared in the same spirit. He was appalled when he realized both she and her family read something quite different into it."

Rathbone could see there was no point in attempting to learn anything more from Wolff. He considered asking neighbors himself, but Monk would be far more skilled at it, and he had other things to do. He rose to his feet and excused himself, thanking Wolff for his time and warning him that their hopes of settling without returning to court were still negligible. He left feeling angry and disappointed, although he could not have named what he had hoped to find.

"What do you want me to discover?" Monk asked as they sat together over an excellent meal of roast saddle of mutton and spring vegetables. They were in one of Rathbone's favorite hostelries; he had invited Monk to join him partly because it was a miserable case he was requesting him to follow, but largely because he felt like indulging himself in an undeniable pleasure, like good food, good drink, a roaring fire and someone to wait upon him with courtesy and a cheerful manner. This particular dining room offered all these things. It was bustling with life, and yet not overcrowded. They had been given a table out of the draft from the door and yet not too far into a corner and not near noisy companions.

"The worst they can find for themselves, or create out of confused and prejudiced observations," he answered Monk's question as the serving girl left a tankard of ale for them and he acknowledged it with thanks.

Monk helped himself to another crisp roasted potato. "I presume you have already spoken to this man Wolff and to Melville himself?"

"Of course. They deny it, but add very little."

"Do you believe them?" Monk was curious, there was no decision or assumption in his eyes.

Rathbone thought for a moment or two, eating slowly. The mutton was excellent.

"I don't know," he said at last. "They are both lying about something. I feel it in Wolff, and I am certain of it in Melville, but I don't know what. I am not at all sure it is that."

"Then what?"

"I don't know!" Rathbone said sharply. "If I did, I wouldn't need you!"

Monk looked amused, even faintly satisfied.

"And I need weapons against Lambert if Sacheverall doesn't settle," Rathbone continued. "And I don't suppose he will. He'll go to Lambert and ask if there is anything I can find. Lambert will swear there isn't. If Sacheverall has any sense he'll speak to Zillah alone and ask her. Whatever there is, or is not, I don't know."

"But you need to," Monk concluded for him, leaning across and taking the last potato.

"Precisely."

"And if there is, would you use it?" Monk asked.

"That is not your concern. Unless, of course, you are telling me you will not look for it if I would."

Monk laughed. "I have often wondered just how hard you would fight if you were tested, which weapon you might decide to use. I was simply interested. I'll learn what I can."

"And tell me what you wish to?" Rathbone said dryly.

"Of course. I presume you are accepting the bill yourself?"

At the nearest table a man roared with laughter.

"Of course. Will you please pass me the horseradish sauce?"

Monk obliged, smiling widely.

Sacheverall sent Rathbone a very clear and tersely worded message that his client would not settle, and Thursday morning saw them back in court, Sacheverall standing in the open space before the high witness-box and facing first the judge, then the jury. He affected to ignore the public benches, now far more crowded again.

"I call Major Albert Hillman."

Major Hillman duly appeared, walking with a decided limp. He stared straight ahead of him, refusing to look at Rathbone or Melville where they sat, or at Sacheverall himself standing feet a little apart, back straight, like a circus ringmaster with his arms a trifle lifted. Major Hillman climbed the steps with difficulty and took the oath.

"I'm sorry to call you on this distressing matter, sir," Sacheverall apologized. "I hope your injury does not pain you too much?"

Rathbone sighed. Obviously it was going to prove to be a war wound, nobly obtained, which was why Sacheverall had drawn attention to it. It was all predictable, but nonetheless effective for that.

"My duty, sir," the major replied stiffly. His distaste was plain in his face and in the downward dropping of his voice.

"Of course." Sacheverall nodded. "I shall be as brief as possible. I would not do this at all . . . had Mr. Melville been prepared to concede the case"—he glanced at Rathbone briefly, and away again—"and admit his fault without necessitating this unpleasant disclosure."

The judge leaned forward. "You have made sufficient apology, Mr. Sacheverall. Please proceed to your evidence."

"My lord." Sacheverall bowed.

McKeever's wide blue eyes did not seem to change at all, and yet even from where Rathbone was sitting, he could see a coldness in the judge. This should not have been a criminal matter, not even a legal one. A domestic sadness, a misunderstanding of emotions, had escalated into something which was now going to ruin lives and perhaps deprive the world of one of its most brilliant and creative talents. One young woman had had her marriage hopes blighted, and no doubt she had suffered a deep and extremely powerful sense of rejection. But she was young, extremely handsome, wealthy and of a charming disposition. She would recover, as everyone does. She could simply have said that they quarreled and she had broken the betrothal. It would have raised a few eyebrows. In a month it would have become uninteresting. In a year it would have been forgotten.

This was ridiculous. Without thinking, Rathbone was on his feet.

"My lord! Before we proceed to drag two men's private lives before the public and suggest matters which cannot be proved, and should not be our concern, over the—"

Sacheverall had swung around, staring with exaggerated amazement at Rathbone.

"My lord! Is Sir Oliver saying that acts of sexual perversion and depravity are not of public concern simply because they do not happen in the middle of the street?" He flung out his arm dramatically. "Is a crime not a crime because it occurs behind closed doors? Is that his view of morality? I hope he cannot mean what he says."

Rathbone was furious. He could feel the heat burn up his face.

"Mr. Sacheverall knows I suggest nothing of the sort!" he snapped. "I ask that we not descend into the realms of prurient unprovable speculation into men's personal lives in an effort to justify acts of misunderstanding, carelessness or at worst irresponsibility. This cannot help anyone! All parties will be hurt, perhaps quite wrongly. They will learn to hate, where before there was merely sadness. They—"

"In other words, my lord," Sacheverall said jeeringly, glancing at the gallery and back at McKeever, "Sir Oliver would like my client to forgive his client and simply abandon the case, with Miss

Lambert's reputation still in question and her feelings ravaged as if all that were of no importance whatever. I fear Sir Oliver betrays all too scant a regard for the purity, the sensibilities, and the true and precious value of women! In deference to his dislike for scandalous suppositions which cannot be proved, I will make no suggestions as to why."

Rathbone took a step forward. "I regard Miss Lambert's reputation as of great importance," he said gratingly, almost between his teeth. "The difference between us is that I regard Mr. Melville's reputation also . . . and Mr. Wolff's. He is no party to this case, and yet he stands to lose a great deal, without proof of guilt, having harmed no one."

"That remains to be seen," Sacheverall retorted. "And as to whether such acts are wrong—or not—that will depend upon another court. But I know what the public thinks!" He all but laughed as he said it, again inclining his head toward the gallery as if he spoke for them and with their approval.

McKeever sighed. He looked at Sacheverall with dislike.

"No doubt you do," he said quietly. "But this is a court of law, Mr. Sacheverall, not a place of public speculation and gossip." He looked at Rathbone. "I regret, Sir Oliver, but passionate as your plea is, it is not an argument in law. If Mr. Sacheverall's client wishes to pursue this line of testimony, I am obliged to allow it."

Rathbone swiveled around to look where Barton Lambert was sitting a little behind Sacheverall, his wife beside him. Her pretty face with its unusual brow was set in extraordinary determination. He had not realized earlier, when she was full of charm and elegance, what power there was in her. He felt certain she was the driving force behind this suit. It was she who understood precisely what damage could be done her daughter if the word was whispered around that a young man who had been in love with her had at the last moment broken his betrothal. Zillah was lovely, wealthy, of perfectly adequate social standing. Whatever fault she had was not a visible one, therefore it could only be invisible, leaving the imagination to rise—or sink—to any level. Barton Lambert might have some pity for Melville. Delphine had none.

Rathbone returned to his seat and awaited the worst.

It came. Sacheverall began to question the major as to his residence, which was the same gracious building as Isaac Wolff, and then took him step by reluctant, unpleasant step through his observations of Killian Melville's visits, the time of day or evening, as far as he could remember them, what he was wearing, his general air and demeanor. He obliged the major to describe Wolff's greeting Melville at the door, their evident pleasure in seeing each other. It was all done with some subtlety. There was nothing whatever to which Rathbone could object. He caught McKeever's eye a number of times, and saw his dislike of the pattern the questioning was following, but an equal resolve to abide by the law.

An hour later, when Sacheverall was finished and turned with a smile of invitation to Rathbone, he had established a regular pattern of visits between the two men and that they frequently lasted for several hours. He could not and would not guess as to what happened within Wolff's rooms once the outer door was closed, but the pinkness of his cheeks and his evident embarrassment and rising anger made his thoughts transparent.

Rathbone rose with his mind in turmoil. He had seldom felt so inadequate to a case or so angry with his adversary. He had often fought hard, and lost more than he wished, but to a better case, and to a man he respected. Indeed, Ebenezer Goode, a man he had often faced, was also a personal friend.

He loathed Wystan Sacheverall, and it was more than just the fact he was winning easily. There was a prurience in the man which repelled him.

"Major Hillman," Rathbone began courteously, walking forward towards the witness stand, "I am sure you would rather not be here on this matter, and I should not press you were there not absolute necessity."

"Thank you, sir," the major said stiffly. He did not know what to make of Rathbone, and it was clear in the expression in his rather plain face.

"Are you acquainted with Mr. Wolff? Do you speak to him if you should meet on the landing or stairs?"

"Yes—yes, I have until now." Hillman was obviously nonplussed.

"But something here has changed your mind?" Rathbone suggested helpfully. "Something that has been said today?"

Hillman looked acutely unhappy. He stood as if to attention, shoulders square, back stiff, eyes straight ahead.

"Perhaps I can assist you," Rathbone offered. "Mr. Sacheverall has suggested a relationship which would be quite improper, and you might find that repugnant to you?"

"I should, sir! I should . . ." Hillman was shaking, his voice thick with emotion.

"Extremely repugnant?" Rathbone nodded.

Hillman was tight-lipped. "Extremely."

Sacheverall was leaning across his table, listening with a half smile on his face.

The jurors were watching Rathbone intently.

Melville had his head down, refusing to look at anyone.

"Quite so," Rathbone agreed. "You are not alone, Major Hillman. Most of us do not care to think or imagine the intimate details of other people's lives. We consider it intrusive at best, at worst a form of emotional illness."

Sacheverall started to his feet.

McKeever gestured him to silence, but his glance at Rathbone warned him that he would not indulge him much longer.

"But before coming here today, Major Hillman," Rathbone said with a smile, "you had not entertained such thoughts? You did not speak pleasantly while at the same time believing him to be practicing the acts Mr. Sacheverall has hinted at?"

"Certainly not, sir!" Hillman said sharply. "I believed him to be a normal man—indeed, a gentleman."

"So it is Mr. Sacheverall who has changed your mind?"

"Yes sir."

Rathbone smiled. "And here were we supposing it was your testimony which had changed his. Thank you for correcting our errors, sir. I am obliged to you. That is all I have to trouble you with."

There was a ripple of laughter around the room. But it was a short-lived victory, as Rathbone had known it would be. Hard on the major's heels was a man of much less repute, a grubby-minded idler with nothing better to do than to watch and imagine. His evidence was as well embroidered. The jury's contempt for his testimony was marked plainly in their faces, but they had to listen to his leering account, and however hard they might have wished to expunge it from their minds, it was not possible. One cannot willfully forget in an instant. And they were sworn to weigh the evidence, all of it, regardless of their own personal feelings, as Sacheverall reminded them more than once.

Rathbone could discredit the man, but it was hardly worth the effort. He had discredited himself. There was no point in trying to shake his actual testimony. To draw attention to it at all, whether to rebut, argue, or deny, was only to fix it more firmly in the jurors' minds.

"No thank you, my lord," Rathbone said when offered his chance to examine the witness. "I cannot think of anything useful to say to such a man."

The luncheon adjournment was brief, only sufficient to eat the hastiest meal, and then they returned to court. An occupant of the building where Melville lived swore unhappily that he had seen Isaac Wolff visit Melville's rooms and remain for some time. No matter how Sacheverall pressed, he would not put an hour to it. Perversely, his very honesty and reluctance made his evidence the more powerful. It was apparent he both liked Melville personally and regarded this proceeding as an intrusion into those areas of a man's life which should remain private.

It was clear in the jurors' expressions that they attached great weight to his word. He refused point-blank, and with some show of temper, to speculate.

Sacheverall dismissed him with almost palpable satisfaction.

Glancing at Barton Lambert, and at Zillah sitting beside him, so stricken with misery and dismay she looked almost numbed, Rathbone had only one more card to play, and it was a desperate one, with only a shred of hope.

He asked for a fifteen-minute adjournment to consult with Sacheverall.

McKeever granted it, perhaps with more pity than legal reason.

Outside in the hall, Rathbone saw Monk and spoke with him momentarily, but he had nothing to offer, and two minutes later Rathbone strode after Sacheverall, leaving Melville standing alone.

"Well?" Sacheverall asked with a grin. "What now?"

"Ask Lambert if he wants to pursue this," Rathbone demanded. He loathed appealing to Sacheverall, of all people, for mercy, but he had nothing else left.

Sacheverall's fair eyebrows rose in amazement. "For God's sake, what for? He can't lose!"

"He can't lose the case," Rathbone agreed. "He can lose his daughter's happiness and peace of conscience. Have you looked at her face? Do you think this is giving her pleasure? She has her vindication; she does not want or need to ruin Melville as well. Ask Lambert if he needs to go any further."

"I don't need to," Sacheverall said with a broad smile.

"Yes, you do!" Rathbone was furious, but he tried to conceal it for his own dignity. "In case you have temporarily forgotten it, you are acting for the Lambert family, not for yourself!"

Sacheverall flushed. "I'll ask him," he agreed gracelessly. "But I shall also advise him. Now, if that was all you had to say, then we should not delay the court any longer." And without waiting for Rathbone to reply, he turned on his heel and marched back to the courtroom, leaving Rathbone to follow.

Sacheverall produced his final witness, and she was damning. She might have called herself an adventuress, but she was little more than an unpleasantly ambitious prostitute, both experienced and astute as to the appetites of men and women. She had no doubt whatever that Wolff and Melville were lovers. She had seen them embracing and her evidence was possibly the more unpleasant because her entire manner showed that she saw nothing wrong in it. She did not imply it was casual or the satisfaction of a physical appetite alone, but she used the word *lovers* because she meant the fullness of that emotion.

There was nothing for Rathbone to do. He was completely beaten. It was not merely in Sacheverall's jubilant face but in the grim disgust of the majority of the jurors as well. Even those few who might have felt either pity or a sense that it was a private matter and not a public concern could not argue the issue that Killian Melville had broken his promise to marry Zillah Lambert because of a fault that lay within himself. He had deceived her as to his nature and his intentions and she had every right to demand and to receive reparation from him for the slight to her honor and her reputation.

Rathbone looked across to where she sat beside her father. Her expression was completely unguarded. Disbelief and confusion were so naked those next to her were for once ashamed to stare. She barely understood what had been suggested. Rathbone doubted she was familiar with much of the intimacy of normal love, let alone that between man and man. Most girls of her age and station learned little before their wedding nights. He felt profoundly sorry for her. She sat rigid, staring straight ahead as if at some disaster she could not tear herself from. He had seen such wide, fixed eyes and unmoving lips when he had had to tell people of unexpected deaths, or that a case was lost and they would face a fearful sentence. In that moment he had no doubt at all that Zillah had truly loved Melville, whether he was aware of it or not. However blindly, for whatever reason, it was a terrible wrong he had done her.

He looked at Barton Lambert beside her. His expression was completely different. His skin was red with anger and frustration. He turned one way then another, ignoring his wife, who was speaking quietly to him, her cheeks also flushed. Had either of them any idea what they had done to their daughter? Had they allowed their anger, their ambition, their intellectual understanding of the injury Melville had inflicted upon her to obscure any sensitivity or imagination to her inner world? She might have to live with the turmoil of thought and the pain of loss, of having been deceived and misled, of wondering what she had done to produce the wrong or why she had failed to see it.

He wondered briefly, and pointlessly, if Sacheverall had actually spoken to Lambert as he had asked. He thought not. Sacheverall was still relishing his victory, standing smiling very slightly, surveying the jury, avoiding the judge's eye.

McKeever adjourned the court, announcing that they would resume again the following morning, when Rathbone could put forward the case for the defense.

There was a scramble to leave the public gallery. No doubt journalists would be weighing what they would say and composing it in their minds as they snatched cabs back to Fleet Street. Rathbone could imagine, but nothing that came to his mind would show a shred of compassion and very little reticence. Killian Melville was a well-known figure; so was Barton Lambert. Zillah was young and pretty. There would be plenty of interest.

Rathbone looked at Melville, who straightened his back slowly and lifted his face. He looked appalling, as if he felt so ill he might faint. It was impossible to begin to imagine what he must be feeling.

"I think we should leave," Rathbone said to him quietly. "We cannot speak here."

Melville swallowed with difficulty. "There's nothing to say," he answered between dry lips. "I never meant to hurt Zillah . . . or Isaac. And I seem to have done both. Zillah will recover. She will be all right." He screwed up his face as if feeling a physical pain deep inside his body. "What will happen to Isaac? Will he be ruined? Will they try to send him to jail?"

This was no time for false hope for Wolff or for Melville himself. Sacheverall's face should have swept any such delusions away.

"They may. If it is prosecuted there is really very little defense. It is something people don't usually bother with—if no one under the age of consent is involved and no nuisance is caused by acts in public."

Melville started to laugh, quietly, but with a wild desperation that warned it would turn to weeping any moment.

For once Rathbone did not even consider propriety, or even what his professional reputation would suffer. He put his hand on Melville's shoulder and gripped him hard, even prepared to support him physically if necessary.

"Come," he ordered. "The least we can do is offer you a little privacy. They've had their pound of flesh; let us deny them the pleasure of carving it off and watching the blood." And he half hauled Melville to his feet, pulling him through the press of people, elbowing them out of his way with uncharacteristic roughness.

Out in the hallway, Melville straightened up. "Thank you," he said shakily. "But I am composed now. I shall be . . . all right."

He looked appalling. His skin was flushed and his lips dry. But his eyes were unflinching, and there was a kind of wild, black humor in them. He still knew something that Rathbone did not. Something that mattered.

Rathbone drew in a breath to ask yet again, then knew it would be a waste of time.

"Do you want me to settle?" he asked, searching Melville's face, trying to see beyond the clear, aquamarine eyes into the man inside. What was there beyond brilliance of ideas, the mass of technical knowledge, the dreams in stone of a thousand generations of history stored and made new? What were the private dreams and emotions of the man himself, his likes and dislikes, the fears, the laughter, the memories? Or weren't there any? Was he empty of everything else?

"I won't marry her," Melville repeated softly. "I never asked her to marry me. If I settle now, say I was wrong when I wasn't, what will happen to all the other men in the future, if I give in?"

"You haven't given in," Rathbone answered. "You were beaten."

Melville turned and walked away, his shoulders hunched, his head down. He bumped into someone and did not notice.

Aching for him, confused and angry, Rathbone hurried after him, determined at the least to find him a hansom and see that he was not harried or abused any further. He caught up with him and escorted him as far as the back entrance. He glared at a couple of men who would have approached Melville, and strode past them, knocking one aside roughly.

At the curb he all but commandeered a hansom and half threw Melville up into it, giving the driver Melville's address and passing him up a more than generous fare.

When the cab was safely on its way, he went back into the courthouse having no idea what he was going to do the next day. When the case resumed he would have to try to find something to change the present opinion. What was there? The last witness had turned the balance beyond redeeming. His only hope was to attack, but what good could that do now? Melville was ruined whatever the result. The only possible advantage would be to save him something financially. And perhaps Barton Lambert, at least, might be willing to do that. He had no need of money.

Rathbone's last hope of achieving that by force, if he could not by appeal to clemency, would be to know something about Lambert, or his family, which Lambert would very much prefer to have kept in silence.

But if Monk could not find it within the next twelve hours, then there was nothing left.

Personally, Rathbone would advise Melville to leave England and try to build his career in some other country where the scandal would not follow him or where they had a more liberal view towards men's private lives. There certainly were such places, and his genius was international, unlike language. Thank God he was not a poet!

Ahead of him, Zillah Lambert was standing next to her parents. He recognized her first, seeing her bright hair, its luxuriant waves catching the light from the lamps above her. She still looked bemused, uncertain about the bustle and clatter around her, like an animal caught in a strange place. He had seen people shocked like that many times. These halls had witnessed so much human agony too raw to be disguised by any dignity or self-protection, too new yet to have found a mask.

Sacheverall walked up to them, still smiling.

Delphine saw him and her expression immediately altered to one of charm and gratitude.

"Mr. Sacheverall," she said earnestly. "I cannot tell you how grateful we are for your diligence in our cause, in Zillah's cause. It has been a most distressing time for all of us, but for her especially." She lowered her voice a little, but since she had moved closer to Rathbone without seeing him, and farther from Zillah, he could still hear her if he gave his attention. "Of course, it will take a little while for her to recover from the shock of all this. Such a revelation is fearful for a young girl to have to hear. She will need all our kindness and encouragement."

"I promise you she will receive it," Sacheverall said warmly. "Her innocence in this matter is quite obvious to anyone. I have been very moved by her dignity throughout this whole ordeal. She is a remarkable person."

"Indeed she is," Delphine agreed, smiling and looking downward hastily, not to seem too immodest. "I admit, Mr. Sacheverall, I am far prouder of her than perhaps some would approve. But how many girls of her age could have borne themselves under this pressure and kept out bitterness from their nature, or hysteria, or a note of self-pity? She has a great sweetness of character."

Rathbone looked past Delphine to Zillah, who must have overheard this exchange. Her cheeks were flushed and her eyes blazed. He could only guess how mortified she felt, the acuteness of her embarrassment. She was still dazed by not only the loss but the utter and public disillusionment with the man she had loved for nearly three years, and here was her mother seizing the moment to praise her to another man, who was very obviously keenly interested.

Sacheverall did not seem to be in the least aware of the clumsiness of it. He moved forward to speak directly to Zillah after the briefest lingering with Delphine, as if a tacit agreement had been understood.

"I am so sorry," he said earnestly to Zillah. "I wish more than you can know that this had not been necessary."

"Do you?" she said coldly. "I am glad you told me, Mr. Sacheverall, otherwise I should not have known. You are a superb actor, sir. I had the strongest impression you were savoring your victory." She looked at him directly, her eyes filled with tears but unwavering.

For the first time he was completely out of composure. It was the last response he had expected. He took a moment to collect his wits.

"Of course you are distressed," he said placatingly. "I cannot imagine how . . ." He was not sure what word he wished to use.

"I can see that you cannot," she agreed, now finding it increasingly difficult to stop herself from weeping. Her anger at him, at her mother, at the whole terrible situation, was now at last releasing the emotion she had kept in check all through the endless and searing days of the trial. "But please do not apologize. It hardly matters. I am sure you have done extremely well the job you were engaged for. We are suitably obliged to you."

She could not have been more effective had she slapped his face.

Rathbone's estimation of her soared. It was more difficult than ever to understand why Melville did not wish to marry her—unless Sacheverall's charge was true. It was the only explanation which made sense. But then, knowing his inclination, he was irresponsible at best for having wooed her, grossly cruel at worst, using her simply to gain her father's patronage and possibly to mask his own affair with Wolff by seeming to have interests elsewhere.

But he would not be the first man of genius to have a moral sense which was distorted by egocentricity into total selfishness. Rathbone should not have been disappointed; it was foolish, even naive. A man of his age and sophistication should have known better.

But the pain of it was startlingly sharp. He wanted to admire Melville. He could not help liking him.

Delphine was talking soothingly to Sacheverall, trying to repair the damage. From the look upon his face she was succeeding. Presumably with Melville excluded, he was an acceptable match. He was the right age, his family was excellent, his career prospects good, and he had more than enough money not to be courting her for merely financial reasons, although such a marriage would undoubtedly improve his situation.

Barton Lambert had taken little part in the exchange. He was standing with his hands pushed deep into his pockets, and two or three times he had looked towards Rathbone as if he wished to speak to him. But it was too late to make any difference now. His whole posture was one of deep unhappiness, and Rathbone guessed he regretted the whole affair. His affection for Melville had been real. It could not be swept away by any revelation, no matter how dark. Emotions do not often turn so entirely in so short a space. The wound was raw, and it showed. He was an unusual man in that he did not seek to alleviate it with anger.

Rathbone admired him for that. Perhaps Zillah did not gain all her refinement of character from her mother.

Rathbone left the courthouse and went out into the bright afternoon with the sharp sun and wind promising a clear evening. Twilight would not be until after eight o'clock. It made the day seem long, the night over so quickly the next morning would be there almost before he had been to sleep. If Monk did not find anything he would have to call witnesses merely to waste time. Witnesses to what? McKeever would know what he was doing, and Sacheverall certainly would.

His only hope lay in there being something, however slight, in the Lambert family history which would persuade Barton Lambert to settle for a modest amount of damages.

He walked briskly towards a hansom, and then at the last moment changed his mind and decided not to ride but to continue on foot until he had consumed some of the energy of anger and frustration inside himself. He had not acquitted himself well in the case, but that mattered very little beside his concern for Melville's future.

If only Melville had been honest with him and told him about Wolff! But he should have guessed it was something like that. Melville was not a very muscular man; he had a visionary's face, a subtle and delicate mind, a poet's imagination. Rathbone should have told Monk all that, and then perhaps Monk would have found Wolff before Sacheverall did, and this scandal at least could have been forestalled. Rathbone had the powerful impression that had Barton Lambert known he would not have pressed the suit.

Perhaps Delphine would not have wished to either. She was not hurt by the revelation, to judge from her manner, but it was certainly embarrassing.

He had dined out and it was nearly nine o'clock when he reached his rooms and his manservant presented him with the evening newspapers.

"I'm sorry, sir," he apologized.

Rathbone saw immediately what had precipitated the remark and the look of distress upon the manservant's somber face. The headlines were lurid, vulgar and aroused speculation even further than Sacheverall had. Not a shred of dignity or honor was left to Melville—or Isaac Wolff either. Even Zillah did not escape prurient suggestions and a note of condescension masked in pity, but lacking any sense of true compassion. She was the catalyst of self-righteous anger, but no thought for her feelings came through the details and the outpouring of criticism, judgment and supposition.

Rathbone was too restless to remain at home. There was a rage inside him which demanded physical action, even if it was completely pointless.

He took his coat and hat and stick, not for any purpose beyond the pleasant feel of its weight in his hand, and went out to visit Monk.

However, Monk was not in, and there was no point in waiting for him in his empty and rather cold room, even though his landlady offered him the opportunity. He left again and went to his club.

He sat and brooded over a single-malt whiskey for nearly an hour, attempting to think creatively, until he was joined by an old friend who sat down in the chair opposite him, bringing another whiskey to replace the one Rathbone had nearly finished.

"Rotten business," he said sympathetically. "Never know where you'll find the beggars, do you."

Rathbone looked up. "What did you say?"

"Never know where you'll find the beggars," the man repeated. His name was Boothroyd and he was a solicitor in family law.

"What beggars?" Rathbone said edgily.

"Homosexuals." Boothroyd pushed over the glass he had brought for Rathbone. "For heaven's sake, man, don't be coy! There's nothing to protect now. Angry with yourself you didn't guess, no doubt, but then you always were a trifle naive, my dear chap. Always thinking in terms of the greater crimes, murder, arson and grand theft, not sordid little bedroom perversions. Looking beyond the mark."

A turmoil of thoughts boiled up in Rathbone's mind, awareness that Boothroyd was right in that he should have thought of it, blind rage at the man's complacency and ignorance of the torrent of pain he was dismissing with a few callous sentences, and then a deeper stirring of a different kind of questioning and anger that these judgments were even a matter of law.

He looked up at Boothroyd and ignored the whiskey.

"I suppose I imagined that what a man did in his bedroom, providing he injured no one, was his own affair," he said clearly and very distinctly.

Boothroyd was startled. His rather bulbous eyes widened in amazement.

"Are you saying you approve of buggery?" he asked, his voice lifting sharply at the end of the word in incredulity.

"There are a lot of things I don't approve of," Rathbone answered with the careful enunciation which marked his icy temper. "I don't approve of a man who uses his wife without love or consideration for her feelings. I don't approve of a woman who sells her body to obtain material goods, or power, or any other commodity, in or outside marriage. I don't approve of cruelty, physical or of the mind." He stared at Boothroyd unwaveringly. "I don't approve of lies or manipulation or coercion or blackmail. For that matter, I don't approve of greed or idleness or jealousy. But I do not believe we should improve our society by attempting to legislate against them. All one would do is turn every petty-minded busybody and every mealymouthed gossip into a spy, a snoop and a telltale."

Boothroyd was staring at him as if he could scarcely believe his ears.

"Of all the things I disapprove of," Rathbone went on, lowering his voice a little, but still just as passionate and just as freezingly angry, "I think that two men loving each other in the privacy of their own homes, involving no outsiders, is neither my business nor is it my interest, and I have no desire to make it so."

"I am surprised you call it love," Boothroyd said with some astringence. "Although perhaps I should not be."

"*Love* is a euphemism for a lot of relationships," Rathbone snapped back, feeling his cheeks burn as he understood what Boothroyd meant, but the rage in him refused to correct it, dear as he knew it might cost him.

"The Bible says it is a sin," Boothroyd pointed out. "I think all Christian men agree."

"So is lusting after a woman in your heart," Rathbone pointed out. "Christ was rather specific about that. Most of us are guilty of it nevertheless. I am, and will probably continue to be. Would you legislate against it?"

"Don't be absurd!"

"Precisely," Rathbone agreed between clenched teeth, his voice crystalline with precision. "There are a great many things which are better left to God to judge, and I think whatever Melville or Wolff does in private is among them."

"You are in a minority!" Boothroyd replied sharply, drinking the whiskey he had originally brought for Rathbone and rising to his feet.

"That does not make me wrong," Rathbone answered him.

"It will make you damned well misunderstood!" Boothroyd warned.

"So I see." Rathbone arched his brows sarcastically and remained sitting. "But I do not find that an adequate reason to change."

"On your own head be it!" Boothroyd turned and walked away, leaving Rathbone furious, embarrassed and frightened, but absolutely determined not to change.

CHAPTER SEVEN

While Rathbone was struggling so fruitlessly in court, knowing he could only lose, Monk was already planning to pursue every avenue into the possible weaknesses in any member of the Lambert family. Zillah herself was the one whose flaws would have most relevance to the issue, so it was with her he began. Not that he expected to succeed. She was almost certainly exactly what she appeared to be, and regrettably, Killian Melville was also what he appeared to be. The whole issue was a tragedy which, with even ordinary common sense, need not have happened.

He began to walk restlessly back and forth across the room.

Zillah Lambert was less than half his age, a child of financial privilege and complete innocence as to the ways of the world. As far as he knew, this was the first misfortune ever to strike her. How could he begin to understand her life?

He would have welcomed Hester's advice, and perhaps even more, Callandra's. But Callandra was still in Scotland and it was too soon to call on Hester again, although she remained curiously sharp in his mind.

His contacts in the underworld of crime and poverty on the borders of the law were of no use to him. Zillah Lambert lived the closed life of girls just turning into women, leaving the schoolroom and preparing for marriage, seeking husbands—and love, if possible. Perhaps they dreamed of glamour, romance, teeming emotions before the steadier years ahead of domesticity and children, of making their mark in society, and eventually of settling with a mature resignation and exercise of power—and, one hoped, serene prosperity. It was a life unimaginable to him, totally feminine, and of a dependency not in the least attractive. But it was apparently what most women wished.

He did not need gossip, but something tangible enough to make Lambert withdraw his case. It was an ugly thing to seek. Monk's sympathies were largely with Zillah Lambert, because however you looked at it, Melville had behaved like a fool. And so had Rathbone for taking the case and allowing it to come to trial. He could not win. He should have settled long before this.

Unless, of course, there really was something about Zillah which Melville had discovered when it was too late, but out of regard for her or for her father, who had been his patron and friend, or even possibly because he could not prove it, he had felt unable to marry her.

Monk owed him at least that possibility.

He stopped pacing the floor, collected his hat and coat and set out to find someone who frequented the same circles as the Lamberts and might give him a word, a remark let slip, anything he could follow which might unravel into whatever it was Melville had learned. He had only a hazy idea who, but certainly they would not come to him while he was sitting in Fitzroy Street.

He was crossing Tottenham Court Road, only half watching the traffic, when a better idea came to him. It should have been obvious from the beginning. If Melville had discovered this blemish, whatever it was, then he should follow Melville's path, not Zillah Lambert's. And that would necessarily be far easier. He changed direction abruptly and strode south towards Oxford Street, passing fashionable ladies, men about business and a steadily thickening stream of traffic. He had a definite goal.

By late afternoon he knew far more of Killian Melville's daily habits, his working hours, which were extraordinarily long, his very restricted social life, and his solitary recreation, which seemed only an extension of his work, by walks taken alone and apparently deep in thought. Melville spent hours in art galleries and museums, but always on his own, except for rare encounters with a dark and slightly eccentric man named Isaac Wolff, who was apparently also an intellectual of some sort, given to study of some artistic work, but of a more literary nature.

His flash of inspiration had not worked. If Melville had learned something about Zillah Lambert, it had been by chance and not in the course of his usual day.

Monk returned home tired and with sore feet and a filthy temper, also a determination not to be beaten. If ordinary intelligence failed, then he had little left to lose. He would resort to bravado and what amounted in effect to lies.

When he had had more money from a regular salary in the police force, even if not a generous salary, he had spent a great deal of it on clothes. From his days as a banker, he still had silk shirts he had cared for, beautifully cut boots and dancing shoes which he seldom wore, two suits of cutaway jacket and tails, several very good gold studs and cuff links. He was too vain to have allowed himself to grow out of clothes he could not now afford to replace.

He dressed with the utmost care, gritted his teeth against the humiliation of possible rejection, and set out for a long and testing evening.

He had no idea where parties such as he required might be held on this particular night. He took a hansom and ordered the driver up and down the streets of Mayfair and Belgravia until he saw a large number of carriages stopping outside a well-lit home and elegant men and women alighting and going up the steps and inside.

He stopped the driver, paid him and alighted also. He was inviting disaster, but he had little alternative left, except to report failure, and he was not going to do that. He hesitated, pretending to look for something in his pocket, until he could walk in with half a dozen people, four of them women, and appear to be part of their group. Indeed, one of the younger ladies seemed to find the idea appealing and he capitalized on it without a second thought.

Inside the main reception hall was already thronged with people, at least a hundred, and more were arriving all the time. It appeared to be a ball, and if he was fortunate the hostess would be only too happy to have another single and presentable man of good height who could and would dance. He traded upon it.

It was nearly midnight, amid a whirl of music, chatter, high-pitched laughter and the clink of glasses when he scraped into conversation with a middle-aged lady in blue who knew Delphine Lambert well and was happy to gossip about her.

"Charming," she said, looking straight at Monk.

Monk had no shame at all.

"How very generous of you," he said, smiling back at her. "If even in your company she seemed so, then she must indeed be exceptional."

The orchestra was playing and the music danced in his head. He restrained himself with an effort.

"You flatter me, Mr. Monk," she responded, clearly pleased.

"Not at all," he denied, as he had to. "I see you in front of me, while Mrs. Lambert is merely a name. She has no grace, no humor, no spark of wit or warmth of character for me to comment on." He looked so directly at her she must take his implication to be that she did.

This was the most gracious attention she had received in a long time. She was not about to let it go. She was quite aware of her friends a few yards away watching her with amazement and envy. She would talk about Delphine for as long as this delightful and rather intriguing man wished her to.

A pretty girl in pale pink swirled by, laughing up at her partner, flirting outrageously for the brief moment she was out of her mother's reach.

A gentleman with ginger hair bumped into a waiter.

"It is not really wit or humor she has," she elaborated, prepared to go into any degree of detail. "Not that she is without it, of course," she amended. "But her charm lies rather in her extraordinary delicacy and beauty. It is not . . ." She thought for a moment. "It is not the beauty of amazing coloring or exquisite hair, although she does have a beautiful brow. Her figure is comely enough, but she is not very tall." She herself was only three or four inches less than Monk's own height. "It is the beauty of perfection," she continued. "Of even the tiniest detail being flawless. She never makes a mistake. Oh . . ." She gave a little laugh. "I daresay it is the sort of thing only another woman would notice. A man might only know there was something less attractive but not be able to put his finger upon what it might be. But Delphine . . . Mrs. Lambert . . . always rises above the little things that trip the rest of us."

The waltz was ended and replaced by a very slow pavane, or something of the sort. The temptation to dance was removed temporarily.

"How interesting," he said, watching her intently as if there were no one else in the room. "You are extraordinarily observant, Mrs. Waterson. You have a keen eye."

"Thank you, Mr. Monk." She blushed faintly.

"And a gift with words," he added for good measure.

She needed no further encouragement. She launched into varied stories not only of Delphine but, with a little guidance, of Zillah as well. She described their social round with some flair. Under Monk's flattery she did indeed exhibit an acute observation of manners and foibles and the intricacies which give clue to character.

A waiter offered them glasses of champagne and Monk seized one for Mrs. Waterson and one for himself. He was more than ready for it. All around them was laughter and color and swirl of movement.

"Only a careful eye could tell," Mrs. Waterson continued, leaning a little closer and lowering her voice confidentially, "but the whole bodice had been taken apart and restitched with the fabric going crosswise. Much more flattering." She nodded. "And her use of colors. It is more than just a flair, you know, in her it is a positive art. Nothing is too much trouble if it will produce beauty."

She was watching him intently, completely oblivious of a couple so close the woman's skirts touched her own, and who seemed to be having a fierce but almost silent quarrel. "You know I have heard it said," she told him earnestly, "that the skill in always appearing beautiful is not so much a matter of the features you are born with, or even of disguising those which are less than the best, but in drawing the onlooker's eye to those which are exceptional. And the others are barely noticed." There was triumph in her face. "Never apologize or appear to be ashamed or attempting to conceal." She raised her chin. "Walk with pride, smile, dare the world to accept you on your own terms. Believe yourself beautiful, and then others will also. That takes a great deal of courage, Mr. Monk, and a formidable strength of will."

"Indeed it does," he agreed, wishing she would proceed to something which might conceivably be relevant to Rathbone's case. "Invaluable advice for a mother to pass on to her daughter."

"Oh, I am sure she did," Mrs. Waterson said with a little lift of her shoulder. "Miss Lambert is quite lovely, and was never permitted to be anything less. The minutest details were given the utmost attention. Of course, nature assisted her beautifully!"

They were playing a waltz again. Could they dance and then return to the subject? No, of course not. It would be forgotten, become forced. He might even lose her altogether. Damn Rathbone!

It was time for a little more judicious flattery. One could not expect a woman to spend above an hour praising another woman.

"Fine features are very well," he said casually, as if it were merely a passing thought. "But without intelligence they very soon become tedious. I could listen all evening to a woman with the gifts of intelligence and expression. I could not look at one woman all evening, no matter how lovely her face."

"You have remarkable perception and sensitivity, Mr. Monk," she responded, her cheeks pink with pleasure. "I am afraid there are very few men with such finely developed values."

He raised his eyebrows. "Do you think so, Mrs. Waterson? How kind of you to say so. I don't think anyone has ever told me such a thing before." He looked suitably satisfied. He refused to think what Hester would have said of him for such playacting. The only thing that mattered was learning something that would help Rathbone's case. And so far he had signally failed in that.

He began again. "It must be tempting to use the power of such beauty, nonetheless, in a young girl with no experience, no maturity to fall back upon." He must not forget that Mrs. Waterson was certainly the wrong side of thirty-five.

"Of course," she agreed.

He waited expectantly, ignoring the young woman three or four yards away gazing at him with bright eyes full of laughter and invitation, obviously bored with her very correct and rather callow partner.

"Perhaps she did not succumb to the temptation?" he said sententiously.

"Oh, I'm afraid she did," Mrs. Waterson explained instantly, and with satisfaction. "One could not help but be aware that she was brought up to regard beauty as of the utmost importance, and therefore she would have been less than human not to have tested its power. And quite naturally it was greater than she expected—or was able to deal with gracefully." She waited to see Monk's reaction. Would he think unkindly of her if she seemed critical?

"How very understanding of you, Mrs. Waterson," he said, biting his tongue. "You speak with the sympathy of one who knows it at firsthand." He said it with a perfectly straight face. Without an ability to act one could not be a successful detective, and he had every intention of being successful.

"Well . . ." She debated whether to be modest or not, and threw caution to the winds. The orchestra was playing with rhythm and gaiety. She had drunk several glasses of champagne, and all she usually indulged in was lemonade. There was laughter and color and movement all around her. Light from chandeliers glittered on jewels and hair and bare necks and arms. Mr. Waterson was very agreeable, but he had far too little imagination. He took things for granted. "In my younger days, before I was married, of course, I did have one or two adventures," she conceded. "Perhaps I was not always wise."

"No more than to make you interesting, I am sure," Monk said with a smile. "Was Miss Lambert as . . . wise?"

She bridled a little. It was not becoming to appear uncharitable. "Well . . . possibly not. She set more store by beauty than I ever did. I always considered good character to be of more lasting worth, and a certain intelligence to stand one in greater service."

"How right you are. And so it has." He accepted a dish of sweetmeats from a passing waiter and offered it to her.

He remained talking for another half hour but learned no more than Zillah's exercise of her charms and the greater attention she paid to her physical assets, under her mother's expert tutelage, than other less well schooled girls of her age. It was hardly a sin. In fact, many might consider it a virtue. It was admired when women took the time and care to make themselves as pleasing as possible. It was in many ways a compliment to a man, if a trifle daunting to the unsure or nervous.

Monk got home at quarter to three in the morning, exhausted. He had a clearer picture of both Zillah and her mother, but it was of no use whatever that he could see. Certainly they possessed no fault that Melville could complain of, and no characteristics that were not observable in the slightest of acquaintance.

He slept late and woke with a headache. He had a large breakfast and felt considerably better.

He saw the morning newspapers but decided he had no time to read them, and if there were anything of use Rathbone would know it anyway and would have sent an appropriate message.

He needed Hester's opinion. She bore little resemblance to Zillah Lambert, but she had been Zillah's age once. That might come to him as a surprise, but surely she would remember it. And as far back as that she would have been living at home with her parents, long before her father was ruined, before anyone even thought of the possibility of a war in the Crimea. Most people would not have had the slightest idea even of where it was. And Florence Nightingale herself would have been dutifully attending the balls and soirées and dinners in search of a suitable husband. So would Hester Latterly. She would know the game and its rules.

It was not far from Fitzroy Street to Tavistock Square and he walked briskly in the sun, passing ladies out taking the air, gentlemen stretching their legs and affecting to be discussing matters of great import but actually simply enjoying themselves, watching passersby, raising their hats to female acquaintances and generally showing off. Several people drove past in smart gigs or other light equipages of one sort or another, harnesses gleaming, horses high stepping.

When he reached the Sheldon house he was admitted by the footman, who remembered him and advised him that Miss Latterly was presently occupied but he was sure that Lieutenant Sheldon would be happy to see him in a short while, if he cared to wait.

Monk accepted because he very much wished to stay, and because he had developed a sincere regard for the young man and would hate to have him feel rejected, even though Monk's departure would have had nothing whatever to do with Lieutenant Sheldon's disfigurement.

"Thank you. That would be most agreeable."

"If you will be good enough to warm yourself in the withdrawing room for a few minutes, sir, I shall inform Lieutenant Sheldon you are here."

"Of course."

Actually, he was not cold, and as it transpired, the footman returned before he had time to relax and conducted him upstairs.

Gabriel was up and dressed, although he looked extremely pale and it obviously had cost him considerable effort. He tired easily, and although he tried to mask it, the amputation still gave him pain. Monk had heard that people frequently felt the limb even after it was gone, exactly as though the shattered bone or flesh were still there. To judge from the pallor of Gabriel's face and the occasional gasp or gritted teeth, such was the case with him. Also, he had still not yet fully accustomed himself to the alteration in balance caused by the lack of an arm.

However, he was obviously pleased to see Monk and rose to his feet, smiling and extending his right hand.

"Good morning, Mr. Monk. How are you? How nice of you to call."

Monk took his hand and shook it firmly, feeling the answering grip.

"Excellent, thank you. Very good of you to allow me to visit Miss Latterly again. I am afraid this case is rapidly defeating me, and I think a woman's view on it is my last resort."

"Oh, dear." Gabriel sat down awkwardly and gestured to the other chair for Monk. "Can you talk about it?"

"I have nothing to lose," Monk confessed. It would be insensitive to speak of Gabriel's health. He must be exhausted with thinking of it, explaining, worrying, having to acknowledge with every breath that he was different.

"The suit for breach of promise . . ."

Gabriel gave his entire attention, and for nearly an hour Monk told him what he had done so far, tidying up his account of the previous evening's encounter with Mrs. Waterson to sound a little more favorable to her. Still, he thought from the amusement in Gabriel's eyes that perhaps he had not deceived him much.

"I am sorry," Gabriel said when he concluded, "but it seems as if Miss Lambert is probably exactly what she appears to be. Why do you think she may not be . . . beyond hope for your client's sake?"

"I don't," Monk confessed. "It is only that I don't like to be beaten."

Gabriel sighed with rueful humor. "It isn't always such a bad thing. The fear of it is the worst part. Once it has happened, and you've survived, it can never frighten you quite the same again."

Monk knew what he meant. He was not really speaking of cases, or even of Melville, but it was not necessary to acknowledge that.

"Oh, I've been beaten before," Monk said quickly. "And in more important cases than this. It is just that this is so stupid. It didn't have to have happened. The man has ruined himself . . . and it is tragic because he is a genius."

"Is he?" Gabriel was interested.

"Oh, yes," Monk replied without doubt. "I was in one of his

buildings. It was not quite finished, but even so it was all light and air." He heard the enthusiasm in his own voice. "Every line in it was pleasing. Not familiar, because it was different, and yet it gave the feeling that it was so right it should have been. Like hearing a perfect piece of music . . . not man created but merely discovered. It reveals something one recognizes instantly." He tried to describe it. "It is a kind of joy not quite like anything else. That is what infuriates me . . . the man has no right to destroy himself, and over something so stupid! An ounce of common sense and it could all have been avoided."

Gabriel bit his lip. "It is surely the essence of true tragedy, that it was avoidable. Someone will write a great play on it, perhaps."

"It's not good enough," Monk said in disgust. "It's farcical and pointless."

"You think Hester can still help?"

"Probably not."

Gabriel smiled. If he thought perhaps Monk had come for some other reason, he was too tactful to say so.

They were speaking of other subjects when Perdita Sheldon came in. She was dressed in mid green with a wide skirt, which was very fashionable, the lace trimming on the bodice lightening it. Had she had a little more color in her cheeks and seemed less anxious, she would have looked lovely.

"Mrs. Hanning has called. Will—will you see her? You don't have to. . . ."

Gabriel obviously did not recognize the name. His face showed only the apprehension he might in seeing anyone.

"Hanning," Perdita repeated. "Major Hanning's wife." She watched him tensely. Her back was stiff, her hands moving restlessly in front of her, smoothing her huge skirt as if she were about to meet someone of great importance, although it was only a nervous gesture because she did not look down to see what she had done. "He was killed at Gwalior."

"Oh . . ." Gabriel stared back at her, breathing in very slowly, his jaw tightening, his lips close together on the good side of his face, the scar curiously immobile. Oddly, it made his apprehension even more evident.

"I'll tell her you're not well enough," Perdita said hastily.

"No . . ."

"She'll understand." She did not move. She thought she knew what she should do to protect him, and yet even that decision was difficult. She had to resolve in order to make it and she watched him for approval. "Perhaps . . . later . . . in a few weeks . . ."

"No. No, I'll see her today." He too had to steel himself.

Monk wondered who Hanning had been and why his widow should call so soon. Was it duty, compassion, or some need of her own?

"I'll ask Miss Latterly." Perdita swung around and hurried away. She had found an answer. If something ran out of control, Hester would be there to take care of it.

Something in Gabriel had relaxed at the mention of Hester's name. He too was relying on her.

Impatience welled up inside Monk. These people were adults, not children, to be needing someone else to deal with difficult encounters. Then he looked again at the lines of tiredness in Gabriel's face, the side that was undamaged. He needed all the strength he could find to battle physical pain and the terrible memories he could not share with his young wife who had no idea what he had seen or felt. India to her was a red area on the map, a word without reality. All he had been taught about the roles of men and women, about courage and duty, responsibility and honor, demanded he support her, protect her, even keep from her the harsher and uglier sides of life. Men did not weep. Good men did not even permit others to know of their wounds.

And it was not Perdita's fault that she was confused and frightened. She had been protected all her short life. She had not chosen to be, it was her assigned role. A few women, like Hester, broke out of it, but it was a long and painful series of choices, and it left them too often alone—and for all the words of praise and gratitude, still faintly despised, because they were different . . . and perhaps threatening. Both Gabriel and Perdita could rely on her now, in their time of need. They would possibly even love her, after a fashion. Perhaps part of them would also resent the very fact that she knew their vulnerability and their failures.

When they were recovered she would leave, and they would choose to forget her as part of their time of pain. And she would begin again, and alone. He had never appreciated her courage in quite that light before. It was an inner thing, a knowledge she would hold inside herself, knowing its cost but for her pride's sake not sharing it.

"Would you prefer to see this lady alone?" he asked, not standing up but facing Gabriel very frankly.

As if he had read at least something in Monk's thoughts, Gabriel smiled back.

"I knew Hanning fairly well, but I never met his wife. He spoke of her, but I gathered she was . . . difficult." A fleeting humor crossed his face and vanished. "They quarreled rather often. I have no idea what to say to her. I don't know if I am being arrogant putting myself to this test. I want to prove to myself that I can do it." He shrugged. "And I shall expect Hester to pick up the pieces if I can't . . . for me and for Perdita. I can see that you care for Hester." He disregarded Monk's sudden discomfort. "It might be a kindness if you would stay—even if it is an imposition. . . ." He watched Monk very steadily. He would not ask, because it would be embarrassing if Monk refused.

Monk did not respond at once. Was his feeling for Hester so transparent? It was friendship, not romantic love. Did Gabriel understand that? Perhaps he should explain? But what words should he use to avoid giving the wrong impression?

"Of course," he agreed at last, relaxing back into the chair. "We have been friends for some time—several years, in fact."

Gabriel smiled and his eyes widened very slightly.

Damn it, there was nothing amusing in that! "She has a good

observation of people, and has been of considerable help to me in several of my cases," he added.

"She is a most remarkable woman," Gabriel agreed. "I find her easier to talk to than anyone else I can think of, even other men who have experienced the same battles and sieges I have."

"Do you!" Monk was stung. Gabriel had only just met her. How could he compare his friendship with her, his dependence, in the same breath with Monk's? Monk was about to make a remark about her professional skills when he realized how rude it would be—and how gratuitously cruel. And an incredible self-knowledge brought the blood to his cheeks. It was prompted by jealousy!

He was startled to hear a sound in the doorway and see Hester standing there. She was wearing blue-gray, the same dress she usually wore when on duty, or one so like it he saw no difference. Actually, he generally took very little notice of what she wore.

She looked at Gabriel with a question in her face, but she did not speak. She hesitated a moment, then accepted his decision and turned to go back and bring Mrs. Hanning.

Gabriel and Monk waited in silence. The clock ticked on the mantel shelf, and the sunlight shone in fitful patterns through the window onto the carpet. A gust of wind billowed the curtains for a moment, then they settled again. It had carried in the scent of blossoms and earth.

Mrs. Hanning walked across the passageway and appeared at the door. She was striking and flamboyant with a rather haughty manner. She had a long, straight nose and very full lips and level brows. Had they been arched she would have been truly beautiful. And perhaps her chin should have been a little firmer. Now she was dressed in widow's black.

She stared at Gabriel, completely bereft of speech. Her gloved hand went up and covered her mouth as if to smother her words so they could not be spoken.

Behind her, Perdita was close to tears. Her eyes swam as she looked at Gabriel, aching for him and helpless to know what to say, how to protect him. Her crushing failure was naked in her face.

Gabriel looked for a moment as if he had seen himself in someone else's eyes for the first time. Monk tried to imagine what it must have been like, the stomach-tearing horror when he realized this was his own face, the outer aspect he would present to the world for the rest of his life. The handsome man who automatically won smiles and willingness and admiration was gone forever. Now he would gain only fear, revulsion, even nausea, the intense embarrassment and pity which made people want to run away. Perhaps he would sooner have died? He could have been buried in India, one of a thousand other lost heroes, and all this need never have happened. It was so much easier not ever to know about such things, not ever to look at them.

Monk should say something. It was his responsibility.

He stood up, smiling at Mrs. Hanning.

"How do you do, Mrs. Hanning. My name is William Monk." He held out his hand. "I am a friend of Gabriel's. I called by to ask his advice on a small problem I am dealing with for a friend. At least, I hope to deal with it. I am not doing very well at the moment."

Mrs. Hanning caught her breath. "Oh . . . really? I am sorry, Mr. . . . Mr. Monk." She was obviously not even sure whether she was relieved to have to speak to him or annoyed. She was also not interested. Her voice was dry, overpolite. "How unfortunate."

"I find him most helpful for clarifying the mind," he went on, as if she had been charming.

It was long enough to give Gabriel time to take command of himself again.

"Good morning, Mrs. Hanning. How kind of you to call." His voice shook only a little and he forced himself to meet her eyes, regardless of what he should see there.

"It was . . ." She had been about to say "duty" and thought better of it. She tried to look at him normally and failed. Her gaze fixed rigidly on his eyes as if she were afraid it would slide off to his disfigured flesh or his absent arm. "It was something I always intended," she finished lamely. "I have just been . . . er . . ."

"Of course," He struggled to help her, hideously conscious of her revulsion. "We were all terribly grieved to hear of Major Hanning's death at Gwalior. We lost so many friends it seemed as if the grief would never stop—stop increasing."

"Yes . . ." She still had no idea what to say to him. If she had had it all clear in her mind before she came, the reality of his injuries had scattered it from her. "It must have been dreadful for you. My husband . . ." She swallowed and gulped. "My husband always mentioned you with great regard." It sounded appallingly formal, as if she were a senior officer's wife making a duty call with no idea and no feeling for the events or emotions of which she spoke. She was floundering, and they all knew it.

Where was Hester? She would know how to say something which could bring them back to honesty. Monk looked over Mrs. Hanning's shoulder and saw first Perdita, ashen-faced, then Hester beyond her. She shook her head minutely.

He nodded, tightening his lips. Why was she letting this go on? It was agonizing!

"He would," Gabriel replied, still holding Mrs. Hanning's gaze, almost unblinking. "He was a generous man, and we were friends. We shared many struggles together, many experiences. We had good friends in common . . . whom we lost." His face was full of emotion and memory. "He loved India. He loved the land, the nights, the smells of spices and dust and everything growing." He half smiled and his voice became even softer. "Once you have felt the heat and life of the jungle you don't ever forget it. Or the markets. The noise, the—" He stopped abruptly. She could not believe him. Unlike Perdita, she had been to India, but only to the sheltered hill posts, and then she had mixed only with other officers' wives.

"I think you are—are mistaken. You must have him confused with someone else." She made herself smile in return, remembering he was wounded. Perhaps his mind was affected. Yes, that would explain everything. The thoughts were as transparent on her face as if she had spoken them aloud.

Monk glanced at Hester. Still she remained silent.

Perdita moved forward, her hands clutched in front of her, her voice trembling.

"I take it you did not care for India, Mrs. Hanning. I am so sorry. That must make your loss doubly hard. I was unable to go, but I always thought I should find it fascinating. Gabriel wrote such marvelous letters, and I have been reading a book lately about its history. Of course, most of what I know is after the British arrived there, but a little about before that too. I should have done it a long time ago. . . ." She smiled at Mrs. Hanning defiantly, daring her to take offense or argue the issue. She came farther into the room. "I should have been so much more of a companion to Gabriel."

Mrs. Hanning drew in her breath. It was impossible to tell whether she was hurt or not.

Perdita knew what she had done, but she was too defensive certainly to retreat.

"Since I didn't go out with him, it is the least I can do now." She smiled, tilting her chin up a fraction.

"Naturally, if you feel it your duty." Mrs. Hanning smiled back with the merest movement of her lips. "Then no doubt it will be of comfort to you. I am delighted you have found something . . . in your situation . . . my dear."

"It is not duty," Perdita corrected her. "It is my pleasure, and naturally it is distressing, of course, because of all the suffering and the wrongs, the injustices—"

"You mean the barbarity of the Indians—the disloyalty!" Mrs. Hanning finished for her.

"No, I meant the injustices we committed towards them," Perdita corrected. "I don't think it is wrong to defend your country. I should want to defend England if Indian armies came here and tried to make us part of their empire."

Mrs. Hanning laughed. "That is hardly the same thing, my dear. The Indians are barbarians. We are English."

"I think if you read the accounts of some of our conquests, you will find that we are barbarous as well." Perdita was insistent. "We were just rather better at it."

"You are very young," Mrs. Hanning said patiently. "I think perhaps someone should advise you more suitably as to your reading material. It is obviously not sound. I am sure your intentions are good." Her voice dropped in tone. "But your doctor will tell you that Lieutenant Sheldon needs peace and rest, and a quiet and loving home, a wife to read of pleasant things to him, or to play a little piano music, not lecture on the history of India. Allow me to guide you, my dear."

"Thank you," Perdita replied. "I am sure you mean well, and it is very kind of you to have come, but I want to learn about India so that if Gabriel wishes to talk to me I can listen with intelligence."

"I think you will find that sweetness of nature is what is required, not intelligence," Mrs. Hanning said with an assured smile. "A man does not wish to discuss serious subjects with his wife. He has any number of friends and colleagues with whom to do that—gentlemen like Mr. Monk." She glanced at Monk briefly.

Monk looked across at Hester. Her eyes were bright with satisfaction. She cared fiercely for Perdita and Gabriel, and their victory was hers. He had not appreciated before how much feeling she invested in her patients, how much emotion filled her. He felt at once thrilled by it and full of admiration for her; he also sensed a kind of envy because it was something wholehearted and generous. There was a warmth in it which was not in his feeling for his clients. He kept a reserve, a coolness, even sometimes an anger. He recognized this difference, a side of Hester which had almost certainly been there always but that he had not seen. He had not wanted to. It was more comfortable to criticize her arbitrariness, her autocratic ways, her too forcibly expressed opinions, her generally awkward manner.

All of which were still there.

This new mixture of emotions was disturbing, and yet too sweet to let go of just yet. It was an astonishing gentleness under the prickling exterior.

Mrs. Hanning had paid her duty visit. It had not been a success. She was preparing to leave—or rather more accurately, to beat a strategic retreat.

Perdita thanked her again for coming and prepared to accompany her downstairs. She walked very straight with her head high and her hands clenched by her sides, betraying her tenseness.

Monk looked back at Gabriel. He was still sitting upright, his shoulders stiff, but there was the beginning of a smile on the good side of his face. In spite of the fear in his eyes, there was also a flare of hope as he watched Perdita's back disappear into the passageway.

Hester came into the room.

Monk wondered if she would refer to it or not. Perhaps it would be clumsy. Maybe it was still too delicate to be caught in words.

She looked at Gabriel, then at Monk, with anxiety in her eyes. Monk realized with a shock that she was not sure of what she had done. She had prompted the confrontation with hope but no certainty. He wanted to laugh because of the knowledge of her vulnerability it gave him. Without thinking about it he stood up and put his hand on her shoulder. It was a gesture of companionship, a desire she should know he understood.

She stiffened, motionless for a moment, then relaxed as if he had often done such a thing.

"How is your case progressing?" she asked him. Her voice quivered almost undetectably.

"Disastrously," he replied. "I came hoping you could offer some advice, although I am not sure anything will do any good now."

"Why? What has happened?" Now she forgot his gesture and thought only of the case.

"Nothing," he said. "That is the point. The case is going to come to a conclusion without Rathbone's having offered a shred of defense."

Hester glanced at Gabriel.

He smiled back, his eyes bright, his right hand closing tightly on the chair arm. They could hear Perdita's feet going down the stairs and Mrs. Hanning's heavier tread a moment after.

None of them spoke. Again the silence filled the room so overwhelmingly Monk could hear a horse's hooves on the road beyond the garden wall and the echo of a dropped tray somewhere far below them in the house, presumably the kitchen. He even thought he heard the front door open and close. Footsteps returned up the stairs. They all faced the door.

Perdita appeared, looking first at Gabriel, then at Hester.

"I was terribly rude, wasn't I?" she said shakily. "I should never have said that to her about being a good companion. Her husband is dead, isn't he?" She gulped her breath and sniffed loudly. Now that Mrs. Hanning was gone she no longer had the courage or the anger to hold herself up.

"Well . . ." Gabriel started.

"Yes, you were rude," Hester agreed with a smile. "I daresay that is the first time a lieutenant's wife has ever insulted her with impunity. It will do her the world of good." She swung around. "Won't it, Gabriel?"

He was uncertain whether to relax, as if it might be too soon—now that the moment of effort was past and quite different control was called for, a different self-mastery. He looked from Hester to Perdita as if he was seeing some aspect of his wife for the first time. Their relationship had altered. They had to begin again, discover, find the measure of things they used to take for granted.

"Yes . . ." Gabriel said tentatively. "Yes—I . . ." He laughed a little huskily. "Meeting her gives me a new feeling for John Hanning. I perceive things about him I didn't before."

"What was he like?" Perdita asked quickly. "Tell me about him."

"Well—well, he was . . ."

Hester took Monk by the arm and led him out of the room, leaving Gabriel to tell Perdita about John Hanning: his nature, his weaknesses and strengths, how he fought, what he loved or hated, his memories of boyhood and home, and how he died in Gwalior during the Mutiny.

Outside on the landing Hester looked at Monk, searching his eyes.

He looked back at her, long and steadily. It was not uncomfortable; neither was daring the other to look away. For once there was no challenge between them, no sense of battle. There was no need for any kind of explanation.

She smiled slowly.

He put his arm around her shoulders, feeling the warmth of her through the thick gray-blue stuff dress. She was stiff and too thin, but then that was how she was. She had been thin the very first time he had seen her in the church with her sister-in-law. He had thought Josephine so much the more beautiful then. She probably still was, and until this moment he had forgotten her.

"How can I help with your case?" she asked, moving away and opening the door to the sitting room.

"I don't suppose you can," he answered, following her in. "Zillah Lambert seems to be a perfectly normal pretty young woman who flirts a little but whose reputation is blemishless. I don't even know what to look for."

Hester sat down on one of the chintz-covered chairs and concentrated.

He remained standing, staring at the window and the budding branches moving in the wind, and the chimneys beyond.

"You still think Melville discovered something about her?" she asked.

"No, I don't think so at all. I think he just decided he couldn't face the prospect of marriage, the intimacy of it, the loss of his privacy, the responsibility for another human being, the—the sense of being crowded, watched, depended upon . . . just the"—he spread his hands—"the sheer . . . oppression of it!"

"Some people quite enjoy being married," she said.

He heard the warning tone in her voice. For an instant, staring at her, he hovered between anger and laughter. Laughter won.

She stared at him. "What is so funny?" she demanded, her eyes flashing.

"Don't force me to explain!" he retorted. "You don't need it, Hester. You understand me perfectly—just as I understand you. None of it needs saying. I want to find something for Rathbone to use to help Melville out of this idiotic mess. I don't say Melville deserves it. That isn't the point anymore. He won't marry Zillah Lambert. He probably won't marry anyone. He has behaved like a fool; he doesn't deserve to be ruined for it. Rathbone won't use anything I find in court, simply to make Lambert negotiate before it is all too late."

She took a deep breath. She was sitting upright, still as if she had a ruler to her back. "Is it possible one of her flirtations went too far, overbalanced into something a trifle irresponsible?"

"How would I know?"

"Well, her parents wouldn't discuss it," she said with certainty. "Her father would probably have no idea, but her mother would. Mothers can read their daughters quite frighteningly well. I don't know why it is, but we all tend to imagine our parents were never young or in love." She shrugged. "Which is probably stupid, when you come to think of it. If there is anybody at all one can be absolutely certain had some experience of intimacy, it is one's mother. Otherwise one would not be here. But at fifteen or sixteen we never see it. I thought my mother the most old-fashioned and tepid of creatures alive." She smiled to herself, her thoughts far away. "I wanted to wear a red dress. There was this young man I thought was marvelous. He had ginger hair and a wonderful mustache. . . ."

Monk held his tongue with great difficulty. He tried to imagine her at sixteen, and resented the young man with the mustache simply for having been there.

"I wanted to impress him," she went on ruefully. "The dress was very daring. He admired Lavinia Wentworth. She had black hair which curled. I thought the red dress would make the difference." She laughed with a ripple of real humor, no pity or regret, her eyes bright. "I would have looked awful. I was so pale, and far too bony to wear red. Mama made me wear white and green. The young man with the mustache ignored me utterly. I don't think he even saw me."

"Lavinia Wentworth?" He had to ask.

"No—actually, Violet Grassmore." She said it as if it still surprised her. "She told me afterwards that he had sticky hands and was the greatest bore she had ever met. Lavinia Wentworth went off with a young man in some sort of uniform. They became very close, but he was unsuitable, I don't recall why. Lavinia's mother took her away to Brighton or Hove or somewhere."

She swung around to face him.

"That's what you should look for! An association her mother stopped. That will be the one to pursue."

"Thank you. I suppose it is better than nothing. But there is so little time."

"Then you had better not waste any more of it," she replied, but she did not stand up. "Would you like a cup of tea, and perhaps something to eat, before you begin to search?"

"Yes," he accepted immediately. Actually, he was very hungry, and not in the least looking forward to what would almost certainly be a fruitless enquiry.

In any event, he joined Hester and Martha Jackson for cold game pie and pickle and a pot of fresh tea, and then a slice each of plum duff. They talked of several things of very general interest. Monk was acutely aware of his promise to Martha to search for her two nieces. He had not even begun, because he had no thought that it would produce anything but further sadness. But sitting at the wooden table in the housekeeper's room with the two women, both so earnest, upright, square-shouldered, a trifle thin, both trusting him, he was trapped into doing it, whatever the result. Martha Jackson was far too honest to lie to. Rathbone's case would not stretch on much longer. There was no defense, and he could not spin it out beyond another day or two. Then Monk could begin to look for the girls.

He smiled at Martha across the table, his conscience eased.

Out of the corner of his eye he saw Hester's lips curve upward. She had read his expression and knew exactly what it meant. He grunted and took more plum duff. If it proved too difficult, or if he found the answer and it was too harrowing, then he would not tell her. What good would it do for her to know if they had died alone, ill, unwanted? Better it remain a mystery, and leave her with her imagination and her hope.

He would not tell Hester either. She was no good at concealing anything.

He had another cup of tea, then thanked them and took his leave. He had perhaps two more days in which to find something useful about Zillah Lambert. Then Rathbone would have to concede defeat. There was nothing more Monk could do to help him. After that he would begin seriously to look for the two deformed children of Samuel Jackson.

At first he had not known where to begin with Zillah. Considering the time he had left, the whole idea was ludicrous. Then he remembered Mr. Burnham's account of Barton Lambert and the aristocrat who had wanted to build the hall and dedicate it to Prince Albert. Apparently, milord's son was enamored of Zillah, and at least for a while, she of him. If such a slip in discretion had ever taken place, this could be it.

It was not so easy to find records of the proposed building, nor of the collapse of the idea; perhaps its ignominy was the reason. He was several times rebuffed, and when he finally learned what he needed to know, he was perfectly sure he had spoken to sufficiently many people that word of his enquiries would be bound to leak back to Lambert himself. He would certainly know the reason for it, and what Monk hoped to find.

What he did find was rumor, gossip, and a little fact. Zillah had certainly flaunted her beauty, encouraged by Delphine, who seemed to get as much pleasure from it vicariously as did Zillah herself. She enjoyed all the usual pastimes: dancing, riding in carriages, swapping tales with other girls, and inventing stories, listening to music, walking, or rather parading, in the park. But she was a trifle more self-conscious than others and never lost her awareness of exactly how to dress to flatter her looks. She was never careless or ill groomed; her glorious hair was always beautifully done or undone. She watched scrupulously what she ate. Perhaps that was the sternest test of vanity. She did not ever allow herself to indulge in sweets or chocolates, rich pastries or cream cakes. If her mother guided her, it was so discreet it remained unobserved.

Yes, she had certainly flirted outrageously with Lord Tainbridge's eldest son. It had very possibly gone beyond what could be regarded as innocent, although if it had been sufficient to sacrifice her virtue, no one was prepared to say.

Monk could only wonder. It might well have been. Young blood is hot, and passion and curiosity are potent forces. Perhaps Zillah was not the virgin she claimed. He could not find himself regarding that prospect with horror, only a sadness that the thought, the idea, should be enough to bring this public ruin on both herself and Melville. After all, it was a purely private matter . . . if, indeed, it was a matter at all.

He left at last to go to Rathbone's rooms and admit that he had nothing certain, only innuendo which might and might not be a weapon if used sufficiently skillfully. He turned over in his mind the subjects of marriage and beauty, and the set of values by which it seemed society judged a woman and led her to judge herself. If a girl was pretty and at least reasonably agreeable, unless some appalling scandal attached to her, she was certain of finding a husband. The prettier she was, the wider her choice, until it came to the aristocracy, where only a ravishing beauty could hope to overcome the barrier of poverty or ignominious family background.

So much depended on appearance. Why? One might suppose man was a creature with only one sense, that of sight. Did one acquire a wife merely to look at? Certainly good looks were most pleasing, a clear complexion, lovely hair, fine eyes. Actually, a beautiful mouth was the feature that most woke Monk's hungers—and his dreams.

But why? Did one imagine that the curve of a cheek or an eyelid actually had meaning? Did a lovely face always indicate a lovely character?

That was idiotic! Any man who still possessed the wits he was born with knew better than that.

In his mind—yes. But in his heart?

What of humor or courage, loyalty, gentleness, and for heaven's sake, intelligence?

He pushed his hands into his pockets and strode across the busy street between hansoms, drays, a wagon piled with carpets, and a coal cart, and stepped smartly up onto the curb at the far side. Unconsciously, he increased his pace.

Hester had all the latter qualities. And yet when he had become enchanted by a woman in these last years that he could remember—and according to the evidence, before that as well—they had been lovely women with beautiful, vulnerable faces who looked as if they were gentle, pliable, as if they needed him and would lean on his strength: utterly feminine women who complemented his masculinity.

He did not like the picture of himself which that painted.

And yet how many other men were the same? Offered a charming figure that suggested passion concealed but waiting, a pretty face that seemed innocent, agreeable, easily pleased, not too critical or too challenging, and one was immediately attracted, seeing behind all this a perfect companion.

No wonder girls like Zillah Lambert strove to fulfil that ideal. It was their prospect to social acceptability and financial security: a wedding ring; their own household; children; a change from dependence upon parents to dependence upon a husband who, with judicious management, might be persuaded to love her, cater to her, even indulge her.

He reached Rathbone's rooms and the manservant let him in.

Rathbone was standing beside the last of the fire, considering retiring for the night. He looked tired and unhappy. His face lightened momentarily with hope when Monk came in, then he saw his eyes and the light in him vanished.

"I'm sorry," Monk said sincerely. He hated this. He had wanted very much to be able to bring good news, not only for his own vanity but for Rathbone's sake, and if he were truthful, for Melville's also. The man who had created so much original and dynamic beauty of form should not be brought down by something so terribly unnecessary.

"Nothing?" Rathbone asked.

"She may have had what amounted to an affair with Lord Tainbridge's son, but there's no proof, only speculation. You could try threatening to suggest it in public, but I doubt you'd do anything but alienate the jury, and Sacheverall ought to know that."

Rathbone stood by the fire, staring into the flames. "I don't think there's any point. Melville is ruined. You haven't read the newspapers, have you?" This was more a statement than a question.

"No. Why?" Monk's heart sank. He did not know why it should matter so much, but it left him suddenly quite cold. "Why?" he repeated, moving closer to the fire himself.

Without looking up at him, Rathbone told him about Isaac Wolff and Sacheverall's evidence regarding him.

Monk heard him out in silence. He should not have been surprised. In fact, he should have found it himself. He should have looked harder at Melville. If he had found it, then he could have warned Rathbone so he would have made Melville withdraw.

"I'm sorry," he apologized. "I was looking for women. I never thought of that. I should have."

Rathbone shrugged. "So should I." He looked around and smiled. "We didn't do very well, did we?"

They stood together watching the fire die for several moments, until the manservant came to the door again. He opened it and stood in the entrance, his face white, his eyes wide and dark.

"Sir Oliver." His voice shook a little. "I am afraid, sir, you have just received a message . . . sir . . ."

"Yes?"

Monk clenched his fists and felt his body chill.

"I'm sorry, sir," the manservant went on, now in little more than a whisper. "But Mr. Melville has been found dead."

Rathbone stared at him.

"I'm sorry, Sir Oliver. I am afraid there is no doubt."

Rathbone closed his eyes and looked for a moment as if he were about to faint.

Monk took a step towards him.

Rathbone put his hands up and waved him back. He rubbed his eyes. "Thank you for telling me. That will be all."

"Yes sir." The man withdrew discreetly.

Rathbone turned to Monk, his face devoid of any shred of color, his eyes hollow with grief and guilt.

CHAPTER EIGHT

Rathbone entered court on Monday exhausted from one of the most deeply miserable nights he could remember. He and Monk had gone immediately to Melville's lodgings, where Isaac Wolff, gray-faced, had met them at the door. There had been nothing anyone could do to help. He had called a doctor, who had assumed death to have been caused by some form of poison and had guessed belladonna, but it would require a full postmortem examination to be certain.

No one mentioned suicide, but it hung unspoken like a darkness over them all. One does not take belladonna by accident, and Wolff was too naked in his grief to make any pretense at lying. Melville had had excellent health, better than most people's. He took no medication of any sort.

Naturally the police had been called. There must be certainty. Even this could not be allowed to pass in private. Suicide was a crime.

Now there was nothing left but loss, not only personal but of one of the greatest, most luminous creative minds of the age. For Rathbone there was also shame for his own failure to have prevented this, a weighing down of guilt, and the last legal formalities of closing the issue. And there was also a colossal rage. He was clenched up inside with it. As he strode up the steps and along the hallway of the courthouse, he scarcely saw the colleagues he passed, the clerks and ushers, the litigants. His feet were loud and sharp on the stone of the floor, his back rigidly straight, his fingernails dug into the palms of his hands.

He entered the courtroom just as they were beginning to consider him overdue, and there was a buzz of attention and disapproval. Sacheverall swung around, his fair face with its protruding ears serenely triumphant. He did not even consider it a possibility that Rathbone had found a weapon against him. A part of Rathbone's anger turned to hatred, an emotion he was very unused to. He noticed Sacheverall smile at Zillah and her uncertain look back at him. There was no question that Sacheverall was pursuing her himself. There was no mistaking the nature of his interest, the eagerness in his eyes, the energy, almost excitement, when he spoke her name or had even the slightest contact with her.

He was moving too quickly, not perhaps for Delphine, but certainly for Zillah herself. There was something indecent in it. Zillah was a charming girl, but the first thought that came to Rathbone's mind was Barton Lambert's money. Perhaps that was unjust, but he was too raw to care.

Sacheverall faced Rathbone and nodded, his eyes bright. If he read anything in Rathbone's expression, he must have assumed it was defeat. He showed no sign of apprehension.

"I apologize, my lord, if I have kept the court waiting," Rathbone said swiftly to the judge. "I was detained by circumstances beyond my control."

Sacheverall let out a slight sound, no more than an audible sigh, but the disbelief in it was obvious.

McKeever caught some sense of Rathbone's emotion.

"What circumstances were those, Sir Oliver?" he asked.

"I regret profoundly, my lord, but my client is dead."

There was an instant's utter silence. No one moved, not even a creak of wood or rustle of fabric. Then suddenly there was uproar. A woman shrieked. Several people rose to their feet, although there was nowhere to go. The jurors looked to each other, eyes wide with shock, unable yet to grasp the full significance of what they had heard.

"Silence!" McKeever said distinctly, looking around the room, then frowning at Rathbone. "I will have order! Sir Oliver, will you please explain to us what happened? Did Mr. Melville meet with an accident?"

"It is not yet possible to say, my lord." Rathbone found it difficult to find the right words, although he had tried to formulate them all the way there. Now, standing in the long-familiar room in which he had fought numberless cases, he was lost to express what he felt.

Press reporters had been expecting a quiet collapse of the struggle and were there only to learn the damages, and perhaps to watch the human ruin as a man's personal life was torn apart. Now they were scrambling for pencils to write something entirely different.

In the gallery a woman gave a little squeal and stifled it with her hand.

"Mr. Melville was found dead last night," Rathbone began again. "At present the cause is not known."

The buzz in the gallery rose.

"Silence!" McKeever ordered sharply, his face darkening with anger. He reached for his gavel and banged it with a loud crack. "I will clear the court if there is not silence and a decent respect!"

He was obeyed reluctantly, but within seconds.

Rathbone looked across at Sacheverall, waiting to see how he would react, if he was as horrified by his own part in this as Rathbone was. Rathbone saw surprise, but not amazement. He thought in a flash that the possibility had occurred to him. If the prosecutor was distressed or ashamed, he hid it well.

Barton Lambert, on the other hand, sitting behind him, looked devastated. His blunt, rather ordinary face was slack with horror, mouth open, eyes staring fixedly. He seemed almost unaware of anyone around him, of Delphine at his side looking embarrassed, caught by surprise, but not grieved beyond her ability to control with dignity. Her head was high, her lips firmly closed, her gaze resolutely forward. She would not satisfy the curious in the gallery by meeting their looks.

Zillah, on her father's other side, had slumped forward and

buried her face in her hands, her hat askew and her bright hair shining in the sunlight from the windows. Her shoulders were hunched and she shook, not yet with weeping but with the deep shuddering movement of horror and disbelief. She seemed hardly able to catch her breath. Her father was still too deeply stunned and overwhelmed by his own emotions to help her, to offer any kind of comfort.

Sacheverall, who so often had his attention upon her, now stood up and went from his table around to stand beside her. He spoke to her, leaning close and putting his hand on her shoulder. He repeated whatever it was he had said, and she sat up slowly, her face ashen, her eyes hollow, burning with tears.

"Go away!" she said quite clearly.

"My dear!" Sacheverall began urgently.

"If you touch me again I shall strike you!" she hissed, and indeed if he had looked at her face at all he must have known she truly meant it.

Delphine leaned across, looking at Sacheverall rather than Zillah.

"I am sure you mean only kindness, Mr. Sacheverall," she said with a smile, but without warmth, "but I think perhaps you had better allow us a short while to overcome our dismay. It has been a very dreadful time for all of us, but most especially Zillah. Please make allowances for her. . . ."

Sacheverall did not withdraw his hand. "Of course," he said with a nod. "Of course it has. I do understand."

"You understand nothing!" Zillah snapped, glaring at him. "You are a—a condottiere!"

"A what?" He was momentarily at a loss.

"A soldier of fortune," she replied witheringly. "A man hired to fight for any cause, literally 'one under contract.' And if you do not take your hand off my arm I shall scream. Do you wish that?"

He removed his hand quickly. "You are hysterical," he said soothingly. "It has all been a great shock to you."

"Yes, I am!" she agreed, to his surprise. "I have never felt worse in my life. I don't think there is anything terrible still left to happen, except your manner towards me."

"Zillah!" Delphine interrupted sharply, then smiled up at Sacheverall. "I think you had better be advised to leave us a little while, a day or two. For all your sympathy, I don't think you do understand quite how fearful this has been to one of innocence in the more . . . elemental feelings of men. It is enough to make anyone . . . a trifle off balance. Please do not take to heart anything that is said just now. Make a little allowance. . . ."

"Of course," he said, smiling back at her. "Of course." He inclined his head towards Zillah and returned to his table.

Zillah hissed something to her mother. It was inaudible from where Rathbone stood, but gauging from the slow flush of Sacheverall's cheeks, he heard at least its tone, if not its content.

McKeever looked at Rathbone expectantly.

"I assume we may have the tragic news from some witness, Sir Oliver? And no doubt we shall have expert witnesses as well? There has been a doctor in attendance?"

"Yes, my lord. I have taken the liberty of requesting the presence of both the doctor and Mr. Isaac Wolff, who found Mr. Melville."

"Thank you. That was most appropriate. It will save the court's time in adjourning in order to send for them." He hesitated, took a deep breath. "Sir Oliver, I would like to express the court's deep sorrow that events have transpired this way. Killian Melville was a brilliant man, and his art was an adornment to our society and all those generations that lie ahead of us. His loss is a tragedy." He did not refer to the case or its outcome. The omission was intentional and marked. Several of the jurors nodded agreement.

"Thank you, my lord," Rathbone said with a rush of emotion which took him by surprise, making his voice hoarse.

Somewhere in the gallery a man blew his nose rather loudly and a woman stifled a sob.

"Call Mr. Wolff," McKeever directed.

Part of Rathbone was sorry to have to put Wolff through this ordeal. The man had had hardly any sleep; he had lost probably the person he loved most to a sudden and profoundly tragic death, almost certainly suicide in despair at the shattering loss of his private life and of his career. Wolff himself might easily lose his professional standing also, his livelihood, even his liberty, if Sacheverall were vindictive enough to lay a complaint. He was haggard with a grief nothing would mend.

And yet the deep burning rage within Rathbone wanted this court, which had accomplished all this, to see what they had done. Especially he wanted Lambert to see. Sacheverall might never feel any regret or shame, but if others saw, then possibly his reputation would sour, and Rathbone desired that with a hunger he could all but taste.

Isaac Wolff came in like a man in a nightmare. His dark eyes were so far sunken into his head he looked cadaverous. He walked across the floor and up the steps to the witness-box like an old man, although he was barely forty. He looked towards Rathbone without seeing him.

The court waited in complete silence. They felt his grief and it held them in awe. It was like an animal thing, raw in the air.

Rathbone had already told him of his own feelings. There was no need to repeat any formal sympathy now, and he did not wish to break the tension by such civilities.

"Mr. Wolff, will you please tell us of the events late yesterday evening which bring you here today," he asked.

Wolff spoke briefly, almost abruptly, except that his voice held no expression, no variation in tone.

"I went to see Melville. I knew he would be distressed after the day in court." It was a simple statement without adjectives, even without expression. It had the starkness of real and final tragedy. He was looking at Rathbone now. Perhaps he knew that Rathbone at least understood the magnitude of his emotion. "I rang the bell of his rooms. There was no answer. I have a key. I let myself in. He was in the sitting room, in the chair by the fire, but the ashes had burned right down. It was obviously three or four hours since it had been stoked. He looked as if he might have been asleep. At first I hoped he was. Then I touched him and I knew. He was cold." He said nothing further.

"What time was that, Mr. Wolff?" Rathbone asked.

There was still silence in the room. Everyone was staring at Wolff. There was a sea of faces, a pale blur as every person's attention was on him.

"Between half past ten and eleven," Wolff replied. There was complete calm about him. Whatever they thought of him would not hurt him now. The worst he could conceive had already happened.

"Did you see anything to give you cause to know or guess the manner of his death?" Rathbone pursued, although he knew the answer.

"No." Just the single word.

"Was anything disturbed?"

"No. Everything was as always."

"Was there a glass or cup in the room, near where he was sitting?"

"No."

"Was there a note or a letter of any kind?"

"No."

"Thank you, Mr. Wolff. If you will remain there, His Lordship may have some questions for you."

Wolff turned slowly towards the judge.

"No, thank you," McKeever declined quietly. "It seems perfectly clear. I am sorry we had to trouble you, Mr. Wolff. The court extends you its sympathy."

At another time there might have been a shadow of humor in Wolff's acceptance. Today there was none. Something inside him was dead and there was no response except words, bare of feeling.

"Thank you." He turned and stepped down, holding on to the banister as if his sight and his coordination were impaired. He made his way to one of the seats at the back of the gallery and someone rose to give him space. Rathbone watched with his heart beating violently in case it were to shun him, but there was so deep a look of pity on the man's face his gesture could not have been misunderstood. Rathbone was suddenly uplifted by such compassion from a stranger, such a lack of judgment of frailty, only the awareness of grief.

He looked at Barton Lambert again. Lambert was shifting uncomfortably in his seat, as if he wanted to take some physical action but could think of nothing which answered his needs. There was a profound unhappiness in every line of him. He turned to Delphine, but she was looking the other way, her chin high, making the best of having to be there in these circumstances, but still aware of being the victor. Nothing so far had taken that from her. Zillah's reputation was vindicated, and that mattered to her above all else.

Zillah herself sat white-faced and quite still, her eyes on Isaac Wolff and then on the judge, although it was impossible to say if she could actually see either of them, she appeared so sunk in her own sense of loss.

"Sir Oliver!" McKeever recalled his attention.

"My lord?"

"Did you say you had also requested the doctor to attend?"

"Yes, my lord."

"Then would you call him."

"Yes, my lord. Dr. Godwin."

There was instant rustling and creaking in the gallery as a score of people craned around to watch as the doors opened.

Godwin proved to be a sturdy man with dark hair and the music of the Welsh valleys in his voice. In total silence from the crowd and from the jury, he swore to his name and professional status, then awaited Rathbone's questions.

"Dr. Godwin, were you summoned to Great Street at about eleven o'clock yesterday evening?"

"I was."

"By whom, and for what purpose?"

"By Mr. Isaac Wolff, to attend his friend Killian Melville, who had apparently died."

"And when you examined Mr. Melville, was he indeed dead?"

"Yes sir, he was—at least . . . at that point I made only a cursory examination. Very cursory."

There was absolute silence in the room.

Everyone was unnaturally still, as if waiting for something extraordinary without knowing what.

McKeever leaned forward, listening intently, frowning as if he did not completely understand.

"Your choice of words is curious," Rathbone pointed out. "Are you suggesting that later examination proved that Mr. Melville was not actually dead?" He asked it only to clarify. He entertained no hope of error.

"Oh no. Killian Melville was dead, I am afraid, poor soul," Godwin assured him, nodding and pursing his lips.

"Can you say from what cause, Dr. Godwin?"

"Not yet, not for certain, like. But it was poison of some sort, and very probably of the type of belladonna. See it in the eyes. But I'll know for sure when I've tested the contents of the stomach. Not been time for that yet."

"Thank you. I have nothing else to ask you at this point."

"No—no, I daresay not." Godwin stood quite still. "But I can tell you something I imagine you did not know."

The room seemed to crackle as if there were thunder in the air.

"Yes?"

"Killian Melville was a woman."

No one moved.

A reporter broke a pencil in half and it sounded like gunfire.

A woman screamed.

"I—I beg your pardon," Rathbone said, swallowing and choking.

"Killian Melville was a woman," Godwin repeated clearly.

"You mean he was—" McKeever was startled.

"No, my lord," Godwin corrected. "I mean she was . . . in every way a perfectly normal woman."

Zillah Lambert slid into a faint.

There were gasps around the gallery. One of the jurors used an expletive he would not have wished to have owned he even knew.

Delphine Lambert gave a scream and jerked her hand up to her mouth. Slowly her face turned scarlet with embarrassment and rage. She stared fixedly ahead of her, refusing to risk meeting anyone else's eyes. She had been completely confounded. It was obvious to anyone who looked at her. Perhaps that, more than anything else, annoyed her now. The shock was total.

No one seemed to have noticed Zillah as she slumped momentarily insensible.

Sacheverall at last reacted. He scrambled to his feet, his arms waving.

"Hardly normal, my lord! Dr. Godwin makes a mockery of the word. Killian Melville was in no way normal. Man or woman."

"I meant medically speaking!" Godwin snapped with surprising ferocity. "Physically she was exactly like any other woman."

"Then why did she dress like a man?" Sacheverall shouted, waving his arms, "behave like a man, and in every way affect to be a man? For God's sake, she even proposed marriage to a woman!"

"No, she didn't!" Rathbone was on his feet too, shouting back. "That is precisely my case! She didn't! Mrs. Lambert was so keen to have her daughter make what seemed an excellent match that she assumed Melville's affection and regard for Miss Lambert was romantic, whereas it was, in fact, exactly what Melville claimed it was: a profound friendship!" He spoke without having thought of it first, something he had sworn never to do in court, but even as he heard his voice he was certain it was the truth. Now, with the clarity of hindsight, it all seemed so apparent. Melville's passion and his silence—her silence—were all so easily understood. Of course he—she—had laughed when Rathbone had asked if the relationship with Isaac Wolff was homosexual. He remembered now how oblique Melville's answers had been. He remembered a score of things, tiny things, the burning level eyes, the fairness of Melville's skin, the small, strong hands, a lack of masculinity in movement and gesture. The husky voice could have been man's or woman's.

He thought ruefully that that must have cost an effort, an aching throat to keep the pitch permanently so unnaturally low.

She must have enjoyed Zillah's company, one of her own sex to befriend. No wonder the relationship was peculiarly precious to her.

Sacheverall was furious, but for once he had no ready answer.

"She was still unnatural!" he said loudly and angrily. His face was red, and he jerked around in gestures too large to have dignity or meaning. He had lost control of the case. Nothing was as he had meant it to be. When he had come in that morning he had had victory in the grasp of his fingers. Now it had all exploded into tragedy and then absurdity.

"She was perverted, perhaps insane—"

"She was not—" Rathbone began angrily, but Sacheverall cut across him.

"She took advantage of Mr. Lambert's generosity for the most obvious reasons, to advance her career, if you can call it that!" He jabbed his finger in the air; his voice was almost a shriek. "She deceived him, lied to him at every turn—then deceived Miss Lambert and abused her feelings for the same crass, greedy reasons, and . . ."

Zillah was recovered now, sitting motionless, the tears streaming down her cheeks, although her face did not twist or crumple. She had the curious gift of being able to weep and remain beautiful.

Barton Lambert rose to his feet.

"Be quiet!" he commanded so loudly that Sacheverall stopped in the middle of his sentence, his face slack with surprise. "He dressed as a man, in that he did deceive me," Lambert went on, lowering his voice only slightly. "I never for an instant suspected he was not one. But I was not deceived in his . . ." He corrected himself: "Her skill. He was still one of the finest architects in Europe, and I'll swear you'll not see a better one in your lifetime!"

Sacheverall burst into laughter, derisive, jeering, an ugly sound. McKeever slammed his gavel down like a gunshot.

"Mr. Sacheverall!" All his passionate distaste of the man was in his face. "Control yourself, sir! This is not a humorous matter!"

Sacheverall stopped laughing instantly.

"It is not, my lord! It is disgusting!" His wide mouth curled exaggeratedly. He still waved his arms as he spoke. "Every decent person in this room must be as confused and offended as I am by this unnatural creature, perverse, deceitful and an insult to all decent women who honor their gender by living up to the highest standards of modesty, decency and—and—are proud to be women!" His gesture embraced the gallery. "Who would not for an instant, a fraction of an instant, deny their womanhood with its sacred duties and blessings, or choose to be different!" He flung his arms out again and turned to face them. "What woman among you is not proud to be wife and mother? Do you want to dress in trousers and pretend to be a man? Do you want to deny who you are, what you are, and spit in the face of the God who made you and ordained you to this—this holy calling?"

"For heaven's sake, sit down!" It was Zillah who hissed at him, glaring through eyes still filled with tears.

He leaned forward, staring at her intently. "My dear Zillah." He lowered his voice until it was tender, almost intimate. "I can hardly imagine the suffering you must be enduring. You have been most cruelly abused. You are the victim in all this insanity, this twisted and terrible masquerade." He moved one hand as if to touch her, then changed his mind. "I cannot say how much I admire your courage and your dignity throughout this ordeal," he went on softly but quite clearly, his eyes intent on hers. "Your refusal to indulge in anger is truly the mark of a most beautiful character. You have a nobility which must awaken a sense of wonder in all of us, a reverence . . ."

"Mr. Sacheverall," she replied coldly, and moving back an inch. "I have lost a dear friend today, in the most terrible circumstances, and I do not care what you think of me, nor do I care for your sympathy. Please do not keep thrusting your opinions upon me. I am sure the court does not care either."

He was startled. It was the last thing he had expected to hear. However, he took it with good grace, determined it was due to her distress and perhaps natural.

"I did not mean to embarrass you," he apologized, turning back to the front of the court. "My emotions made me speak too soon." Before she could answer that, he looked to Rathbone. "I shall consult with my client, of course," he said with a chill. "But I think Mrs. Lambert will feel that her daughter's character has been vindicated in every way with today's revelations. No possible fault can attach to her in anyone's mind. The matter of cost will be dealt with from Mr.—Miss Melville's estate. I imagine that rests with her solicitor."

Barton Lambert jerked forward as if to speak, and Delphine pulled him back again sharply.

McKeever glared around the room and it fell silent.

"I should like to hear more fully what drove Miss Melville to this extraordinary step. And I think we should give Mr. Isaac Wolff the opportunity to clear his name and the question of his own reputation. I call him to testify."

There was a moment's silence, then the usher gathered his wits and called rather loudly for Isaac Wolff.

It took only a few moments for Wolff to come from the back of the court. He stumbled as he climbed the steps up to the witness stand again.

"Mr. Wolff," McKeever said in his soft voice. There was absolute silence in the room. No one in the gallery fidgeted or whispered. The jurors sat with eyes fixed on Wolff, their faces stiff with pity and embarrassment. Neither Rathbone nor Sacheverall stirred. Everyone strained to catch McKeever's words.

"Mr. Wolff, I am sorry to call you again when you must be feeling your bereavement most deeply," he said. "But I feel you are perhaps the only one able to offer us a proper explanation. Why did

Killian Melville spend her life dressed as a man and to all outward purposes living the life of a man? Before you answer"—he smiled very slightly; it was an inner necessity which drove him, an emotion he could not stifle, and certainly one devoid of any shred of humor—"I offer you the court's unqualified apology for its accusation of sexual vice, or any kind of crime on your part or, of course, upon Miss Melville's."

A shadow of very bitter humor flashed in Wolff's eyes but did not touch his lips.

"Thank you, my lord." His voice was too flat to carry gratitude. He did not look at anyone in particular as he summoned the words to answer. His gaze seemed to be over the heads of the gallery, but his vision inward, into memory. "Actually, her name was Keelin. Her mother was half Irish. She simply changed the spelling a little to sound more masculine."

The court waited.

He took a few moments to master his composure. "She was brilliant," he began quietly, but his voice was raw. "Even as a child she was fascinated by beautiful buildings of all sorts. Her father was a keen scholar and the family spent much time in the Mediterranean—Italy, Greece, Egypt, Palestine. Keelin would walk for hours among the ruins of the greatest cities on earth. She has sketches of the Roman Forum, the Baths of Caracalla, the Colosseum, of course. And in the rest of Italy of the great triumphs of the Renaissance, the exquisite simplicity of the Tuscan villas, of Alberti, of Michelangelo's domes and basilicas."

Everyone in the room was listening with eyes intent upon Wolff's face. Rathbone looked at them discreetly. Their faces were filled with emotion as their imaginations journeyed with him, dreaming, thinking.

"But she loved the eastern architecture also," Wolff went on. "She admired the mosques of Turkey, the coolness and the light. She was fascinated with the dome of the Blue Mosque and how the ventilation was so superb the smoke from the candles never made a mark on the ceiling." A shadow of memory softened the harshness of his grief for a moment. "She talked about it endlessly. I don't think she was even aware of whether I was listening or not."

No one moved or made the slightest sound of interruption. McKeever's face was intent.

"And when her father went to Egypt"—Wolff was absorbed in memory—"she went as well. It was a whole new dimension of architecture, more ancient than anything else she had even imagined. She stood in the ruins of Karnak as if she had seen a revelation. Even the light was different. I remember her saying that so often. She always built for light—" He stopped abruptly as emotions overwhelmed him. He stood with his head high but his face averted. He was not ashamed, but it should have been a private thing.

McKeever looked around the room slowly, bidding them await Wolff's ability to begin again without further losing his composure.

Rathbone glanced at Barton Lambert. He seemed like a man in a dream, his eyes almost glazed, his expression hovering between pity and incomprehension. Beside him, Delphine seemed touched with something which could even have been fear, or perhaps it was only the light and shadow distorting her anger. Undoubtably she was still furious.

"Would you like the usher to fetch you a glass of water?" McKeever offered Wolff, then, without waiting for his reply, nodded to the usher to do so.

"No . . . thank you, my lord." Wolff collected himself. He breathed in deeply. "Keelin was always drawing, but she had no interest in being an artist, though naturally it was what her father suggested. She drew only to catch the structures, to see on paper the finished work. She had no interest in drawing for its own sake. She would design her own buildings, not simply record other people's, no matter how marvelous they were. She was a creator, not a copier."

A bitter smile touched his mouth. "But of course no school of architecture was going to accept a female pupil for any serious study. But she wouldn't be thwarted. She found an architectural student who was attracted to her and borrowed his books and papers, asked him about the lectures he attended." A wry expression passed fleetingly across his face, an unreadable mixture of irony, tenderness and pain. "Eventually she took a job as an assistant to a professor, clearing up for him, copying notes for him, all the time absorbing everything he taught the men. She did this for years, and eventually realized that even though she could have passed the examinations she would still never be taken seriously as an architect, never given work as long as she was a woman. She had beautiful hair, soft, shining brown and gold. She cut it off. . . ." In the gallery a woman gasped and closed her eyes, her hands clenched. Her imagination of the cost of it clear in her face.

One of the jurors shook his head slowly and blinked away tears. Perhaps his own wife or daughter had hair he loved.

"She passed herself off as a boy," Wolff said, his voice catching for the first time. "Just to attend a particular lecture of a visiting professor and be treated as a student, not a servant, to be able to ask questions and be addressed directly in answer." He blinked several times, and his voice dropped a tone. "It worked. People thought she was very young, but they did not question that she was a man. She came home and cried all night. Then she made her decision, and from then on she called herself Killian, and to everyone except me, she was a man."

There was a murmur around the room. Several people shifted position with a creak of whalebone, a squeak of leather, a rustle of fabric. No one spoke unless it was in a whisper so soft it was inaudible above the movement.

"It has happened to others in the past," Wolff continued. "Women have had to pose as men in order to use the talents God gave them because our prejudice would not permit them to be themselves. There are two routes open to those who will not be stifled. They can do as many Renaissance painters and composers of music did, have their work put forward, but under their brother's or their father's names . . . or else do as army surgeon Barry did here in England, and dress as a man. How she contrived that and carried it off in everyday life, I don't know. But she did. Some may have known her secret, but the authorities never learned until after her death. And she was one of the best surgeons, a pioneer in technique. Keelin spoke of her often"—he could not mask the trembling of his voice any longer—"with admiration for her courage and her brilliance, and rage that she should have had to mask her sex all her adult life, deny half of herself in order to realize the other half. If sometimes she hated us for doing this to her, I think we have deserved it."

McKeever stared at him, his mouth tightened very slightly, and he inclined his head in a fraction of a nod.

Rathbone felt brushed with guilt himself. He was part of the establishment. He remembered sharply another case of a woman who wanted to study medicine, and certainly had proved on the Crimean battlefields that she had the skills and the nerve, but had been prevented because of her sex. That too had ended in tragedy.

The jurors were uncomfortable. One elderly man blew through his mustache loudly, a curiously confused sound of anger and disgust, but his face betrayed his sense of confusion. He did not know what he thought, except that it was acutely unpleasant, and he resented it. He was there to pass judgment on others, not to be judged.

Another sat frowning heavily, seemingly troubled by his thoughts, his face filled with deep, unsettling pity.

Two more faced each other for moral support and nodded several times.

A fifth shook his head, biting his lips.

"Thank you, Mr. Wolff," McKeever said quietly. "I think you have explained the matter as far as it is possible for us. I am obliged to you. It cannot have been either easy or pleasant for you, but I believe you have done us a service, and perhaps you have dealt Keelin Melville some measure of justice, albeit too late. I have no further questions. You may step down."

As he was leaving the court, outside in the hallway, Rathbone heard footsteps hurrying behind him, and when he turned he was caught up by Barton Lambert.

"Sir Oliver!" Lambert was out of breath, and he looked profoundly agitated. He caught hold of Rathbone's arm.

"Yes, Mr. Lambert," Rathbone said coldly. He did not dislike the man—in fact, he had considered him basically both honest and tolerant—but he was burning with an inner anger and confusion, and a great degree of guilt. He did not want to have to be civil to anyone, least of all someone who was part of the tragedy and might, all too understandably, be seeking some relief from his own burden. Rathbone had none to offer.

"When did—when did you know?" Lambert said earnestly, his face creased, his eyes intent. "I could never be—I . . ." He stopped. He was too patently telling the truth to be doubted.

"The same moment you did, Mr. Lambert," Rathbone replied. "Perhaps I should have guessed, rather than assume the relationship with Wolff was an immoral or illegal one. Perhaps you should have. We didn't, and it is too late now to undo our destruction of her life or recall the talent we have cut off forever."

They were both of them oblivious to others in the hallway.

"If she'd told me the truth!" Lambert protested, his hands sawing in the air. "If she'd just trusted us!"

"We would what?" Rathbone asked, raising his eyebrows.

"I . . . well, for God's sake, I wouldn't have sued her!"

Rathbone laughed with a startlingly bitter sound. "Of course you wouldn't! You would have appeared ridiculous. You would have *been* ridiculous. But if she had come to you as a woman with those new, extraordinary designs for buildings, all light and curves, would you have put up the money to build them?"

"I . . . I . . ." Lambert stopped, staring at Rathbone, his cheeks white. He was too innately honest a man to lie, even to himself, now the truth was plain. "No . . . I doubt it . . . no, no, I suppose not. I thought hard as it was. He was . . . she was . . . so revolutionary. But by God, Rathbone, they were beautiful!" he said with a sudden, fierce passion, his eyes brilliant, his face translucent, alight with will and conviction.

"They still are," Rathbone said quietly. "The art is the same. It remains within the creator if it stands or falls."

"By God, you're right!" Lambert exploded savagely. "Heaven help us all . . . what a bigoted, shortsighted, narrow, self-seeking lot we are!" He stood in the corridor with his shoulders hunched, his jaw tight, his fists clenched in front of him.

"Sometimes," Rathbone agreed. "But at least if we can see it, there is hope for us."

"There's no bloody hope for Melville! We've finished that!" Lambert spat back at him.

"I know." Rathbone did not argue his own guilt. It was academic. Lambert's greater guilt did not absolve anyone else. "Now, if you will excuse me, Mr. Lambert, I have people I desire to inform, and regrettably, other cases." He left Lambert standing staring after him and hurried towards the doors, pushing past people, ignoring them. There was no purpose to be served anymore, but he wanted to tell Monk personally rather than leave him to read it in the newspapers.

Monk was shattered by the news, although he too felt that he should at least have considered the possibility, but it had never occurred to him. He made no trite or critical comments to Rathbone, who was apparently already castigating himself too fiercely. And for once Monk felt a sharp compassion for him. He understood guilt very well; it was a familiar emotion since rediscovering himself after the accident. It is a uniquely distressing experience to see yourself only through the eyes of others, too often those you have injured in some way, to know irrefutably what you have done but not why you did it, not the mitigating circumstances, the beliefs you held at the time which made your actions seem reasonable then.

After Rathbone had gone, he took a hansom to Tavistock Square to tell Hester and—if he was interested—Gabriel Sheldon the outcome.

He was welcomed at the door by the maid, Martha Jackson, and immediately remembered the impossible job he had promised her he would do. It was not the fruitless work that he dreaded, or even the waste of time he could have spent earning very necessary money, but the fact that anything he discovered, even supposing he was able to, would be distressing. Then he would have to make the decision what to tell her and what to tell Hester, who would be less easily deceived.

"Good evening, Miss Jackson," he said with forced cheerfulness. "The case of Mr. Melville"—he did not need to explain the truth here on the doorstep; it was simpler to say "Mr."—"has concluded very tragically, and in a way we could not have guessed. I should like to tell Miss Latterly—and Lieutenant Sheldon, if he cares to know."

She looked surprisingly harassed, and less than interested herself. She stood in the doorway, hesitating as to how she should answer.

"Is something wrong, Miss Jackson?" He felt a sudden wave of apprehension and realized with surprise how much Melville's death had disturbed him. The whole story left him with a sense of loss he did not know how to dispel.

"No!" she said too firmly. She made herself smile, and it was so painful he became more worried. "No . . ." she went on. "Lieutenant Sheldon is not very well today. He had a poor night, that is all. Please come in, Mr. Monk. I shall inform Miss Latterly that you are here. I hope you won't mind if you have to wait a little while? The withdrawing room is quite warm."

"Of course not," he answered; it was the only possible thing to say. He had called uninvited. He followed her obediently into the pleasant, rather ordinary withdrawing room, and she left him to possess himself in patience.

The wait was indeed long, about half an hour, and when Hester finally arrived she too looked tired and a little flustered, her attention not wholly with him.

"Martha told me the Melville case is over," she said, coming in and closing the door behind her. She met his eyes and then saw the tragedy in them. Her expression changed. Now she was filled with apprehension and pity. "Is he ruined? Could Oliver not do anything for him? What happened? Did he change his plea?"

"I suppose so . . . in effect, yes." He found the words suddenly difficult to say. "He killed himself. Isaac Wolff found him last night."

Her face crumpled as if she had been physically hit.

"Oh, William . . . I'm so sorry!" She closed her eyes tightly. "How damnable! Why do we do that to people? If he loved another man, what business is it of ours? We'll all answer to God in one way or another. If we are not hurting each other, isn't that enough?"

"He wasn't homosexual," he said with a jerky laugh. "He committed a greater offense than that, in most people's view."

She opened her eyes. "What?" Then the tears spilled over. "What did he do? Jilt Zillah Lambert? He never accused her of anything. He was scrupulous not to. That was Oliver's problem. What did he do?"

"He deceived the world . . . man and woman," he replied. "Totally effectively. All except Isaac Wolff . . . he knew. But the rest of them were completely fooled . . . all taken in. They can't forgive that. Some of the women might be laughing, a very few, secretly, but none of the men."

"I don't know what you are talking about. You aren't making any sense."

"Killian Melville was a woman."

"What did you say?" she protested.

"You heard what I said. Keelin was her real name, and she was a woman." The anger rang through his voice. "She dressed as a man because no one would allow her even to study architecture, let alone practice it, as a woman. She fooled everyone, except Isaac Wolff, who loved her."

"How terrible!" Her face was filled with amazement and anguish.

For a moment he did not understand. Surely Hester, of all people, could not be so quick to judge automatically and cruelly. His sense of disillusion was so sharp for an instant he could think of nothing else. It was not the Hester he knew, who was so close that her loyalty and her compassion were part of the framework of his world.

Hester was not even looking at him. "It must have been there every day," she said softly. "Pulling at her both ways, until it tore her apart. She was a woman, she loved Isaac Wolff, but she could never marry him. Even by being with him she risked branding him as a criminal." She focused her gaze, meeting Monk's eyes demandingly. "Can you imagine it? Can you imagine the scenes between them? She must have been terrified for him, not knowing which way to turn. And he would have loved her enough to take love, take time together, the sharing of dreams, great things, aspirations and the wonder of thought and idea and passion." She winced as she said it, her eyes bright. "And little things that hurt, the small disappointments." Her voice cracked. "The sudden ache for no reason, the tiredness, the confusion, just the need not to be alone . . . and the jokes, the silly things that make you laugh, something beautiful, a splash of sunlight, a particular flower, a kind act, the ironies and the absurdities, the little victories which can mean so much."

Her voice shook. She took a long, slow breath. Her lips trembled. "And she couldn't! Every time she was with him put them both in danger from prying eyes, people with cruel and inquisitive minds. No wonder she sought friendship with Zillah Lambert. It was at least a moment of sharing something, to see pretty things, a woman's things, perfume, silks, gowns, all the things she couldn't afford ever to have herself. Imagine what she risked if she had ever, even once, worn a dress!"

He started to speak and then stopped.

"Why do we do that?" Suddenly she was savage, her voice thick with emotion. She stared at him as if demanding an answer. "Why do we make rules about what a person should be . . . I mean rules that don't matter? Why shouldn't a woman be an architect, or a doctor, or anything else? What are we so frightened of?" She lashed out with her arm. "And why do we make men pretend they aren't afraid or don't make mistakes, like women and children? Of course they do. We all know they do, we just cover it up or look the other way. It's much easier to admit you were wrong, and go back and do the right thing, than it is to go on adding evasion to evasion, one invention after another to conceal the last, and then you probably aren't fooling anybody, except those who want to be fooled."

He did not interrupt, knowing she needed to say it all. Anyway, he agreed with her.

She scowled at him. "Look at Gabriel and Perdita." She clenched her hands. "He's been taught to be brave, never to explain, never to ask for help. He's been given a hero's image to live up to, and he's riddled with guilt because he thinks he can't. And she's been taught to be helpless and stupid because that's what men want, and all she should do is be a sweet-natured, obedient ornament." Her face was puckered, all her muscles tight. "And she has to sit by and watch him hurt, because he thinks he should be looking after her, and he can't even look after himself."

She drew breath. "And that idiot Athol Sheldon bumbles around telling them it would all be all right if they just behaved normally and forgot the grief and pain and the horror as if it never happened and all those people never died. It's a mockery of the reality of life. It makes me so angry I could . . ."

She was at a loss for words. He could not remember ever seeing that before. He wanted to say something to show he understood and felt the same anger and loss.

He also thought, against his will and with a curious, sharp hunger, of all the things she had said about joy and not being alone, of having the opportunity to share with someone the bonds of honesty and familiarity which are the deepest of all friendships, the losing of the barriers of fear, which divide.

He reached forward and took her hands and held them in his,

quite gently, feeling after a moment her fingers respond. It was not a strong grasp, not a clinging, just a knowledge of the other's being there, a gentleness for which there were no words, perhaps even a memory of many other times when they had felt the same but had remained separate.

It was a clatter of footsteps on the stairs which disturbed them. Hester pulled away slowly, turning to the door as Perdita came in.

"Oh!" she said, seeing Monk. "Oh, I'm sorry. Hester . . . I don't know what to do. It's just impossible. I can't manage this!" She was obviously on the edge of tears, her face pink, and she was breathing rapidly. She behaved as if she had already forgotten Monk was there or simply was past caring.

Hester was on the very edge of losing her temper. Monk could see it in the rigidity of her body, especially her neck. When she spoke her voice was brittle.

"Well, if you really can't, perhaps you had better give up," she answered. "I don't know quite what that means. I suppose you do or you wouldn't have said it. Have the staff look after Gabriel, and you lead a separate life. I don't know whether you could afford it financially. Maybe Athol would help? Or if you ask him, Gabriel would release you from the marriage altogether. He offered to before. You told me that when I first came. Only then, of course, you said you wouldn't dream of it."

Perdita looked as if she had been struck in the face. Her eyes were wide and her mouth slack.

"I'm sure you could marry again," Hester went on ruthlessly, her voice getting harder and heavier. "You are very pretty—in fact, quite beautiful—and you have a very docile and agreeable nature . . . just what most men want—"

"Stop it!" Perdita shouted at her. "You mean I'm stupid and cowardly, and no use for anything but to do as I'm told! I'm fine when everything is all right. I can simper and smile and flatter people and be obedient. I can keep my place and make anyone feel comfortable . . . and superior. But when something goes wrong, and you need a woman with courage and intelligence, I just run away. I don't think of anybody but myself. How I feel . . . and what I want." Her lips were trembling, but she did not stop. She gulped and swallowed, glaring at Hester. "Then you can step in, all brave and unselfish. You know what to do, what to say. You're never afraid, never confused. Nothing ever revolts you or makes you want to run away and pretend it never happened!"

Her voice was rising high and becoming louder. The servants must have been able to hear her as far as the kitchen. "Well, I'll tell you something, Miss Perfect Nurse! Nobody wants a woman who is never wrong. You can't love somebody who doesn't need you, who's never vulnerable or frightened or makes mistakes. I may not be half as clever as you are, or as brave, or know anything about Indian history or soldiers or what it is like to see real war . . . but I know that."

Hester stood very stiff, her back like a ramrod, her shoulders clenched so tight Monk felt as if he could see the bones of them pulling against her dress. He was not certain, but he thought she was shivering. This was what she had wanted, what she had intended to happen when she had provoked Perdita . . . at least he thought it was. But that did not stop it from hurting. There was too much truth in it, and yet it was also so terribly wrong.

"You are lashing out in anger, Mrs. Sheldon," he said in a low, controlled voice. "And you don't know what you are talking about. You know nothing of Miss Latterly except what you have seen in this house. There are many kinds of men and many kinds of love. Sometimes we imagine what we must hunger for is a sweet and clinging creature who will feed our vanity and hang upon our words, dependant upon our judgment all the time." He took a breath. "And then we meet the harder realities of life, and a woman who has the courage, the fire and the intelligence to be our equal, and we discover that those joys far outweigh the irritations and discomforts." He stared at her very hard. "You must be true to the best in yourself, Mrs. Sheldon, but you have no grounds and no right to insult where you do not know the facts. Miss Latterly may not be loved widely, but she is loved very deeply indeed, more than most women can aspire to or dare to accept."

The color burned up in Perdita's cheeks. She was furious and overwhelmed with embarrassment. She did not know what to say, and the rage boiling inside her was only too apparent in her eyes.

Hester, on the other hand, stood as if frozen.

Monk could barely believe he had said what he had. His first instinct, almost taking his breath away, was to deny it, somehow qualify it all so it did not apply to him. The desire to escape was so urgent it was like a physical compulsion.

He saw Hester's back and shoulders, the dress still pulled tight, her neck muscles stiff. As clearly as if he could see her eyes, he knew she was waiting for him to deny his words, to withdraw or disclaim.

If he did, would it be because they were untrue or because he was an emotional coward?

She would not know the answer to that, but he did. What he had revealed was not untrue.

"If you offer Miss Latterly an apology, I am sure she will accept it," he said more stiffly than he intended.

Hester took a deep breath.

"Oh . . ." Perdita sighed. "Oh . . . yes. I'm sorry. I shouldn't have said that. I'm behaving very badly." Her eyes filled with tears.

Hester moved forward. "Not nearly as badly as you think. And you are at least partly right. We do love people for their vulnerabilities as well as their strengths. We must have both, even to understand each other, never mind anything more. Just keep trying. Remember how important it is." Her voice dropped. "Killian Melville is dead. It was probably suicide. Last night."

Perdita stared at her in horror, then her eyes flew to Monk's.

"Oh . . . I'm so sorry! Because of the case? Because of what he was, and because it is illegal?"

"More than that," he answered her. "Actually, Melville wasn't a man at all; her name was Keelin, and she was a woman. She dressed as a man and behaved as one in all respects, except towards Isaac Wolff, because it was the only way she would be allowed to practice her profession and use the talents God gave her." He used the word *God* without thinking about it until he had said it. Then it was too late to take it back, and perhaps it was what he meant.

Perdita did not move. Her face was filled, and changed with growing realization of what he had said, and something of what it meant. Then she shook her head, at first minutely, then a little more, then more again. Then she turned around and went to the door.

"I'm going back to Gabriel. I'll tell him. He'll be terribly sorry. It really is so—so final. It's too late to get anything back now, to . . . say anything, mend anything." And she went out quickly, hand fumbling on the knob to turn it.

Hester finally turned to look at Monk. Her eyes searched his.

He tried to think of something to say which would not be evasive, or banal, nor yet commit him to anything he would regret. His mind filled with Keelin Melville, and Zillah Lambert, and the tragic, destructive farce of beauty and the urge to be suitably married, or if that failed, to be married at all costs, anything but remain single.

"Now you are free to look for Martha's brother's children," Hester said quietly. "But don't run up a debt she cannot pay. Just do what you are able to."

"I wasn't going to charge her!" he said a little sharply. Why had she thought he would? Did she not know him better than that?

"And be careful what you tell her," she added anxiously. "It is almost certain to be very bad."

"Are you paying me?" he asked sarcastically.

"No . . ."

"Then stop giving me orders!" he retorted. He jammed his hands into his pockets. This was going to get worse if he remained. He was not saying what he wanted to, what he meant. He was raw inside with the knowledge of failure, of life and opportunity and brilliance and love wasted forever. Perhaps Hester was too, and it frightened her. "I'll tell you what I find out, if there is anything," he said aloud. "In a day or two."

"Thank you."

He went to the door and turned. He half smiled at her, then went out.

CHAPTER NINE

Monk set about the task of searching for the two children with a feeling of self-disgust for having been stupid enough to accept such a ludicrous case. His chances of learning anything provable were remote, and even if he did it would be something poor Martha Jackson would be infinitely better not knowing. But there was no escape now. It was his own fault for listening to his emotions rather than his intelligence. His fault—and Hester's.

There was only one place to begin: the last news Martha herself knew of them, which was the house where they were born and had lived until their father died. It was in Coopers Arms Lane, off Putney High Street, south of the river. It was quite a long journey, and rather than waste time in traveling back and forth he had packed a light bag and taken with him sufficient funds to stay overnight at an inn should there prove to be anything worth pursuing. He did not wish to spend any more time than necessary on this case, and to be honest, he wished it over with as soon as possible, consistent with keeping his word.

It was a very pleasant day, warm and bright, and if undertaken for any other reason, he would have enjoyed the journey. He arrived in Putney a little before half past ten and found Coopers Arms Lane without having to ask anyone for directions. The tavern after which it had taken its name looked a promising place for luncheon—and for picking up any relevant gossip.

First he would try the house itself, simply to exclude it from his investigations. After twenty-one years no one would remember anything. Probably they would not have after twenty-one weeks.

He found the right house, a modest residence of the sort usually occupied by two or three families behind its shabby, well-cared-for walls. The step was scrubbed and whitened, the pathway swept. The curtains at the front windows were clean, and even from the outside he could see where they had been carefully mended. It all spoke of ordinary, decent lives lived on the razor's edge between poverty and respectability, always aware that the future could change, illness strike with its unpayable bills, or employment vanish.

Had it been the same in Samuel Jackson's day? All the houses up and down the street looked like this one. He felt a wound of sadness as he thought how tragedy had struck, without warning and without mercy. He found he was cold, even in the sunlight, as he put out his hand to lift the knocker.

The woman who answered was not pretty in any conventional sense, but clear eyes and a gentle nature made her appealing. She spoke with a soft Irish accent.

"Yes sir? Can I help you?"

"Good morning, ma'am," he answered with more courtesy than he would have used in his days as a policeman. He had no power to demand anymore. "I am making enquiries on behalf of a friend whose brother used to live in this house twenty-one years ago. I realize it is unlikely anyone will know what became of him now. It is really his children I am concerned with. She lost touch. . . ." He saw the look of concern and disbelief in the woman's face. Twenty years was too long to account for renewed interest now without an explanation. He made himself smile again. "Her own circumstances were difficult. She had not the financial means to employ anyone to seek after them, nor the time or knowledge to do it herself."

"And she has now?" the woman said, skepticism still evident in her voice.

"No," Monk admitted. "I am doing it as a favor. She is in service in a house where a friend of mine is nursing an injured soldier."

"Oh." The answer seemed to satisfy. "Twenty-one years ago, did you say?"

"Yes. Were you in this house then?" The moment he had said it he realized it was a foolish question. She could not be much more than twenty-five herself.

She smiled and shook her head. "No sir, that I wasn't. Sure I was still at home in Ireland then, but my pa was. He worked here, and he lodged over the road with Mrs. O'Hare. He'd maybe know who was here then. Missed us all, he did, and were terrible fond o' the little ones. If you'd like to come away in, I'll ask him for you."

"Thank you Mrs. . . ."

"Mrs. Heggerty, Maureen Heggerty. Come away in, then, sir." And she backed into the passageway, pulling the door wide for him to follow. "Pa!" she called, lifting her voice. "Pa! There's a gentleman here as would like to see you."

"William Monk," he introduced himself. She turned her back to him and was awaiting her father's answer to her summons, so it seemed inopportune to offer her a card.

"Welcome, Mr. Monk. Pa! Are you fallen asleep again now? It's only half past ten in the morning."

A man of about sixty came lumbering from the back of the house, pushing a large hand through thick silver-white hair. He was dressed in shapeless trousers and a collarless shirt with its sleeves rolled up. He denied it indignantly, but obviously to Monk, he had indeed been asleep. He looked like a bear woken from winter hibernation. He blinked past his daughter at Monk standing in the passage, silhouetted against the light from the still-open front door and the sunlit street beyond.

"Sure and what is it I can be doin' for yer, sir?" he said pleasantly enough. He narrowed his eyes to focus on Monk's face and try to read something beyond his beautifully cut jacket and shining boots.

"Good morning, sir," Monk said respectfully. "Mrs. Heggerty tells me you lived in this street twenty-one years ago—in the house opposite this one?"

"Two doors along," he corrected. "On t'other side." His brow creased. "Why would that be interestin' to you?"

"I believe a Mr. Samuel Jackson lived here then," Monk explained. Mrs. Heggerty stood between them, the light on her fair hair, her hands tucked under her apron. "He had two children," Monk went on. "I am making enquiries on behalf of Mr. Jackson's sister, who is at last in a position to attempt to trace those children. Since she is their only living relative, as far as she knows, she has a care that if there is any chance whatever of finding them, she may be able to offer them some . . . some affection, if that is possible." He knew it sounded foolish even as he said it, and wished he had thought of something better.

"For sure, poor little things," the older man said with a shake of his head. "A bit late now, mind you." The criticism was only mild. He was a man who had seen much tragedy of a quiet domestic kind, and it was written in his weathered face and his bright, narrowed eyes as he regarded Monk.

"You knew them?" Monk said quickly.

"I saw them," the man corrected. "Knew them'd not be the right word. They were only tiny things."

"Would you not like a cup o' tea, Mr. Monk?" Mrs. Heggerty interrupted. "And you, Pa?"

"For sure I would." Her father nodded. "Come away to the kitchen." He beckoned to Monk. "We'll not be standing here for the neighbors to stare at. Close the door, girl!" He held out his hand. "Me name's Michael Connor."

"How do you do, sir," Monk responded, allowing Mrs. Heggerty to move behind him and close the door as instructed.

The kitchen was a small, cluttered room with a stone sink under the window, two pails of water beside it, presumably drawn from the nearest well, perhaps a dozen doors along the street, or possibly from a standpipe. A large stove was freshly blacked, and on it were five pots, two of them big enough to hold laundry, more of which hung from the rail winched up to the ceiling on a rope fastened around a cleat at the farther wall. A dresser carried enough crockery to serve a dozen people at a sitting, and in the bins below were no doubt flour, dried beans and lentils, barley, oatmeal and other household necessities. Strings of onions and shallots hung from the ceiling on the other side of the room. Two smoothing irons rested on trivets near the stove, and large earthenware pots were labeled for potash, lye, bran and vinegar.

Mrs. Heggerty pointed to one of the upright wooden chairs near the table and then moved to the stove to replace the kettle on the hob and fetch the tea caddy.

"What happened to the children, Mr. Connor?" Monk asked.

"After poor Sam died, you mean?" Connor resumed his seat in the largest and most comfortable chair. "That was all very sudden, poor devil. Right as rain one minute, dead the next. At least that's what it looked like, although you can never tell. A man doesn't talk about every pain he gets. Could've been suffering for years, I suppose." He looked thoughtfully into the middle distance, and on the stove the kettle began to sing.

Mrs. Heggerty scalded the teapot, then put the tea in it—sparingly, they had not means to waste—and added water to the brim, leaving it to steep.

"Yes, after he died. What happened?" Monk prompted.

"Well, Mrs. Jackson was left all on her own," Connor answered. "Seems she had no one else, poor little thing. Pretty creature, she was. Charming as the sunshine. Never believed those poor misshapen little things were hers. But o'course they were, sure enough. Looked like her, in her own way." He shook his head, his face sunk in sorrow and amazement. Absentmindedly he made the sign of the cross, and in a continuation of the movement accepted a cup of tea from his daughter.

Monk had already been given his. It did not look very strong, but it was fresh and piping hot. He thanked her for it and looked again at Connor.

"What happened to them?"

"Bleedin' from the stomach, it was." Connor sighed. "It happens. Seen it before. Good man, he was, always a pleasant word.

Jackson loved those two little girls more, maybe, than if they'd been perfect." Again he shook his head, his eyes welling over with sadness.

Behind him, Mrs. Heggerty's face was pinched with sorrow too, and she dabbed her eyes with the corner of her apron.

"But always anxious," Connor went on. "I suppose he knew what kind of life lay ahead for them and he was trying to think what to do for the best. Anyway, it never came to that, poor soul. Dead, he was, and them no more'n three and a year old, or thereabouts."

Mrs. Heggerty sniffed.

"What did their mother do?" Monk asked.

"She couldn't care for 'em, now could she, poor creature?" Connor shook his head. "No husband, no money anymore. Had to place 'em and go and earn her own way. Don't know what she did." He cradled his mug in his hands and sipped at it slowly. "Clever enough, and certainly pretty enough for anything, but there aren't a lot for a respectable widow to do. No people of her own, an' none of his to be seen." He stopped, staring unhappily at Monk. "You'll not find them little mites now, you know?"

Mrs. Heggerty was listening to them, her work forgotten, her face full of pity.

"Yes, I do know," Monk agreed. "But I said I would try." He sipped his tea as well. It had more flavor than he had expected.

"Well, you could try Buxton House, down the far end of the High Street," Mrs. Heggerty suggested. "She must have been at her wit's end, poor woman. I can't think of anything worse to happen to a soul than to have to give up your children, and them not right, so you'd never even be able to comfort yourself they'd be cared for by some other person as you would have done." She stood stiffly, her arms folded across her bosom as if holding some essence of her own children closer, and Monk remembered the rows of small clothes on the airing rack and the doll propped up on the stairs. Presumably the children were at lessons at this hour of the morning.

He rose to his feet. "Thank you, I will." The tea was half finished. Leaving it required some explanation. "I know it's futile. I want to get it over with as soon as possible. Thank you, Mrs. Heggerty, Mr. Connor."

"Sure you're welcome, sir," she said, moving to take him back to the door.

A couple of enquiries took him to Buxton House, a large, gaunt building which in earlier days had been a family home but now boasted nothing whatever beyond the strictly functional. A thin, angular-boned woman with her hair screwed back off her face was scrubbing the step, her arms sweeping back and forth rhythmically, her dreams elsewhere.

When he rang the bell it was answered by another woman, so fat the fabric strained at the seams of her gray dress. Her florid face was already angry even before she saw him.

"We're full up!" she said bluntly. "Try the orphanage over the river at Parsons Green." She made as if to close the door.

Looking into her bleak, blue eyes Monk had a sudden very ugly idea, born of knowledge and experience.

"I will, if you can't help me," he replied tersely. "I'm looking for girls about ten or eleven, old enough to start work and easy to train into good ways. I'm setting up house a few miles from here. I'd sooner have girls without family, so they're not always wanting days off to go home. I could try city girls, but I've no connections." He could easily have been stocking a brothel or selling girls abroad for the white slave trade, and she must know that as well as he did.

Her face altered like sunshine from a cloud. In an instant the line of her mouth softened and the ice in her eyes melted.

"I'm sorry, sir," she said smoothly. "I'm fair mithered to pieces to take poor children I 'aven't the means ter care for, though God knows I'm willin' enough. But you can't feed 'ungry mouths if you in't got no food." She straightened her skirt absentmindedly. "It'd be a fair blessin' if yer could take two or three girls, sir. Make room for two or three more wot's infants an' can't do a thing for theirselves. I've got several as is both willin' an able ter please, an' comely enough. Jus' coming inter young ladies, like." She smiled widely and knowingly at Monk. Perhaps in her youth she had been buxom enough; now she was grotesque. His knowledge of her trade made her repellent to him.

He forced himself to look interested. It was difficult to keep the disgust from his face.

"Best young," she went on. "Teach 'em your ways before they get taught wrong by someone else. Come into the parlor Mr. . . . ?"

For some reason he did not want to give his own name. He did not want any part of his true self connected with this business.

"Meachem," he answered, giving her the first surname that came into his head. "Horace Meachem." He must make sure he remembered it! "Thank you."

She opened the door wide enough to allow him in. The thin woman who had been scrubbing the step shot him a look of withering contempt. He wished he could have told her the truth, but it was a luxury beyond him.

The hallway was bare and painted gray. A stitched sampler with several mistakes proclaimed: "The eye of God is upon you." He hoped it was. Maybe there would be more justice in eternity than there was here.

He was led to a parlor decorated in red and a world away from the hall in comfort. She invited him to sit down and sat decorously opposite him, rearranging her bombazine skirts with fat, wrinkled hands. Then she reached for the bell and pulled it sharply.

"I'll have several girls brought for you," she said cheerfully. "You can take your pick. Very glad of a place, they'll be, and the price'll go towards carin' for more abandoned waifs, so we can give 'em a start in life . . . that's no more than a Christian duty."

He loathed what he was about to do. The words would barely come off his tongue.

"I'd like nice-looking girls. At least one will be a parlormaid, in time."

"O' course you would, sir," she agreed. "An' nice-lookin' is wot I'll provide. We don' send 'omely girls for that sort o' position. They goes for scullery maids an' the like, or ter wash pots or such."

"I heard you even took in disfigured girls," he said relentlessly. He wished he could take the girls she would bring. God knows what would happen to them. Perhaps the uglier ones would be better off . . . eventually.

"Oh . . . well . . ." She prevaricated, her sharp, cold eyes weighing how much he might know. He was a customer, and he looked from his clothes as if he might have money. She did not want to offend him. "I don't know 'oo told you that."

He met her gaze squarely, allowing a slightly supercilious curl to his mouth. "I made my enquiries. I don't come blind."

"Well, it's only charitable," she excused herself. "Got ter take 'em all in. Don't keep 'em, mind. If they're bad enough, put 'em in ter work in the mills or someplace like that, w'ere they won't be seen."

He looked skeptical. "Really?"

" 'Course. Wot else can I do wif 'em? Can't carry no passengers 'ere."

The bell was answered by a child of about ten, and the woman sent her off to fetch three girls she named.

"Now, Mr. Meacham," she resumed. "Let's talk money. This place don't run on fresh air. An' like you said, I gotta feed the useless ones as well as the ones wot'll find places."

"Let's see them first," he argued. He could not bear to think of the wretched children who would be paraded in front of him, like farm animals for him to bid on; he knew he could take none of them. "How long have you been here?"

"Thirty years. I know me job, Mr. Meacham, never you fear."

"That's what I heard. But I want to be sure what I'm getting. I don't want any unpleasant surprises . . . when it's too late to bring them back."

"You won't!" she said sharply, narrowing her eyes. "Wot you 'eard, then? Someone blackenin' me name?"

"I heard you took in some pretty badly deformed girls in the past . . . real freaks." He hated using the word.

"When was that, then?" she demanded. " 'Oo said that?"

"Long time ago . . . more than twenty years," he replied.

"So I did, then," she agreed reluctantly. "But it was their faces wot was twisted up. See it as quick as look at 'em, yer did. Didn't fool nobody fer an instant."

"Why did you take them?" he pressed, although he knew the answer.

" 'Cos I were paid!" she snapped. "Wot jer think? But it were all legal! An' I don't cheat no one. No one can say as I did. Sold 'em for exactly wot they was—ugly and stupid—both. I were quite plain about it."

"No one has said you weren't," he replied coldly. "So far as I am aware. I should still like to know what happened to the Jackson girls. I am acquainted with their only living relative, who might be . . . obliged . . . if they were located." He rubbed his fingers together suggestively at the word *obliged.*

"Ah . . ." She was obviously considering her possible advantage in the matter. She glanced at his polished boots, his beautiful jacket, and lastly at his face with its keen, hard lines, and judged him to be a man with a sharp eye to money and a much less discriminating one to principle—like herself. "When they was old enough ter work, I sent 'em ter the kitchens at the pub."

"Coopers Arms?" he said hopefully.

"Yeah. But they din't keep 'em. Too ugly even fer 'im. I dunno wot 'e did wi' them, but you could ask 'im."

"How long ago is that? Ten years?"

"Ten years?" she said scornfully. "Yer think I'm made o' money? Fifteen years, an' I waited even then. They was six an' eight. That's plenty old ter fetch fer yerself. I'd 'a sent 'em sooner if they 'adn't bin so daft. Thought they might grow out of it an' 'ave a better chance." She prided herself on her charity.

"Thank you." He stood up, straightening his coat.

Her face fell. "Wot abaht them girls? Yer'll not find better anyw'ere, nor at a better price!"

"I've changed my mind," he said with an icy smile. "I've decided I'd like plain girls after all. Thank you for your time."

She swore at him with a string of language he had not heard since his last visit to the slums of the Devil's Acre. He walked out of the door with a positive swagger, until he saw the girls lined up in the passage, scrubbed clean, their hair tied back, their thin faces alight with hope. Then instead he felt sick.

"I'm sorry," he apologized. "You're fine. I've just changed my mind." And he hurried away before he could think of it anymore.

It was close enough to noon that he could comfortably walk up to the Coopers Arms and order luncheon and casually make enquiries about the Jackson girls. Could it, after all, be so ridiculously easy that they were still in the immediate neighborhood? It was foolish to hope, and he was not even sure if he wanted to. It might easily bring Martha Jackson more distress. But it was not his job to foresee that and make decisions for her.

Was it?

He had knowledge she could not have. In telling her or not telling her, he was in effect making the decision.

He walked briskly in the bright sunlight up Putney High Street. It was full of people, mostly going about their business of buying or selling, haggling over prices, shouting their wares. Some were begging, as always. Some were standing and gossiping, women with heavy baskets, trailing children, men with barrows spilling out vegetables or bales of cloth, sacks of sticks or coal, bags of flour. The flower girl stood on a street corner with bunches of violets, another with matches. A one-legged soldier offered bootlaces. Two small boys swept the crossings clean of horse droppings. The wail of a rag and bone man drifted across, calling his wares. A brewer's dray lumbered by.

Newspaper boys called out the headlines. A running patterer found himself a spot, and a gathering audience, and launched into a bawdy version of Killian Melville's double life as a perverted woman who dressed as a man to deceive the world. It made Monk so angry he wanted to seize the man by the lapels and shout at him that he was a vicious, ignorant, little swine who made his living on other people's misery and that he had no idea what he was talking about. And if he did not keep his mouth shut in the affair, Monk would personally shut it for him.

He strode by with his fists clenched and his jaw so tight his teeth ached. Every muscle in him was knotted with rage at the injustice. Melville was dead. That was more tragedy than enough. This was monstrous.

Why was he walking past?

He stopped abruptly, swung around, and marched back to the patterer. He did seize him by the lapels, to his amazement, and said exactly what he had wished to, which gathered twice the previous audience and much ribald laughter. He left the man breathless with indignation and astonishment, and resumed his way feeling relieved of much immediate tension.

The Coopers Arms was a very ordinary public house, and at this time of the day, crowded with people. The smells of sawdust, ale and human sweat and dirt were pungent, and the babble of voices assailed him the moment he pushed open the doors. The barman was busy, and he had to wait several minutes before purchasing a mug of stout and ordering pork pie, pickles and boiled red cabbage.

He found himself a seat at one of the tables, deliberately joining with other people. He chose a group who looked like local small tradesmen, neat, comfortable, slightly shabby, tucking into their food with relish. They looked at him guardedly but not in an unfriendly manner. He was a stranger and might prove a diversion from their day-to-day affairs. And Monk wanted to talk.

"Good day, gentlemen," he said with a smile, taking his seat. "Thank you for your hospitality." He was referring to the fact that they had moved up to make room for him.

"Not from 'round 'ere," one of them observed.

"Other side of the river," Monk replied. "Bloomsbury way."

"Wot brings you down 'ere, then?" another asked, wiping the

back of his hand across his mouth and picking up a thick roll of bread stuffed with ham. "Sellin', are yer? Or buyin'?"

"Neither," Monk answered, sipping his stout. His meal had not yet come. Looking at the food already on the table, he was remarkably hungry. It seemed like a long day already. "Probably on a pointless errand. Did any of you know a Samuel Jackson, lived here about twenty years ago?"

The third member, who had not yet spoken, pushed his cap back on his head and looked at Monk curiously. "Yeah, I knew 'im. Decent feller, 'e were. Poor devil. Died. Din't yer know that?"

"Yes, yes, I did know. I was wondering what became of his family," Monk continued.

The man guffawed with laughter, but there was a hard edge to it and his eyes were angry. "Little late, in't yer? Why d'yer wanna know fer now? 'Oo cares after all this time?"

"His sister," Monk replied truthfully. "She cared all the time but was in no position to employ anyone to find out."

"So wot's changed?" the man said, yanking his cap forward again.

A smiling girl brought Monk his meal and he thanked her and gave her threepence for herself. The man at the table frowned. Monk was setting a precedent they would not be able to follow.

"Thank you," Monk said graciously, still looking at the girl. "Do you have scullery maids in the kitchen?"

"Yes sir, three o' them," she said willingly. Any gentleman who tipped her threepence deserved a little courtesy. And he was certainly handsome looking, in a grim sort of way. Quite appealing, really, a bit mysterious. "An' two kitchen maids, an' o' course a cook . . . sir. Was yer wantin' ter speak ter anyone?"

"Do you have a girl with a deformed mouth?"

"A wot?"

"A twisted mouth, a funny lip?"

She looked puzzled. "No sir."

"Never mind. Thank you for answering me." It was foolish to have hoped. The woman at Buxton House had said the publican had got rid of the girls. It might not even be the same publican now. It was fifteen years ago.

The girl smiled and left and Monk began his meal.

"Yer really mean it, don't yer?" one of the men said in surprise. "You'll not find 'em now, yer know? They put people like that away inter places w'ere they can't upset folk . . . they'll be cleanin' up arter folk somewhere, if they're still alive. They wasn't only ugly, yer know; they was simple as well. I saw 'em w'en they was 'ere. There's summink about 'avin' yer face twisted as bothers folk more 'n if it were yer body or yer 'ands. One of 'em looked like she were sneerin' at yer, an the other like she was barin' 'er teeth. Couldn't 'elp it, o' course, but strangers don' know that."

Monk should have kept quiet. Instead he found himself asking, "Where might they be sent to, exactly?"

The man gulped down his ale. "Exac'ly? Gawd knows! Any places as'd 'ave 'em, poor little things. Pity fer Sam. 'E loved them little girls."

There was only one more avenue Monk should try, then duty was satisfied.

"What about his widow? Do you know what happened to her?"

"Dolly Jackson? I dunno." He looked around the table. "D'you know, Ted? D'you know, Alf?"

Ted shrugged and picked up his tankard.

"She left Putney. I know that," Alf said decisively. "Went north, I 'eard. Up city way. Lookin' fer a soft billet, I shouldn't wonder. She were pretty enough ter please any man, long as she didn't 'ave them two little one's wif 'er."

"That's a downright cruel thing ter say!" Ted criticized.

Alf's face showed resignation. "It's true. Poor Sam. Turnin' over in 'is grave, I shouldn't wonder."

As Monk had foreseen, the public house had changed hands, and the present landlord, with the best will in the world to oblige, had no idea whatever what had happened to two little girls fifteen years ago, nor could he make any helpful suggestions.

Monk had acquitted his obligations, and he left with thanks.

———

The obvious course was to tell Martha Jackson that he had done what he could and further pursuance was fruitless. He would not tell her his fears, only phrase things in such a manner she would not wish to waste his time on something which could not succeed.

He arrived in Tavistock Square early in the afternoon and was admitted by Martha herself. The moment she recognized him, her face filled with eagerness, hope that he had come for her battling with fear that it was only to see Hester again and dread that he had something discouraging to tell her after all.

He wished he could free himself from caring about it. It was just another case—and one which he had known from the beginning could only end this way, or worse. And yet the feeling was sharp inside him, not only for Hester but for Martha herself, and above all for Sam Jackson's children.

"I'm sorry, Miss Jackson," he said quickly. He should not keep her in even a moment's false hope. "I traced them as far as working in a public house kitchen in Putney, the Coopers Arms. But after that no one knows where they went, except it was to another job. They weren't abandoned." They might very well have been abandoned, but there was nothing to be served by telling her that.

The stiffness relaxed out of her body and her shoulders drooped. She blinked, for an instant fighting tears. Only then did he realize how much she had truly hoped, in spite of all his warnings. He felt painfully helpless. He tried to think of anything to say or do to ease her distress, and there was nothing.

She gulped once and swallowed.

"Thank you, Mr. Monk. It was very good of you to try for me." She blinked several times more, then turned away, her voice thick with unreleased weeping. "I'm sure you'd like to see Miss Latterly. Please . . ." She did not finish, but led him wordlessly across the hall and up the stairs towards the sitting room which she and Hester shared. She opened the door and stood back for him to enter, retreating immediately.

Hester put down her book. He noticed it was on Indian history. She stood up, coming towards him, searching his face.

"You couldn't find them," she said softly. It was not a question, but her eyes were full of disappointment she could not hide.

He hated having let her down, even though she had never expected the impossible. He realized with a jolt how much her feelings mattered to him, and he resented it. It made him dependent upon her and hideously vulnerable. That was something he had tried all his life to avoid. It had not even happened in a way he could have foreseen and over which he had control. It should have been some gentlewoman in love with him, over whom he could exercise a decent influence and whose effect upon him he could control.

"Of course I couldn't find them!" he said sharply. "I told you that in the beginning. I tried hard, I questioned everyone who had anything to do with it, but there was never any reasonable chance of success. Dammit, it was twenty years ago. What did you expect?" He took a breath, looking at the pain in her eyes. "You were irresponsible leading Martha to hope," he went on.

"I didn't!" she retorted with a sudden flare of temper. "I always said there was very little chance. She can't help hoping. Wouldn't you? No—perhaps you wouldn't. Sometimes I think you don't understand ordinary feelings at all. You haven't got any." She turned away, her body rigid.

It was so untrue it was monstrous. As usual, she was being utterly unjust. He was about to say so when there was a heavy footstep in the corridor outside. A moment later, after the merest hesitation, the door opened and Athol Sheldon stood in the threshold. He was dressed in a smart checked jacket of a Norfolk style and his face was pink with fresh air and exertion. Apparently he had just arrived. As usual, he was oblivious of the emotions of those he had interrupted.

"Good afternoon, Miss Latterly. How are you this delightful day? Good afternoon, Mr. Monk. How are you, sir?" Apparently the expressions on their faces told him nothing. "Gabriel seems a little disturbed today." He frowned slightly. "If I may say so, Miss Latterly, I think you should not have told him the news about Melville. It has distressed him unnecessarily. And, of course, poor Perdita should never have had to learn of such depravity. That was a grave misjudgment on your part, and I am disappointed in you."

The blood rushed in a tide up Hester's face. Monk's emotion changed instantly from anger with her to a rage with Athol he could barely control. He made the effort only because he did not wish to speak without thinking and possibly make the matter worse for her. To his amazement, he found himself shaking.

"Mistaken or not," Hester said between her teeth, "it is my judgment that Lieutenant Sheldon should be treated as an adult and told whatever he wishes to know. He was interested in the Melville case and concerned for both justice and the human tragedy involved."

"And what about Mrs. Sheldon?" Athol demanded, staring at Hester angrily. "Have you given the slightest thought to her feelings, with your zeal to press what you see as your duty to my brother? Have you for an instant thought what irreparable damage you might be doing to her?" His eyes widened. "What about her innocence, her susceptibilities, even her ability to continue as the charming and gentle creature she is and for which he married her . . . eh?"

"It is not possible to protect anyone from the tragedies and misfortunes of life forever, Mr. Sheldon," she replied stiffly. "I don't think Mrs. Sheldon wishes to be locked away. She would be denying the chance to grow up, or to be any use to anyone. No person with a whit of courage wishes to remain a child forever. . . ."

His face was mottled with purple and his eyes were now brilliant with outrage.

"Miss Latterly, you exceed yourself! You have shown much spirit and initiative in going to the Crimea to nurse soldiers, and I am sure much worthy devotion to duty, as you perceive it, but I am afraid you are not suitable for nursing in the home of a gentleman. You have picked up too much of the manner and beliefs of army life. It is most unfortunate, but I must recommend to my brother that you be released as soon as I can find someone to replace you."

Hester was white-faced. For a moment she looked almost as if she might be about to crumple.

Monk was furious. Now he would intervene, whether she liked it or not.

But he was prevented by Perdita herself, who was standing in the doorway, also wide-eyed and extremely pale. She must have heard their raised voices. Now she was trembling as she steadied herself with one hand on the doorframe behind Athol.

"You will not be replaced, Hester," she said huskily, and cleared her throat. "Athol, I appreciate that you no doubt have my welfare in mind, but you will not dismiss my staff, or indeed give them any instructions at all. Miss Latterly is in my employ, not yours, and she will stay here as long as I wish her to and she is willing."

"You are upset, my dear," Athol said after a moment's hesitation in amazement at her outburst. "When you have had time to reconsider, you will realize that what I say is right." He nodded several times to emphasize his certainty.

"It is not right!" she contradicted him, coming into the room and facing him squarely. "Certainly I am upset that Melville is dead, poor creature, and I am upset about the manner of his death—" She corrected herself. "Her death! The whole thing is a most tragic matter altogether. But I am plain angry that you should choose to dismiss my staff without reference to me or my wishes."

"It is for your good, my dear Perdita—"

"I don't care whose good it is for!" she shouted at him. "Or whose good you think it is! You will not make my decisions for me." She took a deep breath and resumed in a normal voice. "And anyway, you are wrong. It is not for my good that I should be shut away from knowing what is going on. What use am I to anybody, especially myself, if life passes me by? Would you allow me to decide for you what you should know and what you shouldn't?"

He laughed abruptly. "That is hardly comparable, my dear girl. I know an infinitely greater amount about the world and its ways than you do."

"Of course you do!" she rejoined smartly. "Nobody told you you should stay in the nursery and drink milk for the rest of your life!"

"Really, Perdita!" He bridled, stepping backwards. "Your complete loss of composure rather proves what I say. You are overwrought and quite unable to think clearly. That is not a matter you should be discussing in front of Miss Latterly and Mr. Monk."

"Why not?" she demanded. "You are trying to dismiss Hester. Should that be done behind her back?"

"Perdita, please control yourself!" Athol was becoming seriously annoyed now. His rather thin patience was worn through. "Have Martha make you a cup of tea or something. This vindicates my judgment that this has all been too much for you. If you are not careful you will take a turn of the vapors, and then you can be no help to Gabriel or anyone else."

"I shall not take a fit of the vapors!" Perdita retaliated. "The very worst I shall do is tell you precisely what I think and feel about your interfering in my household. But believe me, Athol, that could be very bad. Hester is staying here, and that is the end to it. If you do not find that something you can abide, then I shall be sorry not to see you until Gabriel is better and she has been released to care for someone else . . . but I shall endure it. Stoically!" Her face was bright pink, and in spite of her attitude of confidence, she was trembling.

Hester was trying very hard to keep the smile from her lips.

Monk did not bother.

"I am sure your husband will be obliged to you, Mrs. Sheldon," he said quietly. "It is not pleasant to rely on someone and have them dismissed by anyone else, no matter how well intended. And your understanding and feelings regarding the Melville case will no doubt make it much easier for him to bear his own sense of distress, since he will not have to do it alone."

"I will thank you to concern yourself with your own affairs, sir!" Athol said to him coldly. "You have already brought enough distress and disturbance into this house. We should not even have heard of this miserable, farcical business if it were not for you. Women dressing up as men, deceiving the world, trying to ape their betters and living a completely unnatural life. It is a debasement of all that is purest and most honorable in domestic happiness, and those things any decent man holds dear . . . those very values which are the cornerstone of any civilized society."

Perdita stared at him. "Why shouldn't women design houses? We live in them just as much as men do—more so."

"Because you are plainly not competent to do so!" he answered, exasperation sharpening his voice. "That is self-evident." He swept his arm sideways, dramatically. "You run households, that is an utterly different affair. It does not call for mathematical or logical skills, for special perception, individuality, or thought—and certainly not for genius—"

Monk interrupted. "If you have your household accounts kept for you by someone with no mathematical skills you will be in a very unfortunate position. But that is irrelevant. Keelin Melville was a woman, and she was the most brilliant architect of this generation, perhaps of this century."

"Nonsense!" Athol laughed derisively. "When one looks at her work with real perception, one can see that it is eccentric, highly unlikely to last. It has a femininity to it, a fundamental weakness."

Perdita let out a howl of rage and turned on her heel. Then as she reached the corridor she swung around again, staring at Athol.

"I think it is going to rain. You had better leave before you get soaked on the way home. I should not like you to catch pneumonia."

In spite of himself Monk glanced out the window. Brilliant sunshine streamed in out of a dazzling sky. He glanced at Hester and saw her eyes full of deep, shining satisfaction.

Rathbone also encountered society's prejudices regarding Keelin Melville. He knew of nothing else he could do in the case. His client was dead. There was nothing further to defend or to prosecute. There were other cases to which he needed to turn his attention. But tomorrow would be sufficient time.

Today he was weighed down by the sense of his failure.

Unfortunately, he had social obligations which, if he did not attend to them, would make the threads of daily life harder to pick up. He could not mourn the Melville case indefinitely. Perhaps thinking of something else, being surrounded by other people whose minds were occupied with other matters, would make it easier for him. It might prove like a cold bath, agonizing for the first few minutes, then invigorating, or at least leaving him a little warmer afterwards from the chill of grief.

He attended a dinner party at the house of a man who had long been an associate, and perhaps also a friend—at least their acquaintance went back to their earliest days of practicing law.

James Laurence had married well, and his house in Mayfair was very fine indeed. Rathbone could have afforded one like it if he had wanted one sufficiently. He might have had to do without one or two other things, but it would not have been impossible.

But Laurence had chosen to marry and to entertain in society. He also selected cases largely according to the fee he would charge, in order to support his choice. Rathbone did not wish to do that. His rooms suited him perfectly well. Of course, if he married that would have to change.

He went in and found several of the guests already arrived. The chandeliers were dazzling. The sound of laughter and the chink of glass filled the room amid the exquisitely colored skirts of the women, the glitter of jewels and the pallor of shoulders and bosoms.

He was greeted and absorbed into the company immediately. Everyone was courteous and spoke of all manner of subjects: what was currently playing at the theater; the last parliamentary debate and what might be expected of the next; a little bit of harmless gossip as to who might marry whom. It was light and pleasantly relaxing.

Only after dinner, when the ladies had retired to the withdrawing room and the gentlemen remained at the table, passing port and savoring a little excellent Stilton, was the matter of Keelin Melville raised, and then it was obliquely.

"Poor old Lambert," Lofthouse said ruefully, holding his glass in his hand and turning it around so the light fell through the ruby liquid. "He must feel a complete fool."

"It's his daughter I'm sorry for," Weatherall replied abruptly. "How must she feel? She's been taken in completely."

Lofthouse turned to look at him, his tufted eyebrows raised. "She hasn't paid out a fortune for buildings which are worthless now!" he retorted, his voice heavy with impatience.

Rathbone was already raw. His temper snapped.

"Neither has Lambert!" he said very clearly.

Half a dozen people at the table swiveled to look at him, caught as much by the tone of his voice as by his words.

"I beg your pardon?" Colonel Weatherall said with puzzlement, his thin, white hair catching the light.

"I said, 'Neither has Lambert,'" Rathbone repeated. "Any building he has paid for is exactly the same today as it was a week ago."

"Hardly!" Lofthouse laughed. "My dear fellow, you, of all people, know the truth! I don't mean to be unkind, or to make an issue of your misfortune, if that is the word, but Melville was a woman, for heaven's sake." He said no more, as if that fact was all the explanation required.

Weatherall cleared his throat and coughed into his handkerchief.

A ginger-haired man helped himself to more cheese.

"Precisely," Rathbone agreed, facing Lofthouse unblinkingly. "The buildings are exactly the same. Our knowledge of Melville's sex has changed, but not of her architectural skills."

"Oh! Come now!" Lofthouse laughed again, glancing along the table at the others before looking back at Rathbone. "You cannot seriously be suggesting that a woman—a young woman at that—can conceive and draw up technically perfect plans for the sort of buildings Lambert commissioned and had built, for heaven's sake? Really, Rathbone. We all sympathize with your embarrassment. We have all of us made mistakes of judgment at one time or another. . . ." A smile curled his lips. "Although not, I think, of that order . . . or nature . . ." His smile broadened.

Rathbone could feel the rage inside him almost beyond his grasp to contain. How dare this complacent oaf make a shabby joke out of Keelin Melville's tragedy and society's prejudice?

"Lofthouse, I think . . ." Laurence began, although there was a look of humor in his eyes also, or so it seemed to Rathbone. He was not in the mood to consider it a reflection from the chandeliers.

"Oh, come on, my dear fellow!" Lofthouse was not going to be hushed. The port was at his elbow, and extremely good. "It has an element of the absurd, you must admit. When a genius like Rathbone gets caught out so very thoroughly, we lesser mortals must be allowed our moment of laughter. If he is not man enough to take it, then he should not enter the fray!"

Laurence opened his mouth to protest, but Rathbone spoke before he could, leaning forward across the table.

"You can jeer at me all you like. I am perfectly happy to enter the arena and do my best—win, lose, or draw. If my loss gives you pleasure, you are welcome to it!" He ignored the indrawn breath around the table and the looks of amazement. "But I am deeply offended by your making a public joke out of the death of a young woman whose only sin, so far as we know, was to be denied the opportunity to study or to practice her art so long as we knew she was a woman and not a man. She deceived us because we deserved it—in fact, in a sense demanded it."

He disregarded Lofthouse's rising anger or Colonel Weatherall's incredulity, even his host's embarrassment. "And to suggest that the buildings are worth less because they were designed by a woman rather than a man is the utmost hypocrisy. You know nothing more or less about them now than you did last week, when you were full of praise. They look exactly the same, your knowledge of their design and construction and material is exactly what it was before.

You marveled yesterday, and today you mock, and nothing is different except your perception of the personal life of the architect."

"Rathbone, I really think . . ." Laurence protested.

Lofthouse was red in the face. He half rose to his feet, hands on the white tablecloth.

Rathbone rose also.

"You say a young woman cannot do such things," he continued, his tone even more penetrating. "Therefore what she does must be worthless, and what she had done must be worthless because she is a young woman. Actually, she was nearly forty." His voice dripped sarcasm. "But no doubt where age matures a man it merely dulls a woman. I cannot think even you can seriously believe such an argument. You are a hypocrite, and it is bigots like you who drive genius to destruction, because you don't understand it, and what you don't understand you destroy."

He had gone too far, and he knew it even as he was speaking, not that he did not mean it, but he should not have said it. He stared at their shocked faces. He should apologize, at least to Laurence. Perhaps he would tomorrow, or next week, but not today. He was too passionately, irretrievably, angry.

"You're drunk!" Lofthouse accused him with amazement, then ruined the effect by hiccuping.

Rathbone looked at him, then at the half-empty glass beside him, with withering contempt.

There was nothing left for him to do but incline his head in the barest acknowledgment to Laurence, then excuse himself and leave.

Outside he found himself shivering. It was over a mile and a half to his rooms, but he set out walking without even giving it thought, going faster and faster, oblivious of people passing him or the clatter and light in the gloom of carriages. It was only as he was crossing Piccadilly that he realized he did not really want to go home. He did not want to spend the rest of the evening alone with his thoughts.

He stopped abruptly on the curb and swung around, ready to

hail the nearest cab. He climbed in and directed it to take him to Primrose Hill.

When he arrived Henry Rathbone was sitting by the fire with his slippers off, toasting his feet, sucking absentmindedly on an empty pipe, and deep in a book of philosophy, with which he profoundly disagreed. But its arguments were exercising his mind, which he enjoyed enormously. Even losing his temper in such an abstract way was a form of pleasure.

However, as soon as Oliver came in he realized that something was wrong. It did not require a great deal of deduction, since Oliver had left his hat at Laurence's, his gloves were still stuffed in his pockets and his hands were red with cold. It was now pitch-dark, and chilly enough to suspect frost.

Henry had, of course, followed the case and knew of the latest tragic developments. He stood up and regarded Oliver gravely, holding his pipe in his hand.

"Has something happened?" he asked.

Oliver ran his fingers through his hair, something totally uncharacteristic. He loathed looking untidy; it was almost as bad as being unclean.

"Not really, at least nothing in the Melville case," he answered, taking off his coat and handing it to the manservant waiting at his elbow. "I went to a dinner party this evening and lost my temper."

"Seriously, I presume." Henry nodded to the manservant, who disappeared, closing the door silently. "You look cold. Would you like a glass of port?"

"No!" Oliver declined. "I mean, no thank you. It was during the port that I told them they were hypocrites and bigots who were responsible for the ruin of a genius like Melville." He sat down in the other chair, opposite his father, watching his face to see his reaction.

"Unwise," Henry answered, resuming his own seat. "What are you doing now, thinking how to apologize?"

"No!" The reply was instant and sincere.

"Are they responsible?"

Oliver calmed down a little. "They, and people like them, yes."

"A lot of people . . ." Henry gazed at him very levelly.

Oliver's temper had worn itself out and left not a great deal but sadness and a growing feeling of his own guilt.

"You are not responsible for society's attitudes," Henry said, knocking out his pipe, forgetting there was nothing in it.

"No, but I was responsible for Melville," Oliver answered. "I was very personally and directly responsible. If she had believed she could trust me, then she would have told me the truth. We could have told Zillah Lambert, at least, and she would probably have respected the confidence, for her own sake if not for Melville's. Then there need never have been a case and Melville would still be alive . . . possibly even practicing her profession."

"Perhaps," Henry agreed. "Is that what is troubling you?"

"I suppose so."

"Didn't you ask her, press her for the truth?"

"Yes, of course I did! Obviously she didn't trust me."

"What was to prevent her trusting Zillah Lambert, regardless of you?"

"Well . . . nothing, I suppose."

"But years of rejection," Henry concluded. "Years of lying and concealing. You cannot know everything that went before which made her what she was." He reached for his tobacco and pulled out a few shreds between his fingers and thumb, pushing them into the bowl of his pipe. "Perhaps you were unimaginative not to have guessed, perhaps not. Either way, there is nothing you can do now except cripple yourself with remorse. That will serve no one. It is self-indulgent . . . and perhaps you need a little indulgence, but do not let it persist for too long. It can become a habit—and an excuse."

"My God, you're a harsh judge," Oliver said, jerking his head up to glare at his father.

Henry struck a match and lit his pipe. It went out again immediately. His mouth softened, but there was no equivocation in his mild blue eyes.

"Do you want to be invalided out?"

"No, of course I don't. And I'd like a glass of sherry. Actually, I left before I drank more than a sip of the port."

"It's behind you." Henry made another attempt at lighting his pipe.

The following morning a little before noon Rathbone was in his offices in Vere Street when his clerk told him the police surgeon had called with information.

"Ask him in," Rathbone said immediately.

The surgeon came in, looking grave.

"Well?" Rathbone asked as soon as the barest formalities were over.

"Definitely belladonna," the surgeon replied, sitting down in the chair opposite the desk. "Not very surprising. Easy to come by." He stopped.

"But . . ." Rathbone prompted, sitting a little straighter.

The surgeon bit his lips, his eyes narrowing. "But the thing that I find hard to understand, and which brings me back to you rather than merely sending you a report, is that from the amount she took, and the time she died, she must have taken it while she was still in the courthouse." He drew his brows together. "Which can only mean she had it with her, presumably against such an eventuality as . . . what? What happened that afternoon that suddenly became unbearable?"

Rathbone tried to think back. It had been the day Sacheverall had put the witnesses on the stand and exposed what he thought was a homosexual affair. Had Melville known that was going to happen, or feared it? If so, why had she not told Rathbone to plead guilty and settle out of court? She would have saved Wolff's reputation at least. And if she loved him, surely she would have done that?

Had she carried belladonna all the time, just in case?

"Do you know something?" the surgeon asked. "I would guess

she took it after two in the afternoon, and well before five in the evening, probably before four."

"Yes, it probably makes as much sense as suicide ever does," Rathbone answered wearily.

"You do not sound entirely convinced." The surgeon looked at him with a slight shake of his head. "Is there some fact I should know?"

"No. No . . . I am afraid it was a tragedy which may well have been inevitable from the moment Sacheverall called Isaac Wolff to the stand, let alone that damned prostitute. Thank you for coming to let me know in person."

The surgeon stood up and offered his hand. Rathbone took it, and then saw him to the door. He returned to his chair, still with a vague sense of unease, as if there was something unexplained or incomplete, but he could not think what. Probably it was as his father had said, his own sense of guilt.

Nevertheless that evening he went to see Monk at his rooms in Fitzroy Street. He found him brooding over a handful of letters. He seemed quite pleased to be interrupted.

"Trivial case," he said, putting them aside and rising to his feet as Rathbone came in. "You look awful. Still thinking about Keelin Melville?"

"Aren't you?" Rathbone continued, throwing himself into the large chair reserved for clients. "The police surgeon came to see me today. It was belladonna she took. Some time in the afternoon."

"But she was in court all afternoon," Monk said with surprise. "You were with her."

"Well, he was quite sure," Rathbone repeated. "Said it had to have been between two and five at the latest, more likely four."

"What time did she leave court?" Monk pressed. He was sitting upright on his chair. "Is she supposed to have swallowed the stuff?"

"Yes, of course! What else? Pulled out a syringe and put a needle into her arm?" Rathbone said tartly, but his attention was suddenly focused.

"In what form?" Monk asked.

"What?"

"What form was the belladonna?" Monk clarified. "Pills? Drops? Powder? A mixture?"

"I've no idea. I didn't ask. What does it matter now?"

Monk was frowning. "Well, didn't you notice if she swallowed pills, took a drink of water, or had a flask? Someone must have seen. It was about as public a place as you can have, dammit! Why on earth would she do it there anyway? Why not wait until she got home with a little privacy?"

"I don't know." Rathbone was thinking frantically now. "I can't imagine what must have been on her mind. She panicked when Sacheverall put that prostitute on the stand. She realized her evidence would be unarguable, interpretable only one way."

"Then she didn't know Sacheverall would call her until she saw her there?" Monk said quickly.

Rathbone thought back. "No. I don't think she did. I can't be sure, of course, but insofar as I am any judge at all, she had no idea."

"Then why would she have taken belladonna with her . . . in a lethal dose?" Monk was leaning farther forward, his eyes still on Rathbone's face. "And if she did know, why didn't she take it before, and save Wolff's reputation, at least? If she loved him at all, she would surely have done that. It doesn't make sense, Rathbone, not as it is."

"Then find sense to it!" Rathbone said urgently. "I'm engaging you to do it—for me!" He cast aside his personal feelings, even his awareness that Monk must consider him incompetent at best for having allowed the case to come to this tragic end. He refused to think what Hester's judgment would be. He hated asking for favors. The hard edge of his feeling was in his voice, and his awareness of vulnerability in front of Monk, of all people. "I want to know what it was that drove her to kill herself instead of fighting on. Couldn't she have left England, gone to Italy or even the Middle East, or somewhere? With genius like hers she could surely have started again. Anything rather than death. And what about Wolff? She loved him . . ."

Monk was looking at him for once without mockery. Only the faintest spark lit the backs of his eyes.

"I'll find out what I can." Then he did smile. "My rates are very reasonable."

"Thank you," Rathbone accepted stiffly. He felt awkward now, more than a little self-conscious. He stood up, straightening his jacket. It was nearly midnight. He had not realized how long it had taken him to travel to Primrose Hill and back. "I'm sorry to have kept you so late."

Monk stood up also. He hesitated, as if about to offer his hand. It was a peculiarly formal gesture, and at the last moment he changed his mind. "I'll let you know as soon as I find anything," he promised instead, and his face was very grave. Rathbone realized with warmth that he too felt angry and hurt and more than a little guilty.

In the morning Monk abandoned the rather tedious letters in which he had been trying to find evidence of duplicity for a woman who felt her sister-in-law was behaving immorally, and set out for the Old Bailey.

He passed several paperboys. Keelin Melville's death was not on the front pages anymore. A fresh political event in France had superseded her, and there were whispers of a financial scandal in the city.

At the courthouse he went up the steps two at a time and out of a surprisingly sharp wind. The weather had changed and there was a hint of frost in the air. He had been there often enough to know several of the clerks and ushers, too well to deceive them as to his identity or his purpose for being there.

"Good morning, Mr. Monk," an elderly usher said to him before he was a dozen yards inside.

"Good morning, Mr. Pearson," he replied, coming to a stop. "Just the man I was hoping to see."

Pearson looked interested. "Oh, yes sir? Why would that be?"

Monk was one of the more colorful people to enter his world, and his arrival heralded a break in routine. Added to which, if Monk was seeking him, then for a little while at least, Pearson would be more important than merely the efficient, almost invisible functionary he usually was.

"I need to know a good deal more about the last day of the Melville trial. You are very observant of people . . ."

"My job, sir," Pearson answered with suitable gravity, but he stood a little straighter for the compliment. "Times there's little else to do but notice people. What is it you need to know, Mr. Monk?"

"Did Melville leave the courtroom at any time before the hearing ended?"

"No sir."

"Are you sure? Not for any reason?"

"No sir. They'd have had to halt the trial if he'd excused himself. Sir Oliver'll have told you that."

Monk sighed. "I thought not, but he could have forgotten. He is very disturbed at the outcome."

Pearson shook his head. "Nobody likes to lose a case, but for the poor soul to have taken her life is truly terrible. I was very sorry to hear about that. He always seemed like a nice gentleman to me—or I suppose I should say lady, now. I never guessed. Never came into my mind." He looked at Monk curiously, searching his face to see if he felt the same.

"Nor mine," Monk admitted. "The surgeon says she took the poison while she was here in the court, some time during that afternoon."

Pearson frowned. "I don't rightly see how that could be, Mr. Monk. Was she supposed to have swallowed it like?"

"Yes."

"I don't know where. She wouldn't have eaten nor drunk anything in the courtroom. Judge wouldn't allow it. And if she had, anyone would have seen. There's always people looking at the accused, and that's what it amounted to in this case, poor soul. Mr.

Sacheverall went after him something fierce. I mean her. Still can't get it into my head that she was a woman."

A group of junior counsel passed by, glancing at Monk, and one nodded as if he thought for a moment he knew him, then continued on his way.

"Was there an adjournment for any reason?"

"Yes! Yes . . . Sir Oliver tried again with Mr. Sacheverall. I remember that. It must have been then!" Memory quickened Pearson's face. "Must have! No other time. I'm almost sure when Miss Melville left at the end of the day, she went straight out the back way, before the crowds could get at her. Sir Oliver went with her, then came out the front. If she really did take it here, and not after she left, then it must have been during the adjournment."

"Curious," Monk said slowly.

"Sir?"

"Why didn't she wait until she knew the result of Rathbone's talk with Sacheverall? There might have been some better resolution."

"I don't know, sir, I really don't." Pearson shook his head in agreement. "Don't make a lot of sense, does it? Poor creature must have been out of her wits . . . afraid for Mr. Wolff, maybe?"

Monk was not satisfied.

"Do you want to speak with the usher around the corner when everyone left at that adjournment?" Pearson enquired helpfully. "He might have noticed if Miss Melville was given a drink, and maybe took a pill or a powder with it."

"Yes, please," Monk accepted. "I can't think what difference it makes now, but it seems such a pointless time to have begun the process of ending her own life . . . with a poison which acts over three or four hours."

"She was very distressed," Pearson pointed out. "I remember her face. She looked like a person who has seen her whole world come to an end . . . more pain than she can endure." His voice sank and the weight of sadness seemed to droop in his shoulders. He led the way up the wide hallway, stopping twice to ask other people where Mr. Sutton was, and in one of the side rooms eventually found a small man with a narrow chest and bright, dark eyes.

"Oh . . . Mr. Sutton," he said quickly. "This is Mr. Monk. He's looking into how poor Miss Melville managed to take poison without anyone noticing. Seems it must have happened while she was here. Some time in the afternoon. Since they were in court all the time except for the adjournment, it looks like it was then."

"Wasn't then," Sutton said immediately, pursing his lips and looking beyond Pearson to Monk. "Sorry, sir, but I was outside the court all the time and Miss Melville never left the hallway."

"Did anyone bring her a glass of water, or perhaps offer her a flask?" Monk suggested.

"No sir." Sutton was quite firm. "She sat by herself until Mrs. Lambert went over to her and gave her back the gifts she'd given Miss Lambert. I saw a pair of earrings, a gold fob an' a real pretty miniature painting o' trees and such. Had them in a packet. Just opened it up and tipped them all out into Miss Melville's hands. They were dusty as if they had been pushed to the back of a drawer. I hardly think she knew what was going on, that distracted she was."

"Are you certain Miss Melville didn't eat or drink anything?" Monk pressed. It would be easy enough to understand if at this point she had taken a stiff brandy, if nothing else. Any normal person would have waited for the privacy of her own home to take poison. But Melville was a woman. Did women think or feel differently?

He could imagine no reason why they should. Surely agony such as this knew no boundaries of sex!

"What I don't understand," Pearson said, scratching the back of his neck, "is why she did it then. If it was me, I'd have done it the day before, when Mr. Sacheverall brought Mr. Wolff in—that is, if I were going to do it at all . . . which I can't say I would. Although I can't say I wouldn't, not until I'd been there."

"No," Monk agreed, staring at Sutton. "But you saw Melville all the time, and she didn't eat or drink anything? Are you certain?"

"If she had done, she didn't drink from it in that adjournment, sir. I'd take an oath on that myself. She must've took the poison some other way, or more like some other time. I don't want to overstep my place, sir, but maybe the doc got it wrong?"

"Maybe . . ." Monk said, but he did not believe it. "Thank you, Mr. Sutton. You have been very helpful." And with a word of thanks to Pearson as well, he walked back down the hallway.

He spent several more hours confirming what he had been told, but he could find no variation in accounts. Melville had spoken to few people. She had been white-faced, her body rigid, her eyes reflecting the pain she must have felt, but she had neither eaten nor drunk anything.

How had she taken the belladonna which had killed her? And why had she chosen to do it at such a time, instead of either the night before, after Wolff had testified, or that evening, after the prostitute had finally sealed Sacheverall's case?

Any answer he could think of was unsatisfactory, leaving questions in his mind, a darkness unresolved.

CHAPTER TEN

Monk spent a miserable, agitated evening. It would be ridiculous to expect every case to resolve into a solution so absolute there could be no doubt about any part of it. None ever did. There were always unknowns, thoughts he could not fathom. One had to let go once sufficient answers were found to be certain of the truth of the verdict.

But this one troubled him more deeply than most. It was not only the tragedy of it, it was the feeling, the almost certainty, that Keelin Melville had some last secret she had taken to the grave with her, which would make sense of her behavior.

He paced back and forth across his sitting room, ignoring the dying embers of the fire and the rain spattering against the windows, loud because he had forgotten to draw the curtains.

He could understand why Melville had not told Zillah she was really a woman. She had kept the secret so long she could not trust anyone at all, except Wolff, not to reveal it. Perhaps it would only have been a confidence to a girl friend, whispered in exchange for some other romantic secret or dream, a moment's hurt and loneliness eased by sharing. But then what would bind the friend to keep total silence? The chance to share such a dramatic piece of information could be a temptation too great.

No, she was wiser to trust no one. Too much depended on it. And once the case had gone so far, it was too late to hope Barton Lambert would keep silent. If he had told anyone in anger, no matter how much he had regretted it, it would be too late to take it back. Knowledge can never be withdrawn.

Before it all happened, Monk would have thought it trivial. What did it matter whether a person was a man or a woman, except to those who knew that person? The works of art were the same. Why not let it be known, and if there were no more commissions, then leave! Go to Italy, or France, or anywhere one liked.

But Melville had spent twelve years in England, had designed some of the loveliest buildings in the country. She did not want to see them belittled for a reason that had nothing to do with their value. And she had been right. It was happening already, the derisory remarks, the suddenly altered perception when nothing in the reality was changed. She had been prepared to take the chance, and fought to survive in England.

And, of course, once the trial had begun she could not leave. And it seemed she really had believed it would turn out differently.

So what had made her change her mind and take belladonna poison . . . in the middle of the afternoon?

He stopped at the window and stared out of it, seeing only the blur of the rain. Nobody else cared now, except Rathbone, of course, and that was for emotional reasons. He hated failure, and he was not used to guilt. Monk smiled to himself. He was much more used to it, but he liked it no better. The only difference was that for him it was a familiar pain, for Rathbone it had all the shock of the new.

At least Monk imagined it had!

Was that why Keelin Melville had killed herself? Guilt?

Over what? The injury she had done to Zillah Lambert could very easily be explained. It was error, private social clumsiness possibly. Certainly nothing that warranted suicide.

Anyway, wasn't genius rather more self-protective than that? He tried to think back on what he knew of the lives of the great creative people. Many of them had hurt others, been eccentric, selfish, single-minded, impossible to live with happily, sometimes even to live with at all. But it was those around them they injured, not themselves. They were too fired by their passion to make, to build, to create, paint, dance or whatever it was that formed their gift to the world. Sometimes they burned themselves out; sometimes illness or accident consumed them. Many died young.

But he could think of no example of one who had killed himself over guilt regarding his abuse of women. The very idea was almost a contradiction within itself.

Was Melville so different simply because she was a woman?

He doubted it.

Then what?

The rain was streaming down the window now, distorting the lamps of carriages passing in the street below, reflecting in the puddles.

The more he thought about the buildings full of light, the clean lines soaring into the air, the sense of comfort and peace he had felt inside them, the less could he believe Melville would have taken her own life.

Was it conceivable that somewhere, in some way he had yet even to imagine, somebody else had killed her?

Why? Why would anybody want to? What else had happened that day, or the day before, to make her dangerous to anyone? If she had known anything about Zillah that was not to her credit, surely she would have said so before this, long before Isaac Wolff was tarnished by the whole affair, even put in jeopardy of imprisonment, for a crime which now was ludicrous, in light of the truth.

He pushed his hands into his pockets. Below him in the street it was raining harder. The gutters were swirling over their edges. A footman standing at the side of a carriage was soaking wet. His figure in the riding lights was expressive of his utter dejection. A stray dog was splashing about happily.

A man strode by with an umbrella which was ineffectual.

Monk turned away, back to the room and the firelight. What had been the result of Melville's death? The case had been concluded. There was nothing more to say, nothing to pursue. It did not matter anymore whether Zillah Lambert was as innocent as she appeared.

But Monk had already done all he could to uncover any fault in her, past or present, and found nothing. Besides, he really did not believe she would willingly have harmed Melville, far less killed her, even if there was a way to have accomplished it.

Nor had anybody, for that matter. Melville had neither eaten nor drunk anything, by another's hand or by her own.

Was there some other way in which the poison could have been administered? No. The surgeon would not be wrong about whether it was eaten or injected into the blood.

Except that he thought it was suicide, and therefore it had hardly mattered.

But why murder? What threat was Keelin Melville to anyone, except possibly Wolff? If the case had continued as it was, only Keelin herself, and Wolff, would suffer.

Why hadn't Wolff simply told the court she was a woman? The most cursory medical examination would have proved him right, and he of all men knew that! Keelin would not have refused.

The fire was going out. He had neglected it. He bent down and with the tongs picked up half a dozen pieces of coal and put them on one by one. The fire looked like it was being smothered. Damn! It was getting cold and he was not ready to go to bed yet. Also he was angry with his own carelessness. He dropped the tongs and picked up the bellows, blowing gently, sending up a cloud of white ash. He swore again, and tried more gently still.

The reason had to be in what might happen if the case continued. Someone was frightened.

What would happen? Monk would continue to search in the past of Zillah Lambert and her family, but particularly her past romances. Perhaps they were not as very slight and natural as they appeared, no more than most pretty girls might experience. If he had continued, with his characteristic ruthlessness, what would he have uncovered? And who knew about it other than Zillah herself? Her father?

Hester seemed to think it would be her mother, the immaculate Delphine Lambert.

And, of course, the man involved . . . and possibly his family.

But murder! Over a spoiled reputation! Surely Zillah herself could simply have told her father and asked that he settle out of court? He would have been willing enough, if he realized her happiness and the family honor depended on it. He might have been angry for a while, even punished her one way or another, but that hardly warranted murder—in a sane person.

Monk's labor with the fire was rewarded by a spurt of flame. It licked up around the coal and began to burn. He smiled in satisfaction. A small victory—very small indeed.

Tomorrow he would retrace his steps over Zillah Lambert's past. This time he would press harder, not accept any equivocations. He would treat it as if it were murder. The trivial matter of breach of promise was a thing of the past.

He sat by the fire until the coal was entirely consumed, going over the notes he had made on his first investigation. He knew where he would begin tomorrow.

Actually, it took him two days to find the incident he had overlooked the first time—or, more accurately, had considered too trivial and too normal in anyone's life to matter. He still thought it of no real importance. But then he was not of the same level of society as the Lamberts, and certainly not of that level into which they aspired to marry.

He had followed Hester's advice about tracing back the weekly life of the Lamberts to discover a sudden move, probably involving only Zillah and her mother, coming at a time which seemed unplanned, made in haste, and perhaps in other ways inconvenient.

This time he was far more ruthless, pressing people, sometimes with only part of the truth, sometimes frightening them into revealing a fact that with more time to consider they would have kept discreet. The incident had occurred when Zillah was nearly sixteen, a holiday taken without warning, all personal plans disrupted. A garden party—a ball which Delphine had been very eager to attend; indeed, for which she had gone to great trouble to acquire an invitation—had been abandoned. A marvelous gown had to be set aside, to be worn when it was no longer impressive, certainly no longer the forerunner of fashion but rather the trailer behind, seeming a copy instead of an original. Knowing a little about clothes and vanity himself, he appreciated what a sacrifice Delphine had made. There would have to have been a very compelling reason to leave at that time, and a very urgent one.

To begin with, the friendship between Zillah and young Hugh Gibbons had seemed innocent enough, but if Delphine had been prepared to make such a sacrifice, then there must have been more to it. If he pressed he could find it.

It was morning on the third day before he had gathered sufficient evidence to prove it beyond denial. Of course, there was no witness that the two had been lovers in any but a romantic sense. But they had spent much time alone together. Hugh was nineteen, an age when Monk knew the emotions were wild and the blood hot and disinclined to moderation and self-discipline. Zillah had apparently been a willful fifteen-year-old, full of dreams and certain no one else understood them, except Hugh. She had read the great romances in the schoolroom.

By all accounts her parents had been generous and more inclined to indulgence than harshness. Any responsible mother would have done as Delphine had, possibly even sooner. The only answer to such a liaison was to leave the city for a while. Hugh was unsuitable socially—he had no means to keep a wife and no prospects; and Zillah was too young, and utterly impractical. The unplanned nature of the departure made it unarguable that Delphine had discovered a situation which could not be allowed to continue even another day or two, let alone weeks.

Did Barton Lambert know of it? Had it been serious enough for public knowledge of it to ruin Zillah?

But surely if it had, and Lambert knew about it, then he would not have begun the proceedings against Melville?

Had anyone else been concerned? Was there something about Hugh Gibbons? If Monk had pursued him instead of Zillah, would he have found something ugly enough to prompt murder? It seemed highly improbable. He could not imagine what. Another affair, perhaps a child or a rape? What had happened to Hugh Gibbons since then?

Before pursuing that, which might take a long time and be quite fruitless, he decided to speak to Barton Lambert.

It was shortly before one o'clock, and he was admitted readily into the house and, after the briefest hesitation, was shown into the large, very comfortable withdrawing room. French doors opened onto a small lawn surrounded by hydrangea bushes carpeted underneath with tiny white flowers.

The room was warmed by a handsome fire, and heavy brocade curtains framed the big windows and kept the draft from chilling the air. Delphine Lambert was sitting on one of the sofas. She was dressed in vivid blue, her enormous skirts gleaming in the light. She looked calm and happy. Wystan Sacheverall was standing closer to the window only a yard from Zillah; in fact, the frills of her dusky pink skirt covered the toes of his polished shoes. He was looking at her, disregarding Monk's entry as if he were not even aware of it and in any case it held no interest for him whatever. His face was filled with eagerness and he was talking to her, and smiling.

Zillah appeared to be absorbed by something in the garden beyond the glass, a flower or a bird. She did not take her eyes from it even when Sacheverall seemed to be asking a question. Her shoulder was lifted a little, pulling the fabric of her bodice, and Monk could only see the side of her head and the curve of her cheek. As soon as she heard his voice she turned and started towards him.

"Good afternoon, Mr. Lambert, Mrs. Lambert," he said formally. "Miss Lambert . . ."

"Good afternoon, Mr. . . ." Delphine trailed off as if she had already forgotten his name.

"Monk," Lambert supplied. "Good afternoon, Monk. What can we do for you?"

Sacheverall deliberately remained by the window. He stared at

Monk but made no move to come forward. His coldness could hardly be misinterpreted.

Zillah, on the other hand, seemed almost pleased to see him. Whatever had interested her in the garden was instantly forgotten.

"Good afternoon, Mr. Monk. How are you?"

She looked still tired, still hurt, but there was no air of self-pity about her, and no blame towards Monk. Again he was consumed with anger at this whole absurd charade which had already destroyed Keelin Melville and was going to damage Zillah yet further. He even hesitated whether to say what he had come for. What good would it do now?

He looked past her at Sacheverall, who had turned to face the room, watching Zillah. Was it affection in his eyes or enlightened self-interest, plus perhaps a little very natural desire towards an extremely attractive young woman? And she was attractive. She had an unusual mixture of innocence and individuality. A man who loved her might waken all kinds of passions in her, and high among them would be loyalty.

Monk looked beyond her again at Sacheverall and disliked him profoundly.

"What may we do for you, Mr. Monk?" Lambert enquired.

Monk recalled himself. "I am sorry to intrude," he apologized. "May I speak with you alone, Mr. Lambert? I hope it will be brief."

Lambert glanced at his wife.

"Oh, there is plenty of time before luncheon," she assured him. "It is still a trifle cool for me, but I daresay Mr. Sacheverall would like to take a short walk around the garden. Zillah can show him some of our treasures."

Zillah looked at her father appealingly, but he misunderstood. "Yes, of course, my dear," he agreed. "I daresay we shall be no more than half an hour at the most."

Sacheverall offered his arm with a smile and considerable enthusiasm, and Zillah accepted it.

Lambert went to the door and opened it into the hall to usher Monk towards somewhere more private.

Monk excused himself to Delphine and followed.

They went to the study. It was a pleasant room, well furnished with books. A large desk was scattered with papers and there were two cabinets for the storage of yet more papers. Four chairs for visitors faced the desk, and Lambert turned to look at Monk, his brow furrowed, his eyes still filled with his sense of tragedy.

"Well, Monk, what is this about? Is this some further matter to do with Melville?" The absence of title suggested he still thought of Melville as a man. Over the shock of disclosure and all the loss that had followed, he remembered the friend he had known and cared for.

Monk felt a tightening inside himself. A daughter, even as pretty and as charming and as seemingly agreeable as Zillah, was a source for all kinds of fears. Illness and accident were only the worst. There were so many humanly made, unnecessary other traps and snares, even in a young life barely begun.

"What is it?" Lambert repeated, not yet offering Monk a seat.

Monk had been considering where to begin. Lambert was a blunt man. He would not appreciate prevarication.

"I have been looking into Keelin Melville's death," he said directly, watching Lambert's face. "For Rathbone's sake as much as anything. It seems so . . ."

He saw the look of pain in Lambert's eyes.

"So oddly timed," he went on. "According to the police surgeon, she must have taken the poison while she was actually in the court, and yet she was observed all the time, and she neither ate nor drank anything at all. And why then, rather than later at home? Why would anyone choose to take poison in public in order to die in private, when doing both at home would have been so much easier?"

Lambert stared at him, puzzled and now also troubled. It seemed that up until now his emotions had crowded out thought. This came to him as an ugly intrusion, but he did not evade it.

"What are you trying to say, Monk? You are not a man to come here to see me simply to say there are things you do not understand.

You have no need to understand, unless you believe there is something wrong, something criminal, or at the very least, something profoundly immoral. What do you expect of me?" He walked back to one of the chairs, not the one behind the desk but one of those arranged in front of it, and sat on it.

Monk sat in one of the others, crossing his legs and leaning back.

"One possibility troubles me, and I would like to prove it wrong before I let go of it."

"Yes? What is that possibility, and how does it concern me or my family?"

"I am not sure that it does," Monk admitted. "The possibility is that she was murdered."

Lambert leaned forward. "What?" He seemed genuinely not to have understood.

Monk repeated what he had said.

"Why?" Lambert puckered his face, his eyes narrowed. "Why would anybody want to murder Melville? He was the most . . ." He swallowed. "She was the most likable person. Of course, she had professional rivals, but people don't kill for that sort of reason." He waved his hand. "That's preposterous. And no one except Wolff knew she was a woman. You're not suggesting Wolff killed her, are you? I don't believe that for an instant!" Everything in his voice, his expression, emphasized what he said.

"No I don't," Monk agreed. "If it was murder, then I think it was to stop the case from going any further."

"The only person who'd want to stop that was poor Killian . . . Keelin . . . herself." A twinge of pain shot over Lambert's face. "I'm sorry . . . I still find it hard to believe all this. I liked her, you know. I liked her very much, even after she—she . . . damn it! Even after the marriage with Zillah fell through, I still liked him—her!"

Lambert stood up and began pacing restlessly back and forth across the room, seesawing his hands in the air.

"I went ahead with the case because I had to!" He looked at Monk with a desperate urgency, willing him to believe. "I had to protect my daughter's reputation. If I hadn't, people would have said Melville had discovered something about her that made it impossible to marry her. They would assume she was without morals, a loose woman. No one would have had her." His lips tightened. "Do you know what happens to a young woman whose reputation is gone, Mr. Monk? She has no place!" He chopped the air again. "No decent man will marry her. She is no longer invited to the decent houses. Young women with hopes no longer associate with her, in case the dirt rubs off. If she marries at all, it is to a man beneath her, and he treats her as what she is, one of society's castoffs."

He looked at Monk intently, willing him to understand. "Or she stays single, dependent upon her father, while all her friends gain husbands, houses, status—in time, children. Would you want that for your daughter? Wouldn't you fight any battle, any justified battle at all, rather than let that happen? Especially when you know she has done nothing to warrant it."

"I should probably do it whether she had warranted it or not," Monk said frankly. He disliked what he was going to do. Only there was the remembrance that Keelin Melville had been a young woman too, also denied what she wanted most because of the beliefs and conventions of others. There had been no one to feel for her, now not even herself. "What about Hugh Gibbons?"

Lambert's face showed nothing. No man could be so complete a master of himself as to have hidden guilt behind such a bland exterior.

"Who is Hugh Gibbons?"

"A young man who was in love with Zillah some three years ago," Monk replied. "He was unsuitable and the romance had gone too far. Mrs. Lambert took Zillah away, very suddenly, on a prolonged trip to the seaside—in North Wales. Crickieth, to be precise."

Lambert's face paled suddenly. He remained motionless where he was by the window, the light behind him.

"You remember now," Monk said unnecessarily.

The blood rushed back to Lambert's cheeks. He came forward to the desk, leaning over it. "Are you saying my daughter has lost her virtue, sir?"

"I have no idea," Monk replied. "I am agreeing with you that malicious supposition, whether true or not, can ruin a young person, and it would be natural for those who care for them to go to great lengths to prevent that."

Lambert drew in a long, slow breath. "You are accusing me of murdering Melville to hide some damned indiscretion which was caught before it was anything! God Almighty, what kind of a man do you think I am?"

Monk glanced down and saw that Lambert's hands on the desk were shaking and his knuckles were white. He would have sworn that the idea genuinely horrified him.

"I am not accusing you, Mr. Lambert," Monk answered quietly. "I am trying to find out why Keelin Melville chose such an extraordinary time to kill herself, and how. She did not eat or drink anything during the time when the police surgeon says the poison entered her body . . . yet he says it was swallowed. It does not make sense, does it?"

Lambert frowned. He sat down again, this time behind the desk. "No . . . not that I can see," he agreed. "But if she did not eat or drink anything, then how did anyone else poison her?"

"I don't know that either," Monk confessed. "I'm looking for a lot of things. I've seen Keelin Melville's buildings, her dreams, something of what was in her soul. I can't let this go without doing everything I can to understand what happened to her."

Lambert swallowed, his throat convulsing. "Dammit! So am I! I'll retain you if necessary. Nothing we do can bring her back. Nothing I do can alter my part in it. But I can find out what finally broke her, and learn to live with it . . . or if it was someone else, then I'll see they pay." He bent his head and put his hands over his face. "Listen to me! Am I going to find the man I want to punish is myself?"

Monk was overwhelmed by a sudden feeling of empathy with him. They were as different as possible, physically, in pattern of life and fortune, in turn of mind and personality, and yet Monk had stood in exactly the same place: pursuing what he believed to be a monster and terrified that when he found him, it would prove to be his own face he saw.

"Are you not going to punish yourself anyway?" He did not move his eyes from Lambert, and slowly Lambert looked up.

"Yes. But either way I have to know the truth, if you can find it."

"What happened to Hugh Gibbons?"

"What? I've no idea. Can it matter now?"

"I don't know. Can you think of any other incident in Zillah's life which anyone might fear my looking into?"

"I don't fear that." Some of the indignation came back into Lambert's voice. "It could have been tragic, but it wasn't. My wife dealt with it before it went too far. Took Zillah away." There was no shadow in his face, not the slightest duplicity. If there had been anything more to it Monk would swear Lambert knew nothing of it. But then that was entirely possible. A wise mother might well not tell the father of any such thing. She might fear his reaction, his anger, his sense of outrage. He could all too easily lose his temper and, without realizing it, bring about the very disaster his wife was laboring to avoid.

Lambert saw the disbelief in Monk's face. "It wasn't!" he repeated fiercely.

"What about Hugh Gibbons?" Monk said again. "Might he have gone on to become involved with another young woman, and her mother not have acted so quickly, or so effectively?"

"I've no idea. What difference could it make?" Lambert's eyes opened wide. "Are you suggesting Gibbons came to the courtroom and poisoned Melville to stop you from looking into it? That's ridiculous. How? Why didn't we see him? And how would he know about you anyway? What would you have done about it if you had found something? You would hardly have ruined some other young woman just for the sake of it. It wouldn't have helped Melville's cause." His contempt for the idea was plain.

So was Monk's, he had to admit. If it was this incident, then it was to do with Zillah.

The same thought must have occurred to Lambert. He rose to his feet.

"We'll ask my wife and get the whole thing disposed of. Come."

Monk followed obediently, catching up with him at the withdrawing room door. "Would you rather not discuss it with Sacheverall present?" he asked.

"Not at all. He is our family lawyer, and as you may have observed, extremely fond of Zillah. We have no secrets to hide from him." He opened the door and walked in.

Delphine was sitting elegantly on the sofa with a piece of embroidery in her hands, although she was paying it little attention. Zillah and Sacheverall had returned from their walk in the garden. Perhaps it was a little cool. Now they stood over by the window close together, and Sacheverall was talking to her earnestly, gazing at her eyes, her lips. The sunlight caught the brilliance of her hair, shining bronze and gold. They all looked at Lambert as he came in.

Lambert went straight to the point. "Mr. Monk has told me some disturbing things about Melville's death. It seems it is not as simple a suicide as it first appeared."

Sacheverall made as if to interrupt, coming a step forward into the room.

Lambert overrode him. "There are things which need explaining, and we cannot let the matter go until that has been done."

"With respect, sir," Sacheverall argued, "to continue to go over the matter can only cause further distress to innocent people. That Melville should take her own life is easy enough to understand." He shrugged his broad shoulders. "She was obviously a person of—at its kindest—a disturbed mind and unnatural disposition. She realized the great wrong she had done both to Zillah"—he smiled at her and put his hand on her arm—"and to Isaac Wolff. To avoid further dishonor, she killed herself. What further explanation can be needed?"

"A great deal," Lambert answered with a sharpness that surprised Monk, and from the look in his face, Sacheverall also. Only Zillah seemed happy with her father's words.

Delphine looked merely annoyed. "Leave the wretched creature in peace." She shook her head. "As Mr. Sacheverall so wisely says, she was only too obviously disturbed. Pursuing her reasons for taking her life can only distress you, my dear, and perhaps cause you to blame yourself where there is no justification. I have told you over and over that no fault lies with you. You believed what she told you, as did we all." She placed her hand lightly on his arm. "It is not fair to hold yourself responsible in any way. I hate to see you suffer for this. Please . . . let us all put it behind us. No good can come of knowing any more, even if it were possible." She regarded him very earnestly. "And truly, Barton, can we say that her inner turmoil is any of our business? Can we not allow her, at least in death, a little privacy?"

For the first time Lambert hesitated. He glanced at Monk, then back at Delphine.

"What things?" Zillah asked.

Lambert did not answer.

She looked beyond him to Monk. "What things need to be answered, Mr. Monk? Why do you care what happened? Please answer me truthfully. I am very tired of evasions and euphemisms told to protect me."

"You don't need to know, my dear. . . ." Sacheverall said, reaching toward her with his hand.

She moved a step away from him. "I wish to know," she said, still looking at Monk. "Did she kill herself over what we did to her? Was it because of what everyone said about Mr. Wolff?"

Delphine winced.

"We can't blame ourselves for that!" Sacheverall said quickly, a flush of anger marking his cheeks.

Zillah appeared not even to have heard him. She remained looking at Monk.

"I don't know what it was, Miss Lambert," he answered. "If that was the cause, I don't understand why she did not tell the truth. It would have ruined her professional reputation in this country, but there are other countries, and she had lived and studied in some of them. Surely that would have been better than death? The only crime she was accused of was so easily explained."

"Easily!" Sacheverall said with amazement. "Perhaps in your circles, Monk, but hardly in the society in which he—she moved, and among the people who would be her patrons. I think you forget she practiced her profession among the very cream of society, not the sort of person who might regard that kind of . . . perversion . . . as acceptable."

Zillah swung around to glare at him. "It was not a perversion!" she defended hotly. "She did nothing wrong or not . . . normal. She only dressed as a man; she didn't behave as one in—in a personal sense." The color was hot in her cheeks also, but for the embarrassment of having to seek words for something she was uncertain of and which it was indelicate to discuss. "You are trying to say that she was in some way mad, and that's not true."

"My dear Zillah, you have no idea what she may have done . . . in private!" Sacheverall expostulated.

"Neither have you!" she said instantly. "You are suggesting something ugly, but you don't know."

"We know she killed herself," he said gently. "That is unarguable. Young people in good health, with sufficient funds and a stable character, do not take their own lives. It is a crime against God, as well as against the state." He looked calm and satisfied with that answer.

Zillah looked back at Monk. "Is that true?"

"It is part of the truth," he agreed.

"And the rest of it?"

"Zillah . . ." Delphine said warningly.

"The rest of it?" Her eyes did not deviate from Monk's.

"The rest of it is that I wonder if she did kill herself, or if someone else did in order to bring the case to a conclusion before I investigated any further and uncovered something unpleasant," he replied.

She looked completely confused, as if she could see no sense in what he had said.

Sacheverall let out a guffaw of ridicule.

"What were you investigating?" Zillah asked. "About Killian? I—I mean Keelin . . . I don't understand a great deal about the law, but if there was something, surely if she told Sir Oliver, he would have kept it secret? Doesn't he have to, if he was her barrister? Anyway, what could it be?" Her brow darkened. "And why were you investigating her? Sir Oliver was supposed to be defending her. He was on her side!" She was indignant. She felt a trust had been abused.

"No, Miss Lambert," Monk said softly. "I was investigating you."

"Me?" She was amazed. "I have nothing to hide."

"What about Hugh Gibbons?"

"Oh!" She looked away and the color rushed crimson up her cheeks. "Well, that was all rather foolish. I suppose I was indiscreet—"

"Zillah!" Delphine said warningly.

Sacheverall frowned and stood perfectly still. It was the first time he had seemed uncertain of himself since Monk had come in.

Zillah ignored her mother. She was still facing Monk. "I did not behave very well. I should know better now. I would not permit myself to become so . . . emotional. Unless, of course, I were married." She took a deep breath but did not lower her eyes.

Monk found himself feeling extraordinarily partisan towards her. Each time he saw her, it became easier to understand why Keelin Melville had liked her so much she had inadvertently allowed this tragedy to happen.

"Perhaps anyone who is capable of passion is indiscreet at some time or other," he said quietly. He had no idea how he might have erred in his own youth. It was gone, with all his other memories. But he knew himself well enough to be sure it had occurred, and probably often. Not that it was the same for women, of course—at least not to society.

"That is hardly a worthy sentiment, Mr. Monk," Delphine said, looking quickly at Sacheverall and away again. "I would be obliged if you would not express it here. It is not the way we believe—or behave. Zillah was fond of this young man and saw him more frequently than we desired. It was inevitable, since he moved in the same circles. Before he became too enamored of her and overstepped propriety, or we unintentionally encouraged hopes in him that would not be fulfilled, we went for a short holiday to Crickieth, in North Wales." She forced herself to smile. "By the time we returned he had formed an attachment for another young lady, altogether more suitable to his age and situation. The word *passion* is far too strong for such a childhood fondness."

Her words fell in silence, as if they all knew they were a gilding of the truth to such a point as to amount to a lie. Zillah was the only one who seemed unconcerned.

"What has it to do with Keelin's death?" she persisted. "Hugh wouldn't have harmed anyone over me, no matter how ardent he seemed at the time. He said a lot of things he didn't mean. He was hotheaded, but there was no real violence in him."

"Of course there wasn't!" Delphine said urgently, looking at Zillah with warning in her eyes, then at Sacheverall. "It was all very young and innocent, and over with years ago."

"No, it wasn't," Zillah contradicted. "He went on writing to me. . . ." She disregarded Delphine's obvious anger. "I collected the letters from a friend. And there is no use asking me who, because I shall not tell you. . . ."

"You will do as you are told, young lady!" Delphine snapped, moving forward as if to restrain her physically.

"Was he jealous over your betrothal to Melville?" Lambert asked, holding up his hand to Delphine and looking steadily at his daughter, his expression hard and anxious. "Does he still care for you enough to have hated Melville for her insult to you? Tell me the truth, Zillah. He will not be blamed for anything he did not do, but I will not allow Keelin Melville's death to go unavenged if anyone else is responsible for it but herself. We may be speaking of murder. I will have no false loyalties or soft ideas of romance. Your loyalty is to the truth, girl, before all else. Do you understand me?"

"Yes, Papa." She did not flinch. "I wrote to Hugh long after Mama took me to Wales, but I never saw him again, except by chance, and never alone. He says that he still cares for me. Of course, I don't know whether that is true or just his idea of romance. But he wrote very well to me when the betrothal was announced, even if there was some regret in it." She shook her head as if almost certain. "I cannot believe he has it in him to have hurt Keelin, whatever he felt." Her voice was very earnest and she ignored everyone but her father. "He wrote that no matter how it grieved him to see me marry someone else, he still wished me happiness. I believe he meant it." For the first time the shadow of a smile touched her lips. Something sweet had been remembered and it came through even present pain.

Sacheverall stared at her. Perhaps without being aware of it he took a step backward, opening a greater distance between them. The eagerness had gone from his face. Delphine had seen it. Zillah still had her back to him.

"I shall speak to you later about your disobedience," Lambert said to her, but the coldness in his voice was pretense; there was no echo of it in his eyes. "It is up to Mr. Monk whether he chooses to investigate young Gibbons or judges it to be worth pursuing. I have engaged him to learn the truth of Melville's death."

"That, of course, is your choice," Sacheverall said with noticeable chill. "I have discharged my duties in the matter. My final advice to you"—he looked at Lambert, not at Zillah—"is that you consider the matter ended and resume your lives and put it from your mind. You conducted yourselves both legally and morally in a perfectly upright manner and have nothing with which to reproach yourselves. Private mistakes of the past are no one else's concern. I shall not mention them, and I presume Monk is bound by the same constraints, although of course I cannot answer for him."

"You don't need to!" Monk said savagely. "I consider Miss Lambert's reputation to be without blemish."

Sacheverall gave him a curious look, a mixture of contempt for his naïveté and amusement in the mistaken assumption that Monk admired her in a personal sense and would consider courting her.

In defense of Zillah, Monk did not disabuse him.

Sacheverall bade them farewell and took his leave.

The moment he was gone Delphine rose to her feet, her face white, tight-lipped.

"You fool!" she said furiously, glaring at Zillah. "How could you be so unbelievably stupid? You didn't have to say anything about that wretched Gibbons boy! You could have said I took you away because he was pestering you!" She was breathing hard. "You could have said anything at all. A dozen different things would have been perfectly believable and left you with a reputation. Look what you've done." She flung her arm out. "You haven't the wits you were born with! Or at least when you were a child! Sometimes I wonder where you got your stupidity from. It's certainly nothing I've taught you."

She jabbed her finger towards the closed door again. "He would have married you. He was utterly charmed. You were everything he wanted. He has an excellent family, intelligence, good manners and very fine prospects indeed. His reputation is perfect. Do you think I don't look into these things before I let anyone pay court to you? Do you?"

Zillah drew in her breath.

"Well, do you?" Delphine demanded, her eyes blazing. "Haven't I always taken the best care of you, done everything for your interest, for your welfare and your future? Now in one idiotic conversation you've sent another man off out of your life." She gestured towards the door again. "And he won't come back—don't hold any hopes of that. He thought you lost your virtue to Gibbons, and nothing you say now is going to change his mind. He won't look at you again, except with polite contempt. And do you imagine people won't guess why?" Her voice was rising steadily and getting wilder, and unconsciously she was moving towards Zillah. "Two men attracted to you and then leaving you suddenly—in as many months! There's only one conclusion anyone with a jot of sense will draw from that."

"Delphine . . ." Lambert interrupted, moving towards her.

She shook her head impatiently. "Don't be absurd, Barton! Face reality. People may like her, young men may desire her, heaven knows she's beautiful enough, I've seen to that. But they won't marry her. Their mothers won't allow it, whatever they think." She whirled around to Zillah again, her eyes burning in a white face. "Is that what you'll settle for? Being liked and desired while all the eligible men marry other girls? I can tell you, it may be fine for another year or two, but in five years, when they have houses and families and you are still here with us, it will look very different. The invitations will stop coming. You will have more and more time to sit by yourself and consider your idiocy."

"Delphine, stop it!" Lambert commanded.

But she would not be stopped; the heat of passion consumed any restraint. "And when you are thirty, and an old maid, and your beauty is gone, what then? Who's going to keep you? What are you going to do with yourself?"

"I'll keep her, should that arise!" Lambert responded angrily. "And she'll do with herself whatever she chooses."

"There won't be anything to choose from," Delphine pointed out. "Can't you see what she's done? Are you so blind you still don't understand?" There were tears of grief and frustration in her eyes. "One suitor leaving her she might get over, but not two!" Her voice dropped to be deeply sarcastic. "Or are you going to suggest there is something wrong with Sacheverall? He's a woman in disguise, perhaps?"

Lambert was momentarily lost for a reply.

"He was an opportunistic coward who did not love her," Monk

supplied with deep disgust. "And any woman is worthy of more than that." He was so filled with loathing for the whole system of values where beauty and reputation were the yardsticks of worth that he did not trust himself to say more. "It is not a misfortune that he showed his nature before you could no longer extricate yourself from any connection with him gracefully." He said this last to Zillah. He turned to Barton Lambert. "Thank you for your time, sir. I shall learn what more I can about Melville's death, and advise you if it is of worth. Good day." And he bowed to the women and left.

It was later in the afternoon when he was recalling the conversation that he realized how odd were the particular words Delphine had used regarding Zillah. She had almost sounded as if she had not known her in her first year or so of life. She had seemed to disclaim responsibility for Zillah's inherited qualities. Had Barton Lambert been married before, and Zillah was his daughter but not hers? Zillah was apparently an only child, which was not a common circumstance.

Could that be relevant to anything? It hardly affected Melville's death. If he found out, it would be simply from personal curiosity and because he wished an excuse not to go back to the letters and the grievance of the sister-in-law he had been working on before.

It should not be so difficult to find out. He had ascertained earlier that Zillah was not illegitimate because the Lamberts had publicly celebrated a wedding anniversary which ruled that out. But, of course, no one had required proof of the marriage. Perhaps he should have been more thorough then? Of course, it was completely irrelevant now.

Nevertheless, for his own satisfaction he would learn.

It took him the rest of the day, many judiciously placed questions and a lot of searching through papers, but he learned that Barton Lambert, aged thirty-eight, and Delphine Willowby, aged thirty-two, had been married exactly when they had said. But in the parish where they lived there was no record of Zillah Lambert's being born to them, or of any other child.

Some three years later they had moved, and arrived at their new address with a very lovely child of about eighteen months, a little girl with wide eyes and red-gold hair.

So Zillah was adopted. Delphine had married later than most women, in spite of her beauty and intelligence, and perhaps had been unable to bear children. She would not be the only woman afflicted by such grief. It had happened throughout the ages, accompanied by pain and too often public condescension, the kind of pity that is touched with judgment.

Had she married late because she too had suffered some unjust rejection? Was her anger at Zillah rooted in her own experience of hurt?

Suddenly Monk's dislike of her evaporated and was overtaken by compassion. No wonder she had been angry with Melville and been determined, at any cost, to defend Zillah's good name.

Perhaps he owed it to Rathbone to give him this small piece of information and tell him that so far that was all he knew. It was no help, but it was at least a courtesy.

He arrived at noon the next day at Vere Street.

Rathbone was busy with a client, and Monk was obliged to wait nearly half an hour before he was shown into the office.

"What have you learned?" Rathbone asked immediately, not even waiting to invite Monk to be seated.

Monk looked at his anxious face, the fine lines between his brows and the tension in his lips. His sense of failure was acute.

"Nothing of importance," he said quietly, sitting down anyway. "Zillah Lambert was adopted when she was a year and a half old. It seems Delphine could not bear children. She was well over thirty when she married Lambert. That might explain why she is so desperate that Zillah should marry well, and so jealous for her reputation. She knows what it means to society." He added a brief summary of his visit with the Lamberts, and Sacheverall's sudden departure.

Rathbone used a word about Sacheverall Monk was not aware he even knew and Sacheverall would have resented profoundly. He sank back in his chair, staring across the desk. "If we can't find anything better than we have, the inquest on Melville will find suicide." He watched Monk closely, his eyes shadowed, questioning.

"It probably was suicide," Monk said softly. "I don't know why she did it then, or exactly how. We probably never will. But then, I don't know how anyone could have murdered her either. And what is more pertinent, I don't know of any reason why they would. The Lamberts had nothing to hide."

CHAPTER ELEVEN

The inquest on Keelin Melville was a very quiet affair, held in a small courtroom allowing only the barest attendance by the general public. This time the newspapers showed little interest. As far as they, or anyone else, were concerned, the verdict was already known. This was only a formality, the due process which made it legal, and able to be filed away as one more tragedy and then forgotten.

The coroner was a youthful-looking man with smooth skin and fair hair through which a little gray showed when he turned and his head caught the light. There were only the finest of lines at the sides of his eyes and mouth. Rathbone had seen him a number of times before and knew he had no liking for displays of emotion and loathed sensationalism. The real tragedy of sudden and violent death, and above all suicide, was too stark for him to tolerate exhibitions of false emotion.

He began the proceedings without preamble, calling first the doctor who had certified Melville as dead. Nothing was offered beyond the clinical and factual, and nothing was asked.

Rathbone looked around the room. He saw Barton Lambert sitting between his wife and daughter, and yet looking oddly alone. He was staring straight ahead and seemed to be unaware of anyone near him. Even Zillah's obvious distress did not seem to reach him. He did not move to touch her or offer her any comfort even by a glance.

Delphine, on the other hand, was quite composed, and even as

Rathbone watched her, she leaned forward, smiled and said something to Zillah. A slight flicker of expression crossed Zillah's face, but it was impossible to tell what she was feeling. It could have been an effort to be brave and hide her grief; it could have been tension waiting for the pronouncement of the verdict expected by all of them. It could even have been suppressed anger.

Rathbone was feeling almost suffocating rage himself, partly directed towards the court, towards Sacheverall, who was sitting far away from the Lamberts and carefully avoiding looking towards them. But most painfully, Rathbone's anger was towards himself. He had failed Keelin Melville. Had he not, they would not now be here questioning her death.

He did not even now know how he should have acted to prevent the tragedy from playing itself out. He could think of no place or time when he could have done something differently, but taken altogether the result was a failure, complete and tragic. He had failed to win her trust. That was his shortcoming. He might not have saved her reputation or professional standing in England, but he would certainly have saved her legal condemnation and, without question, her life.

Why had she not trusted him? What had he said, or not said, so that she had taken this terrible step rather than tell him the truth? Had she thought him ruthless, dishonorable, without compassion or understanding? Why? He was not any of those things. No one had ever accused him . . . except of being a little pompous, possibly; ambitious; even at times cold—which was quite unjustified. He was not cold, simply not overimpulsive. He was not prejudiced—not in the slightest. Even Hester, with all her ideas, had never said he was prejudiced. And heaven knows, she would have said it had it crossed her mind!

The doctor's evidence was finished. It informed them of nothing new.

The police told of being called over the matter, as was necessary. Melville had apparently been alone all evening. There was no sign whatsoever of anyone else's having entered her rooms.

"Was there any evidence of Miss Melville's having eaten or drunk anything since returning home that evening?" the coroner asked.

"We saw nothing, sir," the policeman replied unhappily. "It seemed the young lady had no resident servant. There was nothing out of place. No food had been prepared and there was no crockery or glasses showing as been used."

"Did you search for any container for pills or powders, Sergeant?" the coroner pressed.

"Yes sir, an' we found nothing except a paper for a headache powder screwed up in the wastepaper basket in the bedroom. We looked very careful, sir. Fair turned the place inside out."

"I see. Thank you. You also looked for bottles, I presume? Even clean ones which might have been used and then washed out?"

"Yes sir. No empty packets, bottles, vials, papers, nothing. And we took away and had tested what was still in use. All harmless domestic stuff as you'd find in most people's homes."

"Very diligent. Have you any idea where Miss Melville obtained the poison which killed her, or where she administered it to herself?"

"No, sir, we have not."

"Thank you. That is all. You may step down."

Rathbone looked around again as the sergeant left and the police surgeon was called. Monk sat lost in gloom. He looked about as miserable and angry as Rathbone felt. There was a certain companionship in their silence. Neither of them had the slightest desire to try to express his thoughts in words. It was a vague comfort for Rathbone to know that he was not alone in his struggle to find meaning in this, in his profound unhappiness and sense of having been helpless and inadequate all the way along.

The police surgeon gave evidence as to his surprise at discovering the deceased was a woman and not a man as she had at first appeared. But she was in every physical way quite normal—indeed, dressed appropriately she would have been a handsome woman, even beautiful, in her own way. He said it quietly and with great sadness.

There was a hush in the room as he spoke. Someone coughed. Someone else stifled a nervous giggle and was instantly glared at. People seemed to be both embarrassed and moved by a deep sense of loss and the finality of death.

"And the cause of Miss Melville's death?" the coroner asked.

"Belladonna poisoning, sir," the surgeon answered without hesitation.

"Can you be certain of that?"

"Absolutely. I found traces of belladonna in the deceased's internal organs. And on examination of the body, every sign led me to consider it as a probable cause of death."

"What were the signs?"

"Widely dilated pupils, exceedingly dry skin, great dryness in the mouth, redness in the face. On examination of the body in autopsy I also found retention of urine and, of course, failure of the heart consistent with the effects of belladonna." There was an uncomfortable shifting in the court as people imagined the distress and the fear; the immediate physicality of it made it so much more real.

"The symptoms before death include increased heart rate," the doctor continued. "Very loud, audible even at a distance from the patient. Often the patient becomes aggressive, disoriented and suffers hallucinations. The police informed me they found one or two items knocked over, consistent with blurred vision."

Rathbone sat rigidly, his shoulders hunched, his fists tight. His mind was drenched with misery as he thought of Keelin Melville frightened, half blinded, knowing she was dying, hearing her own heart pound until it burst.

"Yes . . . yes. I do not argue with your conclusion, Doctor." The coroner shook his head, his voice cutting across Rathbone's thoughts. "If you found belladonna within the body then that is sufficient. How long before death would it have been consumed? I take it it was consumed? It was not injected, or absorbed through the skin, or breathed in?"

"No sir, it was swallowed. Death can take anywhere from a few hours to a few days, depending on the dose."

"And this dose?"

There was complete silence in the courtroom. Rathbone did not look around, but he could imagine everyone waiting. Why? To know what piece of evidence, what revelation or event had finally been more than Melville could take? Did they need the moment of decision?

"A heavy dose," the doctor replied, pursing his lips. "Sometime during the afternoon."

"Are you sure? Could it not have been after Miss Melville returned home?"

"No. It doesn't work that quickly."

"Or in the morning, before she came to court?"

Rathbone found he could hear his own pulse beating. Could it have been that early? Was it over Wolff's disgrace? Perhaps there had even been a quarrel with him?

"No sir," the doctor said with certainty. There was not even a shadow of doubt in his face or his voice. "If she had taken that much before she came to court in the morning, she would have been showing unmistakable symptoms by midday at the latest. No one could have mistaken it. She would have been dead by the afternoon."

"Are you quite sure about that?" the coroner persisted, his face wrinkled with concern.

"Quite," the doctor assured him.

"Can you tell us whether the belladonna was taken in liquid or powder form, or a tablet? Or if it was taken with food?"

"I cannot tell you whether it was liquid or powder, but it was not taken with food. There was very little food in the stomach. The poison probably acted as effectively as it did for that reason."

"How might one obtain belladonna?"

The doctor shrugged.

"The plant grows wild in all manner of places. Anyone could obtain it. All parts of it are poisonous. Various medical powders can be made from it for the treatment of several conditions." He shrugged very slightly. "Even for enhancing the beauty of the eyes. It enlarges the pupils. Hence the name—'beautiful woman'—belladonna."

"Thank you." The coroner nodded. "I have no more to ask you, except whether you can tell us if there is any evidence to show whether the deceased took this by her own hand or not."

"I have no way of knowing. That is a police matter. I can only say I know of no way in which it could be accidental."

The coroner pursed his lips, nodding again slowly. He dismissed the doctor with thanks and sipped a glass of cold water before calling Rathbone to the stand. Even when he sat back facing the court again, it was obvious he was disturbed more than usual by the details and the reality of death.

"Sir Oliver," he began slowly, "you were Keelin Melville's counsel during the case for breach of promise brought by Barton Lambert on behalf of his daughter, Miss Zillah Lambert." It was made as a statement, but he waited as if for a reply.

"Yes sir. I was," Rathbone agreed.

"When did you become aware that Miss Melville was indeed a woman, and not a man, Sir Oliver?"

"After her death, at the same time as we all did," Rathbone answered. He could feel the eyes of everyone in the small public gallery upon him and the heat burned up his cheeks at the realization that they must think him a fool. It was not his reputation that bothered him, but the fear that they were right.

"You have no confidence towards your client now, except that of the truth," the coroner said quietly. "What reason did Melville give you for breaking her betrothal to Miss Lambert?"

"She swore that she had never intended to become betrothed to her," Rathbone answered, looking directly at the coroner and avoiding catching the eye of anyone else in the room. "She said it had happened by misunderstanding, which I had difficulty in believing at the time, but now it seems very readily explainable. I think she was genuinely very fond of Miss Lambert, in a manner of friendship, as one woman may be to another. She must have been extremely lonely." He found it difficult to say, and was not even sure if he wanted to expose such private grief to the stare of others. He doubted himself even as he spoke. "Isaac Wolff was the only person she could trust. Perhaps with Miss Lambert she was able to come closer to the pretty and feminine things she would like to have been able to share in herself but knew she never could. She might have allowed her guard to slip, and without being aware of it have given the wrong impression."

There was a soft murmur from the public section. He did not turn to look, although he could imagine Zillah's face. It might be some comfort to her that the deceit was not meant.

The coroner nodded, still watching Rathbone, waiting for him to go on.

"She was horrified when she knew," he resumed, remembering with painful vividness the look in her eyes. It had been close to panic. He had been impatient with it then.

"But she did not explain?" The coroner's face also was touched with deep sadness.

"No."

"I presume you asked?"

"Of course. I pleaded with her to tell me, in total confidence, if she knew anything to Miss Lambert's discredit or if there was anything in her own life which prevented her marrying . . ."

He heard the faint rustle in the courtroom, but no one laughed.

"She told me there was not." He took a breath. "I did not accept her word. I employed an agent of enquiry to research into both Miss Lambert's past and hers. He found nothing." He owed Monk something better than a bare statement. "If there had been longer, I daresay he would have learned the truth, but events overtook us. It appeared Melville's affair with Mr. Wolff was reason enough. Of course, we now know it was . . . a love between man and woman, not illegal, not abnormal." He had nearly said "not scandalous," but perhaps since they were not married, there would be those who would consider it so. "Such as is usual enough," he said instead.

"What was her frame of mind, as far as you could judge, when Mr. Sacheverall brought Isaac Wolff to the stand and accused him of a homosexual relationship with Melville?" There was a chill in the coroner's voice, and he did not look towards where Sacheverall was sitting.

"She was deeply distressed," Rathbone answered truthfully. "Very deeply. But she denied it to me."

"Did you believe her?"

"I . . . I don't know. I neither believed nor disbelieved. I was concerned with trying to rescue what I could from the situation. I hoped I might persuade Miss Lambert to settle for a small amount of damages, so at least Melville might not be financially ruined, as well as socially and professionally." He found the words difficult to say. They still hurt. The failure was deep and twisting inside him.

"Did you tell Miss Melville your hopes?"

"Of course."

"Do you know of anything that occurred that afternoon which would so alter the circumstances as to make her despair and take her own life?"

"Sacheverall had called a prostitute to the stand in the morning who had sworn that the affair she had observed was of a sexual nature," Rathbone said bitterly, "not the friendship both Wolff and Melville had insisted. But if that was the final incident, then I would have expected her to have taken the poison during the luncheon adjournment, and according to the surgeon she did not."

"Did Miss Melville at any time speak of taking her life, or say anything which led you, even in hindsight, to suppose she was thinking of it?"

"No." Rathbone's voice sank. "Perhaps I should have realized how desperate she was, but I had formed the belief that her art was so precious to her she would have lived to practice it regardless of anything else. I . . . in hindsight, I even wondered if she had been murdered . . . but I know of no way in which anyone else could have administered the poison to her, nor any reason why they should."

"I see. Thank you, Sir Oliver. I have nothing further to ask you."

Rathbone remained where he was. He wanted to say something else, something about the whole ridiculous situation which had brought about a needless tragedy and destroyed one of the most luminous talents he had ever known, not to mention a vibrant, intelligent human being capable of suffering and laughter and dreams.

"It need not have happened!" he said angrily, leaning forward a little over the slender rails of the witness stand, his hands gripping them. "If any of us had behaved with a little more sense, a little more charity, it would all have been avoided. Keelin Melville could be alive now, still creating beauty for us and for our heirs in this city, this country."

There was a murmur of shock in the gallery, and then something which could even have been approval.

He leaned over farther. "For God's sake, why can't we allow women to use whatever talents they have without hounding and denying them until they are reduced to pretending to be men in order to be taken at their true value?"

There was a shifting of weight on the public benches, and a rustle and creak of fabric. People were uncomfortable.

"Why can't we allow people to break a betrothal if they realize it was a mistake," he went on passionately, "without assuming there must be some fearful sin on the part of one or the other of them? Why do we care so much if a woman is pretty or not? If all we want is something lovely to look at, we can buy a picture and hang it on the wall. We do this!" He flung out his arms. "We create a society where people go to law instead of saying to each other the simple truth. And now instead of a broken romance—which, God knows, hurts enough, but we all experience it—we have scandal, disgrace, shame, and worst of all, we have destroyed one of the brightest talents of our generation. And over what? A misunderstanding."

There was definite movement in the gallery now, a whispering, a buzz. Even the jurors were muttering.

Sacheverall rose to his feet, his face red.

"Sir Oliver is being disingenuous, sir, and I cannot sit here in silence and allow it. He knows as well as I do that a young woman's reputation is precious to her. A man who robs another person of reputation steals one of his, or her, most priceless possessions . . . one that can never be got back again." He glanced at the jurors; he did not care about the public. "That is not a false value. It is a very real one."

His expression twisted to undisguised contempt, and he was moving forward from his seat. "Sir Oliver would be one of the first to complain if his good name was compromised. In fact, he may discover after the loss of this case just how painful it can be when people no longer think of you as well as they once did." He was now out in front of the court, not more than a couple of yards from where Rathbone stood. He was a large man and seemed to crowd the area. He moved his hands around, taking up even more space. Everyone was watching him, but the expressions Rathbone could see were very varied, and not all of respect.

"It is natural enough to resent losing a case, especially as dramatically as he lost this one." Sacheverall smiled fleetingly towards Rathbone. "But that was his error of judgment in accepting it and choosing to fight it in the first place. Now he is blaming all the rest of us"—he swung his arms wide to embrace everyone present—"for Melville's misfortune. That is manifestly preposterous. We are not at fault in any way. Keelin Melville chose to behave unnaturally, to deny her womanhood and attempt to follow a masculine profession from which she would, of course, have been excluded had she not practiced such a deception."

There was a rumble from the body of the room, but he ignored it. He also ignored the growing darkness in the coroner's face, the tight pull of his lips and the drawing down of his brows.

"She also deceived Barton Lambert, her friend and benefactor, who had from the very beginning shown her only kindness and a trust she did not honor and did not return." He gestured contemptuously towards Rathbone. "For Sir Oliver to complain now, and accuse society at large, is to show his own shallowness of character and to demonstrate that, far from learning by his error of judgment, he is determined to compound it."

The coroner was so furious he scarcely knew where to begin.

"Mr. Sacheverall," he said loudly and very clearly, "I believe Sir Oliver included himself in his castigation of society. Perhaps your own involvement in these events did not allow you to listen to what he said with the attention which I think was its due. I have heard what has been said here today up to this point, and unless there is evidence yet to come which contradicts it, I cannot help but agree that the death of Keelin Melville was a tragedy which need not have happened. And for you to suggest that she was depraved, that she deceived Mr. Lambert willfully, I find unjustified and most distasteful."

Sacheverall's face reddened, but it was as much in anger as shame. There was no shred of retreat in his attitude, and his chin jerked up, not down.

"Unless you have something to say which is germane to the issue, Mr. Sacheverall," the coroner continued, "you will return to your seat and keep from any further interruption to our proceedings." He raised his eyebrows. "Do you have any information we should know as to when Keelin Melville took the poison which killed her, where she obtained it, or when?"

"No—I . . ."

"Did you observe anything which you have not told the police?"

"No—I . . ."

"Have you anything useful whatever to add?"

"I . . ."

"Then please resume your seat—and do not interrupt us again!"

Sacheverall retreated in ill-concealed fury. There might have been sympathy for him among his peers, or his friends in society.

There was none in the courtroom. Whatever the people there had thought of Keelin Melville in her lifetime, now they had nothing but a sense of pity and an uncomfortable suspicion that they were in some way, no matter how small a way, to blame for her death.

The coroner called Isaac Wolff to the stand. He was obviously in a state of deep grief. His face was almost bloodlessly pale, his eyes had the hollow look of a man who is suffering a prolonged illness, and he spoke quietly and without any lift or timbre in his voice.

The coroner treated him with the greatest courtesy, asking him only those facts which were necessary to corroborate or enlarge upon what was already known.

Wolff answered as briefly as possible, and his bare hands grasped the rail as if he needed it in order to keep his balance. The room was full, for the most part, of ordinary people, and they were too sensible of the presence of loss not to share in it. There was not a sound among them as he spoke. No one fidgeted or turned away. No one whispered to their neighbors.

Rathbone found himself watching Barton Lambert. He too was sunk in a weight of grief. Looking at him now it was naked in his face how fond of Melville he had been—as a friend, as an artist, as a colleague in creating lasting, individual and innovative beauty. It was also clear that his sorrow was touched with an acute awareness of how large his own part had been in this tragedy. His shoulders slumped forward. He did not look to either side of him, as if he preferred to remain islanded away from even those closest to him.

Delphine, on the contrary, sat upright, her eyes wide, her attention sharp and clear. It could not be supposed she was comfortable, but she was enduring the temporary embarrassment with stoicism, knowing the important victory was hers. This was merely part of the price. And there were other battles ahead. Her glance, when it strayed towards Sacheverall, was venomous in the extreme. Rathbone would not be surprised if in due course stories and whispers began to circulate not entirely to Sacheverall's credit. Nothing specific would be said, only looks, intonations of the voice, a question in the eyes. Neither, actually, would he be sorry. In fact, he thought of it with some satisfaction.

After Wolff had finished the coroner called Monk, but only to assure himself that Monk could add nothing. Monk corroborated what he had heard and stepped down again.

The coroner did not retire to consider. There was no need.

"I have listened to all that has been said today." He frowned as he spoke. "It is a case which disturbs me greatly for the loss of a young and brilliant life which had already been an ornament to our culture and would undoubtedly have been more so in the future, had she lived. I have not been satisfied as to exactly how it happened, nor precisely what particular incident turned the balance from discouragement to despair, but there is no other conclusion possible except that Keelin Melville took her own life by swallowing the poison of belladonna while in the courthouse during the case against her for breach of promise." He breathed in and out slowly. "One may only presume that the ruin which the suit brought to her life and career, and to the life of the man she loved, was a pain more than she felt able to bear. We must all live with our own responsibility for our individual parts in that." He picked up his gavel and touched it lightly to its stand. "This court is adjourned."

Monk left after only the briefest word with Rathbone. There really was nothing to say. They both knew before they went in what the verdict would be, and the pain of it would only be made worse by standing around talking about it. They had done their best, and it had not been good enough. Of course, they never expected to win every case. No one did. But losing did not grow easier.

He came down the steps into the street and hailed the first hansom he saw, directing the driver to Tavistock Square. He should tell Hester what had happened in person rather than allow her to read it or hear about it. Anyway, now that it was no longer a cause célèbre it would only be a small item on a back page. She might not even see it.

And he wanted to share the burden of his feelings about it with someone to whom it needed no explanation and who would understand without his needing to tell anything but the bare facts.

He was welcomed as usual and shown into the withdrawing room. He asked to see Hester, and this time there was no waiting. She came after barely five minutes, and a glance at his face told her why he had come.

"It's over?" She came in and closed the door behind her. There was a small fire burning and the room looked gentle and very domestic, shabby enough to feel at ease.

"Yes . . . it's over. Suicide."

She looked at him closely, studying his eyes, his face. For several moments she did not say anything more, simply sharing in silence the complex unhappiness of the knowledge. All sorts of questions and ideas went through his mind as to whether they could have done differently, what he had expected, but none of them were worth putting into words. He knew what her answer would be, and that very fact was comfortable.

"How is Oliver?" she said at last.

He laughed very slightly, abruptly. "Extraordinary . . . quite out of character," he answered, then wondered immediately if that was so. Perhaps Rathbone had instead found a truer part of himself. "He told the court, and the public, what he thought of their general prejudice and of the value of women for their prettiness and docility, and led the way for the coroner to express his highly unflattering opinion of Sacheverall." He remembered it with surprising pleasure as he said it.

She smiled, a slow, sad smile, but with a gentleness he realized he had seen in her often.

"Poor Oliver. He is not used to feeling so violently. I think he cared about Melville more than most of his cases. I've never seen him so angry."

"You admire that, don't you?" he observed. He made it a question, but he knew it was true. If she had denied it he would not have believed her. He admired it too. He had no regard for someone incapable of anger at injustice.

He had thought Rathbone cold, a creature of his intellect, of superb and total control of his emotions. To find he was not so increased Monk's liking for him. He was not sure that he wished to like Rathbone, but even with all its complications, it was a sweeter feeling than contempt or indifference.

"Do you want to tell Gabriel?" she asked, cutting across his thoughts.

"Yes . . . yes, I will. How is he?" He asked because he liked Gabriel; it was not a matter of courtesy.

"Better," she replied, meeting his eyes. "I think the pain is about the same. It will be for a while. But he is sleeping with fewer nightmares now."

"Perdita?" he guessed.

She smiled. "Yes. Slowly . . ."

He smiled also, remembering Athol Sheldon and the look on his face when Perdita had spoken to him the last time Monk had been there. It was a battle she would not win easily, but at least she was prepared to fight it.

Hester led the way from the withdrawing room across the hall and upstairs to Gabriel's room. She knocked on the door.

It was opened by Perdita. She was dressed in soft pink trimmed with wine and she looked very serious and demure in spite of the flattering color. She stared past Hester to Monk.

"Is it more about Martha's nieces?" she asked very quietly, in case Martha should be close and overhear her.

"No, Mrs. Sheldon, it is about the inquest on Keelin Melville."

"Oh." She hesitated only a moment. The old habit of trying to protect Gabriel did not die easily. She had to make a conscious effort to realize what she was doing. She opened the door wider and they followed her in.

Gabriel was sitting up on the bed, but he was fully dressed. It was only the second time Monk had seen him other than under the covers. He realized with a sense of shock how thin Gabriel was. Quite apart from the empty sleeve of his shirt, neatly tucked up and fastened, in the warm room with the sunlight streaming in, the thin cotton fabric showed how his body had wasted even on the other side. Heat, hunger and pain had taken a fearful toll on him. It would be half a year at least before he regained the health he had had before Cawnpore. Monk became acutely curious of his own body with its lean muscles and ease of movement, his energy, the power he did not even have to think of. So much was a matter of fortune. He could have been in the army instead of the police. He might have been in India. He could have been in Gabriel Sheldon's place, and Gabriel in his. Except he would not have had Perdita to care for him and to be responsible for. But he could have! She was just the sort of gentle, charming woman he had fallen in love with so many times.

Gabriel was looking at him, waiting for him to speak.

"Keelin Melville?" he said at last, when Monk was still silent.

"Yes," Monk replied, coming in. "They held the inquest this morning."

Gabriel's face was unreadable. It flew to Monk's mind that Gabriel must have thought of suicide himself in the early days of his maiming and disfigurement. How often had he lain on his back in agonizing pain and helplessness and wished he were dead? Melville could at least have escaped most of her difficulties. She could have left England and started again in a dozen different places. She was young, healthy; she had sufficient means to travel and no unbreakable ties. Wolff could have gone with her, had he wished to. She was whole of body and had her health and very considerable good looks. In Italy or France she could even have lived openly as a woman and married Wolff. Perhaps she would have had to practice her profession through him, give him credit for her creation or her technical skill . . . but was that not still infinitely better than dying?

Why had she given up?

"What is it?" Gabriel asked, watching him.

How honest should he be? There was a difference between the candor of respect and the tactlessness of acting without thought or compassion.

"Suicide," Monk replied. "They brought in a verdict of suicide, although they couldn't decide what actually turned the balance between misery and despair or, for that matter, how or precisely when she took the poison."

Perdita gave a little sigh.

"I'm sorry," Gabriel said quietly. "She must have found it beyond bearing." He looked for a moment as if he was going to say something more, then changed his mind.

"Do you understand it?" Monk asked, then could have bitten his tongue. It was exactly what he had determined not to do. He was aware of Hester just behind him near the door.

Gabriel smiled, lighting the good side of his face and twisting the scarred flesh of the other.

"No. But if there is anything I've learned in all this, it is that we don't understand what makes the breaking point, or what we find we can endure beyond anything we thought we could—for ourselves or for anyone else." He was speaking quietly, the look in his eyes far away. "The damnedest people endure things that seem impossible, and sometimes do it without even complaining. I've seen men I used to think were ordinary, not very special in any way, a bit crude." He smiled ruefully. "A bit stupid even, put up with terrifying injury without crying out. Or walk for miles with their feet ripped raw and squelching blood, and make silly jokes about it." Hester and Perdita had been close together, motionless up to this point. Now Perdita came forward and sat by the bed near Gabriel, sliding her hand over his.

Gabriel tightened his fingers to grasp hers, then went on. "I've seen men I thought were callous and insensitive stay by a dying man they scarcely knew, and sit up all night telling him stories about anything and everything so he wasn't alone, and then when they were so tired they could hardly see straight, get up and dig a hole deep enough to bury him. I've heard illiterate men say prayers that would wrench your heart, and the next minute use language you wouldn't let your father hear, let alone your mother." He laughed, but it was a jerky sound, charged with emotion. "And I've seen men I thought had all the courage in the world lie down and die of a wound that wouldn't have slowed up someone else. I don't know why Melville killed herself. You don't either?"

"No. No, I don't. It . . ." Monk sighed and sat down on the chair at the foot of the bed. "It leaves a feeling of being unfinished, as if there were something else I should know, but I can't think what it is."

"Don't torture yourself," Gabriel said gently. "You may never know. There are lots of things about other people we'll never understand. It doesn't matter. You don't have any particular right to know—or need, except for your own curiosity."

Perdita turned to Monk.

"Thank you for coming," Perdita said with a tiny smile. "I would far rather you told us than we heard it from Athol." She flinched minutely as she spoke his name, more of remembered pain than dislike. She had known him too long not to understand at least part of the prejudices which drove him. "What will happen to Mr. Wolff?" she asked very quietly. "They can't hurt him, can they?"

Gabriel was watching Monk as well, a shadow of concern in his eyes. Odd how beautiful and clear they were above his disfigured face. Monk found himself no longer surprised or horrified by it. Of course, he had never known him before, and that must make a shattering difference. If he had loved a beautiful woman, how would he feel if she were scarred like that? Would he still be in love with her, or only care as a friend?

Hester was not beautiful . . . except for her eyes, and her mouth when she was thinking, and when she smiled, and her hands. She had the loveliest hands he had ever seen, not soft and white as fashion admired, but slender, delicate and very strong, perfectly balanced.

Perdita was waiting.

"No . . ." he said abruptly. "No, it's not a crime to allow someone to masquerade as a man while being a woman. Unless it is for the purpose of fraud, of course."

"But this wasn't!" Perdita said quickly. "She was selling her designs to Mr. Lambert, and it shouldn't matter whether she was a man or a woman for that!"

"Mr. Lambert won't take the matter any further," Monk said with a smile. "Unless he can blame someone for her death—then he will."

Gabriel was surprised. "Can he?"

Monk shrugged. "I doubt it. I thought for a little while it might somehow be murder, but that doesn't make sense, either for motive or opportunity."

"I suppose we should be pleased . . . I think." Hester came farther into the room at last. She met Monk's eyes, searching behind her words to see what he felt. "I don't know if I am. I hate to think of her . . . so . . ." She did not finish the sentence.

Gabriel shot a glance at her over Perdita's head, but Perdita turned also.

"I know what you mean," she agreed. "But we cannot help. If you wish to see Mr. Monk alone for a little while, I shall stay and keep Gabriel company." She smiled self-consciously. "For once we were not talking about India. I have plans to alter the garden a little and I was telling him about it. I shall draw it out, once he agrees. Perhaps I shall even paint it."

Monk bade them good-bye, and Hester took him to the withdrawing room, where the parlormaid served them with tea and hot buttered crumpets. Monk was surprised how much he enjoyed them. He had been too angry and disturbed to think of luncheon.

"So there's really nothing more you can do for Keelin Melville, is there?" Hester asked, biting into her crumpet and trying very carefully not to drop butter down herself.

"No, it seems to be finished," he agreed. "Gabriel is correct:

there are some things we'll never know, and we don't have any right to." He took a second crumpet.

"What are you going to tell Mr. Lambert?"

He looked at her across the tea tray. What did she expect of him? There was nothing to follow, nothing else to pursue.

She was waiting, as though his answer mattered.

"Nothing!" he said a little sharply.

"What other cases have you?" She looked interested, holding the crumpet up regardless of the butter dripping onto the plate.

"Nothing of any interest," he said ruefully. "Trivial things which won't mean anything, people looking for fault when there is only error or inarticulateness." The prospect was tedious but unavoidable. It was part of the daily routine between the larger cases, and it paid his way so well that he relied very little on Callandra Daviot's kindness now. Their original agreement—that he would include her in all the cases of complexity or unusual interest as reciprocation for her assistance in times of hardship—had worked extremely well, to both their advantage.

"Oh, good." Hester smiled and put the rest of the crumpet into her mouth before it lost all its butter. "Then you will have time to look a little further for Martha's nieces."

He should have known she was leading to that. He should have foreseen it and avoided it. How naive of him.

The smile was still on her face, but less certain, and her eyes were very direct.

"Please?" She did not use his name or stretch out her hand to touch him. It would have been easier to refuse if she had. She presumed intolerably upon friendship by not presuming on it at all.

"There is hardly any chance of success," he argued. "Do you realize what you are asking?"

"I think I do." Now she looked apologetic without actually saying so. "It will be very difficult indeed. No one will blame you if you can't find them. Please just look. . . ."

"They're probably dead!"

"If she knew that, then she could mourn them and stop worrying that they are alive somewhere, suffering and alone, and she was doing nothing to help."

"Hester!" he said exasperatedly.

"What?" She regarded him as if she had no idea what he was going to say.

There was no point in arguing with her. She was not going to give up. He might as well agree now as in half an hour, or tomorrow, or the day after.

"I'll try," he said warningly. "It won't do any good."

"Thank you. . . ." Her eyes were soft and bright, and she looked at him with a kind of trust he would never have believed could be so fiercely, uniquely precious.

Monk started out early the next morning without any hope of success. He might trace them from Putney if he was diligent—and lucky. He might even follow the first few years of their unfortunate lives. Would it really help Martha Jackson to know how they were treated, and when and where they died, from what cause? Perhaps it would. Perhaps Hester was right in that it would at least allow her to know there was nothing she could do, so she could begin to leave the worst of the distress behind her.

He packed a small, soft-sided bag with a change of clothes and paid a week's rent in advance, then left Fitzroy Street to travel south and west. He no longer wore his usual smartly cut jacket and elegant trousers. In the places he knew he would be going they would mark him out as a stranger, a target for cutpurses and possibly even garroters. He loathed the feeling of being unshaven, but it helped him to blend less noticeably into the background of those who lived in the borders of the underworld. He wanted to seem a man who should not be crossed, a dangerous man who was too familiar with the territory to be lied to. He also armed himself with a small, sharp knife and as much money as he could spare for food and accommodation, and for such bribes as should prove necessary.

The beginning would be the hardest. It was going to be very difficult indeed to find anyone who knew what had happened to two ugly, slow-witted little girls fifteen years ago. He turned the problem over and over in his mind as he rode in the omnibus along the riverbank and then across the Putney Bridge. The only person who would know would be the landlord who had passed them on, sold them, or whatever arrangement it had been. It would be a waste of his time to bargain with anyone else. Please heaven he was still alive!

It took him all morning and into the early afternoon to track him. He had bought almost a dozen pints of beer or cider for the information.

Mr. Reilly turned out to be a huge man with white hair like a mop head, unkempt and falling over his ears. It also fell over his brow and eyes, but that did not matter because apparently he was completely blind. He welcomed Monk cheerfully. He was sitting in a tattered chair beside the hearth, a mug of ale at his hand where he could reach it without having to fumble. A small black-and-white dog of some terrier breed lay beside his feet and watched Monk carefully.

"What yer be wantin' ter know, then?" Reilly asked cautiously. He was lonely these days, and companionship was precious.

Monk traded on it. "A few tales about the Coopers Arms, when it was yours," he replied, settling into the rickety chair opposite, afraid to let his full weight fall on the back of it in case it collapsed. "What was it like?"

Reilly did not need asking a second time. He launched into one tale after another, and it was the best part of three hours before Monk could steer him towards the two deformed kitchen maids he had sold to a man from Rotherhithe who kept a big public house down by the river and could use some rough help where it wouldn't be seen and no one would mind the twisted lips and the crooked eyes.

"Ugly little beggars, they were," he said, staring sightlessly at Monk. "An' slow with it. Could tell 'em 'alf a dozen times ter do summink, and they still wouldn't. Jus' ignore yer."

"Deaf," Monk said before he thought to stop himself. He was not supposed to know them, or care.

"What?" Reilly frowned at him, taking another long draft of his ale.

"Perhaps they were deaf?" Monk suggested, trying to keep the anger he felt out of his voice, not very successfully.

"Yeah, p'raps." Reilly did not care. He set the mug down with a clunk. "Anyway, I couldn't keep 'em. Upset me customers, and not much bloody use."

"So you sold them to a man from Rotherhithe. That was clever of you." Monk tried to force some appreciation into his tone. Reilly could not see the contempt on his face. "Wonder what he thought when he got them home?"

"Never 'eard," Reilly said, chuckling. " 'E din't come back, that's all I know."

"You never went after him to find out?" Monk barely made it a question.

"Me? Ter Rother'ithe? Not on yer life! Common place. Full o' all sorts. Dangerous too. Nah! I likes Putney. Nice an' respectable." Reilly reached again for his ale mug, which Monk had refilled several times. "What else'd yer like ter 'ear abaht?"

Monk listened another ten minutes, then excused himself after one more attempt to learn the name of the public house in Rotherhithe.

"Elephant an' summink . . . but you won't like it," Reilly warned.

It was late afternoon and the mournful sound of ships' foghorns drifted up the Thames on the incoming tide as Monk got off the omnibus in Rotherhithe Street, right on the river's edge. He could not afford to ride in hansom cabs on a job like this. Martha Jackson's pocket would not stretch to meet his legitimate expenses, never mind his comfort.

It was a gray, late-spring day with the water slurping against the stones a few yards away and the smells of salt and fish and tar sharp in the air. He was many miles nearer the estuary here than in Putney. The Pool of London lay in front of him, Wapping on the farther side. To his left he could just make out the vast bulk of the Tower of London in the mist, gray and white. Beyond it lay Whitechapel, and ahead of him Mile End.

The pool itself stretched out silver in the light between the ships coming and going laden with cargoes from all over the earth. Every kind of thing that could be loaded on board a vessel came in and out of this port. It was the center of the seagoing world. A clipper from the China Seas, probably in the tea trade, rocked gently on the swell, its masts drawing circles against the sky. A few gulls rode the wind, crying harshly. Barges worked their way upstream, tied together in long queues like the carriages of a train, their decks laden with bales and boxes tied down and covered with canvas.

Downriver on the farther side lay the Surrey Docks, Limehouse and then the Isle of Dogs. He stirred with memories of that, and of the fever hospital where Hester had worked with Callandra during the typhoid outbreak. He would never forget the smell of that, the mixture of effluent, sweat, vinegar and lime. He had been sick with fear for her, that she would catch it herself and be too exhausted to fight it.

Even standing there with the cool wind in his face off the water, he broke out in a sweat at the memory.

He turned away, back to the matter in hand. He must find a public house called the Elephant and something.

He stopped a laborer pushing a barrow along the cobbles.

"Elephant an' summink?" The man looked puzzled. "Never 'eard of it. 'Round 'ere, is it?"

"Rotherhithe," Monk answered, a sinking feeling gripping him that the man did not know. Rotherhithe was not so large. A man such as this would surely know all the public houses along the water's edge, by repute if not personally.

They were passed by another group of longshoremen.

"You sure?" The man squinted at Monk skeptically, looking him up and down. "W'ere yer from? Not 'round 'ere, are yer!"

"No. Other side of the river."

"Oh." He nodded as if that explained everything. "Well, all I knows abaht 'ere is the Red Bull in Paradise Street an' the Crown an' Anchor in Elephant Lane—that's just up from the Elephant Stair . . . which you can see up there beyond Princes' Stair. Them two are real close."

"Elephant Stair?" Monk repeated with a surge of hope. "Thank you very much. I'm obliged to you. I'll try the Crown and Anchor." And he walked briskly along the river's edge to the Elephant Stair, where the shallow stone steps led down into the creeping tide, salt-sharp and slapping against the walls, crunching and pulling on the shingle. He turned right and went up Elephant Lane.

He went into the crowded, noisy, steamy barroom and ordered and ate a good meal of pie with excellent pastry. He declined to imagine what the filling might be, judging that he preferred not to know. He followed it with a treacle suet pudding and a glass of stout, then began his enquiries.

He was glad he had eaten first; he needed the strength of a full stomach and a rested body to hear what was told him. It seemed the landlord had paid more attention to the low price than to the goods he was purchasing. When he had got the girls back to Rotherhithe he had put them to work in the sculleries washing glasses and dishes and scrubbing the floors. They had worked from before dawn until the public house closed at night. They had eaten what they could scavenge, and slept on the kitchen floor in a pile of sacking by the hearth, curled up together like cats or dogs.

They were willing enough to work, but they were slow, hampered by partial deafness and by being undersized and frequently ill. After a few months he had come to the conclusion that they were a bad bargain and cost him more than they were worth. He had been offered the chance to sell them to a gin mill in St. Giles, and seized the opportunity. It was a few shillings' return on his investment.

Where was the gin mill?

The publican had no idea.

Would a little money help him to recall?

It might. How much money?

A guinea?

Not enough.

The anger exploded inside Monk. He wanted to hurt the man, to wipe the greedy smile from his face and make him feel for a few minutes the misery and fear those children must have known.

"There are two possible ways of encouraging people to tell you what you need to know," he said very quietly. "By offering a reward . . ." He let the suggestion hang in the air.

The man looked at Monk's face, at his eyes. He was slow to see the rage there. He felt no more than a short shiver of warning. He was still working out how much money he could squeeze.

"Or by threat of something very nasty happening to them," Monk finished. His voice was still polite, still soft, but there was an edge of viciousness in it a sensitive ear would have caught.

"Oh, yeah?" the man said with more bravado than assurance. "You got something nasty in mind, then, 'ave yer?"

"Very," Monk answered between his teeth. He had the perfect excuse. He knew all the details. He had helped pull the body out of the river before he had quarreled with his superior and left the police force. "Do you remember Big Jake Hillyard?"

The man stiffened. He swallowed with a jerk of his throat.

Monk smiled, showing his teeth. "Do you remember what happened to him?"

"Anybody could say they done that!" the man protested. "They never got the bloke who done it."

"I know they didn't," Monk agreed. "But would anybody else be able to tell you exactly what they did to him? I can. Would you like to learn? Would you like to hear about his eyes?"

" 'E 'ad no eyes . . . w'en they found 'im!" the man squeaked.

"I know that!" Monk snapped. "I know precisely what he had . . . and what he hadn't! Where in St. Giles did you send those two little girls? I am asking you very nicely, because I should like to know. Do you understand me . . . clearly understand me?"

The man's face was white, sweating a little across the lips.

"Yeah! Yeah, I do. It were ter Jimmy Struther, in Coots Alley, be'ind the brickyard."

Monk grinned at him. "Thank you. For the sake of your eyesight, that had better be the truth."

"It is! It is!"

Monk had no doubt from the man's expression that indeed it was. He let the man go, then turned on his heel and left.

St. Giles turned out to be only another stop along the way. According to the woman he questioned there, the girls had remained for several years. She was not certain how many, seven or eight at least. Many of the patrons were too drunk or too desperate to care what a serving girl looked like, and the work was simple and repetitive. Little was asked of them, but then little indeed was given. Such affection or companionship as they ever received was from each other. And apparently each was quick to defend the other, even at the cost of a beating. The elder had once had her nose and two ribs broken in a brawl to protect her younger sister from the temper of one of the yard men.

Monk listened to the stories, and a picture emerged of two girls growing up totally untutored and unhelped, learning what little they did by trial and error—sometimes acutely painful error—able to speak only poorly, words muffled by crooked lips, heard by partially deaf ears. They were sometimes mocked for their afflictions, feared for their appearance, as if the disfigurement might be contagious, like a pox.

One woman said that she had heard them laugh, and on two or three occasions seen them play games with one another. They had a pet dog for a while. She had no idea what had become of it.

"Where did they go from here?" Monk asked, fearing this would be the end of his pursuit. No one would know. They were too weary, too sodden in drink to remember anything, or to care. The next bottle was all that mattered.

One woman shrugged and spat.

A second laughed at him.

The third swore, then mentioned the name of a whorehouse in the Devil's Acre, the teeming slum almost under the shadow of St. Paul's.

That was all he could get from them and he knew it. He had already lost their attention. He rose and left.

It took him two days of bribery, questioning, trickery and threats, and several abortive attempts, before he traced the girls to a brothel off a smith's yard in the Devil's Acre. It was a filthy place awash from overflowing drains and piles of refuse. Rats scuttled along the curbs above the gutters and people, almost undistinguishable from the heaps of rags, lay huddled in doorways.

Monk had been there before, but it still made him sick every time. He was hunched up with a cold that seemed to reach through his flesh to the bones. It knotted his stomach and made him shake till he clenched his teeth together to keep them from rattling. It was partly the wind turning and whistling through the alleys and cracks between the walls, partly the damp which rotted and seeped everywhere. Only when it froze did the incessant sound of dripping stop. And partly it was the smell. It gagged in the throat and churned the stomach.

He was too late. They had been there, scrubbing floors, carrying water from the standpipes four streets away, emptying slops in the midden and bringing back the buckets. They had gone the day before.

Gone . . . ! Where? Why?

One answer to that leaped out at him: because he had been pursuing them. He had asked questions, threatened. He had made his intense interest only too apparent. Someone was frightened, with or without reason. Before he began to look for them they were simply two unwanted girls shunted from one place to another, tolerated as long as some use could be made of them. His persistence and ruthlessness had made them important. He had driven someone to try to get rid of them.

Where do you get rid of people you don't want to be found? Kill them—if you dare. If you are sure you can dispose of the bodies. The thought almost suffocated him. His heart seemed to rise in his throat and drive the breath out of him. He grasped the man by the front of his clothes and jerked him off his feet.

"If you've killed them, I shall personally deliver you to the hangman! Do you understand me? If you don't believe me, then I had better see to it myself. You will have a hideous accident! A fatal one—precisely as fatal as whatever you did to those girls."

"That in't fair!" the man squawked, his eyes rolling.

"Of course it isn't!" Monk agreed, not loosening his grip in spite of the man's gasping and struggling. "There are two of them—and there's only one of you!" He grinned at the man savagely, as if a suddenly brilliant idea had occurred to him. "I've got it! I'll string you up, and then when you're nearly gone—when your lungs are bursting and your face is blue and you're almost on fire—I'll cut you down, throw a bucket of water over you, give you a glass of brandy, wait till you're all right . . . then do it again! Once for each girl. Is that fairer?"

"I din't do nuffink!" The man saw death in Monk's face and was nearly sick with fright. "They're fine! They're alive and well, I swear ter Gawd!"

"Don't swear. Show me!"

"They in't 'ere! I sold 'em . . . passed 'em on like. I give 'em a chance ter better theirselves. Get out o' Lunnon and go somewhere better for their 'ealth."

"Where, precisely?" Monk snarled.

"East! Across the water. Honest ter Gawd!"

Monk jerked him up again harshly, hearing his teeth clatter. "Where?"

"France! They're gorn ter France!"

Monk knew what that would be for. From there they would be shipped to God knows where: the white slave trade.

"When?" He slammed the man back against the wall. He regretted it instantly. He could have knocked him senseless, even broken his neck; but then he would be able to tell him nothing. "When did they leave?"

"Yest'y! They went down to the docks . . . Surrey Docks . . . yest'y night." He thought he was staring death in the face. "They'll go out on the afternoon tide terday."

"Ship?" Monk demanded. "What ship? Tell me you don't know and I'll send your teeth out through the back of your neck!"

"The *S-Summer Rose*," the man stammered. "So 'elp me Gawd!"

Monk dropped him and he slid to the floor, lying there sobbing for breath. Monk turned and ran from the room, out across the dripping yard and along the alley overhung with creaking boards and sagging half roofs onto the wider, crooked street. He had about an hour and a half before the tide. He would like to have gone home and changed into respectable clothes and collected some more money, but there was no time.

He stopped on the narrow pavement. It was beginning to rain. Should he go right or left? Where was the nearest thoroughfare where he might find a hansom? Would he even get one in the rain? He had very little money left. Not enough to bribe anyone. It was a good three miles to the docks, even as the crow flies, farther on foot with all the twists and bends of streets. He had not time to go on foot, even if he ran, not and still search the docks for one ship, and that ship for two frightened girls, possibly kept below decks and bound.

He turned towards the river and ran down the next alley and into another broader street. There were drays and carts in it, and one closed carriage. No hansoms.

He started to swear, then saved his breath for running.

Perhaps along Upper Thames Street, the closest one to the water, there would be cabs. It was too far! He needed to hurry. They would have to make a detour around the Tower of London.

He stood on the curb waving and shouting. No one stopped. They all splashed by in the harder and harder rain, going complacently on their way. He started to run eastwards. Queenhithe Dock was a little ahead of him. Stew Lane Stairs were to the right.

A long string of barges was pushing downriver, making slow way. The tide had not turned yet, but it would be slack water soon.

Barges! On the river!

He charged across the street, colliding with a costermonger's cart, extricating himself with difficulty amid an array of curses from several passersby. He yelled an apology over his shoulder and sprinted down Dowgate Hill and along the narrow cut down to the stairs just as the last barge drew level. He yelled, waving both his arms, signaling the barge to slow down.

The bargee must have thought it was some kind of warning. He eased a little, dropping back all the weight that his ships would allow. It was enough for Monk to run and leap. He barely made it. Without the bargee's frantic help he would have fallen back into the icy water. As it was, he was soaked from the waist down and had to be hauled sodden and shaking onto the deck.

"Wot the 'ell's the matter?" the bargee demanded.

"Got to get to the S-Surrey D-Dock!" Monk stuttered, shaking with cold. "Before the tide . . ."

"Missed yer ship, 'ave yer?" the bargee said with a laugh. "Yer'll be lucky if they 'ave yer. W'ere yer bin? Some 'ore'ouse up Devil's Acre? Gaw' lummy, yer look like 'ell! Wot ship d'yer want, mate?"

"*S-Summer R-Rose!*" Monk found he could not control the shaking.

"That ol' bucket! Yer'd be better missin' it, believe me." The bargee bent his back and pushed harder on his heavy pole, steering with almost absentminded skill.

Monk debated for a few moments whether to tell the man the truth or not. He might help . . . he might not give a damn. He might even make his own extra money in the trade.

They were passing under London Bridge.

He was weary of lying. He hated being tired and cold and filthy, and pretending he was something he was not.

"They've taken two girls to sell in France, or wherever they send them after that."

The bargee looked at him curiously, trying to read his face.

"Oh, yeah? What are they ter you, those two girls, then?"

"Their father died and their mother discarded them. They are disfigured, and deaf. Their father's sister is a friend of mine. She's been looking for them for years." It was a slight bending of the truth—in fact, but not in essence.

"Left it a bit late, 'aven't yer?" The bargee looked sympathetic, almost believing.

"They're shipping them out because they know I'm after them," Monk explained. "It's my fault!" he added bitterly.

The bargee regarded the comment critically. "Yer'd be better on something a bit faster'n me," he said with feeling.

"I know that!" Monk retorted. "But you're all I've got."

The bargee grinned and turned to look upstream. He stayed balanced for several moments while they drifted gradually past the bridge and towards the looming mass of the Tower of London, gray turreted against the sky.

Monk was so tense with the passion of frustration he could have screamed, punched something with all his strength as they seemed to move even more and more slowly.

A small, light fishing boat was coming up behind them, skimming rapidly almost over the surface of the water.

The bargee put his fingers to his lips and let out a piercing whistle.

A figure on the fishing boat cocked his head.

The bargee whistled again, waving his arms in what seemed to be some signal language.

The fishing boat changed course to come closer, then closer again.

"Go on!" the bargee shouted at Monk. "Tell 'em wot yer tol' me—an' good luck to yer!"

"Thank you!" Monk said with profound sincerity, and took a flying leap for the fishing boat.

It was farther than he thought, and again he barely made it, being caught by strong hands and amid a good deal of ribald laughter. He told the men on the small boat his need, and they were willing enough to help, even eager. They put up more sail and tacked and veered dangerously through the current and across the bows of other ships, and were at the Surrey Docks half an hour before slack water and the turn of the tide.

They even helped him look for the *Summer Rose*.

It turned out to be a filthy two-masted schooner, low in the water but seaworthy enough to cross the Channel—as long as the weather was easy. He would not have backed her across the Bay of Biscay.

Two of the fishermen came with him, armed with boat hooks and spikes.

Monk led them, facing the captain squarely as they were challenged on deck. He stood arms akimbo, a boat hook held crossways in front of him like a staff.

"You've got two girls on board. I want them. They're taken illegally. Ten guineas reward for you if you give them up . . . a spike in your gut if you don't."

The captain resented the force, but he looked at Monk's eyes, and the size and weight of the men behind him, and decided ten guineas was sufficient to save his honor.

"I'll bring 'em up, no need to be nasty about it. Ten guineas, yer said?"

"That's right."

"Before I sail? I'm goin' on the tide."

"After. You'll be back."

"How do I know you'll be back, eh?"

"I'll pledge it to the harbormaster. I'll leave it with him." Monk lifted the staff a little, and behind him one of the fishermen fingered his spike.

The captain shrugged. He would not have got much for the girls anyway; they were as ugly as sin, and stupider than cows.

He came back less than four minutes later half struggling with two girls of about twenty years of age or a little more. They were matted with filth, clothed in little more than rags, and obviously terrified. They both had mouths with twisted lips drawn back from their teeth in something close to a snarl or a sneer, but their eyes were wide and, even through the filth, clear and lovely. Above the twisted mouths their bones were delicate, with winged brows and soft, exquisite hairlines.

Monk stared at them in shattering, overwhelming disbelief. He was almost choked by it, his heart beating in his throat. He was looking at faces which were caricatures of Delphine Lambert's. Robbed of speech, almost of coherent thought, he simply held out his hands and let the staff fall.

"Come . . ." he croaked. "I've come to take you home . . . Leda . . . Phemie!"

CHAPTER TWELVE

Monk thanked the fishermen, unnecessarily for them. In their eyes the act had been its own reward. One of them had a sister who was blind. His imagination told him all too clearly how such a fate could have happened to her. They even helped Monk find a hansom and get the two terrified girls into it and made sure Monk had sufficient money for the fare to Tavistock Square.

It was late afternoon and still raining hard. They were all filthy and shivering with cold. Perhaps it would have been more reasonable to go around to the back door, but Monk was so fired with triumph he did not even consider it. He paid the driver and helped the girls down onto the curb. He had actually given little thought as to what Martha would do with them, or what Gabriel Sheldon's reaction would be to these two ragged and all but uncivilized creatures brought unannounced to his home. But surely he, of all people, would at least accept their deformities without mockery or revulsion.

All the journey from the Surrey Docks, as he had sought to comfort and reassure the girls, his mind had been filled with the shattering realization that Delphine Lambert must be the same person as Dolly Jackson. The turmoil of emotions in her heart he could barely guess at! Now he set all thought of her aside and knocked on the door, then stood, holding the girls on either side of him, his arms around their shoulders. They were thin, undernourished, nothing like Zillah Lambert. But then Zillah was no blood relative, as he knew.

The door was opened by Martha Jackson. At first she did not

recognize Monk, let alone the two young women with him. Her face showed weariness and impatience, not unmixed with pity.

"If you go to the kitchen door Cook will give you a hot cup of soup," she offered with a shake of her head.

"Miss Jackson," Monk said clearly, grinning at her in spite of himself. He had meant to retain some dignity and detachment. "These are your nieces, Leda and Phemie." He kept his arms around them. "They've had a bad experience, and they are cold and hungry and frightened, but I told them they were coming home and that you would be very pleased to see them."

Martha stared at him, unable to grasp or believe. She looked at the two girls in front of her, their faces wide with wonder, not daring to hope that Monk's words were true. They were dazed with exhaustion and the speed with which things had happened. And they only heard part of what was said. They needed to see a face, read an expression. They had to have words said slowly and with clear enunciation.

Martha searched their expressions, their features beneath the dirt, and slowly her eyes widened and filled with tears. She took a gulp of air and with a mighty effort controlled herself.

"Phemie?" she whispered, swallowing again. "Leda?"

They nodded, still clinging to Monk.

"I'm . . . Martha. . . . I'm your papa's sister." The tears spilled over as she said it, a rush of memory overwhelming her.

"M-Martha?" Phemie said awkwardly. Her voice was not unpleasant, but she found speech difficult as no one had taken the time to try to teach her to master her disability.

"That's right," Monk encouraged her. He looked at Leda, the younger, and he already knew her the more serious, more conscious of her affliction.

"M-Mar-tha?" Leda tried hard, licking her misshapen lip.

Martha smiled through her tears, taking a step forward instinctively, then stopping. It was plain in her face she was afraid of moving too quickly. They did not know her. They might not wish to be touched by a stranger . . . and she was a stranger to them still.

Phemie held out her hand in response, slowly at first.

Martha took it gently, holding out her other hand to Leda.

There was a moment's silence as the lights inside the hallway shone out into the gray afternoon, reflecting in the drifting rain and the cabs and carriages splashing along the street behind the sodden man with hair plastered across his face in dark streaks, his clothes sticking to him, and two gaunt and ragged young women, hair like rats' tails, clothes torn and thin.

Then Leda stretched her hand and gave it to Martha, holding on to her with surprising strength.

"Come inside," Martha invited. "Get warm and dry . . . and have some hot soup."

Monk found himself grinning idiotically. He wanted to laugh with joy.

"I think you had better come too, Mr. Monk," Martha said in a very unbusinesslike tone. "You look terrible. I'll find you some better clothes before you see Miss Latterly. I'm sure something of Mr. Gabriel's will fit you, for the time being. Then I'll let Miss Latterly know you are here."

He wanted to tell Hester himself, see her face when he said he had found the girls. It was perhaps childish, but it mattered to him with a fierceness that startled him.

"I . . ." he began, then did not know what to say. How could he explain what he felt without sounding absurd? Then he remembered Delphine Lambert. "I have something very urgent to tell her."

Martha looked at him doubtfully, but she was too grateful to deny him anything at all.

"I'll tell her you are here," she agreed. She regarded his filthy and disreputable state ruefully. "You'd better wait in the pantry. But don't stand on the carpet . . . and don't sit down!"

"I won't," he promised, then followed her obediently as she led the two girls towards the green baize door through to the servants' quarters, guiding them as they stared in awe. They had never been inside a house so large or so clean—or so warm—in their lives.

Martha pointed to the butler's pantry, which was presently empty, and promised to send the maid up with a message to Hester.

It was less than five minutes before she came down, only the most momentary surprise on her face when she saw his state. She closed the door.

"What happened?" she demanded, her face eager. "Tillie said Martha has two fearful-looking girls with her, wet as rats and about as pretty. Did you find them?" Her eyes were wide, her whole expression burning with hope.

He had meant to be calm, to have dignity, to behave as if he had been in control of himself all the time. It slipped away without his even noticing it.

He did not speak, he simply nodded, smiling so widely he could hardly form the words.

She abandoned any thought of restraint and ran forward, throwing her arms around him, holding him so fiercely she knocked the breath from him.

He hesitated a moment. This was not really what he had intended to do. It was impulsive, too careless of consequence. But even while the thoughts were in his mind, his arms tightened around her and he held her close to him, feeling the strength of her. He bent his head to her cheek, her hair, and smelled its sweetness. She was crying with relief.

"That's . . . wonderful!" She sobbed, sniffing hard. "You are superb! I didn't think you could do it. It's marvelous. Are they going to be all right?" She did not let go of him or look up, but left her head buried on his shoulder and her grip around him as if letting go might destroy the reality of what he had said.

"I don't know," he answered honestly, still holding her too. He had no need to, but it seemed natural. He thought of letting go, of straightening up, but he really did not want to. "I've no idea what she's going to do with them. They're not fit for ordinary service."

"We'll have to find something," she answered, as if it were a simple thing and to be taken for granted.

"That is not all," he said more thoughtfully. He had to tell her the other fact, the one which now was beginning to make such hideous sense.

She was quite still. "What else is there?"

"You remember Martha told us their mother abandoned them . . . Dolly Jackson, Samuel's widow?"

"Yes?"

"I know where she is."

This time she did move. She straightened up and pulled away, staring up at him, her face defiant, eyes blazing.

"She can't have them back! She left them . . . that is the end of it for her!" Her indignation dared him to argue.

"Of course it is," he agreed. "Except that that is not all. . . ."

She caught the emotion in his face, the sense of something new and of vital and different meaning.

"What?" she demanded. "What is it, William?"

"Delphine Lambert," he answered.

She blinked. She had no idea what he meant. The truth had not entered her mind as a possibility.

"Delphine Lambert," he repeated. "I am almost certain, certain in my own mind, that she and Dolly Jackson are the same person."

She gasped. "That's absurd! How could they be? Dolly Jackson was . . . well—" She stopped. He could see in her eyes that now she was considering it. "Well . . . she . . . why? Why would you think that?"

"If you had seen her and then seen those girls, you wouldn't ask. When Samuel died, Dolly Jackson put the two girls into an orphanage and disappeared, to try to improve her position, marry again, presumably as well as possible. She was a very pretty and ambitious woman. She succeeded superbly. She married Barton Lambert, who gave her everything she wanted."

She looked at him with slowly dawning comprehension.

"But she did not dare to give him the one thing he wished: children," he went on. "She had already had two deformed children. So she adopted a child—a perfect child—and she groomed her for the perfect marriage."

Hester did not speak, but her face reflected her sense of awe and pity.

The door opened and Perdita burst in in a flurry of skirts, breathless.

"Martha says you've found the girls! They are down in the kitchen right now!"

Reluctantly, Monk let go of Hester, amazed that he was not more self-conscious of being seen in such a position.

Perdita looked at his filthy appearance with surprise. A month ago she would have been scandalized. Now she was only concerned.

"Is it true? Have you?"

"Yes," Monk answered. "Only just rescued them from being shipped abroad as white slaves." He heard Hester gasp. "I found them actually on the boat." He glanced down at the floor where he had created a pool of water. "I'm sorry. I half fell in the river." He smiled ruefully.

"You must be frozen!" Perdita exclaimed—the white slave trade was not in her knowledge as it was in Hester's. "I'll have someone draw you a hot bath. I'm sure you can borrow some of Gabriel's clothes. Then we must think what to do with these girls."

Hester swallowed, unconsciously smoothing down her dress, now thoroughly wet, also more than a little dirty, where she had pressed against Monk.

"Can you train them to work here?" She turned from Perdita to Monk and back again. "Can you?" There was a faint flush in her cheeks at the presumption.

Before Perdita could reply, Monk interrupted. Hester had not seen them. She had no idea of the reality of their disfigurement, or their deafness, their sheer uncouthness from a lifetime of neglect and abuse. In their entire lives they had seen and heard nothing but the insides of taverns, gin mills and brothels.

"You can't use them as—" He stopped again. How could he

say this? Hester was watching him with anxiety and disbelief. "They're . . ." He glanced down at his filthy clothes, then up at Perdita. There was no point in anything but the truth. "They've spent their lives in gin mills and brothels. They're deaf—and they're disfigured."

Perdita's face filled with horror, then pity. Her chin lifted. "Well, we don't have much company at present, maybe not at all. This could be the very best house in which to train such people." She did not add any note of anger or bitterness, nor was there any in her face. There was no thought of self.

Hester looked at her with a respect which was wholehearted and full of joy.

Perdita recognized it, and it was the final seal upon her resolve. "Shall we go and tell Gabriel?" she suggested. "Then you really must get warmed up, Mr. Monk. You must be feeling wretched."

"Of course," he agreed. He wished to see Gabriel's reaction himself. He could not rest until he did. He followed Perdita and Hester out of the butler's pantry and along the corridor to the servants' stairs, up them and then through the top door to the main wing. He was aware of squelching with every step, and that someone else would have to clean up after him, but perhaps it was worth it this time.

Perdita threw open Gabriel's door. "It's right!" she said without waiting. "He has got them! They're here!"

Gabriel looked at Monk, his eyes bright.

Monk nodded. "They're in the kitchen, getting cleaned up and fed." Gabriel would know what he meant. "They've been on the streets since they were three years old."

Gabriel's face also filled with pity, and a hard, hurting rage. Even his own disfigurement could not mask it.

"We'll look after them," he said without hesitation.

Monk did not argue. He was so cold that in spite of the pleasure he felt, the almost overwhelming sense of exhilaration and relief, he was now shaking and his legs had almost lost sensation. Shivers were running through him and his teeth were chattering.

Hester must have noticed, because she excused them and took him to the guest bathroom and sent for hot water while she then went to Gabriel's wardrobe to find him clean, dry clothes.

Afterwards Martha sent up a bowl of hot thick soup from the kitchen and Monk sat in a chair by the banked-up fire in Hester's sitting room enjoying the heat inside and out, and the savory taste in his mouth of chicken and herbs.

Hester was watching him, her eyes narrowed, her brows drawn together.

"Did you really mean it that you believe Delphine Lambert is the same person as Dolly Jackson?"

He had no doubt. "Yes. If you look at those girls, especially Leda, the resemblance is startling. It is almost a mirror image, only distorted by the mouth. But you can see what she was meant to be. No one could look at them both and not think of it. She had not only one deformed child, Hester, she had two! No wonder she had to leave them behind her if she was going to make her way. She could never admit that to anyone. It's like having madness in the blood. What chance would Zillah have of marrying well?"

"But she's not related!" Hester protested, though her voice was hollow. She knew, as Monk did, that even if they knew Zillah was adopted people would not make that distinction. She was looking at him steadily, searching his face, waiting for him to go on.

"She knew I was looking into the family past, anything I could find that could have put Melville off marrying Zillah. She must have known that if I went on long enough I should find that Zillah was adopted. Perhaps if Melville had gone on fighting the case, I would even have traced her back as far as Putney . . . and Samuel Jackson."

"If Keelin had lived?" She repeated the words in a voice little more than a whisper. "Are you saying that Delphine Lambert could have killed her?"

"I don't know . . . perhaps I am." He watched her face, seeing her eyes widen and slowly belief follow incredulity.

"But how?" she breathed softly. "How did she do it? She was

never alone with her . . . you said so. In fact, you said there was no way anyone could have poisoned her. She didn't eat or drink anything in the court all afternoon." She shook her head. "You couldn't even work out how she could have taken it herself."

"So obviously we missed something." He poked his finger at the table in which his empty soup bowl rested. "She did take it. That is the one thing we can be certain of. It was done . . . whomever by. We missed it."

She thought for a few moments in silence, her elbows on the table, her chin resting on her hands.

"Tell me about the day in court," she asked at length. "Describe it for me as if you wanted me to draw it for you, knowing I wasn't there. Treat it as if I had never been in a court before. Don't leave out anything you saw."

There was no point in it, but he obliged. He told her what the room was like, where everyone sat, how they were dressed and what function they filled. She listened intently, even though most of it was already familiar to her.

"And the adjournment?" she asked. "What happened then?"

He laughed abruptly. "Keelin came out of the courtroom and stood a little to the left of the doorway talking to Rathbone for a few minutes. Then Rathbone left with Sacheverall to go and argue again. I don't know where they went, only that it was entirely fruitless."

"How long were they gone?" she interrupted, looking hopeful.

He shook his head. "About ten minutes, maybe fifteen. But Keelin didn't eat or drink anything, nor did she go to the cloakroom. She was there in the hall all the time, in full public view."

"Alone?" she persisted, refusing to give up.

"Yes . . ." He pictured it vividly, it seemed so unnecessarily, publicly hurtful. "Except that Delphine went over to her with a packet, spoke to her for a moment, then when Keelin held up her hands, Delphine opened the packet and tipped it out into her cupped palms. It was jewelry she had given Zillah. They were dusty . . ."

"Dust?" Hester said slowly.

"Possibly powder . . . I don't know."

"But something?"

"Yes . . . why? It wasn't anything edible. Delphine did not pass her anything she could eat or drink—just the jewelry. She tipped it out so she could itemize each piece and make Keelin acknowledge that she had received it all back—count out each item."

"What did Melville do then?" Hester was leaning forward now.

"She put the jewelry in her inside pocket," he continued. "She looked . . . wretched . . . as if she had been kicked."

Hester winced. "And then what?"

"Then Rathbone came back, spoke to Keelin for a few moments, and they returned to court."

Hester sat for a while thinking silently. It did not seem to make any sense. Monk thought of the afternoon session, the tension and despair. He could picture Keelin Melville safely next to Rathbone, her face tense, the light reflecting in her clear eyes, which were almost the color of aquamarine. Her skin was very fair, spattered with freckles, her features fine but with a remarkable inner power. It was the face of a visionary. And her hands were beautiful too, strong and slender, perfectly proportioned . . . except that she bit her nails—not badly, but enough to make them too short. It seemed to be in moments of greatest anxiety. He could recall her hands in her mouth when . . . Hands in her mouth!

"She bit her nails!" he almost shouted, leaning towards Hester and clasping her hand where it lay on the table, turning it over. "She bit her nails!"

"What?" She looked startled.

He rubbed his fingertips along the tabletop, then put them to his lips.

"The powder . . ." she breathed out the words. "If that was the belladonna, then she put it to her lips . . . into her mouth. Her hands were covered in it from the jewelry!"

"Would it be enough?" He barely dared ask.

"It could be . . ." she said slowly, staring back at him. "If it were pure . . . to act within a few hours. Especially if she ate nothing." Her voice rose a little, getting more urgent. "She didn't wash her hands after touching the jewelry?"

"No. She went straight back into court. I don't imagine at that point she would think of such a thing . . . still less of a taste."

"I don't think it tastes unpleasant," she answered. "Children sometimes eat the fruit by mistake."

"Does it kill them?" he asked.

"Yes, it does, usually. And this would be concentrated."

"Where would she have got it?" He tried to keep the sense of victory out of his voice, but it was there in spite of him.

"An herbalist, or even distill it herself," she replied, not taking her eyes from his.

"There won't be berries this time of the year."

"You don't need the berries. Any part of it is poisonous . . . berries, flowers, roots, leaves, anything at all!"

Monk clenched his fist. "That's it! That's how she did it! By God, she's clever! Now, how can we prove it?" He sat back on the chair. He was warm at last, and very comfortable in Gabriel's shirt and trousers. He felt elated. He knew the truth! And Keelin Melville had not killed herself. She had not died in drowning despair, surrendering. It had not even been directly his, or Rathbone's, failure which had been responsible.

"Is she buried yet?" Hester asked. "Perhaps if they haven't washed her hands . . . under the nails . . ."

"Yes," he answered before she finished. "They buried her." The words hurt. "As a suicide . . . in unhallowed ground. Even Wolff was not permitted to be there."

"God won't care," she said with unwavering conviction. "But without her hands to look at . . . what about the suit she wore? Do you think we could see that? Or did they bury her in it?" There was finality in her voice, as if she expected the answer even before he gave it.

"I don't know, but I expect they did bury her in it. Why would they be bothered to change it? And Delphine took the packet back. She was careful enough for that."

"What about the jewelry itself?" she asked, but without hope.

"It wouldn't prove anything much, except to us," he replied. "Only that she had belladonna in the same pocket . . . not that anyone else put it there. Delphine would simply say that Melville had a packet of belladonna powder in her pocket and it burst or came undone. We couldn't prove otherwise—even if we knew it!"

"Then I don't think we can prove it," Hester said slowly.

"Not—not prove it? We've got to!" He was outraged. It was monstrous! Unbearable! Delphine Lambert had abandoned two tiny children to the cruelty of strangers—two vulnerable, damaged children who needed her even more than most. Then she had murdered the most brilliant, dazzling, creative architect of the age, all to further her own comfort and ambition, and to find a good marriage for her adopted daughter—whether she wanted it or not. Appearance had been everything, beauty, glitter—as shallow as the skin. The passion and hope and pain of the heart beneath had been thrown away. He could not let himself think it could all just happen and no one could call for any accountability, any justice, any regret at all. All kinds of arguments raged through his head, and even as he thought of each one, he knew it was no use.

"Can we?" Hester asked, her face puckered. She had not known Keelin Melville; she had not even been at court this time, as she had in most of the other cases he had cared about deeply. It was strange, and he realized now he had missed her. But Gabriel Sheldon was tied inextricably to it, because Martha Jackson was part of his household, part of Perdita's life, and because he too knew what it was like to be disfigured, to know his face, the outer part of him everyone saw and judged him by so easily, filled people with revulsion, even with fear. He was an outcast of the same kind, a victim of a world where sight ruled so much. Hester understood it.

And she understood Keelin Melville, a woman fighting to succeed in a world where men made all the rules and judged only by the yardstick of their own preconceptions, not by reality of courage or skill or achievement. She had seen others sacrificed to it, and eventually crushed.

"We must!" he said fiercely, leaning farther forward. "We must find a way."

"It's all gone," she pointed out, her mouth tight, her eyes sad. "Will they dig her up again, do you suppose?"

He had to be honest. There was not the slightest chance, not on the belief he had now. No one would want to consider it, to raise such a hideous possibility, face the suit for criminal libel if they were wrong.

"No."

She looked at his empty plate. "Do you want some more soup?"

"No! I want to think of a way to prove what happened to Keelin Melville and find some justice for those two abandoned and unloved children!" He sighed. "And I want some kind of vengeance . . . some balancing of the scales."

She sat in silence for a while again, cupping her chin in her hands.

He waited, searching for an answer in his mind, going over the details of the case, all the questions and answers. He was warm, physically comfortable, but exhaustion was creeping over him and he was finding it harder and harder to concentrate.

The door opened and Martha came in carrying a tray with fresh tea on it. Her eyes were bright and calm and there was a glow in her cheeks. She set the tray down on the table, smiling at him. She was almost too full of emotion to find words.

"Mr. Monk . . . I—I can't . . ." She shook her head. "I just don't know how to say what you've done for me. You're . . . the best man I know. I never truly thought it was possible . . . but you found them. I wish I could give you more. . . ." She was clearly embarrassed, feeling nothing she had was sufficient reward for him.

"I don't need any more payment, Miss Jackson," he said without even having to think about it. "You already gave me sufficient for all my expenses." That was not quite true, but close enough.

She hesitated.

"Except the tea," he added.

She remembered and poured it immediately. It was steaming and fragrant.

"Are they all right?" he asked.

"Oh, yes," she murmured, nodding. "Oh, yes . . . they will be. Everyone's very good. Finding them clothes and boots and so on. Tillie gave Phemie one of her dresses, and Agnes found one for Leda, and a petticoat with frills on it. Sarah gave them both stockings." She blinked hastily. "And she was looking out sheets and blankets for them, and deciding which room would be best. Put them in together, in case they get lonely, or frightened in a new place. And then Miss Perdita came down and she was so nice to them." She said it as if she hardly dared believe it was true. "She said they could stay here all the time."

Monk smiled back at her. "I know."

She hesitated only a moment longer, then excused herself and turned back to the kitchen and the excitement again.

Monk sipped his tea gratefully.

"I wonder what would have happened if Samuel Jackson hadn't died. . . ." Hester said thoughtfully.

"They would have lived ordinary, uncomfortable lives, laughed at by their peers, and possibly found service of some sort," he answered. "Possibly not. He would have loved them, perhaps taught them to read and write. But he did die, so it makes no difference now. We can't undo that. They'll be all right here." He said it with assurance, thinking of the kindness in the kitchen already, everyone trying to help, willing to give of their own few possessions.

"That's not what I meant." Hester was frowning, hardly listening to him. "They would have been laughed at, wouldn't they? I mean, it would have been hard for them, for their family . . . for Dolly Jackson."

"Of course. But she's done very well indeed. She's a wealthy woman in society, beautiful, respected, has a husband who loves her and a beautiful daughter no one knows is not hers, except us."

"Exactly," she agreed, looking at him.

"Hester . . . ?" A thought began in his mind.

"What did he die of?" she asked softly.

"Bleeding . . . bleeding in the stomach."

"What caused it?"

"I—I don't know. Illness?" His mouth was suddenly dry.

"How convenient for Dolly Jackson," Hester said, looking at him very steadily.

He put his cup down. His hands were clumsy, stiff. "Poison?"

"I don't know. But I want to know. Don't you?"

"Yes . . . and I'm going to find out."

"I'm coming with you. . . ."

"I don't know that I—I don't know what . . ." he began.

"I can help." Her face was set in immovable determination. "We'll start tomorrow. When I tell Gabriel he'll insist." She stood up.

"I'm not sure you should. We may be wrong."

She looked at him with eyes wide, her mouth twisted in a mixture of urgency and anger. "We'll need money. I haven't any. Have you?"

"No." He was too tired to argue. And anyway, she was right.

"Then it's settled. I'll go and talk to Gabriel about it, and he'll give us some. We'll start tomorrow morning—early!" She wrinkled her nose at him, and she went out of the room with a swish of skirts, held high. He heard her heels light and rapid along the corridor.

They did start out very early the following day. By half past eight on a blustery spring morning they were in a hansom on the way east and south to Putney. Gabriel had been generous with all he could spare, his only regret being that he was not yet well enough to come with them, and an acute awareness that his disfigurement might prove a hindrance. Meeting strangers was a difficulty he had yet to overcome. It would always be painful. No matter how many times he did it, for them it would always be the first time. The horror and embarrassment would be new.

Now Monk and Hester were sitting side by side in the hansom bowling along at a smart pace through the elegant streets of Chelsea, with the river glinting in the light. To the left lay Battersea Reach, curving away from them. They would pass the gas works and go along the Kings Road with Eel Brook Common to the right. Beyond that was Parsons Green and the Putney Bridge to the south. It was a very long journey.

There was so much to say, and yet he was uncertain where to begin. From Tavistock Square, where he had picked her up, she had told him how Leda and Phemie were this morning, and how changed they seemed already, with clean clothes, washed hair and good food. They were still terrified, expecting each moment to wake up and discover it was all a cruel dream. But they did seem to understand quite a lot, if spoken to slowly and in simple words. The thing that was most apparent was their affection for each other—and their awe and wonder at the thought that Martha actually liked them, rather than simply wished to use them. They flinched if approached too quickly, and it might take some time before they understood that food would be given them regularly and did not need to be stolen or defended.

They were moving away from the river. The street was busy with early traffic, other hansoms, several private carriages. This was an affluent area. Four perfectly matched bays went past at a brisk pace, pulling a magnificent coach, footmen in livery riding behind.

"Where shall we begin?" Hester asked, staring ahead of her. "It all happened twenty years ago. Who will still be there now?"

"Some of the neighbors," he answered. "A doctor must have been called. There'll be a death certificate."

She frowned. She was sitting very straight, her hands in her lap. She looked a little like a governess. She was angry and nervous, afraid they would not succeed. He knew her so well. Anyone else might have thought her rather prim, but he knew she was boiling with emotion, all kinds of fears and furies at the pain and the injustice, and their helplessness to reach it.

"I suppose we could find that," she replied without looking at him.

He was watching her face profiled against the light of the window. What was she thinking about the whole business of beauty and the notion of young women's being too plain to be acceptable, or loved at all, because they were not considered marriageable? Phemie and Leda were disfigured. But what about Zillah Lambert? She was now unmarriageable, in her mother's eyes, because two men in a short space of time had been attracted to her and then at the last moment withdrawn. Perhaps society would discount Keelin, knowing the truth now. But what about Sacheverall? Did it make any difference that he was a shallow, selfish opportunist who had not loved her, only her position and her money? Would she find Hugh Gibbons again? He had not even told Hester about that!

"When she was very young, Zillah had a great romance with a man called Hugh Gibbons," he said aloud.

Hester looked at him with surprise.

He realized his remark seemed to come from no previous thought or word.

"I only say so because he never lost touch with her—I mean, he never forgot her," he amended. "He might still care for her very much. And she obviously thinks of him with kindness. I remember her smile when she spoke of him."

"You mean she might marry him?" she asked.

"Well . . . it is possible."

She turned back towards the window. "Good."

He looked at her and could not read her expression. Had he sounded as if marriage were so important? Zillah, at least, would not be left behind by happiness, social acceptability, living out her days dependent upon other people or earning her own living, pitied by her more fortunate sisters.

That was not what he had meant.

"It will . . ." he began. He was going to say it would matter to Zillah in a way it would not to Hester. But why not? That was a ridiculous thing to say, and insulting. He had no idea how important it might be to Hester to be married. He had always purposely avoided thinking of what hopes or dreams she might have, what secret wounds. He wanted to think of her as she was: strong, capable, brave, well able to care not only for herself but also for others.

And he did not want to consider her in that light; it was too complicated. They were friends, as honest and candid and uncomplicated as if they had been two men, at least some of the time. She was sharper-tongued than most men, quicker of thought, and then sometimes almost willfully obtuse. But she was wise and brave, and sometimes very funny. And she was generous—when it came to care for others, she was the most generous person he had ever known. She just did not know how to be mysterious or alluring, how to flirt and flatter and intrigue. She was too direct. There was nothing unknown about her.

Except that he had no idea what she was thinking now as she stared straight ahead of her. He could see the open stretch of Eel Brook Common through the window past her head.

How could he take back his clumsiness and say something to undo his words? Everything that came to his mind only made it worse, sounding as if he knew he had made a mistake and was trying to climb out of it. Which, of course, was the truth. She would know that.

Better to try something completely different.

"We'll have to see if we can find the doctor," he said aloud.

She looked back at him. "He won't appreciate our suggesting it was poison. We will be saying he was incompetent, that one of his patients was murdered twenty years ago, and he missed it. Even if it is a different doctor, they defend one another. It is a form of mutual self-defense."

"I know that. Have you a better idea?"

"No." She sat silently for a few moments. The sun was shining brightly and the trees and the common were in full leaf at last. They could have been miles from London. They passed several people out walking, women in pale and pretty dresses, splashes of pink and blue and gold, men more somber stems of grays and browns. Two dogs chased each other, barking madly. A child sent a hoop whirling along too fast to catch it. It sped down the incline, bounced over a stone and fell flat when it hit a tussock of grass.

"Hester . . ."

"Yes?"

He had no idea what he wanted to say. No, that was not entirely true. He had a hundred things to say, he was just not certain he wanted to say them, not yet, perhaps not at all. Change was frightening. If he committed himself he could not go back. What did he really want to say, anyway? That her friendship was the most valuable thing in his life? That was true. But would she see that as a compliment? Or would she only see that he was treating her like a man, avoiding saying anything deeper, anything with passion and vulnerability in it, anything that bared his soul and left him undefended?

"Perhaps we'd better just tell them the truth," he said instead.

She sat a little straighter in her seat, uncomfortable as the wheels jolted over a roughness in the road. Her back was like a ramrod, her shoulders stiff, pulling her jacket tight across the seams.

"How much of it?" she asked.

"I don't know. Let's find someone first."

They were coming into Parsons Green and rode in silence through its streets, which were rapidly getting busier now it was mid-morning. They crossed over Putney Bridge. The river was dazzling in the sun, full of noisy traffic, water swirling under the piers as the current gathered speed in the increasing tide.

On the far side, in Putney High Street, Monk alighted and paid the driver with a very generous tip, sufficient to get himself a nice luncheon and something for the horse. It had been an extraordinarily long journey. Then he held out his arm and assisted Hester to alight.

As the cab drew away they looked at each other. The awkwardness was gone. They had a common purpose and it was all that mattered. Personal issues were forgotten.

"The churchyard," Hester said decisively. "That will be the best record of his death. We can go from there."

He agreed. "Which church?"

"Pardon?" She had not thought of that.

"Which church? We passed St. Mary's on the way in. There are bound to be others. I remember a Baptist church on Wester Road, there's a St. John's on Putney Hill. That's three at least."

She looked at him with slight chill. "Then the sooner we begin, the better. St. Mary's is the closest. We'll work along, unless you know anything about Samuel? I don't suppose you know what his faith was, do you?"

"No," he admitted with a slight smile. "But I'd wager hers is as orthodox as possible."

It took them the rest of the morning to ask politely at St. Mary's, visit the Baptist church on Wester Road, go along Oxford Road a few hundred yards to the Emanuel Church on Upper Richmond Road, and then move along that same considerable distance to the Wesleyan Chapel, just past the police station. At least they were saved the journey up Putney Hill to St. John's. In the Wesleyan Chapel an elderly gentleman directed them to the chapel graveyard, and there they found a simple marker that said "Samuel Jackson, beloved husband of Dorothy, died September 27th, 1839." No mention was made of daughters, but that might have been for financial reasons as much as discretion. Carving cost money.

Monk and Hester stood side by side in the sharp sun and cold wind for several minutes. It seemed inappropriate to speak, and unnecessary. Hester reached up her hand and put it very lightly on Monk's arm, and without looking sideways at her, he knew the emotions that were going through her mind, just as they were through his.

Eventually it was an old man walking through the grass with a bunch of daffodils in his hand who broke the spell.

"Knew 'im, did yer?" he said quietly. "Nice chap 'e were. Hard to die like that, when yer've got little ones."

"No, we didn't know him," Monk answered, turning to the man and smiling very slightly. "But we know his sister . . . and we know the girls."

"Them two poor little things! Do you?" The old man's face lit with amazement. "Y'know, I never reckoned as they'd still be alive. Yer didn't take 'em in, did yer?" He looked at Hester, then blushed. "I'm sorry Mrs. . . . ?" He did not know, and left it hanging. "Of course you didn't! They'd be twenty an' odd now. I didn't mean to be impertinent, like."

Hester shook her head quickly. "No, of course, Mr. . . ."

"Walcott, Harold Walcott, ma'am."

"Hester Latterly," she replied. "But I know Martha Jackson, Samuel Jackson's sister. I know her quite well."

Mr. Walcott shook his head, the breeze ruffling his thin hair.

"I always liked Sam. Quick, 'e was, but kind, if you know what I mean? Loved them little girls something fierce."

"They had a terrible time after he died," Hester said bleakly. "But we've just found them and taken them to Martha. They'll be all right now. They're in a very good house, with a distinguished soldier from the Indian army. He was badly injured in the Mutiny, scarred in the face, so they'll not be misused or made little of."

"I'm right 'appy to 'ear that." Mr. Walcott beamed at her. "You and yer 'usband are real Christian people. God bless yer both."

The color was brighter on Hester's face than could be accounted for by the wind, but she did not argue. "Thank you, Mr. Walcott."

Monk felt a curious wrench in his chest, but he did not argue either. There were more important issues, and far more urgent ones.

"You are very gracious, Mr. Walcott," he answered, inclining his head in acknowledgment. "Since you knew Samuel, would you be kind enough to answer a few questions about the way he died? Martha is still troubled by it. It would set her mind at rest . . . perhaps."

Walcott's face darkened and his lips compressed. "Very sudden, it were." He shook his head. "I suppose there in't many good ways ter go, but bleedin's always scared me something awful. Just my weakness, I suppose, but I can't stand the thought of it. Poor Sam bled terrible."

"What did the doctor say caused it?" Hester asked quietly. The situation would not be unknown to her. God knew what she had seen in the battlefield, but looking sideways at her face, Monk saw the horror in her eyes too. Experience had not dulled it. It was one of the things about her he cared for most. He had never known her to deny or dull her capacity to feel. She exasperated him, irritated him, was opinionated, but she had more courage than anyone else he had ever known. And she could laugh.

Mr. Walcott was shaking his head again. The wind was sharper and his hands were turning white holding the daffodils.

"I never 'eard. Not sure as 'e knew for certain," he answered the question.

"Who was he?" Hester asked, trying to keep the urgency out of her voice—and not succeeding.

But if Mr. Walcott noticed he did not take offense.

"That'd 'ave bin Dr. Loomis, for certain."

"Where might we find him?" Monk asked.

"Oh . . ." Mr. Walcott considered for a moment. "Well . . . 'e were gettin' on a bit then. 'E lived in Charlwood Road, I 'member that. Nice 'ouse, wi' a big may tree in the front garden. Smell something marvelous in the late spring, it does."

"Thank you," Monk said with feeling. "You've been of great assistance, Mr. Walcott." He held out his hand.

Walcott shook it. "A pleasure, Mr. Latterly."

Monk winced but kept his peace.

"Ma'am." Mr. Walcott bowed to Hester, and she smiled back at him, biting her lips to stop herself from laughing. All the same there were tears in her eyes, whether they were for Samuel Jackson, for the bereavement which had brought Mr. Walcott here with the flowers in his freezing hands, or due to the wind itself, Monk had no way to know.

He took her arm and turned her to walk back through the

gravestones to the street again, and left towards Charlwood Road. They went for some distance in silence. He felt curiously at ease. He ought to have been embarrassed, filled with urgency to rectify Mr. Walcott's mistake, and yet every time he drew breath to say something, it seemed the wrong time, the words clumsy and not what he really meant to say.

Eventually they had walked all the way along Upper Richmond Road and around the corner right into Charlwood Road and down as far as the unmistakable house with the ancient, spreading may tree leaning over the fence and arching above the path to the front door.

"This must be it," Hester said, glancing up at him. "What do we say?"

He should have been thinking about that, and he had not, not with any concentrated effort.

"The truth," he answered, because he must appear as if he had been silent in order to turn over the matter and make a wise judgment. "I don't think anything else will serve at this point."

"I agree," she said immediately.

She must have been thinking about it. She would never be so amenable otherwise. Why was he faintly disappointed?

He stood back for her to go first up the path.

She saw the brass plate saying "Hector Loomis, M.D." beside the bell pull. She glanced around at Monk, then reached out and yanked the brass knob, a little too hard. They heard it ringing with a clatter inside.

It was answered by an elderly housekeeper with a crisp white apron and cap.

"Good morning," Monk said straightaway.

"Good . . . morning, sir, ma'am," she replied, hesitating momentarily because it was now well into the afternoon. "May I help you?"

"If you please," Monk responded. "We have come a very long way to see Dr. Loomis on the matter of a tragedy which happened some time ago and which we have just learned may involve a very serious crime . . . the crime of murder. It is essential we are certain of our facts beyond any reasonable doubt. Many people may be irreparably hurt if we are not."

"We are sorry to trouble you without warning or proper appointment," Hester added. "If there had been another way, we should have taken it."

"Oh! Bless my soul! Well . . . you had better come in." The housekeeper stepped back and invited them to enter. "Dr. Loomis is busy with a patient this minute, but I'll tell him as you're here and it's important. I'm sure he'll see you."

"Thank you very much," Monk accepted, following Hester to where the housekeeper led them to wait and then left them. It was a most agreeable room, but very small, and looked onto the back garden of what was apparently a family home. Children's toys lay neatly stacked against the wall of a potting shed. A hoop and a tiny horse's head on a stick were plainly discernible.

Hester looked at Monk, the question in her eyes.

"Grandchildren?" he suggested with a sinking feeling of disappointment.

She bit her lip and said nothing. She was too restless to sit down, and he felt the same, but there was not room for them both to pace back and forth, and even though she wore petticoats without hoops, her skirts still took up what little space there was.

When Dr. Loomis appeared he was a mild-faced young man with fast receding hair cut very short and a friendly look of enquiry in his very ordinary face.

"Mrs. Selkirk says you have come a great distance to ask about a crime?" he said, closing the door behind him and looking from one to the other of them with a frown. "How can I help you? I don't think I know anything at all."

"It happened twenty-one years ago," Monk answered, rising to his feet.

"Oh . . ." Loomis looked disappointed. "That would be my father. I'm so sorry."

Monk felt a ridiculous disappointment. It was so strong it was physical, as if his throat had suddenly tightened and he could barely catch his breath.

"Perhaps you have his records?" Hester refused to give up. "It was about a Samuel Jackson, who died of bleeding. He had two small daughters, both of them disfigured."

"Samuel Jackson!" Loomis obviously recognized the name. "Yes, I remember him speaking of that."

Monk's hope surged up wildly. Why else would a man speak of a case many years afterwards, except that it worried him, was somehow incomplete?

"What did he say?" he demanded.

Loomis screwed up his face in concentration.

Monk waited. He looked at Hester. She was so tense she seemed scarcely to be breathing.

Loomis cleared his throat. "He was troubled by it . . ." he said tentatively. "He never really knew what caused him to bleed the way he did. He couldn't connect it with any illness he knew." He looked at Monk earnestly. "But of course we know so little, really. A lot of the time we are only making our best guess. We can't say that." He shrugged and gave a nervous laugh. His pale, blue-gray eyes were very direct. "I think, to be honest, his greatest concern was because he couldn't help, and Samuel was so desperate to stay alive because of his children. And as it turned out, Mrs. Jackson did lose them. She couldn't care for them, poor woman. She was left with almost nothing. She was obliged to make her own way, and she couldn't do that with two small children . . . especially not ones that weren't . . . normal." He looked as if he hated saying it. There was a tightness in him, and his hands moved uneasily.

"She did very well for herself," Hester assured him acidly. "Could Samuel Jackson have died of any sort of poison?"

Loomis regarded her curiously. "Not that I know of. What makes you ask that? Look . . . Mrs. Selkirk mentioned a crime. I think she actually said murder. Perhaps you had better explain to me what you are seeking, and why." He waved to them to sit down, and then sat on the chair opposite, upright, leaning forward, listening.

Monk outlined to him all that he knew about Samuel Jackson, but he began with a brief history of the case of Keelin Melville and her death from belladonna poisoning. It took them nearly three quarters of an hour, and neither Hester nor Loomis interrupted him until he had finished.

"What you are saying"—he looked at Monk grimly—"is that you think Dolly Jackson—Delphine Lambert, as she is known now—murdered Samuel in order to escape her situation because he insisted on keeping the children, and she couldn't bear to have them. She wanted perfection and wouldn't settle for anything less."

"Yes," Monk agreed. "That is what I'm saying. Is it true?"

"I don't know," Loomis admitted. "But I'm prepared to do everything in my power to find out." He stood up. "We can begin with my father's records. He never destroyed them. They are all in the cellar. Do you know exactly when he died?"

"Yes!" Hester said straightaway. "September twenty-seventh, 1839. It's on his gravestone."

"Excellent! Then it will be a simple matter." Loomis led the way out into the hall, calling his intentions to Mrs. Selkirk and instructing her that he was not to be interrupted for anything less than an emergency. "I'm glad you came today," he went on, going to the cellar door and opening it. "We'll need a light. There's no gas down here. I have very few patients today, and my wife has taken the children for a day or two to see her father. He is not very well and does not travel, but he is very fond of my daughters." He smiled as he said it, and his own affection was clear in his eyes. Perhaps that was some of his feeling for Samuel Jackson.

He found a lantern and lit it, then led the way down the narrow stone steps to the cellar where rows of boxes filled with papers lay neatly stacked.

It took them only ten minutes to find the right box for the

month of September in the year 1839, most of the work moving the boxes above it.

"Here it is!" Loomis exclaimed, lifting out a handful of papers. "Samuel Jackson . . ." He held it closer to the light, and Hester and Monk both peered over his shoulder while he read the generous, sprawling hand.

"You are right—he didn't know," Hester said the moment she came to the end. She stared at Loomis. "He wasn't satisfied. He just couldn't prove there was anything wrong. Can we get an order for an exhumation?"

Loomis chewed his lip. "Difficult . . ."

"But possible?" she insisted.

"I don't know."

"Where do we begin?" Monk asked urgently. "We can't just let this go!"

"With the police," Loomis answered, meeting his eyes. "We'll go up to the station and speak to Sergeant Byrne. He'll remember Sam Jackson—and Dolly. I won't let this go, I promise you. But it'll be very hard. . . ."

Hester straightened up. "We'll find Sergeant Byrne, then we'll find the judge."

Monk looked dubious. "The question is, if it was poison, will it still be there to find, even if we can dig him up?"

"Depends what it is," Loomis answered, putting away the rest of the papers and closing the box. He handed all the papers on Samuel Jackson to Hester. "Depends on the quality of his coffin, if it's all dry inside, and what's in the surrounding earth. I don't know what chance we have of proving anything this long after. Arsenic remains, I know that. But this doesn't sound like arsenic. I think my father would have seen that. This was bleeding . . . more like an internal ulcer burst, or an artery, or something of that sort. I don't know why he wasn't satisfied, but from his accounts here, he wasn't."

"Probably because Samuel had no history of earlier illness,"

Hester suggested. "There's no mention of pain before, or difficulty with eating, no nausea or earlier signs of blood."

Loomis looked at her quickly.

"I am a nurse," she explained. Then, as if she recalled the general reputation of nurses as women who scrubbed floors and emptied slops, she added, "In the Crimea. I've done a good deal of field surgery." She said it with pride. It was not boasting but a statement of fact.

Loomis nodded slowly, his face full of admiration.

"Then we had better take these papers and see if we can get Sergeant Byrne on our side, and then persuade a judge that we have reasonable cause to suspect a murder. I warn you, it may be a long and fruitless task, but I am ready, if you are."

"We are!" Monk said without hesitation, including Hester automatically and without even bothering to glance at her.

Sergeant Byrne at the local station was quite easily persuaded. He was a middle-aged man who had known and liked Samuel Jackson, and Jackson's death had shocked him. He took little convincing that there was cause for further investigation. He was more than willing to leave his tedious paperwork and go immediately with Hester, Monk and Dr. Loomis to call upon Judge Tomkinson across the river in Parsons Green.

The judge occupied a large house with an excellent view over a sweep of lawn towards the water, and he did not appreciate being taken from the dinner table.

Loomis had been right in that it was difficult and frustrating to a point close to loss of both temper and hope to persuade Judge Tomkinson to order an exhumation of the body of Samuel Jackson, decently buried, without question, twenty-one years before. He argued with every point they raised, shaking his head and tapping his fingers on the top of his cherrywood desk.

They tried every line of reasoning they could think of, relevant and irrelevant, based on logic or emotion, anger, pity or the desire for justice. The judge dismissed them all, for one cause or another. Even Sergeant Byrne's presence moved him not at all.

Finally, at quarter to seven in the evening, it was Monk's impassioned anger at the death of Keelin Melville which won him over.

"Melville?" the judge said slowly, letting out his breath in a sigh. "The Melville who built that marvelous hall for Barton Lambert? That place full of light?"

"Yes!"

Hester held her breath.

Loomis looked nonplussed.

The judge frowned at Monk. "Are you saying you believe this woman murdered Melville to stop the case, and thus you from pursuing her past, and probably finding these wretched children of hers?" he asked with rising emotion.

"Yes . . . my lord."

"Then—then perhaps we had better find the truth of the matter," the judge said with a sigh. "Not that I imagine it will do any good now. About the only justice you will get will be to spread the news around that she was once Dolly Jackson of Putney and that Leda and Phemie are her natural children." There was a hard edge to his voice. "For whatever satisfaction that may bring you."

"Very little," Monk replied. "It sounds like vengeance, and would hurt her present husband and daughter for very little reason."

"Then you'd better make the best of your exhumation," the judge replied with a tight shrug. "Although if you find poison, that won't help his present family very much."

Loomis took the paper as the judge signed it.

Monk pushed his hands into his pockets. "Thank you."

"It may not help anybody now," Hester acknowledged. "But if he was murdered, we can't look away because it will hurt. It always hurts."

The judge did not reply.

The rest of the evening was spent in frantic organization. They had barely half an hour to eat a hasty supper, then Loomis went to the local police station to inform them of their intentions and show them the judge's order.

When he had gone, Monk searched his pockets, then turned to Hester.

"How much money have you?"

She looked in her reticule. "About two shillings and fourpence," she answered. "Why?"

"We've got to pay the grave diggers," he answered grimly. "It's hard work, and we haven't got the time to haggle. I've only got half a crown and a few pence. We'll need more than that. There'll be the local sexton as well." He looked anxious, his eyes bleak, mouth tight.

She understood his reluctance to ask Loomis. He had given a great deal already. But who else was there? Callandra was still on holiday.

They stared at each other.

"Gabriel?" she suggested. "He'd lend it—even give it. How much do we need?"

"Another thirty shillings at least! Maybe two pounds."

"I'll ask him." She started to move even as she spoke.

"He's miles away," he protested.

"Then the sooner I start, the better chance of being back in time." She smiled with a little twist. "At least we know he'll be at home."

"You stay here," he ordered. "I'll go!"

"Don't be stupid!" She dismissed the idea with unaccustomed brusqueness, even for her. "I know him, you don't. You can't turn up on the doorstep and ask for two pounds."

"And you can't go . . ." he started.

"Yes, I can! Come with me as far as getting a hansom, and I'll be perfectly all right. Hurry up and don't waste time arguing."

For once he conceded, and putting on coats they walked swiftly together along the footpath to the main road, and within ten minutes he had hailed a cab and she was on her way back east again towards London and the Sheldon house.

She sat upright in the back of the cab, her back stiff, her hands clenched in her lap. She felt as if they stopped at every cross street while traffic passed. The horse seemed to amble rather than trot. She was frantic with urgency, muttering under her breath, fingernails digging into her palms.

When at last she got there she ordered the cabby to wait, paid him nothing, in spite of his protests, just so she would be certain he would not leave. She ran across the footpath and up the steps, leaning on the doorbell in a most uncivil fashion.

As soon as Martha answered she greeted her with barely a word, then went across the hall and up the stairs. She knocked on Gabriel's door and, without waiting for an answer, opened it.

"Hello?" he said with surprise. Then, reading her face, "What is it?"

"I need some money to pay grave diggers for an exhumation." She wasted no words on niceties. "Please? I don't know who else to ask. It's terribly important!"

His eyes were level and curious, but without hesitation.

"Of course. Tell me about it afterwards. How much do you need?"

"Three pounds." Better to be safe.

"There's four guineas on the dresser." He pointed to the chest near the wall. "Take it. Just promise me you'll tell me about it afterwards."

"I will! I swear." She flashed him a heartfelt smile. "Thank you." And without waiting any further, she ran out of the room again and down the stairs.

The cabby was standing by the horse, grumbling and staring at the house door.

"Back to Putney," she ordered him, scrambling in again. "As quick as you can! Please hurry!"

In accordance with custom and law, the exhumation was to begin at midnight. Five minutes to twelve found them at the graveyard gates with an ashen-faced sexton, Dr. Loomis, three local police from the station along High Street, including, of course, Sergeant Byrne, three grave diggers, Monk, and after much indignant protest, Hester as well.

It was a chilly night with a damp wind blowing up from the river and the distant sound of foghorns like lost souls out of the rising mist over the water.

The sexton unlocked the gates, and their lanterns swayed as they made their way through and up the path. A constable, blessing his luck, was left on guard in case any curious person should be drawn to investigate what was happening. The grave diggers carried their spades over their shoulders, their feet making soft thuds on the earth path. As if in silent commiseration they walked in unison, unhappy shadows denser against the shifting darkness of the sky.

The sexton stopped at Samuel Jackson's grave.

"Right," he said, grunting. "Yer'd best be gettin' started, then. Nowt ter wait fer."

Obediently the grave diggers set to work.

Monk stood close to Hester, Loomis on the other side, shivering, arms folded across his chest, Byrne beside him. There was no sound but the faint whispering of the wind around the stones and the noise of the spades and the fall of earth.

It seemed to go on forever.

Hester moved a little closer to Monk, and he slipped his arm around her. She must be cold. The lantern light reflected on her face, eyes wide and dark, mouth closed, lips pressed together.

The noise of foghorns drifted up on the wind from the river again.

One of the lanterns guttered out. It must have been short of oil.

At last the spades struck the wood of the coffin lid.

A grave digger standing on the side taking a moment's rest crossed himself.

They put the ropes underneath and began to pull the coffin up, grunting with the strain, and after a short awkwardness, laid it on the earth beside the gaping hole.

It was Loomis's turn to act. He moved forward, rubbing his hands together to try to get the circulation going again.

The sexton opened the lid for him and stepped back.

One of the constables came forward, holding up a lantern but looking away.

Monk could feel his heart beating almost in his throat.

The silence prickled.

Byrne shifted his feet.

Loomis looked in. His skin was garish in the yellow light of the lantern, impossible to read. He moved aside what was left of the clothes. They could not see what he was doing, only the tensing of his shoulders and the expression on his face.

No one spoke.

Monk held Hester even closer, hardly aware that he was almost crushing her.

Minutes passed.

It was bitterly cold.

Loomis looked up at last.

"I'm afraid there isn't enough left to tell anything," he said quietly, his voice hoarse, almost breaking with disappointment. "I can take samples, but I doubt it will prove anything. Too many years . . . it's just . . . gone!"

Hester loosed herself from Monk's grasp and went forward to the coffin. She leaned over and looked in. Byrne lowered the lamp for her. Very slowly she put her hands down and moved the strands of clothes aside herself, going deeper than Loomis had.

Monk waited. He could feel his teeth chattering.

The wail of the foghorn came up from the river again.

One of the constables whispered the Lord's name to himself.

Hester lifted her hand high under the lantern, looking at something in it, showing it to Loomis.

"Glass!" she whispered, her voice catching in her throat.

"Ground glass. It's still here. Under where the stomach used to be. She fed him ground glass. That's why he bled to death!"

Monk felt the sweat break out on his skin, and found he was shaking.

"Got her!" Loomis said softly and with infinite satisfaction. "Sexton, put a guard on this, exactly as it is. On pain of complicity in murder, don't move that body! Do you understand me?"

Very gently, Hester replaced the glass where she had found it.

The sexton nodded. The police moved closer, lanterns wavering, held high.

Loomis rubbed his hands down the sides of his trousers. Perhaps he too was sweating.

Hester turned around and came back to Monk. Loomis and the others were gradually moving away. There was only one lantern left for them to follow.

"We did it," she said softly. She held her hands down, away from him. He had to reach for them to hold them in his. She was so cold they were like ice.

"Yes, we did," he whispered back. "Thank you."

She turned to pull away, but he held on to her. This was not the time, after all they had seen of prejudices and facile judgments, and it was most certainly not the place, but the words came to his lips and would not be stopped.

"Hester?"

"What?" She was shuddering with cold and shock.

He wanted to hold her closer but he knew she would refuse.

"Hester, will you marry me?"

She was silent for so long he thought she was not going to answer, possibly even that she had not heard him. He was about to repeat it when she spoke.

"Why?" she asked, looking at him, although she could hardly have seen his face in the light of the single lantern sitting on the gravestone to their side.

"Because I love you, of course!" he said sharply, feeling vulnerable and suddenly terrified she would refuse. A pit of loneliness loomed up in front of his imagination worse than the yawning grave beside them. "And I don't want ever to be without you," he added.

"I think that's a good reason," she said very softly. "Yes, I will." And she did not resist in the slightest when he drew her closer to him and kissed her again, and again, and again.

ABOUT THE AUTHOR

Among ANNE PERRY's other novels featuring investigator William Monk are *Cain His Brother*, *Defend and Betray*, and most recently, *The Silent Cry*. She also writes the popular novels featuring Thomas and Charlotte Pitt, including *Pentecost Alley*, which was nominated for an Edgar Award, *Traitors Gate*, *The Hyde Park Headsman*, *Highgate Rise*, *Ashworth Hall*, which was a Main Selection of the Book-of-the-Month Club, and *Brunswick Gardens*. "Her grasp of Victorian character and conscience still astonishes," said *The Cleveland Plain Dealer* about the author. Hundreds of thousands of readers agree.

Anne Perry lives in the Scottish Highlands.

39092062163565
2/8/2006
Perry, Anne.
A breach of promise /